MOTHERS' BOYS

FICTION

Dame's Delight
Georgy Girl
The Bogeyman
The Travels of Maudie Tipstaff
The Park
Miss Owen-Owen is At Home
Fenella Phizackerley
Mr Bone's Retreat
The Seduction of Mrs Pendlebury
Mother Can You Hear Me?
The Bride of Lowther Fell
Marital Rites
Private Papers
Have the Men had Enough?
Lady's Maid
The Battle for Christabel

BIOGRAPHY

The Rash Adventurer
The Rise and Fall of Charles Edward Stuart
William Makepeace Thackeray
Memoirs of a Victorian Gentleman
Significant Sisters
The Grassroots of Active Feminism 1839–1939
Elizabeth Barrett Browning
Daphne du Maurier

POETRY

Selected Poems
of Elizabeth Barrett Browning (Editor)

MOTHERS' BOYS

Margaret Forster

Chatto & Windus
LONDON

First published in 1994

3 5 7 9 10 8 6 4 2

Copyright © Margaret Forster 1994

Margaret Forster has asserted her right under the Copyright, Designs and Patents Act, 1988 to be identified as the author of this work

First published in the United Kingdom in 1994 by
Chatto & Windus Limited
Random House, 20 Vauxhall Bridge Road, London SWIV 2SA

Random House Australia (Pty) Limited
20 Alfred Street, Milsons Point, Sydney,
New South Wales 2061, Australia

Random House New Zealand Limited
18 Poland Road, Glenfield
Auckland 10, New Zealand

Random House South Africa (Pty) Limited
PO Box 337, Bergvlei, South Africa

Random House UK Limited Reg. No. 954009

A CIP catalogue record for this book is available from the British Library

ISBN 0 7011 6219 8

Typeset in Bembo by SX Composing Ltd, Rayleigh, Essex
Printed in England by Clays Ltd, St Ives plc

For John and Marjorie,
loyal Cumbrians
who have never
strayed far.

Chapter One

HARRIET BLAMED HERSELF, of course, as mothers always do. There were two dress rehearsals but she didn't recognise either of them as such. If she had realised she was watching a prologue to the real drama, then everything might have gone differently, the parts could have been changed, the scenery shifted . . .

But none of it was acting. All of it was real. Real. It was reality which had to be dealt with. For her, too, presumably. For her, *his* mother, whatever her name was. For both of them.

*

A sunny summer's day. All of it happened on a sunny summer's day, a day following on from a beautifully red sky the evening before, a happy evening, when, for once, there had been no quarrels, no tensions. She remembered – well, she remembered every tiny detail, the way they say you do – but she remembered particularly standing chopping parsley in front of the kitchen window. She wasn't good at such jobs. Hadn't the patience, hadn't the desire to do it properly, as her sister did, knife flying backwards and forwards across the green heap until it was reduced to the finest moss. Her parsley stayed rough. She didn't even have a proper knife, a broad-bladed knife, the sort one can hold at both ends and use to chop effectively. Her knife was short and had a serrated edge. Hopeless. She'd ended up just cutting the stalks off the parsley and half-heartedly slashing the rest. It didn't matter. It was all just going to be sprinkled on top of the chicken and onions and mushrooms already in the wok. To make it look more attractive, to give it colour. Parsley and strips of red pepper. Pretty. It mattered more to her that food looked attractive than how it tasted.

The table outside the window where she was standing certainly looked pretty. There was a PVC cloth on it, a design of red poppies on a black background, and the Spanish plates looked festive. Nobody except for herself much liked eating outside which she could never understand. What was the point of living almost in the country, of having a beautiful garden and views over a lake, if one did not relish them? She only had to see that the sky was blue, that the sun was still coming through the branches of the pear tree which stood close to the house, to usher everyone outside. Sometimes it was not really warm enough. One by one they'd all go back inside, once the food had been served, and she'd be left on her own, stubbornly eating outside, the food cold. But not that evening, the evening before, the evening of the red sky. The air was positively sultry, the shade of the tree welcome even at that hour. Sam smoked, and for once she was not irritated. He hardly smoked at all these days, only what he called 'post–prandially' and not always then. She'd never liked to admit it, but she had some admiration for his control. He loved to smoke, but, conceding the dangers, had cut . . .

That wasn't really what she remembered, all that stuff. It was just that she found it comforting to replay what was reassuring and harmless. The parsley, the tablecloth, the plates, Sam smoking – none of these details was important. Yet her memory droned over them so lovingly and she allowed it to. She could reconstruct the whole banal conversation of that evening, not that it was

2

conversation, only the drifting words families push backwards and forwards to each other, words not formed into sentences or, if they were, not finished. The knife, though. That was not unimportant. The serrated-edged but sharp knife with the wooden handle. They never had their knives sharpened. Her father used to sharpen his on an old stone. Sam couldn't do it, made jokes about his own lack of talent. Sometimes a man came to the door and she'd give him all the kitchen knives she could find and he'd sharpen them, but they never seemed much improved. Serrated knives were hard to sharpen in any case. Once, when one of the knives . . .

Oh, she was doing it again, caught herself doing it. The knife was a crucial memory but not all this rambling on about sharpening. The knife was important because the next day Joe took it. Without permission. It was a lovely sunny day – back again her mind's eye went to the sun, the sky – and he and Frankie went off on their bikes with a picnic. Certainly, she knew they'd gone, that they were going, but she didn't know about the knife. Or the melon. A very fine Charentais melon, at a perfect point of ripeness, sitting in the fridge, awaiting use, for dessert that evening. She'd slice it into moon-shaped slices and place it on a dark blue dish, the better to show the colour, and then have some strawberries and place those between the slices. But Joe took it, instead of an apple or banana, both more suited to the picnic of two twelve-year-old boys. He'd shouted from the kitchen could he take something for a picnic, he and Frankie were going off on their bikes. She'd been delighted. Bikes, picnics – it was what one wanted one's children to do. She hadn't banned the melon. She hadn't even thought of it. And so she hadn't thought of the knife either. She'd heard the cupboard doors bang, and the fridge, and had actually smiled, thinking she knew Joe was swiping some of the strawberries. Well, there were plenty. Let him. He'd take the apple juice and some strawberries and crisps and biscuits if he could find them (she kept them hidden, they were for treats). No sandwiches. He'd be too lazy to make them. She'd heard him whistling and then the kitchen door slamming and she was happy . . .

Happy. Happiness. That was what this was all about, *remembering happiness*, never so acute as before that first time, that warning she'd registered in some vague kind of way but not acted upon, if she could have done, *if*. He came back so slowly. Walked beside his bike, head down, face shielded. She'd thought he'd had an argument with Frankie. Not unusual. They were friends because they were both twelve and there were no other twelve-year-old boys in the same road. They went to the same school, were in the same class, they were even the same height and shared the same birthday month. But they were quite different in both temperament and ability, they had nothing in common beyond those surface similarities. Each tried so hard to get along with the other because each needed a friend. They'd go to see films together, they'd go swimming, watch a video, hang about together, but Harriet, unlike Frankie's mother, had always seen how fragile the friendship was. Put brutally, Joe was too clever for Frankie. Frankie's stupidity annoyed him. And Joe was not physical enough for Frankie to whom sport was everything.

Joe put his bike away and came into the kitchen where she was just about to discover the disappearance of the wretched melon. She'd already decided she'd lost the knife, mislaid it, and was using another to slice bread. He looked shifty, more than frightened, somehow guilty. Not uncommon when he'd quarrelled with Frankie. So she said nothing, didn't even ask how the picnic went. Then she heard him go upstairs and his door closed,

4

quietly. A little surge of anxiety stirred in the pit of her stomach. What now? Always, with Joe, it was a case of what now. He was so volatile, could swing from boisterous happiness to utter gloom within five minutes and not always with any explanation. He'd rage and shout and scream and then be perfectly pleasant. His sudden changes of mood were bewildering. If he'd been a first-born child then she would have thought all this peculiar behaviour something to do with the way she had treated him, but he was second in the family and she had all the confidence of having brought up one other son. No, Joe was different, she'd always sensed it. He was, as one teacher had written on a report, 'a law unto himself'.

She hadn't gone up after him. That was always fatal, with Joe. Impossible to ask the simple question, 'What's the matter?' He hated that enquiry. He'd yell, 'Nothing,' and she might never find out what had happened, if anything had. So she finished slicing the bread and preparing the fish, and then she went to get the melon and strawberries . . .

This was awful, this endless, endless going over of a not very significant episode which had happened years ago. She *must* stop it. She tried to concentrate very hard on the list in front of her. She had four suppliers to telephone within the next half-hour before she went home. She had a little shop in which she sold silk scarves and wall hangings and other artistic presents, most of them made by herself in the workshop behind. She needed more silk, more special dyes, more wood for framing. She could not afford to allow her head to fill with all this pointless reminiscing. Sam said it was unhealthy. She'd asked him if he could truly, truly say he did not do it himself. He said, very firmly, with total conviction, that no, he did not. He wasn't even tempted. The point was, said Sam, all that was history. It was over. The thing to do was to go forward. Otherwise they'd won. And he would not allow them to win. He absolutely would not. She, Harriet, was letting them win, permitting all these memories of before, and even worse of during, to obsess her. What good did it do, Sam asked, in a rage. It was a kind of torture she put herself through. She was a masochist, it was sick, how she carried on . . .

But what he didn't understand was the comfort of it. It was so soothing, remembering *before*, transporting herself out of this permanent misery. Sometimes, when she'd done it most successfully, she'd find herself smiling, such a feeling of lightness inside her. And even coming back to reality wasn't as horrific as might be expected. She came back gradually, like rowing from a calm sea into the beginnings of choppy waves and, at first, no panic, not until the breakers began to crash around her and fear returned. Comfort, she needed that comfort, sometimes quite desperately. As she did today. She closed her eyes and told herself to indulge, to finish the melon–and–knife memory, but to do it quickly. Very well.

Finally, when Joe had not come down for supper, nor replied when she shouted, she had gone up. His door was not locked (he had a bolt on the inside, a bolt he'd insisted on having, for privacy, when he was only eight years old, when it had seemed amusing). She went in. He was face downwards on his bed, his right hand hanging over the edge. She saw he had a cut on it, not a very big one, but bleeding. 'Your hand,' she had said, taking it. 'What happened?' And he had said . . .

No, quickly, she reminded herself, no time, not today, for the *full* memory. So. He and Frankie had not gone up the river path, as he'd wanted to, but to the boring old park. It was crowded, since it was Saturday. They'd tried to find a quiet place, in the bushes at the foot of the slope near the bandstand. They'd drunk the apple juice and then he'd produced the melon. And the knife. He'd been just about to cut the melon when a man suddenly appeared and grabbed it. 'What a lovely melon,' he'd said, and, 'Shall I be mother?' And he'd snatched the knife and slashed into the melon, hacked at it until the seeds scattered and the juice spurted. He'd just gone on stabbing it and they'd watched, terrified, not a squeak of objection. Then he'd put a piece on the tip of the knife and held it out to Joe – 'Open up, open up,' he'd said, but Joe hadn't opened his mouth and the man suddenly opened his own and stuck the knife into his own mouth, scraping the fruit off the blade and cutting his tongue. The blood dripped down his chin on to the horribly smashed up melon lying in the grass. He'd seen their expressions and laughed. 'Blood,' he'd said, 'that's what you boys like, eh? Bit of blood.' Then he'd leaned forward and nicked Joe's hand. Joe sprang to his feet and so did Frankie, but the man held the knife threateningly in front of them and warned them not to move. Then he drew a line down the inside of his own arm and threw the knife away and turned and went running off laughing . . .

There. That was all. Over. She'd got it over. They'd phoned the police of course. So had other people. The man was a well-known nutter, said the police, not to worry, he'd be taken in again. But Joe did worry, about himself, about what he should have done instead of sitting there like a dummy. The man wasn't even very big, and he and Frankie – two of them, to his one – weren't in such an isolated place. The park was full of people within shouting distance. She'd tried to console him. Even Sam had said that keeping calm, as Joe had done, was the most sensible behaviour. 'But I wasn't calm!' Joe had shouted. 'I was scared, that's all.' And he'd gone on to imagine more terrifying scenarios in which he was even more helpless, the man more powerful, the knife used against him, his throat cut . . . For days, weeks, he'd been subdued and then, gradually, he seemed to shake himself out of his terror. Ah, this was the part of the memory, memory No. 1, which she loved, the bit she put herself through it for – *everything went back to normal.*

She took a deep, deep breath. She lifted the telephone and began dialling. Briskly, she spoke to the first person on her list. That was enough for today. She rationed herself severely now: one memory only, and not played to the full, please. And she wondered, always, if *his* mother did the same.

★

'It doesn't make sense,' Alan said, over and over, 'makes no sense at all, that's what gets me.' But Sheila wondered. Maybe it did make sense, more than Alan had the wit to see. He thought if he claimed it didn't make sense, what had happened, then it let him off scot-free. And it didn't. At least she recognised that. None of them was innocent. Leo was their grandson, more like their son, and his shame was theirs. Except he appeared to feel no shame, which was quite the worst part. If only he'd been visibly covered in shame, afterwards. But no. Dry-eyed. Calm-faced. He didn't seem to take in what he'd done, the suffering he'd caused. She'd said to him, 'You've broken my heart, you have,' and he'd smiled slightly. Maybe only a silly smirk, the one he couldn't control when he was embarrassed, but a smile all the same. She would have liked to cry, at that point, but no tears came. She thought over and over again how much she'd like to cry, to sob, to lose herself in tears, but then recollected that it was a decade or so since she'd done any such thing. And what Leo was supposed to have done was too awful for tears. Shock would have dried them up.

Anger, now, was different. Anger had remained with

her all her life. It never deserted her, could always be relied upon to come bubbling to the surface. Anger was her friend, she often felt. She'd reacted, when it happened, with anger inside herself, even if it didn't show, anger towards that daft policeman. The very idea, as if her Leo could be guilty of such a thing. Monstrous. And then, confronted with the appalling evidence, anger against Leo himself. How dare he, how *dare* he. Not how dare he do it but how dare he involve her. It was not fair, but then having Leo at all was not fair, not something she'd wanted. Nor had Alan. He would have said no. It was impossible to say no, but he would have said it. He'd have found a way of dodging. Said, with truth, it was too far. Said it was none of their business – how *stupid* that would have been. Said it was up to John's family to cope. In fact, that was his only real argument: it was up to John's family, it had happened in John's country, they were on the scene. He took no notice of another fact, that John's 'family' didn't exist as such. His mother was dead, his father had never remarried. He had no sisters and only one brother, a half-brother, whom Pat said John had seen only once in his life.

In her letters, that is. Sheila had kept them all. Letters were rare things in her life and to be treasured. Pat was a good correspondent. 'I'll write every week, Mam,' she'd said, and Sheila had wondered what good that would be even if the promise were kept. The very idea of saying goodbye to her only daughter and becoming dependent on letters had made her ill. That was the last time she'd really cried, when Pat went off to Africa, to a country with a strange name she had never heard of and didn't know how to find on a map. 'Barmy,' her own father, Pat's grandfather, had said, and, 'She's a barm-pot.' Which naturally had angered her and she'd sprung to Pat's defence, applauding her sense of adventure, admiring her pluck, getting at her father by pointing out that he'd stayed in his own street all his seventy-two years. 'And proud of it,' he'd shouted at her. 'Proud of it, and you mind yerself or else.'

Then the letters had started to come, not quite every week but near enough, wonderful letters, pages and pages, producing a sense of awe at the very sight of them. Pat described everything – the country, the people, the work she was doing, all in the greatest detail. And she sent photographs so that Sheila could see she didn't live in a mud hut but in a concrete bungalow with a tin roof, in the grounds of the hospital. She could see, too, the people Pat worked with and put names to faces. Her father, and even Alan, shook his head and handed the snaps back without a word, lips tight shut. 'It looks a nice place,' Sheila said defiantly, though she didn't think so at all – the sand blowing about, the emptiness all around, scared her. 'I'm saying nowt,' her father said, and when the shots of lions and elephants arrived he wouldn't look at them. 'Cows and sheep are good enough fer me,' he said, among other stupid things. He irritated her but she knew half her irritation was due to secretly sharing his feelings. Cows and sheep were good enough for her too and so was England. She'd never been abroad in her life. Once, she and Alan had almost taken a package holiday to Spain but then they'd gone off the idea. They were afraid of flying and the bus, which Alan favoured, took too long. These days it was embarrassing to admit she'd never left her own country and so she never did.

But Pat, Pat had been determined to see the world right from a little thing. When she was five, she'd asked for a globe for Christmas, and when she got it she kept it beside her bed and never stopped twirling it round. She'd plot journeys from one place to another and Sheila marvelled at her imagination – even to think of India, of China, made her nervous, but there was Pat, so eager to leave the security of home and venture forth. God knows where the urge had come from. It didn't make sense. She and Alan were so rooted in their home town, so content with what they had. And it didn't seem like rebellion on Pat's part, it wasn't as though she seemed to hate home or them. 'Want to knock them daft ideas out of her head before they tek hold,' her grandfather warned, when Pat reached ten and announced she was saving to go and see the Victoria Falls. Sheila just smiled, serene in the knowledge that Pat could never fulfil these dreams, or at least not for years and years. But those years passed horribly quickly and in them Pat had somehow, on school trips, already been to France and Austria and Italy, which her parents thought quite exotic enough. 'Mebbe she'll settle now,' her grandfather said, but she didn't. Europe wasn't enough. She wanted to go to America and Australia and, of course, Africa. America and Australia, although terrifyingly far away, were at least civilised, somehow safe-seeming. But not Africa. Sheila had always been against Africa and hated Pat to mention it.

No sense at all. Of all the places in the world to want to go to, Africa made no sense in Sheila's mind. She couldn't explain her hostility. It frightened her to think that maybe it was because the people there were black – it wasn't how a Christian should think and it wasn't how any decent person should. She told herself over and over again this was not the reason. She had no prejudice against black people, she knew they were just like anyone else. So what was it, then, this dislike of Africa? The weather, maybe it was the weather. She didn't like the heat. The thought of burning sun made her sick. And the animals, she didn't like wild animals, only domestic pets, cats and dogs. She'd be worried all the time about lions and snakes if she ever went there, not that she ever would. 'You're best off at home,' her father always said, and though she hated agreeing with him, about anything, that was what she thought.

It was the most terrible day of her life setting off on that journey. Terrible. Her insides seemed totally melted, her throat so dry it felt closed up. Her hands shook and she sweated profusely. Nobody, not even Alan, had understood quite what a state she was in. He had wanted to come with her – no, not wanted, had merely thought that he would have to. 'You can't go on your own all that way,' he'd said. 'I'll have to go.' His face had creased with anxiety and horror at the thought. But he was saved by his blood pressure, not that she'd wanted him with her, all gloomy and pessimistic. His blood pressure was sky-high and not responding to drugs at the time and the doctor said there was no question of his undertaking a fourteen-hour flight. So there had been no choice. She had to gird her loins and go alone. That was how she thought of it, in stirring biblical terms, girding her loins. For some reason it gave her courage, a courage her father tried to strengthen. 'Good lass,' he kept repeating, pointlessly. When she hadn't done anything yet. 'Good lass, now.' He was so excited at the idea of Leo, a boy. 'We'll mek summat of him when we get our hands on him,' he announced with relish. 'He's young enough to learn.' His delight when Pat had a son had been marked, all memory of his disapproval forgotten. 'She's done better than you already,' he said to Sheila. 'Better than her mam, better than her grandma – a boy, grand.' The son he had always wanted, fifty years or more too late. It disgusted Sheila to hear him, but his support was more important than she would admit, his encouragement, his approval.

But the actual setting out was agony. She didn't sleep a wink the night before. Even the train to Manchester was an ordeal, though she had taken it several times. She couldn't stop checking and rechecking her tickets, so many of them, and one of them for Leo, for coming back. She didn't feel she could cope and the fear of what would happen if she failed to made her tremble. By the time she'd got to the airport she was exhausted with all the tension, unable even to be sensible and buy herself a cup of tea. She'd never been in an airport in her life and was unprepared for the size and the apparent confusion. Instead of asking for directions – she couldn't ask, she had no voice – she had depended on following signs. The only relief was that the signs to the toilets were very clear and the toilets themselves so clean and tidy. She would like to have stayed there for ever – it was so consoling, washing her hands and face with the pleasant-smelling soap, so soothing watching the attendant slowly and methodically mop the floor. But she had to leave this safe haven and go and find the British Airways desk. Her case trundling behind her, the sort with wheels at one corner which she pulled by a strap, she walked miles and miles until she found the right place. All the time she was reassuring herself that she had plenty of time, plenty of time, she'd allowed far, far too much time to cover this eventuality. But in fact, in the end, she was rushing to the departure lounge, the time somehow having evaporated to half an hour.

She was seated in the middle of the plane, in the middle of a row, exactly where she had not wanted to be, but she hadn't known what to ask for except a non-smoking seat. A woman of fifty-six and she hadn't thought ahead and spoken up. She was furious at her own feebleness but afraid of causing offence if she asked to be moved. The men either side showed no interest in her. Both had brief-cases, both got papers out even before take-off. She closed her eyes and held on to her seat-belt, gripping the buckle with both hands. As the noise of the engines rose in a crescendo she hoped the plane would explode and she would die. Now that it was happening, this flight, that was what she wanted, a crash and death. But the noise steadied and she tried to compose herself for the long, long flight. She knew the number of hours it would take but not how endless each of those would seem. She couldn't sleep, though her companions in the row all snored. The stewardess gave her a blanket and a pillow, but she couldn't get comfortable. Her head pounded, her eyes smarted. And all the time, hanging over her, was the other terror, the fear of arriving . . .

It was all in an attempt to make sense of what had happened that she had taken to examining the past so carefully. She was looking not so much for a solution, or even for clues to one, as for a pattern. She believed in patterns, she believed things were somehow arranged if only the arrangement could be spotted. Nothing as silly as the stars controlling destinies, but a deeper, almost religious belief that nothing was without purpose. Pat must have been meant to go to Africa and meet John and have Leo. She must even have been meant to die, though what kind of sense that was Sheila couldn't begin to see – a young, healthy, happy woman being made to die like that was cruel. Leaving Leo, only three. It didn't bear thinking about and yet she thought of nothing else but the meaning of it all. She didn't want to be told that God moved in mysterious ways. She knew that. It was the mystery she wanted to penetrate. She searched harder and harder, restlessly reviewing what had happened, momentarily pleased if she could spot even a possible meaning to it all.

Maybe it was to give her something to do. That was not the way she wanted to express the feeling she had, but it was how she described it to herself. Crudely, in the most basic terms. She had been a useless person ever since Pat had grown up. She had never had a career, only a humdrum job as a shop assistant which she gave up as soon as she married. Her whole life had been looking after her husband and her child. And she had been quite happy, quite fulfilled, until Pat went away. She had never thought of herself as bored or useless. Now, she saw how empty her days had been and was horrified at how she had accepted the ease of her life. She'd done nothing. Her talent was for that very thing Pat despised: acceptance. She had accepted whatever was given to her. But now all that had gone. She had been made to be brave and, for her, daring. She had been forced out of dullness and complacency. So wasn't that a pattern? Wasn't that meant? But for her only beloved daughter to have to die to achieve such a worthless thing as giving her mother a purpose in life was horrible. She could barely tolerate the thought. Nor could she bear to trace any further pattern in the arrival of Leo and the last thirteen years all leading up to the point where she now found herself more lost than ever . . .

'Are you answering me, or what?' Alan asked. She banged the saucepan she'd been viciously scrubbing for the last ten minutes against the sink. Her heart raced, she felt weak and dizzy. But she wouldn't let him see, didn't want him to know how far away she'd been. It happened more and more often – she simply wasn't there, and when brought back to the present she experienced such a sense of shock. She didn't even know what the question she was supposed to answer had been, but with luck Alan would repeat it, as he duly did. 'I said, it doesn't make sense,' he almost shouted. 'Why won't he see me? What right has he got, eh? I'm going to see about it, that's what.' 'You do,' she said, grimly, knowing he wouldn't. All bluster, that was Alan. Constantly aggrieved that he'd been done wrong and yet never trying to set things right. She hated his whole attitude. He suffered, of course he did, but half the pain of this suffering was for himself. His constant refrain was, 'After all we've done for him.' It was the lack of gratitude he seemed to care about most. He'd whispered, as soon as he had been told, 'Nobody will have anything to do with us.' Quite right. She'd thought to herself it was quite right, and almost gloried in the realisation which caused Alan such distress. She wanted to be cut off, to hide, not to have to face anyone. The most dreadful thing she could think of was the thought of having to face *his* mother in court.

'How was he, any road?' asked Alan. He said it in a bad-tempered manner, turning away from her as she finished the dishes. He was still in his overalls, his hands filthy from tinkering with the car. She knew he didn't really want to know about Leo's welfare. He wanted Leo where he was, behind bars, and he wanted him kept there. For ever. It was Alan's opinion that Leo deserved rather more than he had got. He was very keen on punishment. At one time he had even muttered, 'They should flog him, they should.' Her own father, unsurprisingly, had agreed, but he'd been more concerned about the imagined honour of the family name. 'Thank Christ he didn't have our name, that's one thing.' As if the name mattered. But it had disturbed her at the time, discovering Leo didn't have Pat's surname. She couldn't understand it. If Pat wasn't married, why did she give her son his father's surname? She'd written to ask, worrying that she had no right to, and Pat had written back to say she wanted Leo to have his father's name to show that although his parents were not married both of them cared equally for him. That made no sense to Sheila, but she never mentioned it again. It was only her father, Leo's great-grandfather, who harped on about the name. She wanted to hit him every time he thanked Christ Leo was Leo Jackson and not Armstrong.

How it came to be Jackson Sheila couldn't imagine.

She'd thought John would have an African name since he was African. Before Pat sent a photograph she had assumed, because of his English-sounding surname, that he must be English. And white. Someone out there, like Pat, working with the medical aid programme. It had never occurred to her that this man Pat was in love with was black. She had hardly dared to show his photograph to Alan and had actually concealed it from her own father until she'd heard Pat was expecting. Pat had never mentioned John's blackness. When he was first introduced in her letters it was to say he was a brilliant doctor, he was so gentle, he was so kind, everyone at the hospital loved him . . . And how thrilled she'd been, hearing wedding bells, proud already that Pat was going to be married, she assumed, to a doctor, that this was a hospital romance. That was what she told people, that Pat was engaged to a doctor. She couldn't bring herself to lie outright and say Pat was married, but engaged seemed both safe and fair. Giving the name of Pat's doctor made it sound all right – Dr John Jackson, yes, she met him out there.

He was not handsome. The photograph showed a burly man, the top half of his body more powerful than the legs. He had close-cropped hair, large eyes, a strong face. An African face, obviously. Beside him Pat looked smaller and more fragile than ever. It made Sheila swallow hard just to look at them – *they don't match*, she found herself thinking. They don't. They're opposites in every way. But opposites who, according to Pat, loved each other dearly. And John wrote to her, a lovely letter of his own, beautiful handwriting, saying how he loved Pat and cherished her and was a very lucky man. They wanted her and Alan to go over and meet John, but the journey was too daunting. Instead, Sheila wrote, we'd like you to come home and bring John to meet us. But it never happened, it was too expensive. They were saving for the trip, when the accident occurred. Another year and all three of them would have come over. How that visit would have gone she didn't dare speculate. Maybe John would have won them all over, as he had done Pat. 'Hasn't even done the decent thing by her,' her father grumbled. 'Puts her in the family way and can't even marry her. It's disgusting, he should be ashamed, that's what, in my day, he'd have had to.' No good repeating that it was Pat, for reasons best known to herself, who didn't want marriage whereas John did.

She'd imagined Leo would look like John. There had been only a few photographs, when he was a baby, and after that Pat's camera was stolen. When Sheila saw him for the first time she was startled at how like his mother, not his father, he looked. His hair and his eyes were his father's, beautiful curly black hair and huge dark brown eyes, but his features and frame were Pat's. He was slim, his face quite delicate, his mouth and nose European, not African. And his skin was brown, not black, literally coffee-coloured. He stood, that first time, and studied her, not smiling, looking at her very carefully, too carefully for such a young child. She didn't know what to say or do. She hated to think how she looked, an overweight, grey-haired, white woman, dressed in a flowery dress and an unnecessary pink cardigan, her feet uncomfortable in sandals she'd never worn before and her hair sticking to her head with the awful heat. What had she finally said? She couldn't remember. Something inadequate. But she'd taken his hand, timidly, and squeezed it, and to her great surprise he had taken hold of her other one and done the same. Such a cool hand, to her own hot one. Lovely for her to feel his hand, surely hers felt nasty to him, but he went on clinging to her and it made everything easier.

The people at the hospital were kind. They admired her for coming. She read this admiration as well as pity in their eyes and was upset by it because she knew she was unworthy. She'd come out of duty not love, not love of Leo, her unknown grandson. It was her bounden duty to come and take Leo home, her duty to Pat, to her whole idea of what family meant. But there was resentment there, too, in her, and she was always afraid people would sense this, that someone would divine how appalled she was at the responsibility thrust upon her. She wasn't the adoring grandmother they thought they saw. She was only a middle-aged woman afraid she would not be able to live up to expectations, Leo's expectations. That was what bothered her most – what were this small boy's expectations? What did he think was going to happen? Did he expect his mother and father to return? Did he even know who she was? Well, of course he must know, Pat would have talked of her home back in England and her family, there must be all kinds of information stored in that little head ready to help him make sense of her.

But he didn't speak. Not a word. She stayed in a room in the hospital for a week and he stayed in the children's ward and he didn't speak a word to anyone. Every day she would go to collect him, and he came willingly enough but never spoke, not even hello or goodbye. She wondered if he could speak, if perhaps he was backward, but also knew this was nonsense – Pat had written of all the complicated sentences he could construct and he was only three. Her pride in his linguistic ability had been great. And he spoke English as well as his father's language, she knew that. It made everything so difficult, his silence. Uneasy, creepy. She would hear herself prattling on to him and she sounded so foolish. She took to asking him simple questions in the hope that he wouldn't be able to resist replying but he did resist. The only comfort, the only promising sign, was that he did sometimes smile. And when he did, Pat's dimples appeared in his cheeks making tears come to her own eyes. These fascinated him. He put his finger up and traced an escaped tear or two, and licked it, surprise in his face. But he still didn't speak.

They told her that of course he was traumatised. He'd been in the Land-Rover when it crashed, thrown clear, head-first into soft sand and quite unharmed. But then there had been a time-lapse of perhaps as long as an hour, nobody quite knew how long, before another truck came along. What had Leo done in that hour? Certainly he'd seen the bodies of his mother and father. Maybe he'd touched them. There was blood on his hands and clothes when he was found yet he was not hurt himself. It was too agonising to try to imagine what he had gone through before he was rescued – dreadful, dreadful. So it wasn't surprising he hadn't spoken since. Everyone said this, but Sheila thought it was surprising. She thought hysteria would have been more natural, screaming, sobbing, noise in general, nightmares. Leo, she was told, slept deeply. There were no nightmares. There was no psychiatrist at the hospital – it was only a poor cottage sort of hospital – and no paediatrician, but the nurses, all friends of Pat's and John's, had talked to him and gone over the accident. They had said his mummy and daddy had gone to Jesus and were happy (it was a religious hospital, a Methodist foundation originally). They'd told him his granny was coming for him to take him home with her, and he would be happy too.

Sheila took him, before they left, to his parents' grave. She didn't know if it was the right thing to do or not, but she did it. There was no stone marking the grave and the graveyard was not the place of trees she thought of as a proper graveyard, but there was a wooden cross, Pat and John's names written on it rather untidily in black paint. She could find no flowers to put there – it was the hot

season and the flowers she was assured bloomed in plenty
were all dead. So she stood with Leo, hand in hand, and
stared at the cross, and then she picked him up and carried
him away, patting his back. His face pressed into her neck
and she felt the first stirrings of real love at last. She loved
him. She would love him. He was a poor, sad little boy
and she would be a mother to him.

The first word he spoke was not granny but mummy. It
seemed pointless, when it was such a triumph, to correct
him.

Chapter Two

THE MORNINGS WERE always the worst. Harriet
couldn't understand why. She had expected the
nights to be the worst, had envisaged Joe unable to sleep
or else waking screaming in remembered terror, but no,
he slept soundly. It was the mornings which were bad.

Morning, to her, was a relief. The moment it was light
and she could be up doing something she felt better, was
able to hope a little. Nights for her, since it happened,
were spent staring at the ceiling, becoming intimately
acquainted with the fine crack running across it from the
centre light to the left-hand corner above the bed. It was
never, in their bedroom, or at least to Harriet's eyes, eyes
always good in the dark, entirely black. Almost always
there was enough grey to be able to make out the shapes of
the chest of drawers, the cupboards, the long mirror. She
had grown used to watching the light deepen and the
furniture emerge from its shadowy outline. Beside her,
Sam slept, sometimes snored, and she envied him, then
despised him – to be able to sleep, as he had always done,
as she had once done!

She'd trained herself to keep calm, not to thrash about,
turning from side to side in wild attempts to fool her body
into rest. Instead, she lay on her back, her hands folded
lightly on her stomach, her legs together and straight.
Sometimes she closed her eyes, sometimes she opened
them, feeling them grow heavier as the night progressed.
She knew that of course occasionally she did drift off and

that in some way she must be getting a little sleep. Enough. Enough to keep her going, just. She hadn't taken sleeping pills, not even on the first night afterwards when they had been urged upon her. Joe had. She'd left it to him. Everyone had been most insistent he should take sleeping pills, mild ones, when he came out of hospital, and he had been obedient. Everyone wanted Joe asleep, unconscious. So long as he was staring at them all, dry-eyed, white-faced, mute, they found their own rest disturbed. So he'd taken the pill, that first night home, and the next and the next. He had a bottle of them, beside his bed. It made Sam uneasy. 'You don't think . . .' he'd said. 'What?' she'd snapped. 'Go on, say it, kill himself, take them all?' Sam had flinched, turned away and muttered, 'I only wondered . . .' '*That* was what you wondered,' she had said scornfully, 'and the answer is, you'll be relieved, won't you, that no, I don't think he will.'

What power she had, how Sam, in all this, depended on her. She had only to say she thought Joe would not contemplate suicide for Sam to relax: if *she* thought not, then she was bound to be right because it was she who understood Joe best and was closest to him. That was what Sam thought, what everyone thought. She was his mother. She must know best. But it was all wrong. Joe was no longer her Joe, what had happened had put him way beyond her knowledge. Being alone with him was torture. The burden of his suffering grew heavier and heavier until she felt she must, she *must* put it down. But there was nowhere to put it, it could never be got rid of. And it was in the mornings it was heaviest, when she saw Joe so dead-looking, eyes and limbs so weary, skin pasty, with an unhealthy sheen to it as though covered in luminous paint. Yet he tried so hard. He washed, he combed his hair, he put on clean clothes, and she was grateful. She knew he could have stayed in bed and turned his face to the wall and cowered and given up. That was what made it all so very painful, this evidence that he was struggling, trying to get back to normal.

In the mornings, she had to turn away from him. Her overbright voice made small-talk during breakfast and she could not shut it up. She didn't fuss over food. She was determined not to comment on the fact that he hardly ate a thing at any time of the day and certainly never in the mornings when, before, he had had two bowls of cereal and toast and fruit and was still, then, looking for more. He was strong enough, it was no tragedy if he stopped eating for a while. She saw to it that all his favourite foods were always available but she did not remark upon his lack of interest. It was all too obviously a punishment of some sort to deny himself a hot croissant, to turn aside from the scrambled eggs, done as he loved them, with thin strips of crispy bacon. Sam ate it all anyway, or Louis, if he was at home. Or the dog, though even Bruno seemed affected by the surfeit of luxuries and ate them less than vigorously if they came his way.

He went to school as soon as he was able, when his leg was still in plaster. She hadn't been able to believe he would go until the cast came off, but she didn't want to stop him. 'I might as well,' he said, and she'd taken him and collected him each day. She'd seen how he was stared at. Any boy with his leg in plaster, limping into school on crutches, would have been stared at of course. But these stares were different. She saw how the children stopped talking and gave him a wide berth. Nobody rushed to help him, nobody wanted to sign their name or draw a picture on Joe's plaster. It made her cry to watch him manoeuvre himself into the school followed by clutches of other pupils whispering about him. And what were they whispering? Everyone knew. If only he'd waited until his plaster was off, then he'd have been less obvious, he wouldn't have attracted such attention. She'd almost pointed this out and had been stopped just in time by the expression on his face – the least suggestion that he should keep a low profile and he was furious. Rightly. She'd been weak with admiration, aware of how strange it was to admire one's fifteen-year-old son in this kind of way. And Sam was thrilled. 'That's the spirit,' he'd said, 'he'll show them,' and she'd said, coldly, 'What spirit?' and, 'Show who what?' and he'd said, 'Don't be like that, Harriet, please, it only makes everything harder if we're not friends.'

If we're not friends! Such a silly, babyish phrase. She wanted Sam a million miles away. When, a week later, he had wanted to make love to her – no, have sex with her – she'd hated him. She said to him, that first time, 'How *can* you?' and he had been bewildered, had asked her what she meant, what the connection was between what had happened to Joe and making love. Why on earth should one cancel out the other? There was no point in trying to explain, to explain how *pleasure* revolted her. There was no pleasure in anything for her. But the next time he wanted sex she just gave in and he was pleased. He appeared not to realise that the idea of making love made her want to weep. But she'd let him. It gave her some kind of perverse satisfaction not to throw him off her stone-like body. Except she knew it was a warm, soft, pliant stone and so did Sam. Her mind was not in her body, though. Her mind was watching and hating, curling in every corner with contempt and knowing that if she had been the man this behaviour would have been impossible, she would not have been able even to think of this performance. But Sam saw it as more of getting-back-to-normal. It wasn't that he didn't care about Joe, never for one moment did she think that, but that he was able, as she was not, to resume day-to-day pleasures. His distress hadn't affected his desire. He wasn't held back, he was an expert at closing doors on the past, and proud of it.

Her doors were always open. The past was the place where she still was even if she went quite competently through the motions of the present. She loved the past, could not get through those doors Sam wanted closed and locked quickly enough. Only work blocked out the past temporarily, and the effort to work was mighty. She battled every day with the need to work. Pushing herself to concentrate exhausted her and yet once she had done it the images stopped, the voices ceased. She was like Sam, then. But the difference was that she, unlike him, did not want to succeed in blotting out that agonising past. She knew it was necessary to her, that she literally fed on it. Several pasts, quite separate. The far past, before anything whatsoever had happened to Joe, before even the feeble melon-and-knife incident, that blissful past. Then there was the more serious but still not really dangerous episode, the theft of Joe's Walkman, that nearer but still remote past. And then the last year. That past. The past where she did not want to be and which she hoped one day to bury, as Sam had done.

What she knew she was trying to do was empathise so completely with Joe that she could be with him, know what he was thinking, how he was feeling. She was straining and straining to have been with him, to have *been* him. And she knew this was dangerous. It would lead her into all kinds of delusions and that would not help Joe. She would goad herself into a kind of frenzy trying to go through every minute of that night. It was not like imagining his Walkman being stolen. Then, it had upset her, thinking herself into Joe walking home from the football match listening to his Walkman and the sudden wrench as it was ripped from his head and the fright of the three louts jeering at him and pushing him and tossing the

Walkman from one to another and then running off with it, laughing. She'd been able, then, to empathise successfully and to some purpose. 'Joe,' she'd consoled, 'I *know* there was nothing you could do, I *know* it was all so quick and you were in a daze, don't blame yourself.' He'd cried, with humiliation, and she could feel how he felt. There'd been a curious thrill in being able to understand so completely. 'You shouldn't have been using that stupid thing in a football crowd anyway,' Sam had said. 'It was asking for trouble, you were a sitting target.' Joe had gone mad, demanding to know why he had been a target when scores of boys were walking home from the match on their own listening to Walkmans, why did it happen to him?

At least Sam had not succumbed to the temptation to tell him. She knew why he thought Joe a target, though. Sam thought Joe looked soft. Even though he was quite tall there was something incurably innocent and tender-looking about him, something sweet. Louis had not had this quality, even before adolescence. He was like Sam, stridently masculine in manner. Joe was not feminine, he was not girlish, but he was unthreatening, hesitant, and it was true you could tell this just by looking at him. Every time Sam bemoaned Joe's lack of strength, his sensitivity, Harriet rounded on him and asked him what was so wonderful about being and looking tough. She said she didn't want Joe to 'toughen up', she wanted him to stay the same sweet, if difficult, boy he had always been. Sam said that in that case he was always going to have problems, he'd have to learn how to defend himself, how to conceal his lack of aggression. Then they had quarrelled, about aggression, aggressively. Harriet said male aggression had caused all the trouble in the world and she and her generation of women had tried to rear sons who would not think aggression was part of being male . . . Sam had just smiled.

In the mornings, she fancied she saw that Joe's sweetness had gone for ever. He had aged. His face was drawn, youth had gone. He had an old, old, tired look to him. Nobody would ever again see him as an easy target, and that was what was saddest of all. He had the same cynical expression as his attacker, the same sour pull to his mouth, the same heavily shadowed planes in his cheeks. And had that, she wondered, happened to *that* boy overnight? Was his mother looking at him, when she visited him, and seeing that *her* boy had vanished?

★

Sheila had wanted to apologise right at the beginning. She'd asked everyone to please convey, to his parents, her heartfelt apologies. They'd all – the policeman, the probation officer, the solicitor – said that they would. But she'd never believed them, nor blamed them for failing to pass on anything so insulting as apologies. They were out of order. You couldn't apologise for something like that, it was adding insult to injury. How would she have felt, if it had been the other way round, if *apologies* had been sent to her? Furious, she'd have been furious, hopping mad. She'd have just looked at whoever conveyed those apologies and said nothing. They would have known what she thought of them all right.

In the court, the Youth Court, she and the other mother had been very near to each other. Sheila was shocked, shocked by the whole thing. She realised her head had been full of dark, imposing old chambers and judges in wigs and juries sitting in boxes, everything sombre and frightening. But it wasn't like that at all. The Youth Court was in a new building. They walked up two flights of stairs to it, stairs covered in grey haircord. There were no footsteps echoing down stone corridors. The actual courtroom was quite small, too small. It was a square, plain room with a wooden ceiling lit by artificial light, four globes hanging over the magistrates' seats. It was light and bright and without atmosphere. The bench at which the magistrates sat was made of a shiny light wood and so was the witness box and the tables at which the solicitors and Clerk of the Court sat. She and Alan sat to the left of these tables, on ordinary grey chairs, chairs such as every office had. The other mother sat with her husband and her son at the back, facing the magistrates. They were no more than ten yards away. Only by looking straight ahead could Sheila avoid seeing them, and even then they were in the corner of her vision.

It seemed wrong, this ordinariness, this close proximity, this emptiness. She'd imagined a gallery full of curious onlookers and cringed at the prospect, but now she cringed more at the lack of any public, at the exposure of her and Alan because there were no other people. She felt naked, vulnerable, before a word had been said, and looked down at the pink carpet – *pink*, something else unseemly – with such intensity that she soon knew every fibre of it. She'd hoped she and Alan could just melt into the background, hardly be seen at all, but there they were, targets, a pair of pathetic elderly people, soberly dressed as if for a funeral but this was worse than any funeral. When the other mother crossed her legs or moved her feet Sheila's heart pounded. She feared any movement from over there, she feared some scene in which the other mother leapt across the pink carpet and hit her . . .

Ridiculous. Covertly, she studied the other mother and knew such a vulgar thing would never happen. Class hung in the air and she recognised it. They were so infinitely superior, that family. Handsome, well and fashionably dressed, the mother in particular. She was wearing a suit, a black suit with a shortish skirt showing long, slender legs, and a startlingly white, crisp blouse. She looked cool and immaculate. The man, the father, was a big man, broad-shouldered, dark-haired. He wore a suit too, a grey suit with some sort of thin stripe in it. At least the boy had jeans on, very clean jeans, possibly new, and a perfectly ordinary blue shirt. He was blond, like his mother. Blond, smooth hair and a sweet, gentle face . . .

A buzzer sounded and the solicitors stood up. Sheila jumped, then nudged Alan to stand up with her. She felt obscurely cheated again – a buzzer, such a cheap thing, like one on a television game show, no pomp and majesty at all. Then a door opened and three people walked in and sat down on the red chairs behind the bench, chairs only slightly better than the grey ones in the body of the court. No grand oak chair with a high back and heavy claw feet and arms to it and no bewigged judge. Three desperately ordinary people, two women and a man, all looking slightly sheepish. Then the prosecutor began, a woman the same as Elaine, their solicitor. Again, Sheila felt disturbed. Neither of these women looked right, she hadn't expected women, and young women too, neither she was sure out of their thirties. No gowns. They were not barristers and did not wear gowns. They looked so casual. She knew this ought to have made her feel relaxed, helped her not to be frightened, but it didn't, it made her somehow contemptuous. This was all too upsettingly amateurish, it mocked the serious nature of the business.

She tried so hard to listen carefully but concentration was difficult. She was distracted by silly things, by the sound of the heating system, by the sudden cry of seagulls outside, by the way the Clerk of the Court played with his pen, constantly up-ending it and lightly tapping his papers at each turn. There was a moment of farce when a policeman's walkie-talkie suddenly erupted. He was standing at the side-door, through which Leo would come, and they all heard the static and then a voice calling for attention. He blushed and turned it off and everyone smiled. Then Leo was brought in and put in the witness box, in that flimsy-looking affair, not like a witness box at all. She was looking straight at him but there was no eye contact, his eyes were dead, fixed on some far-off point no one could see. He looked neither nervous nor cocky, just quite still, his hands resting lightly on the ledge in front of him as though he were about to deliver a sermon. He replied calmly and clearly to all the obvious questions – his name, his age, the mere facts. But when he was asked to describe how and why he stabbed Joseph Samuel Kennedy he wouldn't answer. He said, 'I have nothing to say.' Just like that. Asked if he pleaded guilty or not guilty, he said, 'Guilty.' And that was that.

The hardest part was when the magistrates went out – to have to go on sitting there, waiting, when all she wanted to do was slink off, get through that door before the other mother. She stood when the buzzer went once more – hateful, crude noise – but she didn't look up until she was seated again. The male magistrate spoke for the three of them. He didn't make a meal of it, that was one thing. But she despised him for his unimpressive words, she would rather he had made a speech full of fury. He sounded so dreary, mumbling on about 'this sort of thing must be stopped'. Hopeless. And the women either side looked more embarrassed than stern. Leo was sentenced to the maximum sentence, twelve months in a Young Offenders' Institution. She hardly took in where it was.

There and then she'd wanted to apologise. She sat there, fantasising how she would walk up to the mother and touch her on the shoulder of her jacket and she would turn, startled, and Sheila would take a deep breath and just say that she was sorry, so sorry, so very sorry. She wouldn't ask for forgiveness, she would leave straight after saying her bit, she wouldn't wait for the mother to reply. If she replied. (Would she herself have replied if it had been the other way round? No, probably not.) But what stopped her from actually doing what she wanted to do was the thought that it might look like a plea for sympathy. Sympathy for herself: look at me, feel for me, I am his grandmother, his mother to all intents and purposes. And how could she do that? Because she didn't deserve sympathy, and certainly not from his mother. Yet it filled her with horror to think his mother might imagine she did not care, or that she was *not* sorry. Suppose his mother never guessed at how wretched she was? How she blamed herself? How she struggled to make sense of it all? How she felt for her? How she put herself in her position? Suppose his mother thought her as brutal as Leo? That he was from a brutal and brutalised home? That he had never had a chance because he had been unloved and starved and beaten, and that his parents' treatment of him had led to all this?

She couldn't. His mother couldn't think that, not if she'd listened to Leo's solicitor. They hadn't chosen her, neither she nor Alan had a clue. She'd been appointed to take Leo's case somehow. 'Call me Elaine,' this solicitor had said, 'it will make it a bit easier.' But it hadn't, not calling her by her Christian name or anything else. None of it had been easy. Speaking at all had not been easy. She'd replied to all Elaine's questions haltingly, at that first awkward meeting, offering no more than the minimum answer. So much in her head, so little of it emerging in speech. Alan had been more useful. He'd rambled on and on, talked the hindleg off a donkey, repeated over and over that none of it made sense, Leo had had a good and loving home, he didn't know why or how it had all gone wrong . . . Elaine had said it would make a great difference to Leo's sentence, this parental – sorry, grand-parental – back-up, this proof of a solid, decent upbringing, but at the same time she would have to make much of the death of his parents, the trauma of it, the wrench being taken from Africa, his difficulties as a boy of mixed race in an almost completely white community – she would have to, because there were no other exonerating circumstances, were there?

No, there were not. But what Sheila doubted was the wisdom of what this Elaine said she would have to dwell on at length. It was dishonest. He'd only been three. He couldn't remember Africa, or his parents. He had had no difficulties as a mixed-race boy. Well, none she'd known of, nothing significant, surely. Nobody had ever taunted him, or if they had he'd never mentioned it, he hadn't suffered living where they lived or she would have been aware of it. But had she fooled herself? Leo was always a quiet child, even when he did start to speak normally, but she still wanted to convince herself that she would have known about any victimisation. The school would have known. He was a prize pupil, the teachers followed his progress carefully, he was more than noticed. He wasn't popular, she knew that, he had no real friends, which had always troubled her, but that wasn't the same as being persecuted, so that he in turn might have wished to persecute. She would rather Joe Kennedy's mother had heard all this than the stuff Elaine eventually came out with in court, trying to make hearts bleed with the story of the car crash and the not speaking, and the tale of the awful first year. It had embarrassed her to listen to it. She had looked down at her feet, blood thudding in her ears. When she next had looked up, Leo was smiling. She wished he wouldn't. It would be misunderstood. She'd told him often not to smirk and he'd just shrugged his shoulders, indicating that he couldn't help it. What was he smirking at? She hadn't been attending.

Then the court was adjourned and she saw him and his

mother and his father rise, all three tall and handsome and clean and beyond reproach, while she and Alan were so battered and shabby and somehow responsible, defiled by Leo's wickedness. How could she apologise?

*

Joe hated the policemen. He hated the doctor, he hated the solicitor, but most of all he hated the policemen, each one and especially Detective Sergeant Graham.

Harriet disliked him too. She didn't like the way he'd walked into the house in the first place, mock-polite, she felt. She didn't like how he spoke or what he said. 'I'd like to express my sympathy,' he'd said, in an unctuous tone, 'the lad's been through a terrible ordeal, terrible.' And he'd shaken his head and clucked his tongue. She'd been annoyed when she heard Sam offer him a cup of coffee, gratefully accepted, with milk, one sugar. Afterwards, she'd said, 'Why did you have to give him coffee?' and Sam had been rightly surprised. Coffee was always offered to visitors, coffee or a drink, if the time was appropriate. She'd known she couldn't defend her objection.

So Detective Sergeant Graham had drunk the coffee. And stared. He did a lot of staring. She wondered if he thought it made him look compassionate, this solemn stare, and longed to tell him it did not. It made him look foolish. She wanted to slap him. And Sam was always so nice to him, so friendly, so quick to agree that Graham's job, the job of the police in general, was difficult. There were so few clues at the beginning. Joe had seen his attackers only for a minute, only a quick but clear glimpse before they blindfolded him. One was white and big and one black and big, and both had had knives. Well, obviously, they must have done, in view of his injuries. Sam sympathised with how hard it would be trying to catch these two. Graham was pleased, he cleared his throat

34

and nodded and said that he was glad the problems were appreciated and that everyone would be doing their level best.

He wanted to talk to Joe again, at length, on his own. Sam said of course at the same time as she said no. Joe had been through enough, he'd already given his statement to a policeman and had nothing more to add. She wouldn't have him plagued, he needed to sleep. Graham said he was prepared to be patient, he took her point, but he'd have to see the lad himself, preferably soon. She wished he would stop calling Joe a lad. It seemed to be a term of affection but she found it sloppy. What was wrong with his name, what was wrong with 'Joe'?

When he'd gone, that first time, Sam was angry with her. 'There's no need to antagonise the police,' he said, 'for God's sake, it isn't their fault.' 'And there's no need to be so chummy,' she flashed back, 'all matey, as though you had to keep in with them or something.' 'We have to work with them,' Sam said, 'we might as well be friendly, make it easier all round.' He said he didn't see what was wrong with Graham anyway, he seemed perfectly nice and quite couth for a policeman. Sam said it as a joke but she didn't take it as one. And she felt quite triumphant when, on Graham's next call, Louis was there and said, when Graham had left, that he didn't like him. Sam repeated what he'd said about having to work with Graham, and Louis said, 'No, Dad, *he* has to work with *us*.' Exactly. Louis had pin-pointed what she didn't like about Graham or about the way Sam treated him – it was as though, in the middle of all their grief, they had also to take on the burden of handling this policeman, and she couldn't bear it. There was no energy to be friendly, to offer cups of coffee, as though this was a social relationship when it wasn't. She wanted to be formal, distant. It was the only way she could bear it.

35

But she knew what she hated most of all was Graham thinking that he knew the details. He mentioned them once – 'the details are pretty horrifying' – and she found herself flushing. He was always trying for eye contact, wanting to exchange meaningful looks, and she refused to let him. The last thing she wanted was to be close, in any way, to Graham. Once, he'd said, 'You seem hostile, Mrs Kennedy,' and she had denied she was. 'I prefer to be business-like,' she'd said. 'I am a businesswoman after all.' She didn't say this apologetically but as a statement, but he was off, wanting her to talk about her business, about how she ran it, how it was doing, and she was brusque again, telling him in almost as many words that it was no concern of his, surely. He'd smiled and agreed. Then, when he'd stood up, about to leave, he'd said, 'I know how you must feel, Mrs Kennedy. I've got lads of my own.' She'd been so angry, said he couldn't possibly know how she felt, everyone said that and it was *nonsense*, she was sick of it.

Apparently he'd had a word with Sam after that outburst. Suggested his wife should see a counsellor. At least she could laugh at that, if unkindly, contemptuously. A counsellor! How absurd. It made her squirm to hear the word. Stupid people who took a course and then presumed to advise others about how to deal with their grief – dear God, it was outrageous. The last thing in the world she wanted was to be counselled. The word appeared everywhere. 'Seeing a counsellor' had become a cliché, utterly banal. It was the same attitude as the police had towards Joe – *he* should see a therapist. He would never, they said, 'get over it' unless he did, unless he 'talked it through'. Jesus! The soft option, talking, talking to counsellors, therapists, strangers, as though it helped one iota. Joe didn't want to talk to anyone. He'd answered all their questions and that was enough. If he talked to anyone, more than he had already done, it would be to his family. Sam said he didn't know how an educated woman could be so ignorant. He said it was like listening to someone refusing to believe a dentist could relieve the suffering of toothache. Psychiatry was a skilled profession, he said, and she was being typically British, sneering at it. He said he was even willing to go and see a psychiatrist himself, if she and Joe would. She was astonished by this, he immediately had the upper hand for the first time. '*You?*' she said. 'I don't believe it, you, the great blocker–out? Now why would you agree to see a psychiatrist?' And he said, very quietly, 'I have to try to do something, we can't go on like this.'

★

The probation officer was really very kind, kinder than anyone Sheila had yet come into contact with. She hadn't wanted to see any probation officer – wasn't it enough to have had to put up with policemen and lawyers? What on earth did she want with a probation officer? It was like shutting the stable door after the horse had bolted, surely. But apparently the circumstances required that someone called a Through Care Probation Officer be put on the case to liaise between Leo and his family, and over the months Sheila had got used to the occasional visits.

More humiliation, though in fact the first words the probation officer had said, after the usual pleasantries, were, 'You mustn't blame yourself, Mrs Armstrong, you really mustn't, nobody else does.' That had made her smile wearily. 'Don't they?' she'd said. 'How do you know? I'll bet there's plenty as do, not that it makes any difference.' 'Nobody who knows the facts,' said the probation officer firmly. 'Nobody in this neighbourhood who's watched you and Mr Armstrong bring Leo up. Everyone knows what a good home he's had, there's no doubt about that.' And this probation officer, this Helen woman, had touched her hand reassuringly. Surprising, Sheila thought, to do that. Just a pat, but done so spontaneously, or so it appeared. She was a funny little person anyway, this Helen. Small, earnest. She had a dark jacket on with a rose in the buttonhole, a thing Sheila hadn't seen for a long time. She indicated the flower and said, 'Off to a wedding?' and this Helen said no, it was her father, he grew roses and was so proud of them and it pleased him that she liked to wear his roses in her buttonhole.

So she was a thoughtful young woman, she obviously liked to be kind, and it was realising this that made Sheila in the end, after nearly a year, bold. She cut in on Helen's routine questions and said there was one she would like to ask herself and was told to ask away. 'What I want to know is,' she said, 'has *his* mother ever realised how sorry I am? How ashamed? I can't bear her to think . . .' and then she hadn't been able to go on. Not because of any tears, they still wouldn't come, but because she couldn't find the words for what she wanted to say. 'I think about her all the time,' she went on eventually (Helen having said nothing). 'I can't get her out of my head. What she must be going through. If it had been the other way round . . .' and again she had to stop. Imagining it. What was done. She'd vowed not to, never to imagine it. It did no good, it was disgusting, she knew it. But *she* must do it, it would be natural. And her heart must still be murderous towards Leo and perhaps towards his mother, his grandmother . . .

Helen was clearly uncomfortable. She bit her lip and said, 'Well, Mrs Armstrong, I don't know Mrs Kennedy, I haven't had anything to do with her, you see, so I can't say, but if it was me, I mean if I was her, I don't think I'd blame you. I might want to know about Leo's background, to see if I could understand the cause of . . . of what he'd done . . . but I don't think I'd blame you. Parents can't help how their children turn out, can they? I mean, not always. It's too easy blaming them for everything. And I expect she knows that.' All very sensible. Sheila admitted it was. But it didn't help. 'What I'd like,' she said, 'what I've always wanted to do all this time is somehow to let her know . . . not to meet her or anything, but to send some message, somehow, I don't know what . . .' Her voice trailed to a halt. Helen looked so doubtful. 'You don't think it would be a good idea? Maybe you're right, maybe it would seem like a cheek, it might hurt her even more, my thinking it mattered saying sorry, as if it did any good. Oh, I don't know. Nothing's right, nothing feels right any more.'

The same feelings she'd had so many years ago, bringing Leo home. Nothing had felt right from the moment the news of the accident came. Nothing was ever really right ever again, but life went on. That's what people said, life must go on. She'd been so unlike her usual self all that time in Africa . . . no routine, no familiarity, everything strange and out of kilter. From the moment she woke up there was nothing she could recognise – the light was harsh, brilliantly so, that sun blasting its way through the shutters, and then the bare floor, she didn't even know what it was made of, and the sad trickle of water coming from that spout of a tap and no kettle to make her tea. No tea either, not as she knew it. They'd given her a little tin box with some mouldy-looking loose-leaf tea in it and shown her the so-called kitchen at the end of the corridor with its camping stove and told her she could make tea whenever she wished. It felt so terrible, so destructive, the lack of familiarity. She ached to be surrounded by her own things, to have the confidence they gave her. She remembered looking in the little plastic-edged mirror – that was all there was in her room apart from the truckle bed – and thinking, Is that all I am, my kettle, my tea, my cooker, my fridge? Her face was so blank, flat and blank, concealing her terror.

Yet this was how Pat had lived, how she'd chosen to live. They'd shown her the married quarters. Pat and John and Leo had lived in a bungalow in the grounds, which she'd known from the photographs. But there'd been no shots of the inside. Three basic rooms, one with a camping stove in a curtained-off corner, and a cubicle of a bathroom. A proper lavatory, true, but no bath, and the shower was a rusty-looking pipe suspended over a cement trough. This was where Pat had written all those lyrical letters, full of her contentment. Looking round, Sheila had known she would not have been able to enjoy one moment's happiness, not here. Nothing would have felt right. She wouldn't have existed, not unless she'd been able to invent a new persona, which she would not have wanted to do. Again and again in the months that followed she reminded herself of this whenever she saw how lost Leo was. When the cold rain streamed down the windows and she saw his face she remembered that loud sun and understood his bewilderment. Alan said he was only a small child, his memory was undeveloped, he wouldn't notice the difference, but she knew he was wrong. Leo, child or not, didn't feel right, he wasn't himself any more, and it was worse for him because he couldn't articulate his feelings or make sense of anything. Only time would help, which it did, agonisingly slowly, as difficult for her to endure as for him. It would come over her in great waves, nothing was ever going to be the same again, there was no going back. Leo had changed her life irrevocably. Life was about putting up with everything that happened. It would be on her tombstone: 'She Put Up With Everything'.

There were people in the world who didn't. Pat had been one. She'd rejected the life laid out for her at a very early age and gone her own way. Against quite great odds, with little encouragement. 'Look where it got her,' her grandfather had said, 'dead at twenty-six, she should've stopped at home.' Then they'd had a ridiculous quarrel about whether Pat would or would not have met the same fate if she had stayed at home, with Sheila heatedly arguing that there were road accidents all the time in Britain too, and her father blaming African roads and African cars – 'load of rust, stands to reason' – and anything else African he could think of. That was how they got rid of their grief and resentment. But how did Leo get rid of his? She had no idea. Not by crying, anyway. 'He's a brave li'le lad,' said her father, echoed by Alan. 'He isn't a cry-baby, that's one thing, even if he isn't a ray of sunshine either. Has he ever smiled, our Sheila, eh?' Crossly, Sheila said, of course he had and to remember the child had ears. 'I know that,' her father said, 'bonny ears too and a bonny face. He's like his mam, if it weren't for the hair and the eyes, and the colour of him. Pity about that, still, there's nowt can be done, eh Leo? He's a grand li'le lad for all that, once he settles, once he gets ower it.'

It was pathetic, really. She knew she shouldn't get angry. Her father was an old man who'd never even seen a black person before, so perhaps he couldn't help his awful prejudices. She knew this was not true, that he could and should help them, but watching him with Leo she excused him. A child was a child to him and he found it easy to be with children. He got on better with Leo than any of them did, and Leo accepted him as his friend before he accepted anyone else. When Grandad came – it seemed awkward to be correct and say Great-grandad, just as it was to call her Grandma instead of Mam – Leo would rush to greet him,

41

eager to play one of the endless games he could think up. They'd sit on the settee, the old man hauling out of his pockets all manner of string and coins and other unlikely playthings, and she'd remember Pat doing the same thing so many years ago and have to leave the room. There was no pleasure in history repeating itself, only pain. And more pain, wondering where all that love of her father's for Leo had gone. He had seemed to cast him off, instantly, wanted nothing more to do with him now. No question ever of her father's love being unconditional and never-ending. Her father gave to receive, that was the simple truth, and he could cut people out of his heart with no trouble at all. Not for one moment would he be haunted by guilt or regret. 'I wash my hands of him,' he said, and appeared to mean it (though sometimes she was not so sure) . . .

But Helen was talking, had maybe been talking for some time. 'Pardon?' Sheila said. 'I was saying,' Helen said, 'that perhaps you could write to Mrs Kennedy, just to express your sympathy and regret. I can't see it could do any harm . . . though I suppose it might. It might make her angry. And there wouldn't be any point in that.' 'I wouldn't care if she was angry with me,' Sheila said, 'I deserve it, I'd welcome it, really.' A wary look crossed Helen's face and she added, 'But I'd not do it for that, to feel her anger. Oh, I don't know, I don't know at all, it's too difficult, too complicated, nothing is right, there's no right or wrong in any of this, I just tie myself in knots thinking about it.'

Yet as soon as Helen had gone she'd sat down and tried to write a note. After two hours she had got no further than 'Dear Mrs Kennedy . . .'

Chapter Three

THERE WAS SOMETHING about the handwriting on the envelope which alerted Harriet to its contents. Not to what was actually in it, but to the fact that this was a communication from someone she didn't know, a stranger. It was a small, blue envelope. The writing was neat, very small, but faint, written in biro. She was addressed as Mrs Kennedy, no initial. There was no post code.

In a drawer in her desk Harriet had a collection of letters written to her after the attack. Most of them were from friends and family, but some of these, too, were from strangers, sent care of the newspapers. She'd hated them. All these people had wanted to do was say how shocked and sorry they were, but she'd hated them, she hadn't wanted to know how far the news had spread. It was monstrous to think of people she didn't know reading about what had happened to Joe, even if he wasn't named. If he'd been in an accident, a car accident or something, and had been injured in a straightforward way then perhaps she would have felt differently, perhaps she would have been able to accept sympathy, the sympathy of strangers. But not this, not the reactions of people who had read the details and addressed their letters to 'The mother of the boy attacked last Friday'. It was too much.

One of the first things Sam had said had been, 'Can't it be kept quiet?' He was thinking of Joe of course. Or he claimed he was. But it was a silly query and the young policeman had looked at him as if he were mad. 'It's a very serious offence, sir,' he'd said, and, 'We'll need the public's help to find the attackers.' Sam had nodded, but still blundered on, 'I meant just some of it . . .' he'd said, and stopped, and they all knew what he meant. 'No,' she'd broken in, 'of course it can't be kept quiet. How would Joe feel? It would make him think it was something he should be ashamed of, if you're thinking of what I think you're thinking.' But she had noted her own reluctance to speak openly, and so had Sam. There was never any hope of hushing up the full degradation of the violence in any case. It was what had made the case so awful, that and its entirely random nature, the way Joe had been doing nothing, had simply been selected on the spur of the moment, not even as if he were out late at night, as if . . .

So she was used to strangers writing to her. This was only another. A late letter, months after the court case. From someone who had just heard, who had perhaps just been told by someone else. It was bound to go on happening. What surprised her was that, as she held the letter in her hand, knowing what it was, she felt the same distress and anger as she had felt originally. It made her despair. How could she imagine Joe's could have begun to heal when her own wound was still so open? She sighed and was glad she was on her own. Joe was in bed. On Saturdays and Sundays, when there was no school, he clung on to his drugged sleep. He wasn't drugged any more, but that was how his sleep seemed, so very deep, the emergence from it painful and slow. If he'd stayed in bed all day she supposed she would eventually have had to wake him up and would have had to recognise this as a serious symptom which should be attended to. But he always came down about midday, washed and dressed as usual. Always. He never simply turned his face to the wall and gave in, even if he wouldn't or couldn't do the opposite and bound up as once he had done at the weekend. Saturdays he used to be up and off early, to his job, helping with the boats and earning money to save to buy his own car one day. His favourite day, Saturday. Sam's too. Joe at the boat yard, Sam on the golf course and herself walking the dog or shopping. Ordinary, predictable, a small-town life against which she had sometimes kicked. A safe life, good for children, so good Louis had opted for London the moment he had any choice and hardly came home, even in the vacations, he loved the big city so much.

Slowly, she opened the envelope, already planning to send a quick reply then shove it in with the others, her guilty haul, guilty because she didn't know why she kept all those letters she hated. They were nasty things to her, hidden away out of some primitive instinct that they were important however much she grudged them their status. But she'd replied to each one, a curt acknowledgement of thanks, adding she was unable to write more. Once, Joe had caught her dealing with a couple of these letters and he had been furious, disgusted. He'd asked her why she didn't just tear them up and she'd been so embarrassed, stumbling over her reply that when people were so kind . . . '*Kind*?' he'd yelled. She didn't understand his reaction even though she hated the letters too. He'd looked at her so scornfully and she'd made the mistake of adding, 'This is such a caring one . . .' and he'd said, 'Caring, is it? How touching. Nine out of ten for that one? Or maybe eight and a half? What's the handwriting like? And the grammar?' Why did he detest people's concern? But then, why did she detest it herself, saying one thing to Joe, about kindness, and feeling revulsion all the same?

So she'd reply to this one quickly and then really would tear it up. A single sheet, not many words upon it, but the impact startling. She couldn't see to make out those words

45

after the first reading – her vision was clouded, the blood beat in her temples and she had to hold her head in her hands to steady herself. She was sitting down, still at the breakfast table, but felt she might faint, and groped for the cup of coffee steaming in front of her. She gulped some down, clasped the hot cup tightly, licked her lips nervously. When she took up the letter again her fingers were so sweaty they left marks upon it. She read it for a second, then a third time. She closed her eyes and repeated the words aloud. They were not so extraordinary. They were simple, convincing.

Dear Mrs Kennedy,
Excuse this letter disturbing you only I am the grandmother of Leo Jackson. I brought him up from the age of three, after his mother, my daughter Pat, was killed. You won't want to hear from me and after all this time as well, but I just want you to know how ashamed I am and how I feel for you and your son and all your family. I would not have had this happen for the world. Your suffering is terrible to think of. I am so sorry.
　Yours sincerely,
　　(Mrs) Sheila Armstrong

That was all. Short and sincere. Ten out of ten, and a gold star, Joe would suggest sarcastically. She got up abruptly, thrusting the letter into her pocket, and shouted for Bruno. She couldn't stay in, with that letter for company, she had to be out, to walk, to get away to think. But even in the middle of her hurrying she scrawled a note to Joe – she never wanted him to feel deserted, to come down and find the house empty and feel he had been abandoned. From the very beginning – the beginning of afterwards – she'd been convinced Joe needed company at all times.

She walked fast, Bruno streaking ahead once they had turned off the road and on to the path down to the lake. It was early May, the trees newly green, the buds of the rhododendrons just beginning to show purple and the bluebells already swamping the grass like a spreading ink stain. Her cheeks cooled down, her head stopped throbbing. She took deep breaths, and only when she felt perfectly calm did she start to think. She'd seen Mrs Armstrong of course, and her husband, in the courtroom. Pathetic people but dignified. She'd watched them out of the corner of her eye all the time, wanting them to be monsters, to be obviously the scum of the earth, that satisfying cliché, the scum of the earth. But she'd known they wouldn't be, even before she'd listened to how the defence counsel spoke of them. So respectable. He had been a commercial clerk, whatever that was, retired now. She'd always been a housewife since her marriage. They were soberly, conventionally, unfashionably dressed. They would never stand out in a crowd, not even a crowd of four. They were both elderly, very pale, neither wept. She looked down all the time, he stared straight ahead, a little tic working in his left cheek. Both white of course. She knew the mother had been white. Neither of them was called to give evidence, but their presence was commented on by the judge. She noticed Leo Jackson never once looked at his grandparents.

And now the grandmother had written and must be replied to. Swiftly, to be rid of the obligation. She went on walking, climbing the hill, Bruno nowhere to be seen but clearly to be heard, leaping about in the undergrowth chasing a rabbit, and suddenly she felt invigorated, confident, as though she'd just had some good news. It came to her as she reached the crest of the hill and looked down at the lake, a dull, quiet grey reflecting the leaden sky, that she knew exactly what she would do: she would not write. How absurd. She would go and see this Mrs Sheila Armstrong. She felt exultant, excited, almost laughed – she would go and see this other woman, this mother she had wondered so much about. She shouted for Bruno and began descending, hurrying down the stream path as though she had some urgent business to attend to and must get home quickly. Which she had, it *was* urgent, she must go to Mrs Armstrong now, before her nerve failed her, before she had time to weigh up the pros and cons, or consult Sam. Sam would be against it, no doubt about that. She must not tell him, she must go before he came back from golf, simply present him with a *fait accompli* later. If the visit proved disastrous, he need never know, it could remain her secret, and these days she felt she wanted to have secrets from Sam. Maybe she already did. They had travelled so far along quite different roads since it had all happened that she felt removed from him in a way she would never have thought possible in all their twenty years of marriage.

But Joe was up. He was sitting at the table reading her note as though it were written in Arabic. She came to a sudden halt, in every way. 'Oh Joe,' she said, 'you're up. Good.'

'Why?'

'Why what?'

'Why is it good?'

'Well, it's a nice day . . .'

'It isn't. It's cloudy, it's cold. It's a horrible day and there's nothing to do. I wish I could sleep all day. But I can't, and if I don't get up I won't sleep at night, so I have to or I wouldn't.' All the time avoiding her eyes, bending a spoon he was holding, not using it to eat the cereal he'd just drowned in milk. 'Anyway, it isn't a nice day.'

'It was nice out, nice walking. Bruno enjoyed it.'

'Well, I wouldn't, not that I'm going out.' He took a spoonful and pushed the bowl away. 'It tastes funny,' he said, 'I can't eat it.'

'Doesn't matter.'

'It does, actually. It means I've wasted milk. Dad would say I'd wasted milk.'

'There's plenty of milk . . .'

'Oh Mum, stop it, for Christ's sake, *stop* it.' He pushed his chair back, belligerent, turning to look at her, his face quite contorted. 'And what's this stupid note? Why do you write them?'

'It was just you weren't up and you might have wondered . . .'

'Wondered what? What?'

'Where everyone was.'

'Why would I wonder that? Why do you think I need to know where you are? It's a Saturday, I know where Dad is, he's always at the same boring place every bloody Saturday, and I don't *care* where you are, it doesn't matter to me, I'm not a fucking baby, okay?'

'Okay,' she said quietly. She tidied the table and for the sake of something to do took some carrots from the fridge and began scraping them. Her hand shook. She couldn't go and see Mrs Armstrong now. She heard Joe go into the sitting-room and put the television on. Good. Better than going back up to his room. He would stay till lunchtime probably and then Sam would be home, not that his presence would help. The reverse. Sam would be bright and jolly. He'd tell them about how he'd played. He'd suggest things to Joe, how about coming with him to the garden centre, how about this, how about that – Sam would *try* so hard. And Joe would not respond, not even to say no. It was agony to witness. She'd tried to tell Sam not to bother, to just be himself, but that was being

49

himself. Once, Joe had been so close to him, closer than Louis had ever been. Now, Sam coming home for lunch would be a non-event. But it might force Joe out. It might. He might go into the town. It was Saturday and the place was crowded, it didn't need much courage. If he did, then she would go and see Mrs Armstrong after all.

But would it be fair? Now she'd been prevented from acting on the spur of the moment she began to hesitate. Just turning up like that, was it fair? Should she telephone first? And might it not be better to meet on neutral ground? This was exactly what she had not wanted to do, deliberate, allow herself to complicate what had seemed simple. She did it all the time, her head forever full of annoying 'what ifs'. What if Mr Armstrong were at home? What if he stayed and she and Mrs Armstrong couldn't talk? Worst of all, what if Mrs Armstrong hadn't told Mr Armstrong? That would be dreadful, a betrayal. So perhaps Joe's bad temper had done her a favour – she ought to ring first. But was there a telephone number on the letter? She took it out of her pocket and looked: no. She'd have to ring directory enquiries if it wasn't in the book. It would be under Mr Armstrong's initial and she didn't know it – but she could match the address, if it was listed. The town the Armstrongs lived in was a lot bigger than this one but not enormous. An hour's drive away, maybe an hour and a half. Where could she say she was going, if she went? It would have to be somewhere for the day, to visit one of her suppliers. But Sam knew none of them lived far enough away to warrant a day trip. Shopping, it would have to be, to buy something special. For what? What special occasion could she invent? *Oh God, this was what she did not want to do . . .*

She could not telephone until she had the number and until there was no one here in her own house to hear her. She went out that afternoon to the main post office, Mrs

Armstrong's letter in her bag. The number was ex-directory. She ought to have guessed, they would have had to go ex-directory after all the publicity. They would have received hate calls probably, local people always knew who was being referred to. She had never wanted to feel pity for anyone except Joe, but now she began to feel it for the Armstrongs. Agony for them, and none of it their fault. She had never blamed them, never even thought of doing so, they had never been in her mind, there had been no room for them. Or actually, until she saw him, for Leo Jackson. All she had room for was Joe, his injuries, his pain, his misery. It hadn't mattered, at first, who had inflicted the damage. In hospital, she hadn't once thought of revenge and neither had Sam. When the policeman Graham had said, 'I expect you'd like to get your hands on whoever did this,' they both stared at him, amazed. No, they had no wish to get their hands on anyone. All their attention and anxiety was focused on Joe. And even later, in court, months later, when finally they saw Leo Jackson, there was some sort of mental barrier still there.

The worst moment was not the actual sight of Leo Jackson but the anticipation of seeing him. Then, when his name was read out, when the policeman on the door went to bring him through, then her heart had begun to flutter alarmingly and the perspiration to break out on her face. She wanted to see this youth who had so cruelly attacked her son, but she was afraid of her own reaction to the sight of him. She might faint, she could feel she might faint, could feel the dizziness begin. She might cry out, a howl of rage or anguish, she didn't know which sound would rise within her and escape her tightly compressed lips. So the waiting was the worst, the short interval between hearing the name and seeing the boy. Then her agitation subsided rapidly. He was not what she had expected and it was a shock. It calmed her, seeing Leo Jackson. She could not understand it and felt ashamed. He walked so quietly to the witness box, without a trace of that defiance, that cockiness she had expected. And though he was tall, much taller than Joe, and powerfully built, a man's build not a boy's, he was not threatening. His voice, when he took the oath, was low but quite clear and he repeated the words fluently, without stumbling, as if they meant something. He replied politely to the initial questions. Well, he would have been told to be polite, at all costs. But could he have managed to sustain such a well-mannered pose if there were not an innate courtesy? She didn't know. For such a young man he seemed remarkably mature.

Seemed. It was impossible to know. She heard him admit to having taken LSD, to having drunk too much, to having got caught up in a gang, to having attacked Joseph Samuel Kennedy . . . He was admitting it without a trace of emotion. But then, when he was cross-examined, he was suddenly silent. He would explain nothing. He agreed with the facts, that he had, undeniably, been one of the attackers. He had been there, yes. He had held a knife in his hand, yes. But beyond that, nothing. He stood silent, staring straight ahead. Silent, but not insolent. Silent, but not cowed or embarrassed. It was unbearable. She didn't know why but this silence upset her. He shouldn't be silent, he had no right to be. She was here to listen to his explanation and none was forthcoming. She wanted to go up to him and shake him and order him to tell her what had happened. She was horrified to realise that she needed the details, from him, from his lips, every last one. She wanted to hear him explain and justify and apologise and beg for mercy. And he didn't. Until he did so, this distance between her imagination and the reality remained to plague her. It couldn't be real until Leo Jackson had told her it was in spite of what Joe himself had described. When both the Crown prosecution solicitor and the defence solicitor gave up and Leo Jackson was led away she felt such frustration she bit her lip until it hurt. But still she didn't feel any desire to kill Leo Jackson for what he had done, that desire the police called 'natural' and seemed to expect. When it didn't emerge, Graham acted as though he was disappointed. They, she and Sam too, hadn't behaved as they should, there was something not quite right about them, surely.

She suspected Joe might share that view. When Louis came rushing home, straight to the hospital, he'd said, 'I'd like to kill whoever did this,' as he stood and looked at Joe, still in intensive care and all wired up. He'd whispered it, but Joe had heard and he smiled. 'Fucking brute,' Louis had said, tears in his eyes, an unheard-of sign of emotion from him. If it had been Louis set upon, of course, it would never have happened – he was strong and looked it. He wouldn't even have been selected, however random the selection. He wasn't a thug himself but he looked powerful. Joe had always wanted to look like Louis, to play rugby like him and fight like him and just *be* him. Even being Louis' brother, known as his brother, had been enough for a while, though things had changed, inevitably, since Louis had gone away to London. Harriet had tried to get Louis to phone Joe regularly, knowing she'd never get him to write, but it was hopeless, he hardly ever did and Joe minded terribly. But after it happened Louis reinstated himself, though only for a while. He sat with Joe, drove him to and from the out-patients' clinic to get his plaster checked, then off, helped him walk again, entertained him. But he hadn't actually talked to him, not properly. He didn't seem to want to know everything and he hadn't encouraged Joe to talk about it. 'There's no point,' he'd maintained, when she'd asked, but she knew he was afraid. He was like Sam. He couldn't talk about it. Women talked. To each other. She and Mrs Armstrong. She'd have to write, as Mrs Armstrong had done. She'd suggest they meet. And talk.

★

She had never expected a reply, nor any acknowledgement. She hadn't written for that. In her mind's eye Sheila could see Mrs Kennedy tearing up her letter and flinging it in the fire. Or wastepaper-basket. She envisaged the other mother's fury, perhaps, her anger that such a letter should be written at all. It was actually a relief when forty-eight hours had gone by and there had been no response – she'd been afraid to answer the telephone, even though she hadn't put her number on the letter, just in case. And when Alan went to answer it, the few times it rang that weekend, she'd tensed and strained her ears and only relaxed when she heard him naming the caller. Because of course she hadn't told Alan she'd written. It was not that she feared his anger so much as his intense irritation that she wouldn't, as he put it, 'leave go'. That was what he wanted her to do – see sense, face facts, let the past go.

But the past was the present and future too. It had to be lived with. Leo was still their grandson, he could not be disowned. He had to be visited, looked at, talked to, and all the time she was remembering. Months now since she had asked 'How could you?' and 'Why?' Months. She asked him instead about the routine of the prison. It wasn't, in fact, called a prison, she knew that, Leo was too young for a proper prison, but the Young Offenders' Institution was undoubtedly a prison, what else? So she asked about the routine and he replied, in monosyllables, enough for her to glean a few names of jobs and activities and people. She clung on to these, memorised the sequence of events, and knew when, on which day, to ask about the sport, the woodwork, the art. He hated her contrived knowingness, she could see that, but she persisted, forced answers out of him. He never asked her anything. He didn't seem to want to know about Alan, still called Dad, in spite of all the emphasis at the trial on his having no father, or about his great-grandad. Never enquired, so she did not push much information on him. Occasionally she volunteered something Alan or her father had said, but she didn't make a thing of it. Once, when she'd had flu and hadn't been able to go, though she'd been sure to send a message, she'd been upset that Leo hadn't asked her how she was feeling. Not a word. Just stared at her, arms akimbo, as they always were, eyes fixed on her but without contact. She heard herself rambling on about her illness, how she still felt weak, had no energy, and eventually he had broken in. 'Don't come then,' he'd said. Was it out of concern for her? She didn't think so.

She asked about him, asked Helen, the probation officer, naturally, about how he was getting on. Fine. Fitted in well. No trouble. He was taking five GCSEs and working hard. Just as he had done at school – always, reports were excellent. He was clever, everyone acknowledged that. And, except for that one day, when he and an unnamed other did what they did, civilised. He wasn't a lout, he didn't swear and fight. He was a credit to her mothering, except – always except. An isolated incident. Inexplicable was how it had been described. Inexplicable, and likely to remain so. The only time, she was sure, he had ever taken drugs. She'd seen the expressions of disbelief on the faces of the police when she'd said this, but she firmly believed it. Leo had said so. About all he'd said: someone had given him LSD and he hadn't ever taken it before, had no idea of its effect. He claimed not to remember anything that had happened afterwards, not until he found himself holding a knife and Joe Kennedy bleeding at his feet . . . Only none of them had believed him. Alan hadn't, her father certainly hadn't – 'Cock-and-bull, tell us another.' She'd been tempted to put in something about her faith in Leo's story when she wrote to Mrs Kennedy but commonsense had stopped her. It wasn't fitting. A letter of apology ought, in these very special circumstances, to contain no excuses or explanations. It was a gesture, that's all.

Mrs Kennedy's reply astounded her. If Harriet had known instinctively that her strange envelope must contain a letter to do with Joe, conveying someone's sympathy, Sheila was even quicker and more sure about Harriet's when it came. The moment she picked it up. The postmark for a start, such a nice little place, they'd gone there for their holidays once when she was a child. She could still remember her father hiring a boat and rowing her and her sister out into the middle of the huge lake. It had been thrilling. When she heard where the Kennedys lived she had envied them, a lovely place, quiet, leisurely, pretty. So the postmark and the writing and the very quality of the envelope gave it all away. Hate letters had not been written in an italic hand on long white thick envelopes. No. They'd come in buff envelopes, or cheap blue envelopes, the writing hard to read, the address often incomplete. This, she knew, was from *his* mother and she had asked for it, she had brought it on herself. Whatever his mother had written, however much it was going to hurt her, she could only blame herself.

Sadly, she put it in her apron pocket and finished the Hoovering. The roar of the machine dulled the worry she felt. Backwards and forwards across the worn carpet she pushed the Hoover, automatically moving the chairs, getting well into the corners, negotiating skirting boards with care. Alan was out, he'd taken the car for its MOT. There was no reason not to read Mrs Kennedy's letter now. But she finished the Hoovering, put the room to rights, dried the breakfast dishes, put the washing machine on, and then made a cup of tea. Only when the tea was in a mug and she was sitting down at the table, the *Daily Mail* open in front of her, exactly as she would have been doing at this time on any Wednesday morning, only then did she take the envelope out of her pocket and slit it open. She was ready, if she heard Alan return, to slip it back again and appear engrossed. Smoothing the large sheet of paper out – was it typing paper? she didn't know – she was surprised how much Mrs Kennedy had written. At first she feared the very length of this letter. Surely it would be a rant, to be so long, someone working up a head of steam. But no. It was the kind of letter she had never even allowed herself to hope for:

Dear Mrs Armstrong,
Your letter was a great shock and I admit it
distressed me to be hearing from anyone to do with
Joe's attacker, but all the same, after only very
short reflection I was glad to get it.
    Quite frankly, until very recently I've had no
room in my head to think of anyone but Joe and
what he has suffered and is still suffering. I haven't
wanted to think about your grandson, or about
you. But lately I have actually found myself
remembering a great deal I was told about you, and
believe me I at *no* time have blamed you. I know it
must be a nightmare for you too and I am not so
self-obsessed or selfish that I can shut you out of
my mind entirely.
    What I wondered was whether it might be a
good idea to meet? I admit I don't quite know

why. My husband would say it was a bad idea, that there was no point to it, and I fear Joe himself would be angry. But I feel the same need that you perhaps felt when you wrote to me. I can't put a name to it. The horror of what happened continues to spoil my life, however hard I try. Joe is not really recovering as he should. I don't know what to say. It might be a mistake to meet. I don't know what we would talk about. But I felt suddenly so happy you had written and the idea of meeting just came to me. What do you think? I could drive over to you, any weekday.

I will quite understand if you think there is no point. Thank you in any case for writing. It meant a great deal to me.

Yours sincerely,
Harriet Kennedy

The tea was cold. Sheila poured it down the sink, put the kettle back on, made more tea. God knows how long she'd sat there, dazed. In her head she could hear her father crowing, 'You've been and gone and done it now, lass.' She had. How was she to answer this letter? She'd never had anyone write to her so openly in her life, as though already they had met. It was so strange, so eerie. She shivered, and put both hands round the mug she was holding, glad of the reassuring warmth of the tea. This woman was not like her, that was clear. She was highly educated. Comfortable with words. Why did she want to meet? What motive could there be? Was it a trick? Did she want to worm her way in and then somehow strike, somehow make Sheila suffer? Well, if so, that was bearable. She was prepared to suffer. She wouldn't have written her own letter if she hadn't been privately welcoming a measure of deserved retribution. She wasn't stupid. She'd known her letter advertised her willingness to be abused. But what about Mrs Kennedy? What did her letter advertise? Sheila was afraid to speculate. There was no one she could discuss it with, except maybe that Helen person who still paid the occasional visit. But she didn't know when the next call would be due or how to contact her directly. She wouldn't like to do that anyway, it didn't appeal to her. And she couldn't keep Mrs Kennedy waiting, not after a letter like that. It would be rude. Worse, it would be cruel, and there'd been enough cruelty already.

If Mrs Kennedy came, where would they sit? Not in the kitchen. It was poky, there was too much jammed into it. The table was too small, too rickety. So it would have to be in the living-room, and where would Alan go? He was out in the mornings usually, but not absolutely always. And in the afternoons he often watched sport on television and she was out, visiting her father or her sister. Mrs Kennedy wouldn't come in the evening. She'd want to be back for the boy, four o'clock at the latest, so there was no question of the evening. The morning, then, would be best, but what about lunch? It would take her an hour or so to drive here and she wouldn't be leaving until well after the boy had gone to school and she'd tidied up, so, say she left just before ten maybe and arrived about half-past eleven, then what about lunch? She'd have to offer her lunch and then what about Alan? He never missed his lunch, it was the worst part of his retirement, providing his wretched lunch. The afternoon, then, would be better, about two o'clock. Mrs Kennedy would likely have to leave at three to be back for her son. The afternoon was clearly best if only she could arrange for Alan to be elsewhere. But how could she be sure he would be? She could invent an errand for him – no, better still, he could take her father to buy his bedding plants. He'd been on about it, had his list written out, sweetpeas, asters, marigold, stocks and dahlias. She'd fix it for next week, once she'd cleared it with Mrs Kennedy. She'd offer her Tuesday, Wednesday or Thursday next week and then fix it. Once her father had been promised something it could not be unpromised. Alan was resigned to that. He'd go along with it. Even if it poured down, the promised trip would have to take place on the day and at the precise time fixed . . .

She felt exhausted with all the planning, but went and got a sheet of paper there and then and wrote to Mrs Kennedy that she would be glad to meet and could she offer her a cup of tea or coffee any weekday afternoon the following week except Monday and Friday. It was posted within the hour. Relieved, she turned to other soothing, household, tasks, desperate to get into the rhythm of them before Alan returned and spotted something was up. He was not a sensitive man, but forty-odd years of marriage had at least made him an expert on whether she was flustered or not. She didn't want to be flustered but one glance in the mirror told all. Red. Red in the face, when usually she was so pale. The way to deal with this agitation was consciously to relax – breathe in, count to three, breathe out, count to three – and take her mind off whatever was disturbing her. So she ironed, though it was not when she usually ironed, and if Alan was smart he'd register this. She did *not* iron before lunch on a Wednesday morning. Never. She ironed only in the afternoon. It used to be when *Woman's Hour* was on until they mucked the time up. But today she ironed, slowly and carefully, and it worked.

Alan noticed nothing. He was distracted himself. Came in frowning, the tic in his cheek working away. 'One hundred and forty pounds,' he said at once. 'Damned cheek, they charge what they like these days.'

60

'Must have been something wrong,' she murmured.

'Oh, there was something wrong all right but not one hundred and forty pounds worth. It was the labour, that was the expense, that's how they get you.'

'Well, we need a car.'

'I know we need a car, but I don't know how much longer we'll be able to go on running one, that's the truth, not at this rate.'

The expense of the car was a constant worry. It kept him going for hours, working out what was likely to go wrong next with the car and how much it would cost. It was a seven-year-old Ford Escort, beautifully looked after, bought new and treasured by him. Their first new car, almost their first car. The beginning of easier times, they'd thought. Leo had been as excited as Alan. His one ambition then, aged nine, had been to learn how to drive. Alan had promised to teach him as soon as he was seventeen. Together, they washed and polished and cherished the red car and it had opened out their lives immeasurably. It was never too much trouble for Alan to take her anywhere, though when she'd wondered aloud if she could learn to drive he'd been dismissive. She was too old, he said, her reflexes would be too slow. She'd accepted his verdict. Sixty-three probably had been too old. But if only she'd been able to drive, the journey now to visit Leo would be so much less gruelling – it took so long, taking first the train and then buses, changing from one to another. Alan would drive her there, if she asked, but she couldn't bear him to be sitting outside, with Leo refusing to speak to him, closing his eyes and keeping them closed and not speaking at all if Alan insisted on being there.

She mentioned taking her father for his plants when Alan was sitting eating his lunch. He grunted agreement, any day would do, just to let him know, then launched into a lecture about how her father was too old to be looking after a garden, it was too much. He, Alan, was nearly too old himself at seventy-one, a fit seventy-one, but at nearly ninety her father was past it and someone should tell him. Sheila ignored that. As if her father could be told to pack his beloved garden in. Impossible. But he'd missed Leo to weed and mow the lawn and dig. Something would have to be done about that, but not now. She would do a bit herself. Anyone could mow a lawn, it was just like Hoovering, no trouble. They'd have to get someone to weed and dig though, until Leo . . . She caught herself just in time. It was dangerous even to *think* of Leo being released. Dangerous from every point of view. She never, ever, said the words, 'When Leo gets out.' Her greatest terror was just that: Leo out, Leo back in their house, a stranger, secretly a wicked, violent stranger who'd be her responsibility, as he'd been since he was three years old . . .

Would Mrs Kennedy want to talk about that? Would she want Leo mentioned at all? Or was she coming to talk about her son, about Joe? Telling me things, Sheila thought, things I'd rather not know. Maybe she wants to reduce me to tears, not knowing I can't cry, that I haven't cried since Pat was killed. No tears. She might wonder at my lack of tears, think I'm hard. But she might cry, Mrs Kennedy herself, and then what would she do? Comfort her of course. That was what people did. When other people cried, comfort was called for and offered. When they didn't cry the need for comfort wasn't recognised. Nobody had comforted her. Alan and she had silently supported each other, just by being together, by keeping the surface of their life as unruffled as possible, but they hadn't been able to comfort each other. Her sister had tried, she supposed, Carole had tried but only by baking her cakes she didn't want and offering platitudes which were infuriating. Her father had been true to form – never had he comforted anyone. It was a luxury denied to all his children, a foreign language he'd never learned. The nearest he got to it was to say it was no good crying over spilled milk.

Pride. She had pride, that was how she coped, it was her father's version of comfort – you held your Armstrong head high and dared anyone to pity or blame you. And she had done so. There had been no hiding away, however hard it had been to go into shops and walk in public places, feeling herself pointed out as *his* mother or grandmother, depending on how accurate the identification was. She'd wondered, often, what it would have been like if Joe Kennedy had been a girl. Worse, much worse, she was sure. Or if Leo had been only a little older and could have been named in the newspapers. Not that it had made much difference locally – everyone had known. But she was conscious that however hard it had been, and still was, it could have been a great deal worse. Joe Kennedy could have died. The knife wound could have been a little lower, near his heart, not in the shoulder. Or he could have been maimed for life, crippled. It was so near, the next wound, to his spinal cord. What if Mrs Kennedy wanted to go over what had happened? She wouldn't be able to bear it. She never allowed herself to reconstruct the attack. The policeman had wanted them to read Joe's statement but they'd refused and in court they had managed not to listen when it was read out. She knew enough. She didn't want details. But maybe that was what Mrs Kennedy wanted, why she was coming, to shove the details down her throat . . .

All of a sudden, she felt panic-stricken and, leaving the table, she went to write another letter.

Chapter Four

HARRIET SAW THE anniversary creeping up and was determined to ignore it. It was silly to think of it as an anniversary anyway, inappropriate if technically correct. She had deliberately chosen *not* to note the actual date at the time and had succeeded so successfully that all she could now be sure of was that it had been in the first half of June. Light nights. No need to worry about Joe being out in the dark, not that she had ever worried much. There was no danger, and he was a boy. So many times she had thanked God she had no daughters, recalling with heavy feelings of guilt the agonies she'd put her own mother through. Only sons, about whom one did not need to worry in the same way, and certainly not in this small lakeside town. No clubs, no areas of danger. Everyone knew everyone else, except in the summer with the tourists and trippers, and the occasional invasion of gangs from the big towns, just looking for trouble.

But she watched the nights lighten, the days lengthen, and it was no good pretending it was not almost a year since her life had changed. Such a long time, such a short time. The drama of it all had carried them so far along – the thing itself, the recovery of Joe from the physical injuries, the arrest of Leo Jackson, the long wait for the trial – all that had taken months. Always, there had been something they'd been waiting for, something that had to be got over before the horror was done with. And between the crucial events there had simply been gaps which were somehow filled in without being real time. Real time had only returned so recently. Even then she was unconvinced. There was another boy, out there somewhere, never identified or caught. Perhaps he had been the instigator. Leo Jackson wouldn't say, not even to shift some of the blame from himself. The defence counsel had tried to make much of that, had talked about her client's sense of honour, but this had been quickly demolished by the prosecution. Honour? To do what he admitted he had done to another innocent boy younger than himself? No question of any honour. But still the fact of his accomplice getting away with it meant that even now everything was not completely over. There was what Detective Sergeant Graham called, with his love of clichés, 'unfinished business'.

The worst part of this was Joe's continuing fear. She knew he thought the other attacker might find him again. Against all reason, he had the idea that this other boy would want to do it again, exulting in the fact that he'd got away with it once, scot-free. This time he would be killed. The fear of death had been utterly real. Joe had only spoken of it once, eyes full of tears, shaking, weak after his release from hospital, overwhelmed to be home again and instead of happiness and relief more wretched than ever – 'I thought I would die, Mum.' The two knives, the strong arm round his neck, the smell of one of the attackers, beery, sweaty, and the words, the obscene language, the verbal as well as the physical violence, the demand for money, or else. He'd given it so quickly, willingly, only two pounds, maybe less, he didn't know, it was all in small change, and then everything had got worse not better, he'd known they would kill him – one of them had said, over and over again, that he would – and he'd wet himself, the urine seeping hotly down the inside of his jeans, and . . .

'No, no.' Harriet said it aloud, alone in her little work-room. Never, never, did she allow this, no going over what had actually happened, it was disgusting to do it. But as the time of the attack approached she couldn't help doing it, partly to see if it felt any less dreadful, whether she *could* imagine it just as acutely but find it caused her less agony, that the pain had faded just a little, that she could take herself through the whole half-hour and flinch a little less. But she couldn't. The nausea still rose in her stomach, her flesh still crawled, the crying still welled up inside her throat. Nothing had got better in all this time for her, who had not gone through this, so how could it have got better for Joe? It was not proving true, that time healed, that the memories of even the most horrific things faded. Someone had mentioned the sufferings of those who, at Joe's age, had survived Nazi concentration camps, who had suffered repeatedly far, far worse experiences and survived to rebuild their lives and be happy people. She'd hated that person. It wasn't a competition in suffering, she'd told them, she didn't want to hear about other victims, they had no relevance to Joe. What Joe wanted to do was forget and he couldn't and neither could she. Ever.

The trouble was, others forgot so quickly. They'd forgotten at school, Joe said. Not that he talked much about it, but sometimes he'd repeat something someone had said and marvel at how it showed that what he'd gone through had been forgotten. In class, they were studying *A Clockwork Orange* and were asked to write an essay on how the author conveyed terror with special attention to the use of language in the portrayal of violence. Joe had hardly been able to read the novel at all. He shook and cringed and felt sick but forced himself through it. Then when it came to writing the essay he read over and over again the descriptions of men and women being beaten up and the thugs, Alex and Dim and Pete and Georgie,

66

enjoying it. He showed Harriet his essay, for which he had been given an 'A' with the comment, 'Well done, an excellent appreciation of Burgess's intention, quotes exactly right.' She looked to see what he had quoted. 'Dim was very, very ugly,' she read, 'and like his name, but he was a horror-show filthy fighter and very handy with the boot.' And then a longer passage – 'Pete held his rookers and Georgie sort of hooked his rot wide open for him . . . Georgie let go of holding his goobers apart and just let him have one in the toothless rot with his ringy fist and that made the old veck start moaning a lot then, then out comes the blood brothers, real beautiful. So all we did then was to pull his outer platties off, stripping him to his vest and long underpants . . . and then Pete kicks him lovely in his pot.' Harriet couldn't bear to read what Joe had made of all this, how he had earned his 'A'. She sat, tears barely held back – Joe was so angry if she cried – and he told her how oblivious the teacher had been, and all of the class, of how, for him, this was no academic exercise. He was incredulous at how short memories were and how nobody related the descriptions in the novel to his experience. He felt humiliated, couldn't stay in the room. And he couldn't watch anyone being attacked in any film or video or TV programme – he had to dash out when friends laughed or cheered on the assailants. Violence wasn't *real* to them, it was a story. They didn't feel the blows, the pain, the edge of the knife. And they were always full, his friends, his contemporaries, of what they would do in similar circumstances, how they would have brought into play their Karate training or Judo moves, they'd have kicked like this, and twisted away like that . . . None of them understood.

Harriet saw how Joe's whole nature had changed and was still changing as a result of such an experience so young. The young didn't believe in evil, not really. They didn't think the world a bad place, however much evidence they saw on television. That was the great comfort of being young, especially young in a loving and safe environment. But Joe had lost that. Not only did he now know the world was cruel and this cruelty random, he believed there was nothing else. He couldn't see good any more, he had no faith in luck. His vision was black, he had proof that evil existed. It was no use expecting Joe to 'get over it'. He could indeed resume, superficially, normal life, he had done it with impressive speed, but what he couldn't do was recover his youthful ignorance and natural optimism. It had gone, nearly a year ago, in half an hour. Nobody seemed to understand this except herself. In her treatment of, and attitude to, her son she felt she had to keep at the forefront of her mind, always, that half-hour. Her patience was limitless because of it, her tolerance never-ending.

This was exactly what was wrong, Sam argued. She let Joe ride rough-shod over them, put up with his snarling bad temper, his moods, his lack of any kind of co-operation. She was condoning his absolute obsession with himself and it was doing him no good. That was how Sam always ended – 'You're doing him no good.' Sam's way was, as he put it, 'to treat him as normal, as you used to'. To which, of course, she'd replied that Joe was not now normal, and Sam was fooling himself if he thought so. He'd pushed and pushed himself to act normally, and succeeded, but he was in no normal frame of mind. While his leg was broken, while he was recovering from his ruptured spleen and the knife wounds, Sam had been all sympathy, but now that Joe was battling with his broken confidence and his ruptured faith in life and his wounded self-esteem, Sam's sympathy was evaporating. He said things like, 'Joe is wrecking our lives,' and, 'Joe only wants to make us suffer because he did,' and, worst of all,

'Joe is making us into enemies.' Enemies. It was not true. She and Sam could never be enemies. But she recognised some truth in what Sam had been trying to say – they were more separate. She was totally bound up in Joe and he was not. And Joe did indeed play on that, consciously or not. He had turned against Sam, moved away from him, and there was nothing she could do about it. For the moment, she was Joe's.

Sam resented this quite openly. He didn't agree with the way she treated Joe, he couldn't match her overwhelming absorption in their son and nor did he want to, but he felt excluded and was envious, it seemed to her, of her dedication. It left him on the outside of the unhappy little world she and Joe had made their own. Even his strength, his physical height and weight, told against him in an obscure way. She and Joe were uncomfortable with it, uneasy when Sam did anything at all that showed how powerful he was. He almost wished he could shrink, become slight and unnoticeable. They seemed to look at him with such distaste when he carried heavy loads of logs into the house, or cut the big hedge in the garden. They made him feel brutish, just for being a strong man, and there was nothing of the brute in him. It was as though they were blaming him, somehow, and feeling this made him miserable. But his misery was not recognised as such. It came out in uncharacteristic displays of bad temper. The Sam they knew, and had depended on for his good humour, did not behave like that. He began to pick on small transgressions – Harriet's failing to report the loss of her front-door key, Joe's borrowing of his tracksuit bottoms – and blew them into major sins. He wouldn't listen to explanations. His moodiness caused problems at work. There were four other architects in his firm and a great deal of shared work was done. Sam had always been the one who connected best with each of the others and also the one whose social skills with clients had been greatly valued. His new intolerance made him less reliable and, after a while, his colleagues resented this. He found he had to make a huge effort to appear to be his old self again, and the strain of doing so told when he was at home. But Harriet had no sympathy for him. Instead, she was harder on him, he felt.

Once, he had forgotten to pass on a message from Detective Sergeant Graham about the results of the DNA test carried out on Leo Jackson, and Harriet's fury had goaded him into saying he was being 'got at'. How she had sneered, how she had scorned him, claiming the only person he cared about was himself, poor, poor little Sam, being 'got at', how dreadful. They had a furious row, which in itself was so unusual that the effects were felt for days afterwards. Their whole relationship was based, in fact, on Sam's refusal to argue. His method of expressing anger or resentment was generally to retreat into silence or literally to disappear, to go out of the house until whatever had brought him and Harriet to the brink of a verbal fight had cooled down. But when she taunted him at that point he was suddenly so furious and hurt that for nearly the first time in his married life he swore at Harriet. He called her a sanctimonious bitch, he accused her of deliberately turning Joe against him, and when she in turn said he was an insensitive brute who cared only about himself he almost hit her. He couldn't bear her to think she was the only one who suffered, but she would neither acknowledge nor allow that he too had the right to his own brand of pain, no less severe in being different in kind from hers. He felt persecuted by them, by Harriet and Joe, and he didn't understand why, what had he done?

Nothing. Harriet knew that Sam was guilty only by the sin of omission, of not allowing the attack on Joe to submerge all else in their lives. Once he had left the house each day, once he was working, she suspected the weight of their tragedy lifted for him. She wished it was as easy for her. Only for a short while was she able to put Joe if not out of her mind then at the back of it. At first, she'd thought she'd never work again. How could she, when her concentration was so fractured? She spent six weeks at home, nursing Joe, and her business almost collapsed. She'd had no one to whom she could delegate properly other than the girl she employed in the shop, and she was incapable of doing more than keep that unimportant part ticking over. The real business, the designing, the supervising of the out-workers, depended on her, and without her it collapsed. And when she'd gone back into her work-room she'd thought herself finished, not an idea in her head, all creativity dried up, paralysed. She'd kept herself going only by keeping new designs embarrassingly simple. Even then, she'd been so slow, it had taken her days to print a poppy on a plain white scarf. She couldn't *see* a poppy and yet that was all she could think of to use. A poppy. Blood-red. A symbol of suffering. It had taken her weeks to come out of this sterile phase and when she did, when the first few hours had flown and she'd forgotten about Joe for all of them, she'd felt guilty at how much better she felt. Whatever was in her was not dead, it still stirred, pleasure was there, pleasure and satisfaction and the old sense of achievement. She cried to feel it. If only Joe could feel it, but there was no sign of that kind of inner recovery, which, even at her most miserable, sustained her.

She wondered if Joe marked the date. He didn't mention it. She didn't. Nobody did, except her sister Virginia. 'A year next Saturday,' Ginny said, sitting in her kitchen. Harriet ignored her, turned away and took refuge, as usual, in being busy preparing food. 'Don't ignore me, Harriet. Why shouldn't I say it? It isn't healthy not to, you *should* talk about it.'

71

'I'll decide that,' Harriet said.

She and Ginny had only recently, since their mother's death, grown closer again, though they had always lived in the same place, the place in which they were born, and had always seen each other every week with monotonous regularity. Ginny had no sons. She had two daughters, one a year each side of Joe's age. She'd been infuriatingly fond of saying, '*Think* if it had been one of my girls, I can't bear the thought,' and then going on to bear it, many times, aloud. 'A year, and you're thinner than ever,' she went on, watching Harriet carefully. 'You'll wear yourself out, what with all this and work. You should have a holiday, get right away. I've always said so.' She had indeed, over and over, like a litany. So had a great many other people, urging her and Sam to take Joe and get 'right away'. No one knew how much she would have liked to think a simple thing like a holiday would work – sun, blue skies, different surroundings, why not? Because Joe didn't want to. He wanted to stay at home.

Partly to shut Ginny up she blurted out, 'I've written to his mother, but don't tell Sam. Promise?'

'Whose mother?'

'His – well, his grandmother.'

Ginny stared at her. It was satisfying to see her first puzzled and then appalled. 'You don't mean . . .'

'She wrote to me first, about being sorry.'

'*Sorry*? I thought you hated pity.'

'I do. This wasn't that kind of sorry. She wanted to tell me how sorry and ashamed she was. So I wrote back. I'm going to see her, I hope.'

'Oh, Harriet. Oh, Harriet, I'm sure it isn't a good idea, really, I'm sure it's dangerous.'

'How could it be? Where's the danger?'

'It will only upset you. I mean, what good could it do? Think about it.'

'I've thought about nothing else ever since her letter came. I think she was so brave.'

'For writing to you?'

'Yes. Imagine, imagine if it had been your grandson, son really, that's what she thought of him as. Imagine how you'd feel.'

'I certainly wouldn't write to the victim's mother, and especially not months after my son, grandson, whatever, had been tried and convicted and sentenced, that's the bit that's fishy, so long after.'

'But don't you see, that shows she's doing what I do.'

'What?'

'Thinking about it, all the time, making herself ill with it, not able to understand it or forget it, feeling desperate . . .'

'I don't think it shows any of that at all. You're getting carried away. If you see her it will start everything up again.'

'Don't be stupid, Ginny . . . it can't start everything up again, nothing's died down. That's the point, seeing her just might resolve something.'

'What?'

'I don't know.'

Ginny looked at her sister, scrutinised her intently. Too thin. She'd lost at least a stone, probably more. Her face was thin too, drawn. She didn't look pretty any more. Her looks had always depended on animation and now there was none. It was pitiful to see her so lethargic. People wondered if she was ill. People in this small town, who'd known her and Harriet all their lives, stopped Ginny in the street and asked if her sister was all right. It was even rumoured that she had had a nervous breakdown, which Ginny firmly denied. Harriet hadn't *had* a breakdown but was surely having one all the time, a breakdown made all the worse because she wouldn't admit to it. What was a breakdown, anyway? Ginny had always wondered until the last year had shown her. It wasn't a collapse, a sort of sustained faint. It was what Harriet was enduring, a permanent sense of great pressure, an inability to relax for one single moment, it was living in a state of crisis all the time. Joe was attacking her, using her, every day, and she let it happen. She'd been in this very kitchen and heard Joe swear at his mother viciously, heard him heap contempt on her for her supposed stupidity. That, Ginny suspected, was only the half of it. 'He needs a good slap,' Ginny had once said, furious with Joe at the sight of her sister's distress after one scene when he'd yelled at her. Harriet had just looked at her, and afterwards her unthinking remark had created a barrier between them. For her to have said Joe should be slapped was quite unforgivable.

Ginny supposed it was. She was sorry she'd said it, as though Joe were a three-year-old who'd deliberately broken another child's toy. But she found, on reflection, that she wasn't sorry at the thought behind what she'd said. She agreed with Sam. Harriet was too soft, too indulgent, towards Joe. She'd made herself into his whipping boy. Everything Joe said and did was excused because of what he had suffered – Harriet had made him into a special case for life and it was wrong. Joe traded on it. He knew his mother's heart bled for him and he appeared not to want to protect her. She was so cheerful with him too, never let him guess, so far as Ginny could tell, how wretched he was making her. Sometimes she thought how effective it might be if Harriet did let go, if she really did collapse so that Joe could take his turn and be the strong one. She'd discussed it with Sam, poor Sam, shoved out by both of them, and he'd shrugged and said Harriet would say she was the rock Joe clung on to and if she sank then he'd have no hope. It had made Sam irritable to report this and Ginny even more irritable to hear it. Both of them had agreed that Harriet was very wilful.

This crazy scheme of visiting the attacker's mother, or whoever she was, was the perfect example of such wilfulness. How like Harriet, acting before she thought something through to its likely conclusion.

'You haven't really thought about this, Harriet,' Ginny began again.

'I have. Carefully.'

'What about Sam? What about Joe? Have you thought about what they'll say?'

'I told you, they won't know.'

'How can you be sure they won't find out? The woman might phone – who knows – she might turn out to be a nuisance, they could become involved.'

'They won't, it won't be like that.'

'I'll come with you.'

'What?' Harriet laughed, turned round. Ginny looked so grave, so serious. 'You certainly will not.'

'I think I should, you don't know what you're going into, you'd be safer . . .'

'Ginny, it isn't pistols at dawn, for God's sake, grow up, it's just a meeting between two women . . .'

'One of whose son almost murdered the other's.'

'Ginny!'

'Sorry, but that's how it has to be put to make you see this isn't *normal*, Harriet, it's very abnormal. You have to be careful, you know nothing about this woman . . .'

'I do actually. So do you. I heard plenty, in court. She's an elderly, decent, responsible woman. Her daughter was killed in Africa and she went all that way to bring her grandson back and look after him, all that way, a woman who'd hardly ever left her home town never mind her country. On her own, she went on her own, she flew for the first time. She was the best mother anyone could have been to that boy.'

'We don't know that . . . but anyway, what *is* all this

75

passion for her, Harriet? I don't understand it. It's as though . . .' Ginny stopped. She couldn't think what she meant. She thought that maybe she'd been going to say it was as though her sister was in love with this stranger, this Mrs Armstrong. She was glad she'd pulled herself up because that wasn't really it. It was more that Harriet seemed to want to latch on to this woman in some way that seemed suspicious. After all, why would anyone want anything to do with the mother, or grandmother, of the boy who'd nearly killed their son? She noted Harriet didn't say, 'As though what?' when she stopped half-way through that sentence. She didn't ask her to explain. That could only be because she herself knew Ginny was right, there was something odd going on even if it couldn't be articulated. 'Anyway,' Ginny said, lamely, 'I think I should go with you.'

'No. I don't want company. I want to meet her on my own, on my own terms.'

'She might have someone with her.'

'I doubt it, I don't think so.'

'At least tell me when you're going.'

Harriet laughed. 'So you can send out a search party if I don't come back?'

They both looked at each other. These trigger words. Ginny's husband Michael had organised the search party that found Joe. It was upsetting how Sam had resented the fact. Sam hadn't thought any search party necessary. 'Good heavens,' he'd said, annoyed, 'it's only eleven o'clock. He'll be staying at a friend's, he's just forgotten to phone.' Even after all the likely friends had been contacted Sam had thought a search party melodramatic. He didn't like Michael. He thought he was bossy and he hated all the keep-fit stuff Michael went in for. But Harriet had been so worried and Michael happened to come to the house to collect Ginny, and she hadn't been able to resist his eagerness to go and look for Joe. That was all it was, until midnight, just Michael being over-helpful and going off to look for Joe. It didn't turn into a search party until an hour later, and Sam was right, there had been something repellant about Michael's zeal, about the almost gloating way he'd said he'd organised a search party. Sam, worried himself by then, only refusing to admit it, hiding behind bad temper, raging at Joe's lack of consideration, had still declined to be part of it. He said it made more sense to ring the police, which he did, but before the police had even arrived Michael had found Joe and rung for an ambulance and administered vital first aid. He must have been, said Sam later, in his glory.

Watching Harriet's face after she'd joked about a search party, Ginny felt unbearably depressed. Her sister surely could not go through the rest of her life being thrown off balance by the association of simple words. She saw her face change, shut down, and the memory begin unrolling, and instead of compassion she felt exasperation. This had gone on too long, she had to snap out of it. She knew perfectly well what an offensive thought that was but it was true. Joe wasn't dead. Every day there were cases in the newspapers where teenagers, children, had been attacked and had died. There must be something Harriet hadn't told her that made the attack on Joe worse than it seemed, something she gathered Joe might not have told anyone except his mother, but she knew it wasn't anything to do with sex. That had been Ginny's first thought when Harriet had hinted at something too appalling to speak of, but when she'd tried to ask if it was sexual assault, Harriet had said no, very firmly. In Ginny's opinion this extra horror couldn't therefore be so bad, but she had been wise enough not to say so – Harriet too obviously thought it very bad.

So, however much Joe had suffered, and she didn't deny

he had, she'd seen his injuries, seen how broken in spirit he was, he wasn't dead, or maimed, nor had he been sexually assaulted. As her mother would have said, and as Harriet had herself at one point tearfully agreed, there was a great deal to be thankful for. But she'd forgotten that. She didn't, these days, seem thankful for anything. She'd let Joe drag her down so low she was unable to get up again. Ginny wondered if she dared say, 'It isn't so terrible, Harriet.' Harriet was determined to think it *was* terrible and could see no hope of Joe's real recovery. Once, she'd said to Harriet that it would take time for Joe to come to terms with what had been done to him and Harriet had gone quite mad, screaming how much she loathed that meaningless phrase 'coming to terms', she hated it, everyone used it without thinking, it was jargon, it was slick, and even to dignify it with a meaning, which it didn't deserve, it was still stupid, there were no terms to be arrived at . . . On and on she had ranted, and Ginny had been alarmed. She'd never used the words again and every time she read them she remembered Harriet's objections and had begun to think them valid.

She tried, now, to think clearly and simply. If Harriet couldn't joke about search parties without being overwhelmed by memories, all of them bad, then what it meant was that she couldn't consign those memories to the dustbin of her mind. She couldn't say, 'It happened, it is over, now we go forward.' And what was stopping her from doing that? Ginny decided to tell her, there and then.

'You're thinking of Michael's search party that found Joe, aren't you,' she said, quite loudly, not at all in the usual soft, sympathetic tone she reserved for Harriet now.

'Don't talk about it,' Harriet said, going back to her fussing over food.

'Yes, I will talk about it,' Ginny said. 'I'm tired of it. You don't know what you're doing to yourself, all this punishment. It's got to stop some time, and it won't until you admit it all happened and *it is over*. It is, really.'

Harriet leaned over the sink, gave up scraping carrots so furiously. 'You've seen Joe, Ginny,' she said, voice thick with tears. 'How can *you* of all people say it's over? It isn't. Nobody understands. It really isn't, it never will be, he'll never be the same, never.'

Ginny went over to her and turned her round and put her arms round her. 'God, you're skin and bone,' she complained, then, 'Look, Harriet, I'm not clever, I know I annoy you and say clumsy things, but I'm not saying Joe can ever be the same, all I'm saying is what's wrong with being different, a different Joe but just as good, just as happy as he was? And, darling, he wasn't ever easy, was he, between you and me? He always had problems, didn't he? No, no, don't hate me, I just meant you've been dealing with Joe since the day he was born, trying to understand how difficult he is. This didn't make him difficult. You always said he was complicated, hard to make happy, but now you're blaming it all on the attack, you've stopped believing he can absorb what happened and pick himself up and in spite of it sort himself out, and he always would have had to do that . . . oh, I'm talking rubbish, I'm sorry, big mouth, it runs away with me, but it's *you* I worry about, Harriet. You, not just Joe, not even mainly Joe.'

Harriet cried. Ginny held her, feeling like their mother. Large, well-padded, just like her mother, and Harriet fragile, enviably slim all her life, and now stick-thin, brittle, not pleasant to embrace. She wondered, fleetingly, holding her sister as she was doing, what her love-life was like after all this. It wasn't something they ever talked about, but she sensed Harriet's hostility towards Sam and knew it must cause problems. Sam had a dour look to him, he wasn't like himself at all, but Harriet all too clearly had little time for him. She had time only for Joe. It was fortunate Louis was not at home or he would surely have resented his mother's total concentration on Joe. He'd always been over-indulged, but then he was the youngest and got away with it. The youngest and meant to be a girl, she always thought, though Harriet fiercely denied this, said she had hoped it would not be a girl, positively prayed for a second son, dreaded a daughter.

She'd been ill, having Joe. No trouble with Louis, an easy pregnancy, easy birth. But with Joe she'd threatened to miscarry all the way through, until the sixth month, and even after that there had been problems. She'd had to have a caesarean, which distressed her – she worried it made a difference to the bond with the baby, though everyone had assured her this was not so at all, or not necessarily so. Then Joe didn't look like Louis, who had been a big, healthy, beautiful baby. Joe, joked Sam, was the runt of the litter, a five-pound weakling with a wobbly neck. Harriet had fretted over him from the very beginning and even when, by the time he was two, he was nearly as strong and lively as Louis had been, she had never quite relaxed. He was like her, she thought, and she didn't want him to be, she wanted him to be like his brother, who was like his father and their father's family, all Kennedys with their easy-going natures, lovers of sports, outdoor types, direct and straightforward in temperament. Joe, as Ginny had observed, was never any of those things. Sandwiched as he was between her two girls, she'd seen a lot of Joe as a child and she knew what he was like. To her shame, it had even slightly pleased her that at last Harriet knew what it was like to have a child who was introspective, a mass of strange fears, a child who was always hard to please and seemed frighteningly mature in all kinds of unexpected ways – just like her elder daughter Natasha. She'd got so sick of Harriet boasting that she never had a broken night with Louis, never had a real tantrum from him, never had a qualm about his going to school, whereas she, Ginny, had found Natasha's first five years a test of endurance. Then Joe came along and changed all that.

'I'm getting as bad as you,' Ginny said, after she'd stood comforting Harriet for several minutes, after her sister had stopped weeping and was fumbling around with the wretched carrots again. 'I spend half my time wallowing in memories, not here at all, wondering how things happened. Oh, not Joe,' she went on, hurriedly, as Harriet made a small gesture of protest. 'Natasha, I was suddenly thinking about Natasha. Remember how she used to cry? All the time, for everything, cry, cry, cry, it drove me wild. Do you remember? I thought it was me, how I moaned I must be a rotten mother, I must be doing something wrong. Then she just stopped. I don't even know when. And now she's the most cheerful, confident girl imaginable. It's amazing how they change.'

'Oh Ginny,' Harriet said, smiling, 'for God's sake, you're so obvious, spare me, please.'

'But I didn't mean anything. I was just rambling on, honestly . . .'

So they both ended up laughing, and things felt a little better.

'I'd better go,' Ginny said. 'Laura will be home.'

'How's she getting on?'

'Fine. They said there's no change. It isn't even as bad as they first thought and it might not get any worse, they can control it.'

'Good.'

Ginny hesitated, and then, door already open, said, 'Well, at least tell me when you *have* been to see her. Promise?'

'Promise,' Harriet said. But she knew she wouldn't.

Ginny was under the impression that tears were a good thing. Harriet was sure she'd just gone off humming to herself, convinced that 'a good cry' had helped. But it didn't. Crying was exhausting and at the end of such bouts of weeping she was no better off, nothing whatsoever had been achieved. 'It's letting steam off,' Ginny always told her, at her most confidential, as though imparting some great truth newly discovered by her. 'It lets the pressure on your nerves relax, go on, cry.' What rubbish! All it did was give her a headache and red eyes. Eyes so red-rimmed and bloodshot she'd have to think of an explanation when Joe came in. She never let him see her cry, never. She didn't want him to think he was the cause, and so add to all the other burdens he carried. Even while visiting him in the hospital she'd been completely dry-eyed. It was Sam who'd cried, when he first saw Joe, and she'd despised him for it . . . it was no time for them to cry. Joe didn't want or need their tears, she was sure of it. He wanted them composed and capable. He himself was the only one who had any right to cry and he never did, except once.

When Joe came in from school she was using the age-old trick of peeling onions to explain her red eyes. 'These onions,' she gasped, 'the juice is spurting into my eyes.'

'Wear goggles,' Joe said, quite amiably.

'Good idea, but I've nearly finished.'

He sat down at the kitchen table, slumped. She shot furtive glances at him. Pale, as usual. That frown, so heavy, so permanent now.

'There's a skiing trip,' he said, 'next January.'

'Oh.' She didn't ask if he was interested, that would be fatal.

'It's to Austria, not that crap French place.'

'Sounds an improvement.'

'Louis went there, remember? In his fourth year, before they changed it to the crap place.'

'Oh yes.'

'What do you mean, "Oh yes". Why don't you just say what you want to say? Ask it for Christ's sake, ask me if I want to go, that's what you want to know, isn't it? It's so *false* how you talk to me, all this fucking politeness and *handling* me, be careful, Joe might bite.'

'Well then, *do* you want to go?'

'Obviously!' he yelled. 'Jesus! Why the hell would I mention it if I didn't?'

'It might just have been idle chat . . .'

'Idle chat? I don't *do* idle chat, idle *chat*!'

'Sorry.'

'Sorry? Why? Why are you sorry? I've been rude and you're sorry. What's going on?'

'I'm sorry I annoyed you. I . . .'

'Why can't you annoy me? What's so special about me that I can't be annoyed? Eh?'

'I just meant I seem to say the wrong thing all the time . . .'

'Then shut up.'

He slammed out of the kitchen and up to his room. Another slam. The tears came again, horrifying her. He couldn't help it, she knew he couldn't, that was how all his misery came out, in that kind of ugly way. He didn't behave like that with anyone else, only with her. Even when he was foul to Sam it wasn't in that way. She just had to take it, show him she could bear anything and not flinch. She was the one person who loved him so much, *so* much, that no matter how she was treated by him, that love would endure. Sam, of course, when she'd tried to explain this, had said it was high-minded nonsense. He said Joe needed boundaries set beyond which he could not go. If they didn't exist, he'd go on riding rough-shod and it would do him no good. But she knew Sam was wrong. What Joe needed was what she, and she alone, gave:

83

unconditional understanding and devotion, exactly what she would have given if she had been Leo Jackson's mother, though even to imagine that made her panic. Would she? Would she truly? If Joe, not Leo Jackson, had stabbed a boy? Had kicked and beaten him? Had watched while he was made to do that other thing?

The truth was that she didn't know. The truth was, that was the real reason she wanted to meet Mrs Armstrong, to see if *her* mother's love stretched that far, could encompass such a nightmare. And if it did, she wanted to feed off it. Ginny was right, it wasn't healthy, it was suspicious, it was abnormal. The very excitement she felt at the prospect of this meeting with *his* mother, his grandmother, was indeed sick. But was Mrs Armstrong's gesture equally sick? Did it spring from the same sources? She didn't know. The fact that Mrs Armstrong had so swiftly followed her first letter, saying she would be happy to meet, with another, cancelling the arrangement, showed her own confusion and doubt. But Harriet was going to ignore the cancellation. She'd replied before she got it, saying she'd arrive, as suggested, at two p.m. on Wednesday next. In the cancellation letter Mrs Armstrong had put, 'Please let me know you have received this and understand.' She was ignoring that. She wasn't letting Mrs Armstrong know anything of the sort. She was going to pretend she never got that letter and if in the interval before next Wednesday another arrived she'd ignore that too, however mean it would be to do so. She'd already set the trip up. Sam had been told. She didn't know why she'd bothered to make up a convincing story because he wasn't the least bit interested. He just said, 'That'll be a nice day out,' and that was all. She'd told Joe too, and he'd said, predictably, 'Why are you telling me? So you might not be here at four p.m. next Wednesday . . . for God's sake, Mum.' She was going, even if Mrs Armstrong closed the door in her face. As well she might.

Chapter Five

Sheila's father, Eric James Armstrong, retired butcher, liked both of his Christian names to be used. He was very attached to the James and would reply 'Eric *James*' if his name was called out in a clinic, for example, 'Eric *James* Armstrong is correct,' and glare. He lived on his own in a small terraced house only a few streets away from both of his daughters. People were always telling him he was a lucky man, surrounded by his family in this day and age, and he'd growl, 'I'm no bother to any of them, that's one thing.' It was true. He was no bother. A worry, a scourge, an irritation but, on the surface, no bother. At the age of eighty-nine he fended for himself without any help, kept his little house as clean and tidy as his wife (dead twenty years) had always done, washed his own clothes, even the bedding, in the bath, in spite of both daughters begging him to be sensible and let them do his sheets and towels in one of their automatic washing machines. He walked half a mile a day to get his shopping and, secretly, to place the bets he would never admit to – his only official bets were on the Derby and the Grand National. He was always smart, shoes burnished, trilby at an angle or cap pulled firmly down, and the stick he'd started to carry at seventy often used as a weapon in a bus to correct some unruly child.

He insisted on boarding buses even though he was regularly offered lifts. He had his bus pass and he liked to use it. 'I'm independent,' he was fond of declaring loudly, and using buses was part of the independence. Getting on and off was a performance of his, agonising to watch – he had such difficulty hauling himself up the two steep steps and then balancing while he showed his pass. Sometimes the drivers would say, 'It's all right, Grandad,' as he fumbled for his pass and he'd frown at them and say they were not doing their job if they didn't inspect his pass and he'd report them. The whole bus would heave a sigh of relief when at last he was settled and begin to tense when they knew Mr Armstrong's stop was coming up. Help was not allowed. Everyone would have to watch while he stumbled and staggered to the dreaded step, and many of those who knew him best would be obliged to close their eyes while he negotiated them once more.

But they all admired him now, even those who once had disliked him as intensely as they had liked his wife Jane. It was an area of the town which had remained surprisingly stable over several decades – people really had been born and lived all their lives in this district and, in spite of the town itself growing and changing since the war, whole generations of families still lived in the same rented houses their great-grandparents had first inhabited. It was what Pat, Sheila's daughter, had found so awful and stifling, but it was what her grandfather loved. He was proud of the stability of the area. 'No need to move,' he would declare, 'there's everything anyone could want right here, mek no mistake. "East, West, Home's Best" I alus say.' He hadn't been east or west, or even north or south, but he was quite confident. Anyone moving was a fool as well as a traitor. 'They'll be back,' he'd growl, 'tail between their legs,' and when they were not, when they wrote saying how much they loved wherever they'd gone, he didn't believe them. They were liars all.

His daughters, Sheila and Carole, indulged him these days. Both had been dominated and bullied by their father, but they stood up to him, met threats with disdain, anger with their own anger. The worst thing Eric James could say of either of them was known to be, 'By God, you're nowt like yer mother, *nowt*!' and if either of them dared to yell back, 'Good, who wants to be?' they'd get beaten with a strap. It was practically a hanging offence not to want to be like the saintly Jane and, of course, really they did want to be like her, they adored her, they just knew that they couldn't match up. The truth was, they were like Eric James – tough, brave, independent, needing nobody's protection. Not that he admired them for it. Everything was wrong about them. Their mother was small and delicate with fluffy, mousy hair and beautiful skin, whereas they were both big-boned, big-Armstrong-boned, and tall, with their father's alarming dark eyebrows which they spent many painful hours in their adolescence plucking. They were Armstrong women, like Eric James's mother, the mother he never talked about and usually claimed not to be able to remember, but the few photographs which had survived told the whole story. Armstrong women, fierce, challenging, handsome but needing a strong hand, especially Sheila.

She recalled actually fighting with her father when she was small, six or seven, hitting his thighs with her fists and being picked up by him and held kicking and screaming, but pinioned by his great hands so that she was like a marionette. She'd shrieked she hated him and once she'd spat in his face, and first he'd laughed and then he'd shaken her and called her a little cat and then he'd slapped her, though only across the legs, and pushed her out of the door where she'd collapsed, sobbing for her mother, who finally was allowed to come and bring her inside and put Vaseline on the red marks. 'You shouldn't goad him,' her mother would say, tired and defeated, and Sheila would hiccup that it was his fault and say again that she hated him. 'You don't,' her mother would say, firmly. 'You're as alike as two peas in a pod, that's the trouble.' By the age of twenty Sheila had been bound to acknowledge that her mother was right. It was dreadful to think, but she *was* like her father and there was nothing she could do about it except try to make herself less like him. Whenever she caught herself losing her temper in an irrational Eric James way, or sneering as he sneered, without cause, she would pull herself up and deliberately change tack. The older she got, the more she found she could do it, and by the time she married she was of the opinion that she had actually succeeded in changing her own nature.

Alan had been part of the process. Her father was beside himself when she announced she was going to marry Alan Armstrong. At first, before she brought him home, Eric James had been charmed by the coincidence of the surname, common though it was in their part of the world. 'Must be good stuff if he's an Armstrong,' he smirked, and enquired about Alan's parentage, clearly hoping there would be a connection. There wasn't. Alan was from a different kind of Armstrong family. No big bones, for a start. All of them were on the short side, and bones were so well covered they were not much in evidence. Sheila was actually an inch taller than Alan, another cross against him. Her father wouldn't credit she'd got involved with what he called a midget. 'Why'd yer go for a bloody midget?' he'd roared. 'It beats me, I can tell you, a lass marrying a chap shorter.' She hadn't liked Alan's lack of height herself, in fact, but when her father made it sound like a deformity she'd defended him passionately, even to absurd lengths. 'I hate big men,' she'd declared, to her six-foot-two father, 'big hefty men – ugh, who wants them.' Eric James had laughed. 'Oh aye?' he'd said, and turned away, disbelief written all over him. She was five-foot-nine, Alan five-foot-eight, not a midget at all, but at her wedding, walking down the aisle one way on her father's arm and the other on Alan's, she'd known which looked best.

She loved Alan for everything in him that was not like her father – his quiet nature, his patience, his good humour, his constant kindness. She didn't mind what even her mother called his 'softness', implying his lack of power, of drive and ambition. It was true, Alan had little drive. She would even admit he was lazy. Not lazy enough to lose his not very demanding job, but just lazy enough not to make much progress. He had a little money when they married from his mother's side of the family, and Sheila believed this small inheritance was part of Alan's trouble. They bought a house outright with it when they married and it wasn't until much later that any worry about money at all had ever had to enter Alan's head. He'd been cautious, put the rest of his inheritance in a building society, and the interest had enabled them to live as his actual salary would not have done. No car, not for a long time, but no need for Sheila to work. In this kind of secure, cosy life her transformation had been complete, the shadow of her likeness to her father banished for ever, she hoped.

Until Pat was killed. Then, she felt Eric James stirring in her – his determination, his stubbornness, his courage. For the first time in her life she had despised Alan, his helplessness, his conviction that nothing could or should be done. Her father had been in the house when they'd heard. Having his dinner, as he did every Sunday – dinner at Sheila's, tea at Carole's. Alan had answered the telephone while she and her father had gone on eating roast beef and Yorkshire pudding – 'not bad, but not as good as yer mam's' – and he hadn't stopped wolfing it down all the time Alan was stuttering out the terrible news. He'd gone on eating till he'd finished the whole

89

plateful. Then, as Sheila sat transfixed, he'd got his khaki handkerchief out and passed it over his brow and said, 'Oh hell,' followed by, 'Damn, damn,' and a shaking of his head. An eternity she'd sat there, aware he was watching her furtively. She knew why. He was waiting to see if she'd break down, he was terrified she would cry, then what would he do? He, who had never offered a crumb of comfort to anyone, only said, 'It can't be helped,' and, 'There's nowt can be done,' intent that his own fatalistic attitude should prevail and act as a brake on all emotion. So she hadn't cried, but not because of him, whatever he thought.

He'd shuffled off home. Without touching her. Without any embrace. He'd said he'd be there if he was needed and made his way home where he then proceeded to telephone the entire family, not just Carole, but cousins, aunts, the lot, to tell them. He told Carole she'd best get round to Sheila's at once – so she could offer what he could not, presumably. He thought he'd done well. 'Did Carole come?' he'd asked, later that evening, ringing before bed. 'Yes.' 'Thought so,' he said, triumphantly, 'good lass.' She hadn't bothered arguing. But later there had been plenty of arguments. Over Pat's body, for one. He thought it should be brought back and buried where her grandmother, his wife Jane, was buried. It was proper, he said. She told him what it would cost and he didn't blanch. He still thought it proper and said he'd pay out of what he'd saved for his own funeral. He shook his head in disgust when they told him the two bodies had been buried already out there. Only over the matter of Leo had he been any help. 'Lad's family,' he'd said, 'can't get round that, blood's blood, there's no choice. Lad's lost his mam, nowt worse, nowt worse.' He'd visibly toughened and stiffened while Alan pleaded that to bring a mixed-race three-year-old-boy back here would be cruel. 'Cruel?' Eric

James said. 'Cruel to leave him, yer mean, without his mam. He needs our Sheila, no getting away from it.' When Alan said it was Sheila he was concerned about, she was nearly sixty, it would be hard taking on a three-year-old – Eric James had interrupted, banging his stick and saying, 'Nearly sixty? She's an Armstrong Armstrong, they don't give up at sixty. She could tek on any number of three-year-olds and never blink an eye, what the devil are yer talking about, eh?'

He hadn't been able to wait to see Leo, whatever his loud former opinions of the colour of the child's father. All that was forgotten. Leo was Pat's lad and that was that. Right had to be done by him. And, of course, he loved children, at least until they were seven. He was even good with them – all his grandchildren had adored him. His own daughters might have no memories of any tenderness, of games played and attention devoted, but his granddaughters did. He'd have gone with Sheila to claim Leo, breaking his own proud record of never having left his own country, if only he'd been younger. He said so frequently, glaring at Alan. 'Good job *she's* got backbone,' he'd said, pointedly. 'Very good job.' All the way through the planning of Sheila's daunting journey he'd praised her for 'sticking to it' and, though bewildered by all the strange place names and the timetables he couldn't understand, he'd pushed her on as hard as Alan tried to pull her back.

When she returned, her father was there, at Manchester airport, with Alan, to greet her and Leo. It was the greatest gesture he could make, to drive with Alan all that way at his great age to a city he was afraid of. Nothing Alan could say would persuade him that this ordeal was not called for – he'd be better off at home, instead of subjecting himself to unnecessary effort. But no, he wanted to be there, to give the little lad a real welcome, to let him see what was what, as he mysteriously expressed it. And so, when she and Leo came through the customs hall and out into the arrival lounge, walking unsteadily, her legs cramped from being so long in the plane, and Leo tired, the first face she saw was that of Eric James, peering over the barrier, looking fierce. He didn't smile when he saw her – smiling was not his forte, and indeed when he did smile his lips never looked comfortable and slid as quickly as was decent into their normal grim line – but instead raised his stick. He was the last person she wanted to see. She wanted comforting Alan, quiet Alan, or Carole, who'd be so good at taking charge.

Having her father there made everything twice as difficult. He walked so slowly with his stick and was forever pausing to shout indignantly, at some fool he accused of trying to trip him up. 'Git away with yer!' he'd bark, but his voice was lost in the general hubbub. Leo didn't even notice him. He was being carried by Sheila, his face buried in her shoulder, half asleep. She sat in the back of the car with Leo's head now in her lap and the rest of his small frame curled on the seat, covered with a rug. Her father sat in the front, instructing both her and Alan. 'That's it, let the lad sleep, best thing, don't waken him,' to her, and, 'Tek yer time, tek yer time, no hurry,' to Alan. Every now and again he'd turn round, with immense difficulty, cursing his seat-belt and half strangling himself with it, and look at Leo. 'Small,' he muttered, 'like Pat, nowt of our Armstrongs in him.' She didn't reply, kept her own eyes shut, but it didn't put him off asking questions. 'How's he been, the lad?' She managed to say, 'Fine,' which brought forth a stream of 'Good lad's'. Later, it was, 'Hot, was it, eh? I'll bet.' She nodded. 'Lad'll notice the difference, bound to.' His desperation to talk, to bring himself close to Leo, was so marked that even in the midst of her overwhelming weariness she felt sorry for him. Awful, she reflected sleepily, to want to communicate concern and affection and be unable to, all that unused pent-up feeling inside him which he wouldn't acknowledge as emotion.

All through the first trying month Eric James had trumpeted, 'I met them at the airport, I was right there when the li'le lad landed on British soil.' It was as though he'd attended a coronation at least. The rest of the family had come to meet Leo, but none of them managed it without Eric James accompanying them. He took it upon himself to organise all the visits, ringing each member of the Armstrong Armstrongs up and telling them when they could go to Sheila's, calling for him on the way, 'Because the lad's used to me, I'd best be with yer.'

Sheila hadn't the energy to defy him, just let it happen. Leo was awake most of the night, and so was she, sitting reading him stories, cuddling him, giving him soothing drinks, being there with him as her only concern. Alan swore she hadn't slept a full night in their bed since her return. Not that he complained – he understood Leo's need of his grandmother. In fact, it was all exactly as he had predicted: Sheila became a mother all over again, gave herself to it wholly, nothing and no one else mattered. Slowly, she brought Leo round to accepting his new circumstances, saw that he received such love and devotion that he could be in no doubt that he was safe and secure. And Eric James helped. He was part of the routine, regular as clockwork, part of Sheila's own regime of concentrated attention. Alan was kind but distant all the same – he could not help standing back, being unsure, whereas Eric James had such zest for the job of making Leo love him too. Not that he ever used that word, or thought of what he was doing as bidding for, as well as giving, love. Leo was simply a source of endless fascination to him.

93

Until he was seven. Four years of complete harmony between the old man and the boy and then the first cracks began to appear. Faint, hairline cracks in the beautiful relationship, nothing to worry about. But Sheila saw them and worried. The first time she heard her father say, 'Yer don't do what I do, yer do what I say . . . now then,' she groaned. Leo was clever. He was curious. He wanted explanations for everything, reasons, justifications. To be told not to do something his beloved grandfather was doing simply because the old man said so and without any rationale being given annoyed him. Logic was something Eric James never bothered with, but it held great attraction for Leo from an early age. Then there was his rejection of some of the more babyish games Eric James had invented. This caused offence. 'You please yerself then,' his grandfather would say and shuffle off in a huff, his disappointment only too evident. Worst of all was the clash of what could only be called 'standards'. 'If he hits yer, you hit him harder, knock him to the ground, kick his teeth in, that'll learn him,' Eric James advised when Leo got into his first fight. Leo stared at him. 'I don't want to fight,' he said. 'It's not what you want, lad, it's what yer've got to do or yer'll end up a pansy.'

'What's a pansy?'

'Yer'll know soon enough.'

There it was again, reasons, explanations, *never* given. But Leo did fight. When he came home with a split lip, blood all over his lower face, but not crying, Eric James was delighted. 'What's the other fella like then, eh?' And when Leo reported his assailant had indeed had his teeth kicked in and was still writhing on the ground, bawling, his grandfather was elated. 'Good lad, good lad!' he chortled. What he failed to observe was Leo's unhappiness with his own victory and his disapproval of his grandfather's joy. It didn't feel right, nor did it feel right to follow Eric James in his constant small methods of cheating – jumping queues, getting into cinemas free by a side-door, silly, unimportant things, but they added up. Eric James was no shining example of grandfatherly rectitude and the more clearly he realised this, the more hesitant Leo became in partnering him as he had once done. By the time he was thirteen, Eric James was becoming an embarrassment. Leo was big by then. He'd turned, against all expectation, into an Armstrong Armstrong after all (nobody mentioned any Jackson side). He was tall, broad-shouldered and already powerfully built.

'Be a boxer,' Eric James urged. 'Darkies mek good boxers.'

'I'm not a darkie,' Leo said, 'and don't use that word.'

'I'll use what word I bloody well like,' roared his grandfather. 'Don't you be ordering me about, lad.'

'I wasn't, I was just saying . . .'

'Niver mind just, niver mind that, remember yer manners, show some respect to yer elders.'

'I will if they show respect to me,' said Leo, and in the background Sheila had smiled and secretly urged him on. But when Leo was upset later, and said how he hated his grandfather calling him a darkie, she'd defended him, to her own surprise.

'He's an old, old man, Leo,' she said soothingly, 'it doesn't mean anything, really. You've got to remember he's lived a narrow life, he doesn't think . . .'

'Well, he should.'

'I know he should, but he's set in his ways, it's too late to change him now, don't hold it against him, it's only ignorance.'

'*Only* ignorance?' Leo queried, morose and sour, suddenly.

It wasn't easy for him from then on. She watched him

retreat into himself, bit by bit, lose all the former openness which had been so attractive. He'd always been quiet, but never sullen, quiet in an attentive, alert way, whereas now he was sunk in some kind of gloom she couldn't penetrate. She didn't believe he knew himself why his personality seemed to have suffered some sea-change. Her sister Carole said they were all the same, all boys went like this, but Sheila wondered how she could know when she had only daughters herself. The physical change alone was so violent and alarming – at sixteen Leo was over six feet and weighed thirteen stone. His shoes were size twelve, no sweater had arms long enough. And he wasn't beautiful any more. Everything about his features seemed to coarsen and his eyes, once huge in the small face, seemed to narrow and shrink as the rest of him grew bigger. He filled their small rooms, knocked his head on doorways, was clumsy where he had been strikingly graceful. She found it all so difficult to take, and so, she sensed, did he.

But they were still close, still friends. He was a good boy, helpful, thoughtful. Carole was always commenting on it – 'Catch any of my lot doing my shopping,' or, 'Clean my windows? You must be joking.' He looked after her, did Leo, without drawing attention to what he did or seeking reward or praise. They talked too. Often they had serious conversations, not that she could keep up with him, he knew too much, he was too clever. But he listened to her, gave weight to her uninformed opinions, never told her she was stupid, as Carole's children had done. He loved her, she knew he did, though he'd long since outgrown the stage when he could openly tell her so, when he'd flung his arms round her neck and clung to her and kissed her and said, 'I love, love, love you, mam.' Maybe she should never have begun correcting him, making him realise she was his grandmother. It made him upset, it was as though she was betraying him in some way and at the same time reminding him his mother was dead. He couldn't remember a thing about her, about Pat, absolutely nothing at all, nor about the accident. His earliest memory was of her, holding out her hand in that hospital room. That, and the plane and being given a teddy-bear by the stewardess. His life had started with her.

He did once say, 'What would have happened to me, if you hadn't gone for me?' He'd been about eight or nine when he asked that. She ought to have been prepared for this inevitable question, had an appropriate answer ready, but she wasn't and hadn't. She was startled into truth and said she didn't know. Then she'd added how kind everyone there had been and that she was sure he would have been well looked after. 'But who would have been my mam?' he'd said, quite panicky. She'd sat down with him, glad he could still be cuddled, just, and told him there were questions in everyone's life which could not be answered and it was no good torturing himself looking for them. She had come for him and that was all that mattered. At least she was ready for the next alarm – 'Could anyone come from Africa and take me back there?' It was such a relief to be able to be emphatic and say this was quite impossible, he belonged only to her and Alan. It was Alan, whatever his views, who had seen everything was done properly. She even showed him the adoption papers, and he was satisfied. But gradually, in adolescence, Africa loomed larger in a different way. He wanted to know about his father. He liked being told he was a doctor. But about John Jackson's family she could tell him nothing. She'd never known much, and though all Pat's letters had been preserved and she passed them on to Leo on his sixteenth birthday, they held surprisingly little concrete information, few facts. Most of them were full of lyrical descriptions of the landscape and the animals and sunsets. 'She loved Africa,' Leo said, quite puzzled, and Sheila had agreed. Pat did love Africa. So Leo began to think he should go there and see for himself, and her great dread grew that once he was eighteen he'd up and go and leave her for ever, just like Pat.

Now, she supposed, he would never get the chance. He wouldn't be granted a visa, probably, not with his record. 'Send him back to Africa,' Eric James at one time had said, with such cruelty. 'That's where he belongs, in the jungle, carrying on like that, just an animal.' Her hatred for her father had been so overpowering she had almost fainted with the pressure of it, the sheer burning pressure inside her. For once his mighty age, his physical frailty, had not protected him from her contempt. 'I think *you* should go back, to you own home, if that's all you have to say,' she'd said.

'Well, yer can't deny it, bloody disgrace, acting like that, like an animal . . .'

'You know nothing about it.'

'I know he damned well did it, I know that, and so does the rest of this town.'

'I don't want to talk about it.'

'No wonder, neither do I, and neither does he, not a word to say for hisself.'

'Exactly.'

'Eh?'

'Nobody really knows what went on, Leo hasn't said.'

'He didn't deny he was there and he had a knife and he bloody used it, he didn't deny it and he couldn't, not with them finding the knife and his prints and the blood matching and all the . . .'

'*Dad*! For pity's sake! I can't stand it, stop it!'

He'd stopped. Shuffled off. Later, she'd realised it was his own pain speaking, the only way he could release his grief. They'd never spoken of it again. She and Alan never spoke of it, not after the first awful night. They agreed it did no good. And that was what terrified her most about Mrs Kennedy wanting to come . . . she might want to speak about it, the actual crime, go over it. Maybe she even knew more. That policeman, the Detective Sergeant, he'd hinted at something more and her heart had raced. He was always hinting. Smug. Actually tapped his nose with his finger and said he got feelings, call it sixth sense. He dared to tell her he had one about Leo, about why he'd done it. He insinuated it was something unpleasant, this reason. She refused to ask him. He could keep his suspicions, whatever they were, to himself. Nor would she volunteer any hypothesis of her own. She stuck to what she had always said: Leo was a good boy, always had been. She was his grandmother who had been like a mother and she *knew*. It was impossible for her to have brought this boy up for thirteen years and not to have known him through and through. Yes, she had to accept the evidence of Leo's guilt, but she didn't have to accept this meant he was rotten and evil. For one night, for forty minutes, yes, it was indisputable, but not before, not ever, and that must mean something. 'Mothers,' the policeman had said, smirking, 'they're all the same when it's their little lamb.'

But Leo didn't seem to want her loyalty and faith in him. He was like a zombie, he couldn't talk to her any more. If Mrs Kennedy was coming looking for explanations she would get none. She could talk about Leo's upbringing, about Leo's character and so forth, but there was nothing at all she could tell her about the attack. If she started on it, Sheila had made up her mind . . . she would show Mrs Kennedy the door. Clearly, the woman was going to come. There'd been no reply to her second letter, retracting the previous invitation, and meanwhile Mrs Kennedy's own reply, saying she'd come on

Wednesday, had arrived. She must just accept that she'd made a mistake in agreeing and get it over with as quickly as possible. She was nearly seventy years of age, she ought to be able to deal with it, behave with some dignity. She took the trouble to have her hair done on the Monday and though she wasn't so foolish as to buy anything new to wear, she had her best dress dry-cleaned. She didn't want to look pathetic and shabby. Mrs Kennedy had seen her in court all sombre in grey. Her best dress was a bright blue and she was glad, she didn't want to look down-trodden, she wanted to show life went on and, although sorry and ashamed and miserable, that she was trying.

And she baked two cakes to offer Mrs Kennedy a slice, a Dundee cake, her special, and gingerbread. She made sure both were produced on Sunday for tea so that a good bit of both cakes had been eaten and they wouldn't look obvious. She wasn't going to use her best china from the cabinet, nor was she going to sit in the living room. Too stiff, too far apart. The kitchen was small but friendlier. They could sit at the table, under the window, with the sun coming in and the geraniums visible in the window-box. She would *say*, 'Would you rather go in the living-room, or is the kitchen all right?' and she was sure Mrs Kennedy would choose the kitchen, with the question so cunningly put. Any woman would. Then it would be easy making the tea. She didn't have any real coffee or a coffee-machine and didn't want to offer instant, even if everyone else did. This was a tea household and tea it would be, unless Mrs Kennedy was very forthright in declining it. Then, the instant coffee would be produced. None of these things mattered, Sheila knew that, neither to her nor to her guest. They were irrelevant – tea, cake, best dress, hair – irrelevant, but not unimportant. They set the stage. It was all unnatural and the right props helped . . .

By the time two o'clock on Wednesday came, Sheila was quite calm.

Chapter Six

SHE WAS AT THE END of Mrs Armstrong's street by
one-twenty p.m. A street of small, terraced houses
opening straight on to the pavement. Rows of them, all
absolutely straight, running off a shopping thoroughfare.
There was a railway bridge nearby and the trains could be
clearly heard shooting over it. She'd passed two factories,
enormous red-brick edifices with high, small windows.
There were no trees anywhere, no gardens, and yet these
narrow streets were not entirely bleak. She noticed all the
doors were brightly painted and most had brass knockers.
The windows sparkled and some had window-boxes on
the whitened sills. There was no litter at all, not a speck of
dirt anywhere. It was as though someone regularly
washed and polished the grey stone of the pavements and
the very tarmac of the road. Harriet drove along it a little
way then turned into another street and parked. She
couldn't sit in the car for a whole forty minutes, so she got
out and began to walk with as much sense of purpose as
she could muster along this street. Unfortunately, it was a
dead end and she was obliged to turn round and retreat.
The wind was whipping her hair and though she did not
care about such things she didn't want to arrive at Mrs
Armstrong's house looking bedraggled, so she was
obliged to get into her car once more. She brushed her
hair, staring at herself in the small mirror fixed to the flap
which hung down in front of the passenger seat. In it, she
saw reflected a woman coming out of a house and

stopping to look at the strange car curiously. Of course, in this kind of street any stranger or strange object would be noticed.

It was silly to have arrived so very early, but she had been afraid of not being able to find the street and of being late and therefore flustered. She'd allowed twice as much time as she could realistically expect the journey to take and was still glad of it. She wanted to be calm and her composure was always threatened by anxiety over punctuality. She was calm now. Calm, but nervous. She hadn't the faintest idea what she was going to say and the onus would be on her. Mrs Armstrong had, after all, tried to cancel this meeting, she'd thought better of it. She might be angry at being tricked, or what she could, with every justification, regard as being tricked. Or she might not be there at all, not having received any acknowledge-ment of her last note. I must, Harriet thought, be prepared for anything, and I must, above all else, betray no emotion. This meeting was not about emotion. Even if she did not know what it was about, it was not about that.

With another twenty minutes to go, she took out the folder of press cuttings. These repelled Sam, and Joe did not even know about them. She didn't know why she had clipped and kept reports, first of the attack, then of the capture of the unnamed Leo Jackson, then of the court case. She'd done it furtively. All the cuttings were from the *Daily Telegraph*, their own daily paper, and from the local paper. There were no photographs alongside any of the pieces, because both boys were too young to be named. Really, these cuttings, she now saw, did not amount to much. They were quite pathetic. Front-page news in the local paper, but only in a side column, and a mere paragraph on page three of the *Telegraph*. The facts were stated and that was about all. Except there was a description of Leo Jackson's upbringing. His grandfather was quoted as saying none of it made sense to him and his grandmother – 'known as his mother' – as reflecting he had always been a good boy. It was astonishing how little attention there had been.

But then the attack and Joe's fate were run-of-the-mill. Detective Sergeant Graham had tactlessly pointed this out in a mistaken attempt to be comforting. Run-of-the-mill. Random violence was run-of-the-mill, quite ordinary, nothing to get excited about. Run-of-the-mill or par for the course, Graham as usual wasn't fussy about his clichés. He had been trying, Sam maintained, to reassure them that because what had happened to Joe was not unique, then his recovery was not impossible. 'People get over it,' Graham had said, 'they think they won't but they do. And he's young, the young heal quicker.' How it had enraged her. He knew nothing about Joe and yet could confidently assert he'd heal quickly and eventually forget. He hadn't the faintest inkling of what all this had done to Joe. Once, he had even said, sanctimoniously, 'It's you I'm worried about, Mrs Kennedy, you're taking it hard.' He'd shaken his head sadly and attempted to engage her in one of his soulful, meaningful stares. She'd turned away, rejected his ghastly sympathy. He'd boasted to her about how he lectured – *lectured* – to police audiences on 'How to Treat Victims of Random Violence' and she'd almost vomited on the spot at the very idea of such a thing – it was disgusting.

She wondered if Graham had visited the Armstrongs. Probably. And how would he have behaved with them? Would it have made any difference that they were the grandparents of the aggressor? Maybe not, maybe the self-importance, the evident relish of his role, would have been the same. It was something, she supposed, she could discuss with Mrs Armstrong, but she didn't think she would. Ten minutes to go. There was no harm in being just a little early. She started the car and reversed and turned back into the right road. The Armstrongs' house was nearly at the end. There was plenty of room to park. She pulled up at the very end of the road. She walked quite briskly to the front door, which opened before she could ring the bell.

'Come in,' Mrs Armstrong said, standing well back, with the door opened to its fullest extent, as though she wanted to convince Harriet there were no lions waiting to pounce.

'Thank you.' Harriet stepped inside and waited. Mrs Armstrong made little clucking noises as she went ahead. 'I thought in the kitchen, it's quite cosy, but if you'd rather . . .'

'Oh, in the kitchen,' Harriet said, and saw Mrs Armstrong's approving little smile.

The kitchen was small. Cosy means cramped, Harriet thought. Hardly room for the table between the cooker and fridge and cupboards. The table had a cloth on it, an embroidered cloth, she was sure Mrs Armstrong had made it herself, and a white jug of some pink flowers, she didn't know what. Mrs Armstrong went straight to the kettle and put it on. It boiled at once, showing it had already been boiled in anticipation. Harriet wondered if she should say she didn't like tea and rejected the idea – this was one occasion when she would have to force it down. Except for the faint hiss of the water as it was poured into the yellow china teapot there was silence. The fridge sprang into life, whirring croakily.

'You sit down,' Mrs Armstrong said, 'I won't be a minute.'

Harriet sat, facing out of the window. Thank God she could at least recognise geraniums. 'Cheerful, your geraniums,' she said, as Mrs Armstrong set the teapot down and got cups out of a small wooden cupboard.

'My husband is fond of geraniums. Anything bright he likes. Milk?'

Harriet said no. Mrs Armstrong's dress was a very bright blue. She was a big woman. Funny, when in court she hadn't seemed so. Her hair was white, cut short, too short, a rather masculine haircut which didn't suit her. She should have had a bun, Harriet decided, and a middle parting. Her features were quite fine, but the brutal haircut made them look coarser. She was suddenly aware that she'd been sitting there for a long time without speaking, not even to say thank you for the tea she hadn't wanted.

'Mrs Armstrong . . .' she began, but was instantly interrupted.

'Sheila. I know I'm old, but I'm not old-fashioned.'

'I'm sorry, Sheila then, I just thought you might prefer me to be formal since I've barged my way in . . .'

'No, I let you come, even if I changed my mind, I knew you'd still come and I let you. I could have stopped you.'

'Yes. You're very kind.'

'We could all do with a bit of kindness.' Sheila saw how Harriet's hand trembled as she replaced her cup. Replaced it without even taking the smallest sip. Maybe it was too hot. Tea without milk, tea newly poured and not cooled by milk, would be. She surely knew that. Now she was clasping her hands together under the table and clearing her throat. Sheila knew that noise. It was the same noise she had once made herself when she'd been trying to stop herself crying in the days she could cry. Crying would do no good. If this woman had come to sit and cry it would be hopeless, a waste of time. She couldn't help her. 'Have some cake,' she urged, 'it's home-made.' She expected it to be rejected, but a slice of Dundee cake was accepted quite eagerly and actually eaten. 'I don't bake so much now, with only Alan and me to eat the stuff. And my Dad, he enjoys a bit of cake when he comes.'

105

'Does he live near?'

'Too near, I sometimes think.' They both smiled. 'He's nearly ninety,' she went on, 'and a cantankerous old chap, he's difficult, always has been. Are your parents alive?'

'No. They both died five years ago, quite young, one after the other, both of cancer.'

'Young?'

'My mother was sixty-six, my father sixty-eight. Not young really, I suppose.'

'No.'

Harriet closed her eyes. Leo Jackson's mother, she remembered, had only been in her twenties when she was killed. How crass she had been to comment on her own parents' supposed youth. She looked hurriedly at Sheila, whose face was impassive, and decided not to apologise, it would make matters worse. She must get on, she hadn't come here to talk about her dead parents. Ten minutes had gone already – she could see her hour ticking away on the kitchen clock in front of her. This wouldn't do. 'It was good of you to write,' she said, trying to look Sheila straight in the eye.

'I should have done it before. I thought about it enough, but I wasn't sure . . . it seemed . . . I thought it might make things worse, coming from me.'

'No. It made things a bit better. Because they haven't been, lately. They've been very bad again.'

'Sometimes it's like that. When my Pat was killed – well, it was terrible, I don't want to talk about it even now, but a year later it seemed worse. I never could understand why. People seemed to think I was over it, but I wasn't. I hadn't even started.

'Started?'

'To get over it, like they expected. I didn't even want to get over it. That's all people want, they want to know you're getting over it, eh?'

'Yes. They do.'

'But your boy isn't dead.'

'No. I've a lot to be thankful for. That's one of the problems. People tell me all the time I've a lot to be thankful for. They didn't kill him.'

Sheila got up abruptly. 'More tea?' she asked, loudly.

The clock in the next door living-room chimed the half-hour. Good. Half-time. No score. She wouldn't let it run to extra time, that was one thing, couldn't afford to, not with Alan and her father due back.

'No, no more tea, thank you. I'm sorry.'

'Sorry? Oh, you don't want to worry about that . . .'

'No, I mean mentioning killing. I didn't mean to, I didn't mean to mention what happened in any way,'

'It's only natural, you couldn't be blamed if you did.'

'But I didn't, I don't want to. It's pointless. It's nothing to do with you, with us, all that.'

'I'd like to be as sure.'

'Did I sound sure?'

'Well, you said it. It can't be true, though, is how I feel. It would be a relief, but I can't think it's true, for me. For you, yes, but not for me.'

'Why?'

'Bound to have something to do with upbringing, bound to. He couldn't just turn into a monster. We went wrong somewhere.'

'And I did.'

'Oh, now!'

'I did. I must have done. I've blamed myself over and over. There must have been something about Joe, and then, how he reacted . . .'

'No, no.'

'I didn't mean to talk about it.' Harriet managed to gulp some of the now cold tea. Her dislike of the taste braced her. 'My husband doesn't know I'm here,' she said.

'Neither does mine.'

'He'd be angry.'

'So would mine. He'd say I was daft, writing in the first place, he wouldn't like it at all.'

'The thing is, Sam thinks I'm wallowing in it all, I mean he thinks everything would be all right if I'd just go along with pretending it was.'

'How old are you?'

'Forty-five. Sam's forty-six.'

'Old enough to know about men. They're all the same. Can't face up to anything even when it's staring them in the face. When our Pat was killed, Alan never spoke of it, of what was going on in his head. He cried, mind. He cried a lot, and I suppose that isn't typical.'

'Sam doesn't cry, or only once, seeing Joe in hospital . . .' Harriet saw Sheila's expression and stopped. It was impossible. Everything, with Sheila, came back to her grief over her daughter's death and everything with herself to Joe's suffering. How could they talk to each other without plunging into this overriding pain?

'I can't cry,' Sheila said, though her face looked so ready for weeping. 'It's odd. Everyone else cries except me. People think it's funny, they think I'm hard, or those that don't know me, like that policeman. He thought I was hard-bitten, definitely.'

'Detective Sergeant Graham?'

'I can't remember his name. Lean chap, like a whippet, hair brushed straight back.'

'Graham. I hated him.'

'Only doing his job, as they say. Thrilled with himself, he was, took a pleasure in it. He had the place turned upside down. I scrubbed it from top to bottom afterwards. I shampooed the carpets, all of them, not that feet leave marks on carpets, I just felt they did. I felt like moving, selling the house and moving.' Sheila stiffened at the memory she was invoking. Her back went very straight and she lifted her chin in the air so that to Harriet she looked suddenly threatening. She never knew how the police had got on to Leo, though Alan said it would have been easy enough – how many black kids were there in this small city? If a gang with a black kid had been seen in Joe Kennedy's area, if a gang had been recognised, in that pub where they'd called in, as being from the city, then the police wouldn't have had to do much detection to think of Leo. All the trouble in their city started in its one nightclub and Leo, on his own admission, had been there. Easy, as Alan said. But she'd been so confident when she opened the door, and saw two policemen there on Sunday morning. Yes, she'd said, quite unworried, yes, Leo Jackson lived here and yes he was at home, if still asleep, and yes they could see him, she would call him – but they had brushed past her and gone thundering up the stairs . . .

She brought herself back with difficulty to the present and looked at Harriet with embarrassment. It was so quiet. They were both so quiet, sitting there. The smallest clink of a teaspoon on a saucer was shockingly loud, the faintest movement of a hand seemed to screech in the still air. 'I felt like moving,' she repeated, and then again, 'I felt like selling the house and moving.' She saw recognition in the other woman's eyes. She knew this woman, why there had been this pause, why Sheila had completely withdrawn for a few minutes and now she was helping her pretend nothing had happened, that there had been no gap in their stilted conversation.

'Yes, Sam suggested that,' Harriet said. 'He thought I'd like it, but I didn't. Where could we move to that was so peaceful and nice?'

'I used to go where you live for my holidays, well, a couple of holidays. Lovely it is, you're right. Lovelier than this, but we've lived here since we were married, all these years. We couldn't move.'

'I don't think it does any good anyway. It's just running away. It might work on a superficial level but not a deeper one, where it matters.'

There was another long pause. This time Sheila was alert. She couldn't think what to say and she could see that Harriet was equally at a loss. She studied her, quite openly, quite boldly. Rude. Her stare, for that was what it undeniably was, could be called rude. There was a sense of defiance in it, she knew. She was defying this woman to blame her and yet it was blame she wanted to face. She could see no blame, not a speck. She saw barely contained distress. Harriet quivered, visibly quivered, her eyelids fluttering rapidly all the time, her lips trembling, as though they were stuttering though no sound came from them, and even her hair seemed to give off movement. The tension was unbearable. It is my house, Sheila thought, and I must stop this, I must think of something very ordinary to say.

'You work, don't you?' she finally said.

'Yes, I have a small business. I design and print fabrics.'

'That must help.'

'It does, if I can concentrate. I couldn't, at first, and then I pulled myself together, but now it's slipping again, the concentration, I mean. I seem to spend half my time wandering in the past. It's silly . . .'

'It's natural. I do it, I've always done it.'

'No, but it isn't natural, not how I'm doing it now. I can't explain, I use it like a drug and it has the same kind of effect, it makes me stupid. My sister says it's not natural.'

'Are you close?'

'Quite. More now. She's very straightforward, very practical. I was always the dreamer. She lives near, we see a lot of each other. She's been very good, really. She's got her own troubles, one of her girls, she's got two daughters, the younger one has diabetes . . .'

'That's nasty.'

'Yes. So Ginny, Virginia, that's my sister, she tends to get exasperated with me – you know – everyone has troubles and they just have to adapt. I admire her, she's wonderful. I have terrible daydreams. I'm ashamed of them, in them I think which would I rather, Joe has diabetes or gets attacked, as though you could compare them, it's terrible.'

'If I could have Pat back, I'd swop anything. I'd even trade lives, other people's for hers.'

They both stared at each other again for a long time. Harriet's eyes were full of tears now, Sheila's clear and unblinking. Each took in the other's intensity. Sheila reached out her hand and touched Harriet's, her hand cold, Harriet's warm. The lightest of touches, hardly a touch at all, and hastily withdrawn. The clock next door struck three. Both of them started. Harriet sprang up, Sheila got to her feet more slowly, wondering how a whole hour could have passed.

'I must go,' Harriet said, suddenly embarrassed. 'Joe will be home, it's quite a long drive and I like to be home when he gets in, even if it annoys him. Thank you for letting me come.'

'I wish I thought it had done you some good, dear.'

'Oh, it has. Just talking.'

'At least it hasn't done harm, I hope.'

'No, no, certainly not. Maybe one day you'd like to visit me? We could have a walk, by the lake, if you like it, you said you did, didn't you?'

'Yes, I do like it. Maybe one day.'

They were at the door. Sheila felt she'd never see Harriet Kennedy again and was sorry. Twenty-five years between them, but it didn't seem like that. She was even sorrier for her now than she had been before. In court, Harriet had seemed aloof and confident, a class apart, and class had been in the air all the time. Now it wasn't. Different accents, different clothes, different generation, but the sum of these differences didn't add up to the gulf it should. Sheila felt the stronger. She didn't feel so old and beaten any more. This younger woman was in worse shape and she felt compassionate. Not one angry or resentful word had passed Harriet's lips, not a mention of any hatred for Leo, no feeling of utter revulsion towards him and all who were connected to him. She realised how relieved she was not to have had to talk about Leo, not to have been called to account. Everyone else, family, friends, neighbours, police, probation officers, strangers – all had wanted to call her to account, to explain, to find reasons. That was what she had dreaded this meeting would be about and she had been ready to take her punishment.

She watched Harriet drive away, giving a little wave and a smile, and when she went back inside the house seemed dreary. She went upstairs and took off her blue dress and put on a skirt and blouse. Harriet had worn some sort of big shirt over leggings. Unusual clothes, not really suitable for a woman in her forties, except that these days being in your forties meant nothing . . . Her thoughts drifting in a banal, aimless way, Sheila eyed the bed longingly. She wanted to lie down upon it and give herself up to pointless, comforting, meanderings about clothes and hair and looks and fashions and memories of what her mother had worn and she had worn and Pat, Pat in her arty phase, coming back in all that junk from India, cheesecloth was it, light stuff you could see through, floaty stuff . . . she'd had precious few clothes when she was killed. Nothing colourful. A few pairs of shorts and trousers, some shirts, a couple of plain dresses, ordinary. Nothing worth keeping, nothing to get sentimental about, nothing of any significance to save for Leo. But then he was a boy, he wouldn't have wanted anything, it would have been embarrassing. She'd taken the photographs and the pearl necklace they'd given Pat on her twenty-first, the one she'd never liked and clearly thought a waste of money, money she could have used to travel. And a ring, a silver ring. They said it had been on her finger. She'd tried it on but couldn't even get it on her little finger. So small and thin Pat had been . . .

The front door going jerked her out of her reverie and she hurried down the stairs, heart thudding as though she'd been caught out in some minor crime.

'Sheila?' Why, if she wasn't in the kitchen and immediately visible, did Alan have to sound so alarmed? It annoyed her.

'What?' she called, bad-temperedly.

'Oh, you're there.'

'Of course I'm here, where'd you expect me to be, Timbuktu?'

'What's up?'

'*Nothing's* up. For heaven's sake.' She bustled into the kitchen, put on her apron, though there was no need, boiled the kettle again, fussed about. There were still two cups on the table.

'Company?' Alan asked, staring at the cups.

Dear God, their lives, *her* life was so predictable that the presence of a second cup was worthy of attention.

'Carole,' she said briskly.

'Oh? On a Wednesday? What was she wanting?'

'She just dropped in.'

'Carole?' said Alan, incredulous. 'Just dropped in?'

'Oh my *God*,' she shouted. 'Are you an echo or something? Can't my own sister have a cup of tea without the heavens falling in?'

Alan stared at her, concerned. 'What's she been saying to upset you, eh?' he asked quietly.

'She hasn't upset me. She hasn't said anything. She was just passing.'

'A likely story. She was snooping, I'll bet, seeing what was what. She won't leave well alone. Take no notice of her.'

'I won't,' said Sheila, almost laughing now at the way Alan could get everything wrong and think himself so clever. He'd had words with Carole who, like her father, had been blunt over Sheila visiting Leo. Carole thought she shouldn't. She said Sheila was making herself ill over those visits. Even though Alan agreed, he'd been irritated at his sister-in-law thinking it was her job to point it out.

'Any road,' Alan said, 'we got all his bedding plants and I've left him happy as Larry putting them in.'

'That's good.'

And then it was over, the brief period of alarm, though she didn't know why she'd been alarmed, she wasn't afraid of Alan. Never, ever, had she felt afraid of Alan. Not like her father. They'd all been afraid of him until well into adolescence and even now he had the power to make them all, if not afraid, then apprehensive. He was old, he was frail, he had no power and yet he dominated them still. The only person he'd failed to terrify at some stage was Leo. Leo had been brought up not knowing what fear was. Never beaten, never smacked, never shouted at. But then he'd never needed to be. Docile, Leo was always docile . . .

She'd lied now. Told a straightforward, unmistakable lie to Alan. She might even get found out. Next time Carole and Alan met, he'd mention it. He wouldn't be able to resist it. But she didn't care – let him find out. A woman of her age was entitled to a secret and if guarding it meant lying, then so be it. Anyway, it was already in the past, a one-off thing, hers.

★

All the way home Harriet went over and over every word that had been said and was horrified by their emptiness – nothing, in effect, had been said, which was why she couldn't understand the comfort the interchange had brought. Sheila Armstrong was a nice woman. No evil could possibly have been nurtured by her. She'd been friendly and yet kept her distance. She hadn't seemed to mind that Harriet didn't know what to say, that she couldn't articulate why she had wanted to meet. It was as though the older woman had been waiting and was glad the waiting was over. They hadn't talked at all about what had happened, the very thing that gave them any reason to be together. Nor had they talked about their boys.

That, thought Harriet, was what I was afraid to ask, about *him*. That was what frightened her, knowing that she wanted to know so badly. At first she hadn't even thought of the attackers, but now she thought of them all the time. All these months and now they rose in her mind, shadowy figures, huge and menacing. She'd only seen Leo Jackson, not his more dangerous accomplice, but she felt she hadn't seen him at all, she didn't equate him with the brute in her imagination. He, the two 'he's', were elsewhere. She sickened herself wanting to know every last detail about them, to explain it all away once she knew, once it was not all without a history. Yet she'd asked nothing, nothing at all. She hadn't seen his room, for example. She blushed, alone in her car, driving along, to think she had wanted to see his room. What kind of a room did a brutish boy have? What would be on his walls? What clues would there be?

She stopped the car half a mile from her home in a lay-by from which the neck of the lake could be seen. She had to calm down, this was no good. Revulsion for her own curiosity made her tremble. If Sheila, Mrs Armstrong, had been a different woman . . . she would never have been able to ask to see his room. It could only have happened if she had been urged to, as proof that Leo Jackson was a good boy until one half-hour of madness . . . 'Look at his room,' another woman might have said. 'Look at those posters of elephants and whales, all he ever thought about, my Leo, was animals and what he could do to protect them, look at his books, look at the *National Geographic Magazine*, it was all he ever read, we got him the subscription for his birthday, look at those models, he carved them himself, and that trumpet, he played it so well, look at . . .' She could hear a shrill voice in her head, a voice quite different from Sheila Armstrong's, she could hear it going on and on and see herself, actually *see* herself, wandering round this mythical, ridiculous room she'd designed for Leo Jackson, full of things mentioned in court . . .

Horrible. It was horrible, her need. She dreaded Joe, or even Sam, finding out. The last thing Joe wanted was to have Leo Jackson made into a human being. When he'd first spoken coherently he had gone on and on as to *why* this had happened – 'I wasn't doing anything. I hadn't done anything to them. I was just walking down the street, it wasn't even dark or late. Why did they pick on me?' – and she had tried to console him by saying there was no reason it had happened to him but that there would be reasons why those who had attacked him had come to be so vicious and cruel, and he'd shouted at her that he didn't want to hear one word of justification, not one word, he didn't want to hear his attackers were from broken homes and had been made to suffer all their lives and were just doing as they had been done by, he didn't want to hear that shit. He'd sobbed. She'd been scared of how violently he'd reacted. Then, when it turned out that Leo Jackson at least was not from some terrible deprived background, his anger had again startled her. It hurt him more, not less, that there were no obvious reasons for this other boy to have taken part in such a crime. Listening in court to all the praise for Leo Jackson – his excellent school record, his trumpet playing, his love of animals – had almost driven Joe mad. Then there was the heavy play made of his mother's and father's deaths, the attempt to arouse pity for him. It drove Joe frantic, as did the sight of the boy. Tall, yes, and well built, powerful, yes, but a heavy, intelligent, calm face, not handsome but not brutish, definitely not brutish. And Joe badly needed him to be a brute.

Staring at the lake in the distance, Harriet wondered how abnormal was her reluctance to let Leo Jackson go. It wasn't something she could discuss with anyone. She had fantasies in which she visited the boy. She sat in front of him – she'd seen the films, the television programmes, she knew the set-up – and asked him questions. Not about what he'd done but about why. All those questions others had asked him to which he had not replied a single word. But he'd tell her. In her fantasy, he told *her* everything. She was so near to him. She could see the pores in his skin, so near she could feel the slightest breath he took. She was excited, her heart pounded as she waited for his answers and he gave them, his voice low and indistinct, he told her how he'd been just hanging about, lonely, bored, he'd only gone into the club out of desperation and at first he'd hated it, he'd been going to leave straight away, but then the comfort of it, the darkness and noise and crowds and himself anonymous had begun to appeal and he'd stayed, and then he'd been seen by someone in his class, not a friend, just someone, and he'd had a drink with him and then another, and after that he'd begun to feel happy, light-headed, after only two halves of beer, and he'd got in a gang and was swept along by them and glad to be with them, and then he'd somehow been in a car and driving very fast and arriving he didn't know where, some pub, and suddenly he was outside, in the fresh air and with someone he didn't know who gave him something to take, and he took it thinking he wasn't himself anyway and he might as well and next minute he had a knife in his hand . . .

No! What nonsense. It could not have been like that. If only, if only she could know how it had been. She wondered if he had told his grandmother. Was Sheila Armstrong the only person who knew? Would *she* be the only person Joe would tell? Well, she had been. She was the only person, his mother, to whom he had confided that last, appalling detail. He said he would never, ever tell anyone again in his whole life. Sometimes she thought that was the whole basis of what was now wrong between them, that she alone was to know this final thing which haunted Joe most . . . Michael had seen him, covered in blood and excrement. She and Sam had not. By the time they had reached the hospital Joe was in the operating theatre. Michael and the policemen and the ambulance crew and the nurses and doctors – they had all seen poor Joe, all recoiled at the sight of him, his thin naked body, filthy, his hair matted with the shit rubbed into it . . . He was clean when she saw him. White sheet below him, white sheet drawn up to his waist, white bandages, everything white. She hadn't had to see the filth. They told her, but she didn't have to see it. Only picture it, imagine it . . . had they defecated actually on to him? Had they, or one of them, done it in a corner and then picked their own dirt up and smeared it over Joe's hair? Had they made him do it? She didn't know, she couldn't ask. Detective Sergeant Graham could and did. He told her. He said he had to know. And Joe had told him. But he hadn't told Graham that he'd eaten it. He hadn't told them that. He'd told her, screaming and sobbing one night, blurting it out, watching her, seeming to hate her as he said it, said one of them had urinated into his mouth and he'd swallowed half of it and choked and then the shit . . . his underpants, used as a gag, pulled out and then the shit packed into his mouth, his lips forced closed over it, gasping and choking and swallowing . . . then vomiting, on and on, and hearing laughter . . .

The lake was blue but misty, the hills shrouded in mist. All that was beautiful and peaceful and serene was before her. Nature did heal, but only those parts it could reach. It healed her eyes and her ears but not her heart. She could feel her eyes less sore, less strained, washed by gentleness of the landscape, and her ears were rested, the silly voices of her fantasies stilled by the silence. But deep inside was the same hunger to resolve this conundrum which plagued her so and no amount of looking at lakes or hills could help. Her instinct was so strong, she knew that if only she could get to Leo Jackson and his partner then she would be satisfied. She loathed the mystery, the vagueness, the lack of reality when what had happened had been so very real. She couldn't let Sheila Armstrong go. She'd thrown away this opportunity and must not allow another to be wasted. Next time, she'd be direct. She knew the woman now, knew the sort of person she was dealing with. She could trust her. She could confess, and ask for her help. As simple as that.

Joe was there when she got in. He was sitting watching tennis on television. She called out to him but he didn't reply and she was glad for once to be ignored. She didn't want to lie to him. It mattered less about Sam, for whom she'd already invented the scenario she'd decided on. Sam could take a lie or two, it wouldn't really bother him if he found out, not the fact of the lie anyway. But Joe despised lies, even small ones. All his childhood he'd been implacable. 'You said' were words forever on his lips –

'You *said* it was ice-cream for pudding,' and when she'd had to confess she'd just discovered that there was none, 'You *lied*!' Silly, really, then. They'd made fun of him, called him little Georgie Washington. He had such standards, Joe. She'd been proud of him. But it was exhausting all the same, his rigid attitude to so many things.

He came through after a while, the television left on in the background, and just stood watching her. She felt she ought to say something but everything she thought of was no good, none of the normal pleasantries now sufficed, they were not any longer part of the currency of chat. She waited, trying to edge herself towards some harmless observation, but he made it so difficult. That was what Sam resented most, how *difficult* Joe made things. His brooding, unhappy mood affected them all and they couldn't tell him to snap out of it. He never asked them anything about themselves, their lives, their jobs. Everything was in-turned. But today he was visibly hovering, hanging about, wanting something if only she could decide what. If she said the wrong thing she'd never find out but if she waited too long he'd give up and disappear. She risked sarcasm, a little normality.

'You wouldn't be wanting something, would you, squire?' she asked him. He actually smiled.

'I think I'd better go on the skiing trip. The money has to be in, the deposit part, tomorrow.'

Careful, she told herself, not too much enthusiasm now. 'Well, that's fine, good, I'll write the cheque. How much is it, the deposit?'

'Fifty pounds.'

'Right. Get my bag, it's on the table, I'll do it now.'

'I'll pay you back. I'll start at the boat yard, if he'll have me.'

'Of course he'll have you . . .'

'Why? Because he's sorry for poor little Joe?'

'No, not at all, because he said you were the best part-time worker he ever had.'

'That's boost-Joe's-ego time, isn't it?'

'Why do you have to turn everything? Of course I'm not trying to boost your ego, or . . .'

'That's lucky, it would be rather hard, I haven't got one, lost it, dunno where, must look for it, have you seen my ego?'

She eyed him warily. Was he making a joke? Was he being skitty? Was it safe to laugh?

'Why are you looking so worried?'

'I wasn't. I was just wondering if I remembered to buy some more cheese.'

'Liar.'

'No, I really was, the thing is I went . . .'

'Stop it, Mum. Spare me.'

'Then *you* spare *me*.' What had she said? 'What I mean is, you're so, so . . .'

'So?'

'I can't think what I mean. You know what I mean anyway. You jump on me. I can't say anything without your taking it the wrong way.'

'What's the right way?'

'Oh Joe, don't start that, all that playing with words, you know what I mean.'

'So you keep telling me. It's boring.'

'Well, here's the cheque.'

'No questions asked.'

'Why should I ask questions?'

'Because you want to. You want to know why I want to go skiing all of a sudden, why the change of heart, does it mean I'm *getting better*. That's what you want to ask. You'll tell Dad, and he'll say, Oh good, he must be *getting better*, about time he *got over it*, and you'll tell him not to be

so sure and it isn't a case of my *getting better*, oh, you'll tick
him off, and then you'll say that all the same it does look
hopeful and it will do him good to get right away, you
always thought a holiday would help . . .'

'Joe, please, I wish you wouldn't.'

'And I wish *you* wouldn't. Look, you want to ask so *ask*,
can't you?'

'All right. What persuaded you?'

'Boredom. I don't expect to enjoy it, but it will use up
time. I have to fill time up with something. If I'm not
going to have the whole thing over I have to start filling
up time. Holidays, working at the boat yard again, that'll
fill up the time.'

She was silent. Any pleasure she'd felt in him wanting
to go skiing was spoiled. He soured everything. She knew
he was watching her, a funny little half-smile on his face.

'You don't like that, do you?'

'Of course not.'

'You don't like the truth, ever.'

'Who would, if that's the truth?'

'There's no "if" about it, Mum. I'm sorry, but that is
the truth.' He went upstairs, she thought, with an air of
triumph.

It was clear enough, she supposed, what 'the whole
thing over' meant. Suicide. Well, it was absurd, she knew
he didn't mean that, he was just being melodramatic. He
would never, ever kill himself, not because he'd been
attacked and degraded. She wasn't even frightened, not at
all. If he'd been deranged enough to do that he'd have
done it long ago, not now. That kind of talk was merely a
sign of the usual adolescent depression, the sort she'd
suffered from herself, that awful feeling that there was no
point to life, so why bother? One had to be patient with
that kind of feeling and it would gradually go, it always
did. Activity dispelled it, which was precisely why this

skiing jaunt was a good thing. It was only a pity it was so far off, the trip – if only something nearer in time would turn up. But if he was going to start working at weekends and in the holidays again, to earn the money, then that would be activity too, that might achieve something and at least get him out of his room . . .

The telephone broke into her ramblings but she didn't mind, she was feeling cheerful as she answered, expecting Sam or Ginny. 'Mrs Kennedy?' he said, and she knew the voice at once, even after all this time. 'Detective Sergeant Graham here. I'm sorry to bother you, but there's been a development. We've got a suspect for the other attacker. Can I come round now, or when would it be convenient?'

Chapter Seven

DETECTIVE SERGEANT GRAHAM didn't need to look at the Kennedy file. He knew every detail of it, remembered every date and fact and then some more. From the very beginning of the case it had felt different to him and it was all down to those two women, to Mrs Kennedy and Mrs Armstrong. Neither of them was typical. Time and time again he lectured police cadets on how there was no such thing as a 'typical mother', but nevertheless there was. A typical mother of a victim, a typical mother of an attacker. He'd seen them both, scores of times. The victim's mother stunned then hysterical, wanting vengeance, only satisfied with a quick arrest, a Crown Court conviction and a long sentence; the aggressor's mother, entirely disbelieving, then either blindly loyal to the idea of the son she held in her memory, who bore no comparison to the boy himself, or else wanting to distance herself from him, disown him.

But Mrs Kennedy didn't fit the pattern. Her name was Harriet but she never asked him to call her by her Christian name. That was his first failure. Usually, he established a rapport fairly quickly and the use of first names confirmed this. Rapport of any kind with Mrs Kennedy had been impossible. He could see she thought he was stupid and he didn't mind that – if she wanted to regard him as stupid, then let her. He knew he wasn't, he knew it was a defence mechanism, an obvious one. She had to hate someone for the ordeal her son had gone through and he was handy. He'd bowed to it, hadn't resented it. But what he did resent was this mother's assumption that he was insensitive. She wouldn't give him credit for sharing her feelings. He'd told her he had two lads of his own, grown up now, and that he knew how she felt, and a look of absolute contempt had crossed her face. She'd almost spat at him, and that he did mind. The trouble was, she wouldn't accept sympathy. That was very untypical. Usually, sympathy, sincerely conveyed, worked a treat. Not with Mrs Kennedy. She was visibly offended by it.

In the first week he'd been at the Kennedy house every day. The boy, Joe, came home on the fifth day, his injuries not as bad as at first feared and the family anxious, and able, to take over the nursing. He had never been made welcome in that house. He was offered tea or coffee, and it was excellent coffee when it came, always in a cafetière, none of that instant muck policemen usually rated, but he wasn't welcomed. Even after he'd applied all the relaxing techniques he had learned, the atmosphere never lightened. Mrs Kennedy did not want it to. She wanted to stay stiff, formal and hostile. So he had to battle against that all the time and it was hard work. It would have been unprofessional to take it personally, but it felt personal, he felt discriminated against as a man, not a policeman. Of course, he showed none of this unease. He went on being polite, responding to Mrs Kennedy's wish. That was how he had been trained.

But he couldn't work out the dynamics of the family. It was tempting to think Mrs Kennedy was the boss. She did most of the speaking, she controlled access to the boy. Mr Kennedy was much more pleasant. He smiled, was prepared to discuss the weather, the garden, all the usual ways into communication. He deferred to his wife over anything to do with their son, but all the same he was no push-over. Graham was not at all sure Mrs Kennedy really ruled the roost here. He caught Mr Kennedy looking at her warningly several times and the unspoken warning carried definite indications of strength. What went on between them when they were alone he could only imagine, but what he did imagine were arguments, heated ones. But he could tell they were a devoted couple, the Kennedys. The tension between them was all to do with the aftermath of their son being so brutally attacked.

Couples often split over this, over the reaction. He'd seen father and mother driven apart, usually because one took it harder than another, but also because they'd differ over how they should behave. One would suppress anger and grief, the other drown in it. One would want to confide in him, the other not. But in fact neither of the Kennedys confided in him. Mr Kennedy might be friendlier but even he wouldn't really give, there was no hope of a real heart-to-heart. He wanted him out of the house as quickly as possible, just as his wife more obviously did. They both thanked him but there was not any real gratitude for a job well done. When Leo Jackson was arrested and admitted his guilt there were no congratulations, no recognition that the police had been successful.

Not that he wanted thanks. If he did, he'd be a fool to have chosen to be a policeman. But he expected intelligent, middle-class people like the Kennedys to acknowledge how hard his station had worked to catch the attackers and how well they had done to get one of them so quickly. It had been annoying as well as puzzling that they hadn't seemed all that elated. They should have been. Catching the criminal in a case like this was vital for the psychological welfare of the victim. That was another thing he stressed in his lectures: in every case of a random, violent attack the victim will be helped to recover only if the attacker is caught and punished. It was obvious, but it needed emphasising.

They'd worked so hard, if only the Kennedys knew how hard. He hadn't needed to suspend all leave – the whole station gave up time off of their own accord. The atmosphere had been tremendous, the sense of urgency exciting. He'd tried to calm this excitement – it wasn't healthy, getting too worked up – but he'd failed. It fuelled itself. Those who'd been first on the scene told the others the state they'd found the boy in, and then there were the photographs taken before he was cleaned up. That kind of thing simply didn't happen on their patch. There had never been a case like it and the one terror was that they wouldn't be able to solve it themselves. The whole pride of the station hung on it and the relief when they got Leo Jackson was great, the air of celebration almost indecent. They'd known the attackers were not local and to have located and arrested one of them so far out of their own area was a triumph.

He'd broken the news to the Kennedys himself. He'd gone to their house barely able to keep the smile off his face. 'I've got some good news,' he'd said, when Mrs Kennedy opened the door. She stared at him blankly, didn't ask him in, and because he was impatient to tell her, and make her happy, he pushed a bit, said, 'Can I come in?' which he shouldn't have done. She took him into the sitting-room and stood there in the middle of the room and because she didn't ask him to sit down he was irritated and said, 'Is it all right if I sit for a minute?' Maybe he'd been a little sarcastic, but he hoped not. She apologised, said of course, and would he like some coffee. He declined, knowing it gave him pleasure to do so. 'Husband at work?' he asked. Yes, he was, due home in an hour or so. He asked how Joe was and was told he would soon be out of intensive care. She didn't ask him what the good news was, which astonished him. He had to mention it again – 'I've got some good news.'

'Yes, you said.'

'Don't you want to know what it is?'

'Of course. It's just that I can't think of any news that could be good, I'm afraid.'

'That's a pity, because it *is* good news, Mrs Kennedy, make no mistake. It's news your lad needs – we've arrested one of the attackers and he's confessed, admitted it.'

There was dead silence. She was still standing, hadn't sat when he had. She swallowed several times, he could see her throat moving, and then smiled slightly, a bitter smile. 'Well,' she said, her voice husky and maybe – he was not sure – tearful. 'Well, I'm glad, if it's good news. Good.'

He was exasperated. 'Surely,' he said, 'you want whoever did those awful things to your son to be caught and punished?'

'Yes, I suppose so, yes, I do. But it seems so irrelevant. What good does it do?'

'A lot of good. It'll help Joe. If we didn't catch anyone he'd be afraid they were still out there and he'd know they'd got away with it. Believe me, it makes it all much worse not to catch the offenders.'

'Yes, I can see that. I'm sorry.'

He stood up. 'Well, I just wanted to tell you myself. I'll be visiting Joe in hospital tomorrow.'

'Why?'

'I'll need to talk to him again and . . .'

'Oh no!'

'Mrs Kennedy,' he said, as patiently as possible, given his growing exasperation, 'we'll need Joe to identify our suspect.'

'But you said he'd confessed.'

'He has, but it doesn't make any difference. We need Joe to verify it was him. You needn't worry, he won't have to confront him, it's all done behind mirrors, behind glass. He just needs to look and point.'

'But he's ill, he has a broken leg and all those knife wounds and bruises. He's in no fit state . . .'

'We'll show him photographs first, we can wait for the ID parade till next week, or as soon as we can arrange to get him to the station as comfortably as possible.'

'Oh *God*.'

She sat down suddenly, at last. 'There will be a trial,' she said, stating, not asking.

'Of course.'

'Joe will have to appear.'

'Probably, almost certainly.'

'When?'

'Oh, a while yet.'

'It'll drag on and on, he'll be put through more and more.'

'There's no way round that, Mrs Kennedy, and in fact going through a trial often helps, it's cathartic.'

She laughed and echoed, 'Cathartic?' as though it was the funniest word she'd ever heard, or at least in his mouth. He decided it was time to leave.

And now, all these months later, he would have to return to the Kennedys and go through the same thing again, except not quite the same. They'd arrested one Gary Robinson, but he hadn't confessed like Leo Jackson. He was denying everything at the moment, and Leo Jackson had never named the other one. It all depended on Joe to identify him to make the case tight, even though they were sure. All the evidence could be called circumstantial by a clever counsel – Leo or Joe, preferably both, were needed to clinch it. At least Gary Robinson had no mother to complicate everything. He *was* typical:

fostered from the age of two, petty crime from the age of ten, convictions for assault, burglary and drug-dealing by twenty. A nasty bit of work, a pleasure to bang up. He'd been shopped, they'd never have got him any other way after so long. In all respects he fitted Joe's observant description. He was still drug-dealing, still terrorising customers and exacting punishment for bad debts. But the debtor who'd shopped him wouldn't do in court. He'd be a disaster, they wouldn't dare produce him.

He wasn't going to tell either the Kennedys or Joe all this. He wanted Joe down for an identity parade as quickly as possible without too many explanations. This time he was going to be as cool and distant as Mrs Kennedy, quite abrupt in fact. He only wished he could get to the boy without going through the parents but, of course, he couldn't. There'd be all that time he'd have to spend fencing with the mother before he got to the son and even then it would be no picnic. The boy was a nightmare. If his mother was difficult Joe was even harder to handle. He was clever, sharp, made a brilliant statement and he'd been brave, whatever his own opinion of himself. In the appalling circumstances in which he'd found himself he'd been sensible, even if he saw his own commonsense as something to despise, as being pathetically submissive. He could have been killed. Gary Robinson had all the makings of a psychopath – if it was Gary Robinson, bad to be already convinced, a sign he was slipping and must watch himself.

He'd had to question Joe himself at the very beginning, while he was still in intensive care the first twenty-four hours. That was always difficult. The nurses didn't like it and the family hated it, but he'd managed ten minutes with Joe on his own. There were things he'd had to find out, questions difficult to ask in front of a mother, any mother, never mind Mrs Kennedy, and he wanted them over. Joe, although with his leg in a hoist and tubes and bandages everywhere, had been alert and not, in those few minutes at least, in pain. 'Joe,' he'd said to him, keeping his voice soft and low, remembering his own instructions to cadets, 'Joe, I know you were stabbed and beaten, but I have to ask you this, did they do anything else to you? It doesn't matter what it was. You can tell me, don't be embarrassed.' He'd tried to put compassion into his tone, to establish trust, but he'd seen outright rejection in Joe's eyes. Still, he'd replied, perfectly audibly and distinctly. 'No,' he'd said, 'no. They took my clothes of' – he noted the eyes filling now with tears – 'but they didn't do anything.' The boy might be lying, but he said, 'Good.' It was still possible the state he'd been found in didn't mean what he thought it meant. There had been his nakedness, the wounds and then the other, the filth. He asked him again, to be sure. 'They didn't interfere with you sexually, Joe?' The boy had closed his eyes, almost shouted, 'No,' and a nurse came to turn him out. He'd questioned the doctor, of course, and the police surgeon: no evidence of any interference, so that was that and thankfully he could leave it alone.

Sometimes he'd thought he should bring this up with Mrs Kennedy. Did she imagine something worse than the obvious injuries? It was as though she did, the way she was always hinting and then drawing back, and it crossed his mind that she hadn't been able to ask Joe and he hadn't volunteered the information because he couldn't see she wanted it. Was it the excrement, then, that distressed her so? Joe was smeared in it when they found him, blood and urine and excrement. 'Covered in shit,' the horrified young PC had reported. Mrs Kennedy knew that. Everyone did. It was in the newspapers, it made the crime even more disgusting. Joe couldn't have denied they'd – or one of them – pissed and shat on him, even if he'd wanted to, because too many people had seen his poor body, too many had been involved in cleaning him up, making him presentable before his parents saw him. Just in case his parents didn't know, he'd told them right away that, as well as two knife wounds and a broken leg and bruising, Joe had been rolled in excrement. Maybe it was from that moment Mrs Kennedy had hated him, but what else could he have done? Somebody had to tell her, and he'd known very early that it was this final degradation which would be hardest for the boy to recover from. 'The loss of self-worth,' he warned his cadets, 'is the hardest blow of all – never forget it.'

He'd never forgotten it himself but it had done him no good. Maybe something was still held back. He'd grown tired of his own suspicions, of the way his antennae bothered him. Mrs Kennedy didn't think he had any, didn't realise he could pick things up. She was making it harder for the boy, he'd picked that up. And her agonising put another burden on him. The boy saw what all this had done to his mother, it added to his guilt and shame. The fact that she didn't appear to make an open show of her suffering, that on the contrary she was determined to deal with it by hiding it from him, if not everyone else, only made it worse. The message she gave out was: *We* do not collapse, *we* do not crack up, so Joe was obliged to follow her lead. He never cracked up. He was always composed, went straight back to school as soon as he was able, consistently underplayed his distress. And he'd had no counselling or psychiatric help – fatal. He knew it surprised people how in favour he was of counselling, they didn't expect it from a solid policeman, but he'd thought of training as a post-traumatic stress counsellor himself. Pity he hadn't the time.

Right, he had to take the Kennedys on, forget they had resented him. Then he'd have to go and see the other mother, the grandmother rather, and see if she could help over getting Leo Jackson to talk. Everything had changed, surely, with the arrest of Gary Robinson. There was no need for Leo to keep quiet as he'd done almost from the moment he was arrested. It had been a very strange scene that morning. A quiet street, a quiet part of the town where decent lower-middle-class people, who owned their own houses, lived. Mostly elderly people who'd lived there a long time. No skimpy curtains. Lace curtains, very clean looking. Freshly painted door, shining knocker. And the door was opened by a rather imposing older woman, neatly dressed, calm, showing no evidence of guilt or even concern. He'd been momentarily embarrassed to be disturbing her Sunday morning. Then they'd gone up and there was the boy, asleep, still in his bloodstained clothes. The woman had turned deathly pale, so pale he thought she might have a stroke. They'd made her sit down, in the boy's room. She watched as they woke him up. She saw him nod his head when the question was put to him, in official language with all the names and times. He admitted guilt immediately. The look on the face of Mrs Armstrong was disturbing. Disbelief, of course, but anger and horror too, horror struggling with revulsion. He'd been concerned for her, suggested that the constable with him should find her husband who, it turned out, had gone off early, fishing, but she was furious with him at the suggestion. The boy had his eyes closed. He was sitting up but his eyes were closed, his head turned away. 'This is a mistake, you'll see,' the grandmother had said and had shaken off the help he and the constable had offered her to get back downstairs.

They took him to the police station and charged him there. Mrs Armstrong never said a word all the way there and neither did the boy. He wouldn't look at her. Only when it was time to leave him did she say, 'You've broken my heart, you have.' It was moving, the way she said it. Very moving. So quietly, without any vehemence. Wearily. And he could see the boy was crying, though the tears were almost completely trapped behind his still shut eyes. Once his grandmother had left, the tears dried up. The boy became what he could only call proud. Lifted his head up, opened his eyes and made a short statement. He described going to the club, drinking, accepting drugs, falling in with a gang he didn't know at all, driving off with them, and then suddenly finding himself standing holding a knife and on the ground a naked boy whom he did not know either. So he dropped the knife and ran. He maintained he didn't know how he got home, how he covered the forty miles. And then he wouldn't utter a word, except to ask if the boy on the ground was dead.

He wouldn't say who he'd been with, though he agreed he had not been alone – he remembered that, at least. Graham had told him 'Don't think you're a hero, taking the blame on your own, because you're not. You're an even bigger coward. Whoever it was you know fine well he will do it again, and next time it'll be your fault, understand? Your fault.' But it had made no difference. According to Mrs Armstrong the boy hadn't talked even to her. Well, that would have to change.

★

She didn't know how to tell Joe, but he had to be told, at once, and he had to be at home when Graham arrived. It was so hard to say: 'That policeman is coming again – they've arrested someone they think was the other attacker and they want you to go to an identity parade.' Easy words, impossible sentence. She could imagine his reaction. He'd be overwhelmed, everything would rush back, she'd see it in his face and her own flesh would tingle at the memory. It was dreadful to put him through all this, and suppose it was for nothing? Suppose it was the wrong man? The effect of everything being dragged up again would be devastating, just as he was getting over it. But there – she knew she contradicted herself. If, as she was always saying to Sam, he had not got over it, if those words were ignorant and offensive, how could she argue that the ID parade would drag it all up again? It wasn't buried, it never had been, it was still on the surface for all to see.

She was weary by the time Joe came home. To make it worse, he was cheerful, he was actually smiling a little, he came in as he used to do, throwing his bag of books on to the floor and going straight to the fridge for something to eat. She had a sudden vision of him rushing in from his first day at the comprehensive, thrilled with it, all excited and full of news, rushing because he had so much to tell her, the words tumbling out, his whole face alight and animated – there was no one like the young Joe, so eager to share his pleasure or pain. She used to listen to him for hours, prattling on, amused, adoring the way he acted out all the people in his little history of the day. Never any need to ask Joe what had happened – he wanted to tell it all, in strict order. There was such passion about him then. Passion was all she could call it, passion of the right sort, meaning energy, spirit, warmth . . . He was talking to her, his back to her, as he looked for one of the yoghurts he liked. 'Old Ralph says I can start next Saturday,' he was saying. 'You were right, he *did* say I was the best casual he'd ever had. And he's put up the rate to £3 an hour. Good, eh?' She could have cried. Inside, she did cry, conjured up an image, to distract herself, of the tears flowing backwards, down through the flesh of her cheeks, leaking out at the corners of her mouth . . .

'Joe,' she said.

'Yeah?'

'Detective Sergeant Graham is coming in about half an hour. That policeman, you know. They've arrested someone else. They need you to go to an identity parade as soon as they can organise it.'

He went on eating the yoghurt. That was something. But his face went dark and closed. Carefully, he scraped the inside of the container, carefully put it in the waste bin, carefully washed the spoon he'd been using. Then he just walked out of the kitchen and up to his room.

She'd handled it all wrong. Harriet put her head in her hands, and pressed her eyes with the palms of her hands, till her eyeballs ached. Her funereal tone – all wrong, she should've been throw-away or at the very least matter-of-fact, and there she'd been, quavery, doom-ladened. And she should have said something first about Ralph and the boat yard, she should have shown her delight and shared in his. But no. Heavy-footed. Like Detective Sergeant Graham. She looked at the clock. He'd be here any minute and she'd have to shout for Joe. She'd so wanted them, the two of them, to be together, to be sitting quietly, united to face this. Now Graham would know they were not. He'd see her face. He'd register why Joe had to be shouted for . . .

He was prompt as ever. 'Afternoon, Mrs Kennedy.'

'Hello. Come in.' She bent her head, avoided his eyes. She took him into the kitchen, which she had never done, simply because she needed its protection, needed things to do while all this was going on. She hadn't had time to adopt a glacial front. 'Excuse me,' she said, 'I was just preparing something to go in the oven.'

'Carry on.'

She carried on, knowing he was watching every move, longing to be cosy and chatty. She chopped onions, carrots, the usual, and piled them on top of the meat in the casserole and then put it into the oven. She washed her hands swiftly, dried them on kitchen paper.

He said, 'It's been a long time since I've seen you. How's Joe been?'

She swallowed, blushed. She couldn't possibly sum up for this man how Joe had been. She shook her head, tried to make an expression of hopelessness on her face, to convey how hopeless it would be to answer. It gave him the advantage, somehow.

'Is Joe in?' he asked.

'Yes. He's doing homework up in his room.'

'Good lad.'

There was a pause. He raised his eyebrows, inclined his head. It was up to her. For once, he was not disposed to pretend they were friends. There was a new air of briskness about him which disconcerted her. She went to the bottom of the stairs and shouted for Joe. He came down at once, for which she was pathetically grateful.

'Joe,' Graham said, 'how are you?'

'Fine.' But he didn't look fine. Harriet wondered if he'd been sick, but surely she would have heard him dash for the bathroom. She was amazed to see he'd changed his clothes. Did that also indicate he'd vomited, had needed another shirt?

'Good. Now, your mother will have told you we've arrested a man we think was the principal attacker' – he paused, but when Joe said nothing, added – 'so we'd like you to come to the station and go through an identity parade. I know it's an ordeal but we'll make it as painless as possible. What happens is . . .'

'I know,' Joe said, 'I know what happens. I've done one, remember?'

'Of course you have,' said Graham, shaking his head. 'Well, we don't want to disrupt your schoolwork more than we need to, so if one day next week is better than another . . .?'

'Tuesday,' Joe said, expressionless. 'Tuesday morning.'

'Right. We'll try for that. We've got enough on him anyway to put him away for a long time.'

'Is that all?' Joe said.

Graham looked startled, said rather tightly, 'Well, yes, I suppose so.'

Joe just went. He should have been more polite, Harriet thought. There was no need to be so rude. But then she knew she'd given him the lead, *she* was what could be called rude.

Graham was on his feet. 'I'll be off,' he said, 'I'll ring you on Monday to confirm Tuesday is on and fix a time. I'll come and collect Joe.'

'No, I'll bring him.'

'There's no need for you to be involved this time, Mrs Kennedy . . .'

'Of course there is! I'm not letting him go through that on his own, good God, the idea.' She'd raised her voice and sounded aggressive. 'I'm sorry, it's just you don't seem to realise . . . you don't seem . . .'

'Oh I do, Mrs Kennedy, I do. I was just suggesting Joe himself might find it easier to handle it if . . .'

'Yes,' said Joe's voice from the landing. They both went to the stairs and looked up. 'I'd rather go on my own, Mum,' he said, and then went into his room and closed the door. She put a hand over her mouth. She felt she'd been slapped. Graham was considerate, he walked quietly to the front door and only as he opened it said, 'Don't worry, Mrs Kennedy, it's normal. I shouldn't worry, just let him have it his own way,' and he left.

★

In the car on the way to the Armstrongs' house, Graham felt pleased. He didn't want Mrs Kennedy there. She was a disaster, all emotion, though she thought of herself as

138

controlled. The boy would do better without her. He'd seen so many victims walk fearfully down the corridor and look through that glass at the suspects and almost faint at the sight of their attacker. Some did faint. Some screamed or cried. Some had to be persuaded to open their eyes at all. Even the odd one who strutted through it and triumphantly pointed out their torturer suffered a backlash as soon as it was over. Mothers, if they were there – and if the boys involved were young enough, they had to be – made it all worse.

He badly wanted to be at this ID parade himself. He wanted to handle the whole thing and go through with Joe, but it was not his job, the Duty Uniform Inspector would object. It struck him that apart from that ten minutes in the hospital he'd never seen Joe without his mother around. Even when she'd been in another room you could feel her presence around the boy, hovering, anxious, defensive. Joe had been younger, of course, not quite sixteen. Now he was nearly seventeen, more able to detach himself from his mother, if he wished. He'd grown but he'd lost weight, and lost some of his looks. There was a hunched look to him, but then lots of adolescents hunched their shoulders to hide their height or just so they didn't stand out. It didn't necessarily mean anything and nor did the very dark shadows under the boy's eyes. There were dark shadows under his mother's too. Whatever went on in that family they certainly were suffering, they hadn't got over it, and if that mother carried on as she was doing they never would.

Ringing the bell at the Armstrong house, he knew he wouldn't get a welcome here either, but he had never expected one. There'd been no need to make any but the most basic contact with the Armstrongs. They weren't his concern, this elderly couple. He'd felt sorry for them but he hadn't got involved. Their plight was common enough and it didn't really interest him. So many parents he'd known who absolutely denied their son could have done whatever he'd done even with a signed confession before them. 'You must have beaten it out of him,' some of the more disbelieving and enraged said. Another effect of the tabloids and television. He'd registered, though, that Mrs Armstrong was a formidable character. She'd stared at her grandson for a long time after he was charged. She didn't ask *why*, that was what made her different, she didn't ask what had got into him, or wonder aloud what she'd done to deserve this. She just sat and stared and finally she got up and said that one sentence: 'You've broken my heart, you have . . .' and left the room. No tears. Not a single tear. He'd been very impressed.

'Mrs Armstrong? Detective Sergeant Graham,' and he showed his card, though he could see she remembered him perfectly well. 'Can I come in a minute?'

She led him into the living-room, without speaking. He was direct. 'I've come because we think we've got the other man, who attacked Joe Kennedy. Now you'll wonder why I've come to tell you that and the reason is I need your assistance. We need this man positively identified, which we hope young Joseph Kennedy will do for us, but we need your grandson to name him too. It would simplify matters a great deal.'

'Leo won't talk.'

'Yes, I know that, but he might now, now this chap's caught and he's going to go down for drug-dealing anyway.'

'I meant he won't speak to me, not a word. Haven't they told you? Every visit now, for ages, he just sits silent.'

Graham hesitated. He hadn't been told this, though there was no reason why he should have been. How lucky this mother didn't get upset. She had her arms folded across her chest and was regarding him with absolute detachment, as though he were a pedlar trying to sell her dusters she was never going to buy.

'Oh,' he said, 'well then, no, I wasn't aware of that, but all the same, could you try this name on Leo? Could you visit him early next week, Monday or Tuesday, and just put the name Gary Robinson to him? Watch his reaction? It would help a lot. And it might be in Leo's interest. This Gary is a real villain, he was the one, not your grandson, who . . .'

'I know,' she said, steadily. 'I don't need you to tell me that. I've always known Leo could never have done half he was supposed to have done, but it doesn't make any difference, does it? He was there, he aided and abetted, and he's paying the penalty. It doesn't excuse him even if it is proved this Gary person did the worst, and it doesn't help Joe Kennedy.'

She wanted him out of her house now. Having him standing there, radiating self-importance, enraged her, but she wouldn't let him see her anger. He wanted to use her, that was all. He wanted his case tidied up. She was supposed to be eager to 'help', what he called 'help', but it was only to help himself. He wasn't in the least concerned as to how this visit was affecting her, nor would he give a thought, after he left, to any distress he might leave behind. She'd told him Leo would not speak to her and he'd just passed over this, he hadn't paused to understand the heartbreak. What, she found herself suddenly wondering, was he like with Harriet Kennedy? Did Harriet receive different treatment? Well, if she did, her need was greater.

'You will at least mention the name, Gary Robinson, to him? If he says nothing, fine, nothing is lost. I'll tell the officer present to be watching him . . .'

'They watch him anyway. We're always watched. I'm never on my own with him.'

'Do you think you could get the name out of him if you were?'

There it was again, the sheer *eagerness* to get a result, the total passing over of the pain behind her statement. Who had brought this man up? Who was his mother? 'I've no idea,' she said.

'Because it could be arranged, if you felt willing to take the risk and wouldn't mind being searched, before and after, by a woman officer, of course, and then . . .'

'I would mind.'

'What?'

'I would mind being searched. I wouldn't agree to it, before or after.'

'It's just a regulation, a precaution . . .'

'No, it isn't. It isn't just anything. I'm an elderly woman and I refuse to be searched.'

'That would present difficulties, but maybe . . .'

'Maybe you could get round them if you thought it was worth it?'

'Maybe.'

He hadn't even detected the sneer in her voice – it was remarkable. She was about to refuse any deal vigorously, when she heard the back door open and her father call out her name. 'In here, Dad,' she shouted, and he came grumbling through the kitchen, complaining his supper wasn't on the table as it should be on a Friday evening, what was she playing at. She said nothing, let him come in and see Detective Sergeant Graham.

'Oh,' Eric James grunted, 'company. I'll go.'

'I was just leaving,' Graham said. 'Thank you, Mrs Armstrong, I'll be in touch, and if you change your mind . . .'

'She won't,' Eric James flashed back, 'she's my daughter and yer won't catch her changing her mind. Who are yer, any road?'

'Detective Sergeant Graham.'

'Oh aye, I remember yer, you put our lad away, right?'

'I arrested and charged him, yes.'

'Wasn't that enough for yer then, eh? Come back for more? Because there isn't any, there's the door . . . out!'

Sheila could have laughed at Graham's face, but her father's fury was too pathetic. He was trying to be the old Eric James, he actually clearly thought he *was* his former self, and the effort was pitiful to watch. The voice that should have been a bellow, loud enough to make the ornaments shake in the china cabinet, was a mere hoarse whisper and the arm flung out so dramatically shook. It was so sad to see him playing the role he had loved to play and finding he hadn't the strength. He might collapse in a heap, he might have a heart attack and die on the spot in front of this policeman. And Graham was not to know this performance was in any case a sham. He sounded like Leo's champion instead of his condemner. She watched Graham leave without attempting to apologise to him and heard the front door going with relief.

'Damned cheek,' her father said. His face was scarlet and there were beads of sweat on his forehead. 'What's up? Why was he here?'

'Come and get your supper,' she said, and led him, quite tenderly, back into the kitchen.

★

Once home, Graham tried to slip into his usual weekend routine, but he could not shake off the depression that had come over him, confronted by that silly old man. Everyone's enemy, the police, no question. No good being in the force, he always told his cadets, if you want to be liked, because you won't be. Liking is not important. What *is* important is impartiality. If you can't be impartial you'll never be a good policeman. And he himself was a

143

good policeman. He knew he was. Good at detection, good at human relationships. It was simply that those two mothers, those two women, Mrs Kennedy and Mrs Armstrong, hadn't sorted themselves out yet, that was all that was depressing him.

The moment he had identified the cause of his depression he felt better.

Chapter Eight

O N SATURDAY, LOUIS came home, his term
finished. She met him at the station, excited as ever
at the thought of seeing him, of having him at home even
for a short time. He'd warned her his stay would be short
– he was off the following Thursday to America where
he'd got a vacation job in some camp. He was home to
dump his stuff, wash his clothes, that was all. And she
assured herself, with a vehemence which made Sam smile
cynically, that she didn't resent it. Other mothers might
complain their houses were treated as hotels, but she
didn't mind, she was proud of how tolerant she was, how
free-and-easy. It was the way, she was convinced, to stay
friends with her sons, by not being clinging, not making
them feel guilty that they wanted to be somewhere else
other than home.

Every time she met him after a long absence, she loved
that moment before she recognised Louis – only a
moment, a flash of a stranger, before familiarity broke
through. He looked so attractive and interesting, she felt
herself wondering who he was, this young man with the
deep-set eyes and Spanish good looks, and then when she
saw it was Louis she felt so proud. She walked up to him
and kissed him and he let her, good-humouredly, no
longer embarrassed as once he had been. He had his bike
with him and a huge rucksack and two enormous holdalls,
so it took ages to get everything to the car and load it. He
wanted to drive but she was firm – Louis' driving scared

her, he went far too fast. The bike on the roof-rack worried her, even though he swore it was firmly fixed. They chatted as she drove, desultory chat, giving each other information and not much else, using the time to slip back into mother/son mode. She'd long ago realised that Louis had made it, he was gone, had cut the umbilical cord so completely it might never have existed. Good. She always told herself, *good*. As it should be. He was fond of his family, she was sure, he cared, he'd never just disappear, but he was no longer bound to them. Others now came first. Charlotte whoever she was. Sam referred to her as 'the oracle', because Louis was always quoting her when he did come home. They hadn't met her yet. Louis had been about to bring her home when there was all the Joe horror and since then no time had seemed right.

'And how is Charlotte?' she asked eventually.

'Fine. We're sharing a flat next year.'

'Oh. With others?'

'No, just us. It's only small, a glorified bed-sit really, but we were lucky to get it. It's near the college, we'll save a fortune on fares.'

'So you're an item, you and Charlotte?'

'We've been an item nearly a year, Mum,' said Louis wearily, slightly sarcastic. 'You just haven't noticed.'

'How was I meant to notice when I haven't met her?'

'I told you.'

'You didn't.'

'Mum, let's not start. It doesn't matter. I don't blame you.' He was sighing in that insulting way she resented.

'What do you mean, you don't blame me? For what?'

'Oh God . . .'

'No, I want to know, for what? What are you not blaming me for, Louis?'

'I only meant I know your mind's been on other things,' he said, with an exaggerated patience, which maddened her. 'You've been obsessed with Joe, it's natural . . .'

146

'Good heavens, I haven't been so obsessed I wouldn't have taken in that Charlotte was serious if you'd told me.'

'It wasn't like that, I didn't tell you, there was nothing to tell . . .'

'It sounds as if there was . . . is.'

'Jesus, Mum.' He was rubbing his face with his hands, exasperated and sighing again. Pointedly he looked out of the window and made some remark about the weather.

She was upset, made a mess of changing gear going up a hill and he winced. When eventually she had controlled the car and was driving smoothly she tried again. 'Well, I'm sorry, Louis,' she said, 'but if it was my fault I didn't pick up the signals, it wasn't because of Joe, it was because I truly didn't recognise them.'

'I know. I've said, it doesn't matter.'

'It *does* matter. I don't like you to think I'm so wrapped up in Joe I've no time for anyone else . . .'

'I don't mind, I understand . . . calm down.'

'Don't talk to me like that, as if I were mad or a baby, or something, so patronisingly.'

'Right. Let's start again. Charlotte and I are, and have been, for nearly a year, an item, and I obviously didn't make that clear, so it's clear now.'

She wanted to go on, having it out with him about this supposed lack of interest of hers due to Joe, but she didn't want to arrive home arguing, it would be bad for Joe. She was silent for a mile or so, struggling to be calm. Louis whistled. He seemed so superior, but she must ignore that. He hadn't asked about Joe yet, but she must tell him what was happening. She cleared her throat, went straight into it. 'They've arrested the other attacker, the one they think actually did the stabbing.'

'Really?'

'They think so. Joe has to go to the police station on Tuesday, to an identity parade.'

147

'How's he taking it?'

'Hard. He won't talk about it.'

'Well, why should he?'

'Maybe he'll talk to you?'

'I doubt it. He's gone off me these days.'

'He's gone off everyone, that's the trouble. Just as things were improving, only a little, but they were. He's back at the boat yard from today and signed up for a school skiing trip . . .'

Louis listened only vaguely. On and on she rambled, half incoherently, this about Joe and that about Joe, all worked up and blinkered. It wasn't that he didn't care about Joe because, of course, he did, he'd thought of nothing else himself for months and only Charlotte knew how upset he'd been. But not like his mother. She was driving herself crazy. Every time he came home it was worse – she was always thinner, more tearful, more distracted and tense. He didn't know how his father stood it. And as for Joe, it must be hell for him. Exactly what he didn't want or need, all this maternal *angst*, all this devoted concentration of feeling. Yet it was true, nobody else except her could cope with Joe. He'd tried. He'd had him for the weekend, laid on all kinds of events and treats, rallied all his own friends to be good to him, and it had all been a disaster. Right from the moment he'd met him at Euston. He and Charlotte had set out with such goodwill, such concern. They'd been over and over how they imagined Joe would be feeling and how they could best respond. 'He won't want to be treated as delicate,' Charlotte had said, and he'd agreed. So they'd been deliberately casual, no big deal welcome. But the moment Joe saw Charlotte he'd seemed to stiffen up and resent her. She was so friendly, too, so *nice* to him, but he replied to her in monosyllables. He'd muttered, 'Is she going to hang around all the time?' when they were going back to the college. It had been awkward, but Charlotte had been brilliant, she'd gone off on her own even though they'd planned to stay together the whole weekend. But her absence hadn't made Joe any happier. Louis had taken him for a drink and he wouldn't speak to anyone, just stood there all sullen.

Charlotte laid on a meal for them in her room on the last day. He wasn't going to cancel it, he knew she'd go to such trouble to cook what he'd told her was Joe's favourite meal, spaghetti alla vongole. It was delicious but Joe didn't say so, he hardly even thanked her. Then all Charlotte had said, after they'd eaten, was, 'How are you feeling, Joe?' and he'd gone *mad*, absolutely mad, had asked her what the fuck she meant. Even then Charlotte had made allowances. She'd said, very softly, she had only wondered . . . but she hadn't got any further. Joe had leapt in, red–faced, and suggested she only wondered if he still smelled of shit. It was ridiculous, stupid. Charlotte had been totally bewildered because, of course, she hadn't meant that at all. After that, Joe just wanted to get home to his precious understanding mummy.

It was trite to think it, but Joe *was* spoiled. His mother said they had both been spoiled, if spoiled meant loved and over–indulged. But Joe still was. He was handled with such care, allowed totally to dominate the family from the beginning, all on account first of his frailty and then because of his difficult temperament. Now, of course, there was no hope of its ever ending. Special treatment until the end of his life. Not that he envied him, who could, but it was true that sometimes lately he had begun to resent his mother's lack of worry about *him*. Not worry, exactly, he didn't want to be the object of worry, and he cared more now about what Charlotte thought than his mother . . .

'You're not listening, Louis,' his mother said.

'I am.'

'Then say something.'

'There's nothing to say. I can't do anything.'

'Just be aware, that's all.'

'Mum, I could hardly be anything else, could I? Not with him looking like he looks and all that. No wonder you're exhausted.'

'Who said that? I never said I was exhausted . . .'

'I can see you are. You and Dad need a holiday . . .'

'Oh, I couldn't . . .'

'. . . leave Joe?'

'Well, I couldn't, not yet, it would be heartless.'

'If you say so.'

'He couldn't be on his own.'

'He wouldn't have to be. He could go to Ginny's.'

'He'd hate that.'

'I could stay with him, after I get back from America. There's three weeks spare, no problem.'

'It's nice of you, Louis, maybe we could, we'll see, see how things are later on.'

So at least they arrived home amicably. Sam was back from golf and his pleasure in greeting Louis showed Harriet how much he welcomed an ally. There was a ganging-up feeling immediately, Sam and Louis straight into sports talk, football teams, cricket fixtures, swopping opinions and news. Louis was glad to be rid of her exclusive company, she knew. He didn't like being trapped in the car with her, obliged to listen to her droning on. He and his father wouldn't discuss Joe with each other. They certainly would not, perish the thought. Anything but.

It was evening before they were all together, with Joe being at the boat yard all day. The meal went well. She knew even thinking like that – 'the meal went well' indeed – was a sign of how unnatural the atmosphere still was, but nevertheless there was an awareness that it had done. They didn't eat outside, she somehow didn't have the heart to suggest it, though Louis teased her – 'What, inside, Mum, when outside the sun is shining, what's up?' She just smiled and let it go. Joe looked at her curiously and she started talking quickly, afraid he would follow up Louis' observation. Louis had held court, naturally. He'd talked about the past term and about the job he was going to and about Charlotte. She and Joe had exchanged looks and Joe rolled his eyes without Louis seeing, and she was so happy. Please, she found herself pleading inwardly, please let it stay like this. Please let this happiness stay, let it not escape, let it last and last and never be interrupted, I will give anything to keep our life like this again. Anything.

★

Train, bus, bus. The same tedious journey she knew by heart. Sheila read on the train, but on the two bus journeys she looked out of the window and listened to other people's conversations. She sat towards the back, and the two women in front of her on the first bus were oblivious of her presence. It was extraordinary how trivial their talk was – they were so animated about cardigans bought to match skirts and grandchildren with measles and the trouble they had finding a new window-cleaner yet there were so many unemployed . . . She marvelled at the zest with which they exchanged all these stunningly boring bits of inconsequential information. Her sister Carole was like that, *hours* she could chatter on with nothing at all communicated of value. Sheila never interrupted her. She had always let Carole carry on, like a stream, understanding that the source of all this was unstoppable. She wished she could do it, take up yards of her life with nothing. Instead, she spoke little and liked what she said to

151

be of use. Alan said she brooded. Maybe he was right. She knew she thought about serious things and was unlike Carole, or the women in the bus. 'A penny for them,' Alan would sometimes say, and she'd alarm him by replying truthfully, 'I was thinking about bombs,' or, 'Those starving children in Ethiopia, I was thinking about them.' Never the price of meat, the colour of knitting wool. Never.

On the second bus, the special bus, the one on which everyone was going to the same place for the same reason, there was almost no talking from anyone. They all sat silent, all of them, except two, women and children. Now Sheila gazed at the fields and hedgerows in peace. Wild roses threaded through the green, honeysuckle cascading over the hawthorn, foxgloves standing sentinel. Pink, white, red, purple. All mixed up and beautiful, all disordered and glorious. One good thing about her father, he loved nature. Eric James knew all the wild flowers. He'd walked the two of them as children, her and Carole, down lanes and little roads like these and pointed them out. They'd had competitions collecting them. He'd done the same with Leo. Taken him and shown him the wild flowers and picked brambles later. When he'd become old and arthritic and he'd had to give up long walks, Alan had dropped the two of them off for their rambles and picked them up later. Leo loved it, almost into his teens. The rambles only really stopped because Eric James wasn't up to them.

Once, Leo fell in a river. He was only four, very small and slight still. He was hardly in the water before Eric James was in after him – there was never any danger. He'd taken his tweed jacket off and wrapped the shivering boy in it and carried him home, white with anxiety while all the time vowing there was nothing to worry about. He'd suffered far more than Leo. It was the first indication of

152

how much Leo meant to him and Sheila had noted it and adjusted her opinion of him without ever saying a word. Soft, he'd become. Clucked after that boy like a mother hen. So where had it all gone, that feeling? She looked round the bus surreptitiously. All these women were doubtless plagued by the same thoughts: why had this happened, why had all the love led to this? But maybe not. Sheila turned back to the view from the window. Maybe a good many of them knew the answers, unlike her. Drugs. One drug, anyway. That was her only answer, but it left many more questions to ask. Why had he taken *any* drug? Why this one, a dangerous one? What was his need, to experiment so suddenly, to get himself into the clutches of this Gary Robinson?

She was going to try. There was no reason why she should but she was going to do as she had been asked. She would mention the name and see if there was any reaction. Detective Sergeant Graham might think she was doing it to oblige him, to do what he thought was her duty as a good citizen, but that wasn't the reason. Her own curiosity was the spur – she wanted to see if the old Leo could be stirred into life. She might also tell him about Mrs Kennedy's visit. Why not? And about her own letter of apology which had prompted their meeting. She might lie and say she'd seen Joe too. Now why would I want to do that, she thought, shocked, surprised at herself. Good gracious, what was happening to her? How silly. It wouldn't interest Leo anyway. He didn't care, she was sure. The first few visits he'd spoken little but at least he had said something. And he'd learned to look at her. They'd learned to look at each other, rather. That had been the hardest stage, learning to bear each other's scrutiny. His eyes had gone everywhere except towards hers, darted all over the place, resisted her own. He was so nervous. Steadily she'd focused on him, willing him to look at her straight and true, and finally, a fleeting glance at first, instantly recoiled from, they had locked their eyes together. The relief made her feel faint, just to know he – her Leo, her boy – was still there. Whatever had happened, whatever he'd done. She was so happy to renew this contact that she was not going to endanger it by at last asking the questions she so wanted to. Later, later there would be time, the right time.

But it never came. The first question she asked, after several weeks, was why wouldn't he see Alan, his grandfather. He wouldn't answer. 'He feels it,' she told him, 'it makes him feel bad. He's still your grandad.' He just shook his head. It was peculiar. Alan was so harmless, why should he ban him? All she could think was that he would feel more ashamed in front of Alan than in front of her and she couldn't fathom why, if that were true. Surely she was the one he'd feel most guilt about? She was closer, she'd done most for him. For once Alan was right, it didn't make sense. But it was a mistake to have asked that question. He started just sitting there, only replying, if she asked something, with a short factual answer. Never offering any information. Then he'd stopped altogether, for no reason she could discern. He'd gone stoical. She could only assume he'd put himself in a trance to get through his sentence.

In her bag she had two books, a magazine and some paper. Nothing to eat. No cigarettes or sweets. This was what the other women had, usually. All kinds of treats, to make the institution diet more palatable. But she knew Leo didn't want such things. He was quite content to be deprived. So she brought books, which she had great difficulty choosing, and magazines, which were easier. His *National Geographic* and a music magazine. She stood every month in W.H. Smith's trying to choose the paperbacks. Nothing violent, nothing pornographic. She went for travel books, journeys people had made, and adventure stories. Leo never said if he liked them but once, when she'd remarked that it was a waste of money buying the books if he didn't read them, he had actually said, 'I do.' So she went on bringing them and she always fancied he took them eagerly, though never passing any comment on what they were.

Today, she withheld the books, kept them in her bag as she sat down. They were lucky, there was no one right next to them on the left, and on the right was a prisoner who was whispering intently to his visitor. Sometimes it was so noisy that her head ached and it seemed pointless trying to talk at all, especially with so little response from Leo. Or sometimes there were such distressing things being said, quite audibly, that she was silenced. Women telling boys they couldn't go on coming, it was too much, and the boys crying, or women saying they'd lost their job and couldn't pay the rent and the other children were ill – dreadful litanies of hardship. But today she was lucky. The whole atmosphere was quite subdued, nothing nasty going on and the guard not breathing down their necks. She leaned forward, trying to look Leo in the eye, but he evaded her and deliberately looked over her head. She just suddenly said it, straight out, without so much as the most cursory of greetings – 'Gary Robinson!'

His eyes locked with hers immediately as they hadn't done for months, fright clear in them. She smiled, and sat back. 'They've arrested him,' she said. 'I thought you'd be interested. For something else, drug-dealing, but they're sure he stabbed Joe Kennedy. He'll be going to prison anyway, but if you identify him as well as Joe Kennedy it would make everything easier.' He said nothing, but lowered his head. 'I'm not saying any more, Leo,' she said softly. 'No need, is there? I needn't go on about it. But now they've got him it's up to you. Just think of that boy having to . . .' He rose suddenly, pushed his chair back so that it clattered on the floor and the guard leapt up. She heard him say, 'I want to leave,' and the guard telling him to sit himself down and behave and think of his grandmother. He stood there, his back to her, stubbornly refusing to return to his place. A supervisor was coming over. She took the books and magazine out of her bag and put them on the table, then she got up herself and walked slowly out, to make it easy for him.

★

Waking at dawn the next morning, Harriet lay very still. Their bed creaked terribly these days – she only had to turn over, or Sam to move, and this dreadful creaking started. Something to do with the screws attaching the wooden headboard to the sides. An awful, whining noise. She realised she'd slept well. They'd gone to bed just after eleven and she'd been asleep ever since. Five, maybe six, hours' sleep. A record in the last two years. The boys had gone up at the same time. All of them in their beds, tucked up metaphorically if not actually, and asleep well before midnight.

She used to love wild nights in the winter when the boys were small, wild winds bashing the house, roaring through the trees outside, rattling the window frames, and all of them safe and warm inside. She'd shiver, and turn to Sam, and there would be something exciting and yet reassuring about their security in the middle of a storm. She missed that. When Louis first went off to university she'd hated wild nights. She'd wondered where he was, if he was out in the rain and cold, and wished him back in his bed, under her roof. With Joe it was worse. He wasn't out very often beyond ten at night, hardly ever, but when he was she couldn't go to bed. The wind, the rain, they increased her fear for him a hundred-fold and her imagination tortured her with visions of him once more jumped on and stabbed and . . . which was silly. It had been summer. Light, not late. No wind. No rain. It was a perfect summer's day . . . NO!

She slipped out of bed as quietly as it allowed her and into the bathroom. She ran the cold tap and splashed her face and cleaned her teeth, then crept downstairs. Bruno stirred and growled and she went to him and patted him and he turned over and went back to sleep. So lovely, all of them asleep, safe, content, upstairs. She opened the porch door and the sun shot in, shafting itself through layers of mist to find her face. She stood, eyes closed, the sun's warmth not yet strong, and breathed deeply. She was resolved to be happy. Today she would start consciously being happy, leaving the past alone, quite alone. If it came and tapped on the door of her memory – that insecure, flimsy, thin door – she would run out the other way, into the future. She would think about Louis and his Charlotte. There were fantasies there aplenty. What did Charlotte look like? Louis must have given her some idea. And what did she read? Was she a scientist, like Louis? She longed for him to get up so she could ask . . .

Today they would go on a picnic. Like old times. The boys would indulge her. They would climb something and have a picnic on the top, maybe swim when they got down, or even go to the sea, it wasn't far. Just them, against the world. It would do Joe good. With Louis there he wouldn't refuse and Louis, only home for four days, wouldn't refuse either, she was sure. She began thinking of the picnic, what she had in the fridge and larder. She took bread out of the freezer, French bread, it would have defrosted by the time they were ready to set off. She would aim for half past ten. It was only half past five now. Plenty of time. At eight she would take Sam coffee and wake the boys, offer it to them. She would be happy. She would tell them to get up and greet the glorious day and make ready for a climb and a picnic. They would groan and protest, but not seriously. She'd walk between them, small among three tall men, though she was not small, and feel such pride. She was a romantic. It was true. All the ugly realism of the last year couldn't wreck her innate romanticism. She'd let it rip today, nothing would spoil it . . .

The lake would be busy. Holidaymakers, trippers, would stream in, choking the small town, but it didn't matter, they knew, the locals, how to avoid the crowds. They'd leave all those sweating hordes, louts many of them, louts who had no place here, for whom there was nothing, no amusements, nothing. God knows why they came . . . She opened a window and bit her lip, hard. Key words. Louts. She had to keep off them. 'Louts,' she said aloud, out of the open window, looking into the circle of lawn with its spotlight of sun dead centre. 'Louts – who cares?' Louts, clouts, shouts – it was only a word. She would deny it power. She walked swiftly out into the garden and raised her face to the sky, now clearing of mist, the blue deepening by the minute. Birds, sheep, faint sounds of the waterfall nearby. She'd been so foolish imprisoning herself in all that pain and misery when she could have turned to this and drawn faith from it, faith that *this* was greater than *that*, that *this* could not be ruined by *that* . . .

Sam surprised her. He came down, in his tracksuit, an hour later, as she was drinking coffee, sitting outside under the pear tree. He didn't speak. He smiled, waved a hand, and went running off, Bruno with him. Half past six and Sam out running! Even happier, she went and had a shower and dressed. She'd aged. She knew that. All that had happened had aged her. Not white hair, nothing like that, not even a matter of more lines. No. She had aged as

Joe had aged, by something disappearing. There was a deadness in her face, a lack of light and movement. Always afraid to be overtaken yet again by sudden grief she kept a curtain of inscrutability over her face. She must draw this curtain aside, not be so wary of expression. Otherwise she'd suffered no irreparable damage. The loss of weight was no bad thing.

Joe could do the same. She knew he could. He was younger, much younger, and it should be easier.

But then, when Sam came back, all red-faced and pleased with himself, when he'd showered and was outside with her, hair still wet, face still hot, she cried. Again. She'd made more coffee, heated croissants, set everything out prettily on a tray, as she liked to do, taken it and put it on the small white, iron table under the tree and sat herself down and heard Sam say, mockingly, but meaning it, 'Ah, this is the life,' and then she wept. All her promises gone in a moment.

'No!' she sobbed, as Sam put his arms round her. 'No, no. I'm *not* crying, I'm not, I'm happy, really. I don't know what it is.'

'Hay fever?' said Sam, and she started to laugh.

'Oh yes,' she said, 'that's it, hay fever.'

*

Sheila wasn't sure what to do. There would be a report, after a commotion like that. Questions would be asked and, doubtless, if Detective Sergeant Graham was at this time wanting access to Leo, he'd be told what had happened. Except nobody could possibly have heard her say Gary Robinson's name, nobody except Leo. She should ring Graham but she didn't want to, and what, after all, did she have to tell him? Only that Leo had been startled by the name and all too obviously recognised it. But where was her proof? She had none. Leo hadn't

159

spoken. She couldn't see that she had anything worthwhile to tell Graham.

Her father was in when she got back, the last person she wanted to see. He was sitting in her kitchen, scowling at the cat. 'Wants putting down,' he said, nodding at the cat, 'put out of its misery.'

'She isn't miserable.'

'Course she is. A cat wi' three legs not miserable?'

She didn't rise to that. He knew perfectly well that their cat had long since adapted to the loss of its leg. Every now and again he did this, picked on the cat. It was code for something, doing this, but she couldn't be bothered to decipher what.

'Where've you been, then?' he asked, watching her, both hands resting on his stick and then his chin on his hands.

'Out.'

He smiled, or gave what passed as a smile. His sour old face resisted smiling as usual. 'Out where?'

'Visiting.' She couldn't quite bring herself to say it was none of his bloody business.

'Who? Carole?'

'Yes, Carole,' she lied.

He was delighted. 'That's funny,' he said, banging his stick, 'I've just come from Carole's and I niver saw yer. Funny, eh?'

'Very funny.' She got on with making some tea, for him too, of course, though it was unlikely he'd drink it. A cup with his breakfast, a cup for his midday meal, and that was the end of tea for Eric James. He could bore people for hours telling them how once he'd also had a cup with his supper, but had given it up to control what he claimed was his night-time incontinence. He loved that 'incontinence' word, pronounced it perfectly and with a flourish.

'What brings you here on a Saturday?' she risked asking.

Since he was the King of Routine she felt the question not just permissible but expected.

'I'm wanting Alan. My mower's stuck and I can't git it to move. Tried all afternoon and I can't, so I've come for Alan to lend a hand.'

A likely story, as likely as her own about visiting Carole. 'Well you'll have a long wait,' she said, complacently, 'because he's gone fishing.'

'Oh aye, I forgot.'

Liar. He never forgot anything, unfortunately.

'Ring Peter,' she advised. 'Shall I ring him now?'

'No, no, Peter's no good wi' machines, doesn't like getting his hands dirty.'

'I'll tell Alan to come round when he gets in. Or tomorrow.'

'Might rain tomorrow.'

'So?'

'I want my grass cut.'

'All right, I'll send him later.'

Still he went on sitting there. She hated him looking at her, scrutinising her. It must be wonderful, she thought, as she often did, to have a father who was wise, to whom one could turn. Old and wise and ready to impart his wisdom. Eric James was just old. Not wise. Life had taught him nothing, so far as she could fathom. There were no obvious benefits to his almost ninety years. His attitudes – you couldn't call them principles – were exactly the same, she was sure, as when he had been a boy. Maturity had no meaning other than in the strictly physical sense. All experience of life, such as it was, seemed to have glanced off him. He had proved impervious to it.

'You've been to see that lad,' Eric James said, glaring at her, making a statement, not asking a question.

'I have.'

'It's not time, you'd just been.'

'True.'

'It isn't allowed, two visits in a week.'

'No.'

'What was special, eh?'

'I don't know what you want to know for,' she said, quite aggressively. 'You said you've washed your hands of him . . .'

'Of him maybe, but I didn't say owt about you.'

'Same thing.'

'Don't be daft, 'tisn't same at all.'

'It feels like it to me. You can't separate us that easy, he's my grandson and always will be, whatever he's done. Not like you, you said . . .'

'I know what I said. Now then, I know what I said all right.'

He'd shouted. He was trying to browbeat her, as he always did, the habit of a lifetime. But he was upset. That was what always puzzled her, that she could see through the bluster that he was upset and that she immediately didn't want him to be. His distress in turn upset her and it had no right to. He was old, old, vulnerably old, and it made all the difference.

'Look, Dad,' she said, 'I told you what's happened, you saw the policeman here. I went to mention a name to Leo and watch for his reaction. It was a special visit with a special purpose. And I'm tired, I want to put my feet up.'

'Put them up, I'm not stopping yer.'

She went into the living-room and sat in an armchair and did indeed put her feet up on a stool and closed her eyes. She heard him shuffling about and felt mean, leaving him there.

'I'd best be off,' he said, calling from the kitchen.

'I'll send Alan,' she called back. She hoped Alan would be a long time. She wanted the house to herself, she wanted rid of both men. She heard the back door close and then the clang of the gate and sighed. Peace. Peace to wonder what she should do. Her conscience was such a plague, she was always wanting to do the right thing. That's how she'd brought Leo up, to want to do the right thing. So had Alan, if not as forceful in his example. Only her father, wicked old Eric James Armstrong, had relished directing Leo the other way. But who could blame an old man? Nobody, not she anyway. He hadn't been an evil influence on Leo, far from it, he'd made the boy feel loved. She had been the influence, she knew it.

Once, Leo had said to her, cheekily, that she was too good to be true and added she didn't know the real world out there. He'd come back from the supermarket with change for a twenty-pound note and not the ten-pound note she'd given him for the jar of honey and six eggs. He liked to go shopping for her, in fact he loved shops, especially supermarkets. How old had he been? Maybe ten, maybe younger, desperate to go on errands, and so she'd sent him for the honey and eggs, and though it was ridiculous, with a perfectly adequate shop on the corner, had agreed he could take the bus and get them at the supermarket. He'd laughed, been thrilled, at the mistake with the change. She'd made him go back. What a struggle that had been. He'd said he'd look silly, it was a *supermarket*, they would think he was mad, the girl wouldn't even remember. She'd gone with him full of moral virtue, and watched him go into the supermarket and up to the check-out. Only later, much later, she'd found the money in a tin of draughts in his cupboard. He'd somehow tricked her and kept the change and all she could do was console herself with the thought that at least he hadn't spent it, it had become tainted money.

It was right, her duty, to inform Detective Sergeant Graham of Leo's reaction, however slender her evidence of his registering the name. She ought to tell him before this identity parade he'd mentioned, before Joe Kennedy was put through that ordeal. She wondered if they would make Leo go too, whether he was willing or not, so they could see his reaction for themselves. But Leo would not now react. He was forewarned and would give nothing away. Unless, of course, fear betrayed him, his own possible fear of this Gary Robinson. If they made him go, she would insist on going too. Could they stop her? She ought to try to make a bargain with them while she was in a position to do so. She'd been there when Leo was put on parade himself, put in that line-up of eight others. She'd stood by him, waited with him, felt the humiliation acutely. There was no doubt, of course, he'd already made his statement, but for some reason they weren't satisfied and wanted him in the line. He was so much more presentable than any of those other eight. He stood straight, tall, apparently unafraid. Hard, they called it. 'He's a hard one,' a policeman had murmured. 'Doesn't give a toss.' But he was wrong, she knew he was. Leo was not hard. Whatever he'd done or not done – he would not enlighten them, beyond confirming that he had been there, and Joe Kennedy himself was not clear who exactly had done what – he was not hard. He had the trick of being able to make himself seem not there, but that wasn't hardness. At moments of stress or grief he could do it, make his inner self disappear, go quite remote from everyone, even her. He'd had it from a small boy, right from when she'd claimed him. It was his secret weapon, this ability to go into a kind of trance, become untouchable.

She missed Pat. Sitting there, she missed her so much she ached. If only Leo had been a girl, none of this might have happened. She could have stayed close, as she'd done with Pat, even when they were so far apart. Pat never retreated from her like this. Nothing she'd suffered on Pat's account had been like this pain with Leo. She'd always felt she knew Pat, however much she changed, and she didn't know Leo at all. It was wrong to blame this on what had happened. That had made everything worse, but it hadn't been the cause. Maybe, in fact, the cause had been Leo's own sense of having broken loose, of drifting, of looking for something she could no longer give him? Maybe the cause was her? Maybe that would make the sense Alan had always been looking for? It was somehow all her fault, this muddle.

Chapter Nine

LOUIS ANSWERED THE TELEPHONE, offhand, annoyed it wasn't Charlotte ringing. He left the receiver dangling and shouted, 'Mum, for you,' and Harriet went to it without an idea who it would be, quite unconcerned and in a hurry, because she wanted to get things ready for the morning. Sheila Armstrong's voice took her by complete surprise. At first, even given the name, it meant nothing to her and then she realised and apologised, and immediately she felt all the tension which had drained away during this happy weekend return. 'How nice to hear from you,' she said, automatically.

'I'm sorry to disturb you . . .'

'No, no, not at all. I wasn't doing anything, really.' How strange the woman's voice sounded, the local accent so strong, and yet when she'd visited her she'd never noticed that it was so pronounced.

'It's just I wondered if you could spare me a few minutes . . . if you can't it doesn't matter, I'll manage.'

It was the 'I'll manage', the evident embarrassment, that caught Harriet's attention. 'Of course I can,' she said, 'you carry on.'

'I was hoping we might be able to meet, soon, only it would be easier to talk, but if you're busy, or don't fancy it . . .'

'That would be fine. When were you thinking of?'

'Well, today, if possible . . .'

'Oh, today's a bit difficult, and tomorrow . . .'

'I know. It's that parade. He told me, the police chap. It's about that, about the identity thing, I wanted to pass on something, but not to him. It's nothing, really. I'd just like to pass it on . . .' Her voice trailed off.

Harriet felt dismayed at her own agitation. She didn't want to see Sheila, she didn't even like talking on the telephone now that she'd decided to put all that behind her. Sheila Armstrong was part of 'that'. But she'd started it, she couldn't be hostile when the other woman had not been hostile to her. And there was this 'thing' she wanted to pass on.

'We could meet half-way,' Sheila was saying, naming a town. 'I have to go there anyway, I'm going by train, we could meet at the station, if you could get there.'

'If it's important . . .'

'I don't know if it is. Oh, maybe forget it, I shouldn't bother you. I can ring that policeman . . .'

It was the weariness in the voice which decided Harriet – the same aching weariness she had felt herself, weary of thinking, weary of remembering, weary to the point of mental standstill and seeing no help anywhere. 'No,' she said, 'we should meet, I want to. I can be at the station by twelve, will that suit? In the buffet, if there is one, or the waiting room?'

'Grand.'

Her whole day was now wrecked. She'd planned to keep herself extra busy so as not to think about tomorrow. Joe was not mentioning it. He looked and sounded better after the weekend and with Louis around she didn't feel she was carrying the whole weight of worry about how he'd react to the identity parade. Louis might even go with him. It hadn't been discussed but she convinced herself it was a possibility and it made her feel pleased to imagine it. Brothers, solidarity among brothers. Louis had been so willing but Joe so resistant – he wouldn't accept help, was

167

suspicious of any offered and most of all of Louis'. Louis somehow had let him down, though she couldn't see how. But perhaps, come the morning, come the arrival of Detective Sergeant Graham, Louis would count again. She wasn't going to put it to Louis – best if it happened naturally. That showed how far she'd come, she decided. All the way through this last year she'd been trying to organise support for Joe. She was through with it. She would *not* get Louis in a corner and whisper, 'It might help Joe if you . . .'

It was easy getting to the station. As usual, she was early, and she had time to inspect the buffet and waiting-rooms. Dismal. They made her shiver. The ladies' waiting-room was utterly empty except for a bench, a wooden bench with a hard, black leather seat running along one wall. The floor was covered in dark brown lino which had great cracks in it – a dreadful place, she was unable to do more than poke her head round the door. The buffet was hardly better. It was brighter and lighter but small, only six red-topped plastic tables all crammed together and a strong smell of hamburgers hanging over everything. She didn't want to sit there either. But just beside the station, in a side-street, she found a long, narrow café, flowered cloths on the round tables and posters on the walls. She didn't go in, but it would do. They could be private in there and not be overwhelmed by the dreariness of the setting.

If Sheila Armstrong cared about settings, if she noticed them. I don't know anything about her, Harriet thought, waiting on the platform outside the buffet. Nothing about her tastes, her likes and dislikes. It takes so long for those to emerge. She tried to visualise Sheila's house, the kitchen in which they had sat, and could hardly remember a thing. Geraniums in a window-box, that was about all. She should have asked Sheila to her house but she hadn't

168

wanted to, for all sorts of reasons, not just because of Joe. She hadn't wanted Sheila to invade her own territory, to then become another memory. She didn't want to have had *his* mother in her house, and that was so wrong, she was ashamed. It showed yet again how guilty she felt about meeting Sheila at all. Sam would have known it would end up like this, an imposition, a rash act leading to complications. Ginny too.

She could hardly pick Sheila out, even though there were only a few people walking down the platform, wasn't sure it was her until she was almost upon her and then she was embarrassed not to have recognised her. It was that coat, the grey coat she'd worn in court, it made her invisible. At home, the blue dress had changed her into an individual and now she was back to being a blur. It was awkward meeting, much more awkward than it had been the first time. Neither of them was in charge, nobody was taking the lead, showing the way, offering tea. Harriet didn't know whether to shake hands or just smile. She was glad she'd worn a dress with pockets, so she could keep her hands in them until the last minute. Sheila wasn't smiling. She looked older, she was nervous, hesitant. Harriet felt sorry for her. It flashed into her head that Sheila looked like a victim's mother, not she. The noise was great for a few moments while one train departed and another arrived, and she pointed at the exit and took hold of Sheila's arm to propel her along. When they were outside she explained about the café and they walked there, two abreast, formal and silent.

It was a relief to be sitting down, as far away from the counter as possible. Nobody else was there, except the girl in charge who couldn't have shown less interest. Deliberately, Harriet ordered a pot of tea, though there was a wonderful smell of coffee and she longed for it. Until it came, they hardly spoke, but once the liquid was poured into their cups and steamed satisfactorily in front of them, Sheila looked more relaxed. 'I'll get to the point,' she said, 'you'll want to be off.'

Harriet said nothing. This is how I must have seemed, she was thinking, so needy, so nakedly wanting comfort. She dreaded appearing patronising, so she kept quiet, played with her teaspoon.

'I went to see my grandson yesterday,' Sheila said, 'in . . . you know . . . in there. The policeman asked me to.' She dropped her voice lower on 'policeman', though there was no one to hear. 'He wanted me to put to Leo a name. The one – you know – tomorrow . . .'

'Yes.' Harriet didn't want to say it either.

'I didn't say I would but I did. And there was no mistake, it *is* him, it was him. Leo wouldn't say so but I saw. I should tell the police, really.' She sounded so depressed at the idea that Harriet found herself saying, 'I'll tell them. But it won't stop them wanting to hear it from you.' She took a sip of the tea. 'Well, I suppose Joe will identify him too. And that will be that. After another trial, all that to go through again. I wonder if he has a mother, this brute?'

Sheila said nothing. Harriet Kennedy seemed a different person to a month ago. Calmer, not so excitable. Maybe it was where they were, in this odd café, maybe she thrived in impersonal places, whereas I shrink, Sheila thought, I am not at home. She is. It was a mistake coming here. She didn't know why she'd set this ridiculous meeting up. The sooner it was over the better.

'Does the name mean anything to *you*?' Harriet was asking.

'No. Nothing.'

'He wasn't a friend of your grandson's?'

'Leo didn't have friends, not close friends. He preferred being on his own, always did. His grandfather, well, his great-grandfather, my father, was his best friend once, and then me. Or I thought so.'

'I wonder how he got mixed up . . .' Harriet began and was startled to see Sheila struggle to her feet.

'I'd better be going. I only wanted to pass on . . .'

'Please, I'm sorry, what did I say? Finish your tea, please, at least finish that cup.'

Two women came into the café, laden with shopping, talking loudly. Sheila looked at them as they settled down, strewing their belongings around, ordering soup and bread and a salad, taking over the place. She was glad they had come. Noise, a bit of life, that was what was needed, instead of this agonising atmosphere between her and Harriet Kennedy. She was able to compose herself under cover of the sudden action. She finished her tea and said, 'I'm sorry, dear. I just can't bear being asked about how Leo came to do what he did, I can't stand it, even from you, even nicely put in a roundabout way. It gets me on the raw, I don't like to think about it.'

'Of course. It was my fault. I wasn't thinking.' Harriet paused, not wanting to make the same mistake again. Very, very gently she said, 'Your Leo, he didn't necessarily do anything horrific to my son. It upset Joe they didn't get the other one. They even said in court . . .'

'I know what they said. It doesn't make any difference. Leo knows it doesn't. He was there, he watched and he had a knife in his hand . . .' Sheila shook her head.

'All that to hear again,' Harriet said, suddenly appalled, and then blurted out, passionately enough to make the two new arrivals pause and turn round, 'I don't want to see or hear him.'

'No,' said Sheila, 'neither do I. I dread it.'

'I didn't want to see either of them, and then when your Leo was arrested, I suddenly did. I wanted to see him, just to know, even if it made it all a hundred times worse. I wanted my nightmares to have their faces, their proper faces, in them.'

'I didn't want to see your boy. Looking so decent. Hearing all that, and Leo there, part of it. Terrible, terrible. His life's ruined, he'll have to live with it all his life.'

'So will Joe.'

'Oh, I'm not making comparisons, I'm not doing that, I know it isn't the same, but for your boy it was an accident, it could have happened to anyone, he hasn't got to live with being part of evil. I never believed in evil, never. But now I do. It's everywhere, everywhere, and no stopping it.'

The other two women were laughing uproariously, red in the face with mirth. Harriet cleared her throat. There didn't seem anything comforting to say and she didn't even know if she should be trying to offer comfort. But even while Sheila was saying it she was registering her own surprised disagreement. Surely, she should be the one saying that about evil? But she couldn't. She didn't believe in pure evil, some evil force existing without cause. She rejected it. All evil *must* have causes, even this random evil which had selected Joe. There must be a reason why this woman's grandson had assisted in the attack on Joe and why the other one had perpetrated his crimes. If only these causes could be identified, the evil would be understood if not condoned, certainly not condoned. But she couldn't come out with any of this in front of Sheila. It wasn't right, it would sound sanctimonious. Sheila's burden was different. Her grandson, whom she was convinced was tainted with evil, would be released soon and then she would have to live with him, start battling with how they were to live together. Her own life was already soured, embittered, wrecked by the knowledge she had of him. And her sense of failure was complete. It made Harriet suddenly appreciate how absurd her own sense of having failed Joe was – *this* was failure, Sheila's guilt.

'It's all so unfair,' Harriet said finally. 'It's awful for you. And for me.'

Sheila gathered up her few things and stood up. 'I'd best be getting back,' she said.

'Now?' said Harriet. 'But I thought . . .'

'I didn't want to drag you all the way, I just pretended I was coming here, it was no bother anyway.' She smiled slightly. 'Silly, eh? At my time of life. My husband would say I was going potty.'

They walked together back to the station and shook hands, wanting some contact but not an embrace.

'I'll keep in touch,' Harriet said.

Sheila nodded, clearly disbelieving. She'd have to ring Detective Sergeant Graham herself. She'd always known she would. Pathetically, this had only been an excuse to meet Harriet again. A mistake.

*

Detective Sergeant Graham was at the station by eight o'clock, anxious to check the arrangements for the parade himself. This caused offence. It looked as though he didn't trust his subordinates, which was true, he didn't, not to get every detail right, every tiny detail, as he always did himself. They were quite capable of having at least two in the line-up several inches shorter and a stone lighter than Gary Robinson. He wanted all eight to be six foot and thirteen stone with shaved heads and an earring. The officer on duty, already furious at this interference, looked appalled when he emphasised this – it was asking too much, they'd be combing the streets for days. 'Comb them,' he'd said.

The resulting bunch were obviously a nasty-looking crowd, though he was told one was a medical student and

173

another a dancer. The sight of all of them lined up, half of them smirking, the others sullen, in a hurry to get their money, their £4 each, and run, was formidable, and that was without Gary Robinson yet. Graham wanted to see him on his own first, make sure he understood what would happen if he went on not co-operating. He knew the type, full of themselves, not in the least intimidated by being handcuffed or banged up. All swagger, even now, with a definite gaol sentence looming. He matched him eye-to-eye, stood in front of him and glared. He'd like to hit him, certainly. Perfectly correct, he'd like to do him violence. And Gary Robinson knew he would like to and knew he wouldn't do it, and the pleasure of knowing this was all over his face. A horrible face, fat, big mouth, squashed nose. Graham thought of Joe Kennedy, having to look at this powerful, strutting figure and remembering. It was enough to make anyone sick. 'I want him at number three,' he said.

They were all lined up, ready to go. Gary Robinson kept back, separate, until they were walking in. Graham felt the uneasiness in the air. The other men, the innocent men, worried at this point, they were infected by the tension, they started imagining being picked out wrongly and not being believed. It was dramatic, an identity parade, always. The whole station loved it. And in this case everyone wanted Gary Robinson picked out and put away for life if possible. When everything was ready, Graham went to see Joe.

The boy had his brother with him. He'd just come out with Joe, when Graham drew up outside the Kennedy house, and assumed he could come, but he was polite enough, like his father, and anyone was preferable to the mother. He'd liked the way the brother, Louis, kept talking on the way, not being chatty exactly but throwing out laconic remarks about things he saw out of the

174

window of the car which Joe seemed to find amusing. He wasn't as worried about the boy, this Louis. He didn't radiate anxiety like the mother. He even told Joe off when he banged the car door too hard getting out at the station. Now the mother, Mrs Kennedy, she'd have let that go, shot him an apologetic look perhaps but wouldn't have wanted to upset Joe by referring to it. Once in the station, he saw Louis was interested. He pointed out a notice to Joe and they both laughed. Far, far better than that mother. The boy was as relaxed as it was possible to be at the moment. All that might change, of course, but at least they were going into this ordeal with a victim in a state of composure and not gibbering with apprehension to such an extent that he would not be able to identify his own face if it were shown to him.

He was watching Joe very, very closely, as they stood together looking through the mirror. No young face was ever really impassive, he reflected, though he recalled Leo Jackson's, the exception that proved the rule. Adults, certain adults, could train themselves, but there was something so fluid about an adolescent face that the muscles and nerves responded to the faintest reaction of the person. Joe was trying so hard to be expressionless but already, as the first in line walked into the room behind the mirror, his mouth was twitching and his rate of blinking had increased rapidly. The moment Gary Robinson lumbered in, the effect on Joe was dramatic – his face flushed, his eyes widened, he was so agitated his finger literally shook as he pointed it and said that was the one, number three, definitely. But Graham kept him there. He made Joe watch all the other five, front-on, sideways, both sides. However cruel, he wanted Joe to see Gary Robinson from every angle. He asked him again and again if he was absolutely certain, again and again to look carefully. Only when the whole line had moved out did he let Joe go. Everyone was elated of course. Smiles all round, the news passed on quickly. For a moment it was as though Joe, too, shared in the elation . . . he smiled as he told his brother he'd identified the principal attacker, and when Graham patted him on the back and said, 'Well done, Joe,' he seemed pleased. But this euphoria faded before he left the station. Sitting in the car with Louis, waiting to be taken home, Joe leaned back on the seat, closed his eyes and was suddenly tremulous. 'I don't want to go home,' he said to Louis. 'Not yet. I don't want Mum to see me. I feel sick.' The driver looked through his driving mirror at Louis, waiting for his instructions. Louis didn't seem to have any. He frowned, said, 'Mum will be at work, won't she? She said she was going to go.'

'She won't, though,' Joe said. 'She'll be there. I know she will. I can't stand it.'

'How about a walk then, and a cup of coffee? Then we could just get a bus.'

'Okay.'

They walked up the river, self-consciously. Not a normal activity on a Tuesday morning, two brothers walking up the river, neither saying much. Joe had his head down, kicked stones. Louis had his up, looking at the river and wondering why he'd never fancied fishing. He yawned. 'I'm sorry I'm boring you,' Joe said furiously, 'let's go home.'

'Don't be stupid, I couldn't help yawning, for Christ's sake. Don't be so bloody touchy.'

'I am boring. All I think about is what happened and it's ages ago. I'm pathetic. All I do is whinge. It isn't even as though it was all that awful . . .'

'It was awful all right, you needn't worry about that.'

'. . . hundreds of people go through much worse, they end up scarred for life.'

'You're scarred.'

'I'm not . . . don't start that, all that crap, that's what Mum does, poor little Joe, all this stuff about . . . if my arm was cut off people would realise, but because it's my mind . . .'

'What?'

'Oh nothing, she gets muddled, she means I am scarred, only it's in my mind.'

'Maybe she's right?'

'She's *not* right. It's just self-pity, that's all. I just wallow in it, going over and over it, I'm sick of it, *sick* of it. I wish I'd never said a word.'

'Wouldn't have mattered if you hadn't, you'd have been found, you'd have been taken to hospital, how could you have said nothing?'

'I mean about the rest, what he made me do.'

'Do?'

'Stop echoing me, I hate it.'

'What else can I do when I don't know what the fuck you're on about? What rest? What did they make you do? Why is it nobody in this family tells me anything?'

'It isn't the sort of thing you tell. And I didn't, just Mum.'

'All this mystery, that's what I'm sick of. How can I understand if I don't know, eh?'

'You'll only laugh.'

Louis stopped walking abruptly. Joe had already gone another few yards before he caught up with him again. He took hold of his arm and pulled him round quite roughly. 'Why would I laugh at anything to do with what happened? You're an arrogant little bastard, Joe, do you know that? You're the only one with any feelings, of course, sensitive little Joe, and I'm just a rugger-playing hearty, that's it, isn't it? No point in telling old Louis anything, or Dad, it's only Mum and her precious little flower who really feel anything. Right. Fine. Let's go home. I'm fed up. Anyway, I've got things to do, I'm off on Thursday.'

'Exactly.'

'And what's that supposed to mean?'

'Why are you surprised you haven't been told things? You don't care. You just drop in now and again and pretend you do. You can't wait to fuck off again.'

They'd turned and were walking back, Joe now the one with his head thrown back, Louis grimly watching the path. It hardly took them any time to get back to the bridge, and the sudden noise of traffic was a relief to both of them. They found the bus stop and when it came got on and sat at the very back. Joe felt better, Louis worse. As the bus approached the terminus Louis said, 'I'm sorry I shouted. I shouldn't have. Sorry.' He'd always been good at saying sorry. He apologised easily. Not like Joe, who never did say sorry. The best Joe could ever do was try to show he was sorry. The scenes there had been when he was a child trying to get that simple word out of him . . . 'It doesn't matter,' Joe said now, 'I know I'm a pain.'

'You're not. I'm useless. Charlotte says it too. I'm clumsy, I always say the wrong thing at vital moments.'

'It wasn't a vital moment . . .'

'It felt like it. I just blundered on, instead of listening and waiting. Charlotte says . . .' Joe gave a groan. 'What's wrong?'

'You just go on about Charlotte as though she were one of the family but you haven't even brought her home yet.'

'I know. There never seemed a right time, what with . . .'

'Me. Thanks. Spoiled a beautiful introduction, sorry, I can't take you home, my baby brother's freaked out, it's all rather unpleasant, too horrid for your tender ears, my darling, let's wait until it's all over and my family's presentable again . . .'

The bus stopped, Joe leapt up and was off it in a flash and running down the street. Louis didn't bother chasing him. He could have caught him easily but he wasn't going to. He couldn't cope with Joe. He felt exhausted and he'd only been with him on his own for an hour. Walking slowly after him, Louis suddenly felt a new admiration for his mother. How had she stood it? All this self-laceration of Joe's, all this flaring up over nothing, taking things the wrong way.

He couldn't wait for Thursday and flight.

★

Harriet was proud of herself. She really had managed to treat Tuesday like an ordinary day and had not only gone to work but had worked well. She didn't even watch the clock and wonder what was going on at the police station. This was the new her, the other side of the turned-over leaf. It amused her to be concentrating on using a four-leafed clover as a repeat pattern on some beautiful silk she had dyed a misty purple. Luck. Hope. She was going to be optimistic and her optimism would surely affect Joe. It was Sheila Armstrong who had the problems now, not her. If this Gary Robinson was the one then he'd be convicted and sent to prison for a long time and Joe could really go forward. Detective Sergeant Graham had been right, the arrest of Joe's real attacker was good news. There would be room to think about other things in life. Holidays. She and Sam would have a proper holiday, somewhere exotic, maybe the West Indies, where Sam had always wanted to go. It would be an act of faith, faith in Joe being able to do without her. He was seventeen, nearly, and should be treated as independent . . .

It was incredible how different she felt. She hadn't retreated into the past now for nearly a week – all her fantasies ran into the future and it was such a pleasure.

Detective Sergeant Graham rang Mrs Armstrong himself and thanked her for letting him know of her grandson's reaction to the name of Gary Robinson. In the event, he told her, it didn't matter so much because Joe Kennedy had made a positive identification. They could now proceed without Leo's help, even if he could still tell them a great deal which they'd like to know should he decide to speak. She was not to worry herself, he said.

Sheila smiled as she put the phone down. What did the smug Graham know about worry? But she was glad to have been told about Joe identifying that thug. Very glad. His mother would be relieved. There would be a lot in the local paper about it, going over everything again, especially since Gary Robinson was twenty-two and could be named. She would have to brace herself for the stares and nudges. They'd go over the whole thing from beginning to end. Well, she didn't care about how she was treated, she really didn't. She was locked into herself, had been for years. It was her father and Alan and even her sister and her husband who would be resentful, who would talk about not being able to walk into shops for the shame, for the odium attached to them.

She was surprised when the probation officer, the Helen woman, turned up again. She said she'd just come to see how things were, 'in general'.

'That's kind of you,' Sheila said, allowing a note of sarcasm to creep into her voice. 'Well, in general, we're soldiering on, thank you.'

'And how's Leo?' Helen asked. 'I can't get much out of him myself.'

'You'd have to ask those who know,' Sheila said, quite tartly, 'and that isn't me. He looks fit enough, though, doesn't he?' Helen hesitated.

'The thing is, Mrs Armstrong,' she said, 'this trial of Gary Robinson might alter things for Leo.'

'How's that?'

'Well, it was never clear what part Leo had actually played in the attack on Joe Kennedy, beyond being there.'

'That was enough. And he had a knife in his hand, don't forget, they found it, with his fingerprints on.'

'Yes, but it could turn out that Leo *did* nothing, that in a way he was a victim like Joe, that this Robinson used him.'

Sheila stayed silent. Her head swam – the mere notion that Leo might have been a sort of victim too, which had never occurred to her, or anyone else that she knew of, made her dizzy. She couldn't help a sudden surge of excitement sweeping through her body, but she was at pains to conceal any reaction from Helen.

'Joe Kennedy never really incriminated Leo,' Helen was saying, 'he just said he was there.'

'Well,' Sheila said, trying to convey her disgust.

'It was the prosecution implied Leo had actually stabbed Joe too,' Helen argued, 'because of his fingerprints being on that knife they found and Joe's blood on his clothes, and when he didn't deny it, when he would only say he was there and nothing more . . .'

'That's right, so there you are. If he hadn't done anything he would have said so, wouldn't he? He would have denied it.'

'He probably can't actually remember what he did or didn't do, he was under the influence of . . .'

'I know what he was under the influence of, thank you. Out of his mind. And how did he come to take that stuff? That's bad enough.'

'Anyway, Mrs Armstrong, all I'm saying is that a lot more may come out at this Robinson trial and it may put Leo in a different light. I just want you to be prepared. He may not be as guilty as he seemed. He's been his own worst enemy, keeping quiet.'

Sheila told no one about Helen's solicitous visit. She hugged this secret to herself as something both too unbelievable and too wonderful to give voice to. Taking drugs was one thing, especially the drug Leo had taken, even if perhaps only once, who knew, but it was nothing compared to taking part in the attack on Joe Kennedy, actually assisting. She felt suddenly worried that she had never firmly stated her opinion that Leo had done nothing. She hadn't. What she'd said was that she couldn't *believe* he'd done anything. That was different. Maybe if she'd been more confident and sure, maybe if in front of Leo, she had said to the police, 'Leo never harmed Joe Kennedy, I *know* he didn't,' Leo would have talked. But then, there was the evidence – Joe's hairs on Leo's clothes, Joe's blood on them, showing, surely, the boy had tried to fight him off. The truth was, she had not shown that absolute faith in Leo's innocence which a mother might be expected to show. She had allowed herself to be persuaded that Leo, in some sort of frenzy, under the influence of drugs, had indeed hurt Joe Kennedy. Oh, the agony if this turned out not to be true! If all along Leo had never touched Joe but had kept silent because he feared that in his hallucinating state he had done (and the hairs, the blood . . .?)

The last person she wanted to see was her father, but it was Friday, it was his evening for high tea. God, these routines, these rigid routines, she was so tired of them. If she rang up to tell him not to come that would only lead to further trouble – why, what was wrong, etc. She protected him, he, who had never protected her. She protected him now from anything unpleasant because he was old.

And he was at his most annoying that particular evening.

'Something funny going on in the garden,' he grumbled, shovelling in his meat, 'half the tatties haven't come up.'

'Oh?' she said, bored, yet glad to be on such a harmlessly absurd topic. 'Why's that, Dad?'

'How should I know?' he said, aggrieved. 'Seventy year I've planted tatties and they've alus come up.'

'Maybe you planted them upside down.'

'Don't be daft, doesn't matter how tatties are planted, they come up. Any road, I didn't plant them. Just ask yerself what was the new element this year, just you ask yerself that.'

'Alan? Did Alan put them in for you?'

'Aye.'

'Oh *Dad*, you can't be accusing Alan of stealing your potato plants . . .'

'Did I say so? I did not, niver said a word. But he's the new element. Leo did them last year, and the year before, and they all come up and they alus come up when I could plant them meself. That's all I'm saying, that's all.'

'I'll tell Alan.'

'You'll do no such thing!' And he glared at her. 'You'll get the back of my hand if you do any such thing. He's a good lad, your Alan, nowt wrong wi' him. You leave him alone, mind.'

She told Alan as soon as he came in, after Eric James had left. He laughed. But he had his own preoccupation, equally trivial, equally real to him.

'The car's not sounding right,' he said. 'I'm worried, it's a knocking sound, sounds bad, could be something major. When I'm going over forty it starts, this knock–knock in the engine.'

'Well, take it into the garage.'

'That's what I'm trying to tell you. I'll have to take it in and it might be something major, and then what?'

'Then you have it mended.'

'Cost, Sheila, cost.'

'You just have to pay it.'

'It could be hundreds.'

'Then sell it.'

'Sheila, you can't sell a car with an engine knocking, see sense, for heaven's sake.'

She kept quiet, let him drone on after that. What the hell did she care about potatoes or car engines? All this in her, bursting to come out, all this longing to share her doubts about Leo's guilt, and she was condemned to idiotic ramblings with her menfolk. She couldn't bring herself to interrupt Alan, to tell him to shut up and listen, because there had been an important new development, that the arrest and identification of Gary Robinson had changed everything, had *possibly* changed everything. She ate with Alan, she washed the dishes, she watched the news, she went to bed with him and she said nothing at all.

'You've been very quiet this evening,' Alan said to her before he put the light out. 'Anything up?'

'No,' she said, 'nothing.'

Chapter Ten

UNTIL LOUIS DEPARTED, the pretence could be maintained, but Harriet knew that was what it was, a pretence, a sham. They all connived, even Joe himself. Sam was the only one entirely taken in. 'Well,' he said, with such immense satisfaction on Tuesday evening, 'that was another pleasant family meal.' She said nothing. 'It was, wasn't it?' he persisted, no shadow of doubt in his voice, merely seeking agreement. 'If you say so,' she said, not wanting to let him see her dismay, but wanting to keep up her own optimism, that tender plant she had only just begun to nurture. She tried again. 'It was pleasant,' she said, 'no arguments, anyway. And after such a day . . .'

'Did they tell you about it?' Sam said, anxious now. It was awful that he was used to receiving all news of any importance through her.

'Not much. You should have asked them, asked Louis, anyway.'

'I thought maybe I shouldn't . . . everything seemed okay, I thought I'd leave well alone. What did Joe say?'

'Nothing really. He just said this Gary Robinson was the one, and he didn't want to talk about it. So we didn't.'

'But was he upset?'

She didn't know how to answer. Joe had been alone when she got in, but outside, in the garden with Bruno, just sitting under the pear tree, slouching against it, doing nothing. Everything was easier outside, always. She'd gone and got a chair from the shed and joined him. Determined to be open and direct, in keeping with her new resolution, she said brightly, 'How was it? Was it him?' and he nodded. She waited, and when he added nothing, when the silence grew and she couldn't stand it any longer, she asked him where Louis was. He shrugged. She felt annoyed, Louis shouldn't have left him, not after he'd been through such an ordeal, *she* wouldn't have left him, and then she checked herself. There was no reason why Louis should have played nursemaid, keeper. Joe was nearly seventeen, it was absurd. Louis had his own life, friends to see, things to buy and do before he went. She stroked Bruno who moved away, closer to Joe. She laughed, pleased. 'Easy to see who he likes best,' she said. Joe didn't move a muscle. She felt the same old feelings begin to overwhelm her, feelings of panic and misery, and fought them. 'Right,' she said, bouncing up, 'I'll get on with the supper. We'll have it outside.'

When Louis came home he was whistling and she could have blessed him for his cheerfulness. She drew him into the kitchen, away from the window through which Joe, still under the tree and motionless, might see them. 'How was it?' she asked. Louis told her. He went over the effect of the parade on Joe and then the walk they'd had. 'So I fucked it up,' he ended, 'he wouldn't tell me and he ran off. So I just let him. I wasn't doing any good. Sorry.'

'Not your fault,' she said, automatically, then, 'he's in the garden, not speaking, just lying there.'

'Let him.'

'But he doesn't really want to, he wants company, anything to stop him thinking. It'll be churning around in his mind . . .'

'Mum, please.'

'What?'

'You can't do it for him.'

186

'What's that supposed to mean?'

'Oh, you know.'

Then Charlotte rang, and Louis raced upstairs to talk to her on the extension.

So she didn't know how to answer Sam. Yes, Joe was upset, clearly. But what did 'upset' in this context mean? It wasn't a case of being upset. He just wasn't there any more, he was remote, ugly in his self-absorption. His power frightened her all over again. One person only but with the strength of thousands. She had never known misery could dominate in such a way. She couldn't bear to look at him, couldn't bear to feel him in a room with her. No comfort was possible and that was the worst thing. Suddenly, hatred stirred in her, hatred for Gary Robinson, and an alarming surge of violence came with it. She saw Gary Robinson in her mind's eye and she hit him and then she had him stripped and she taunted him and she laughed when she saw the fear in his face . . .

'Well,' said Sam, 'we've had a good few days. Good weather, good meals, good chats and I suppose even the outcome of the ID parade was good. Things are looking up. Pity Louis is going off. Joe will miss him.'

'Only because he breaks up the atmosphere,' she said, 'only because Joe doesn't like being alone with us.'

'Oh, I don't know, they get on well, I thought, they seemed quite close. I'm sure Louis helped Joe . . .'

'He didn't. He doesn't. Joe always thinks he will, but he doesn't. I wish he did.'

'Pity it wasn't Joe going off.'

'You're always saying that, wanting to be rid of him.'

'That's not true. I mean I don't want to be rid of him, I want his mind taken off the past, I want to see him giving himself a chance of being happy . . .'

'And happiness to you is the old thing, activity.'

'Yes, a lot of it. At least if he were active, with others, there's a possibility he'd be diverted . . .'

'Diverted?'

'Harriet, stop it, you're doing it again, jeering, treating me like a moron. I *know* it sounds as if I'm making light of what happened and its effect on Joe, but I'm not. But having him hanging round here all summer with nothing to do but . . .'

'He's going to work at the boat yard.'

'Part-time, that's all. And not in the evenings. It isn't good for him, he needs to be forced into company . . .'

'You can't force Joe into anything.'

'Quite. He calls the shots.'

'Oh, don't talk in such silly jargon, this isn't some stupid melodrama. It's Joe's tragedy, this strength, it's what's got him through all his exams last year, kept him going, when anyone weaker would've cracked. But it's what keeps him from being able to be helped, he can't show weakness, he thinks he has to deal with it himself . . .'

'He's got you.'

'I'm useless. I make things worse.'

'Don't be silly . . .'

'No, I do. I make them worse. He's told me. At school, he manages perfectly. It's at home, with me, that's when it's bad.'

'Because he can be himself. That must be a relief, surely, to . . .'

'No, it isn't a relief. It's a burden. I'm a burden for him.'

'Harriet, what the hell are you on about?'

She stopped. She didn't know what she was on about, but rambling on to Sam she felt she'd stumbled on a truth others had been trying to get her to see: she was a burden to Joe. Her pain for him was a burden, her agonised concern a stone round his neck. He couldn't get free of his memories, he couldn't get free of her. So she said yes to Sam, she said she'd go away with him, for the weekend of

188

their wedding anniversary. They ought to celebrate and a party was out of the question. She couldn't cope with that kind of celebration, it was too much when there was so little joy in her. Nor did she want to go far. Scotland, that was far enough. Maybe Edinburgh. Their anniversary was in August, they'd go during the Festival and have a weekend of plays and events, of liveliness. Joe could go to Ginny's. But when she told him, Joe refused. He said he would stay at home, he wouldn't hear of going to Ginny's or anywhere else. She wondered if Louis would be back and flew to the calendar where she'd made him write down his dates. August 16. Their anniversary was the 15th. Sam wanted to go on the 14th, return on the 18th.

Could she leave Joe for two nights, alone in the house? Nothing had happened in the house. It was a test.

★

'We'll go out for the day,' Alan said, 'that'll buck you up.'

Sheila smiled wearily; it was so ridiculous. It was how Alan thought: simply. She was quiet and listless, unlike herself, so a day out and Bob's your uncle, she'd buck up. 'All right,' she agreed, 'we'll have a day out.'

It was marvellous the way his expression changed. 'Sunday,' he said, 'we'll go to the Lakes on Sunday. Keswick, have a sail on Derwent, eh?'

'No,' she said, 'not Keswick, it'll be crowded on a Sunday, this time of year. Ullswater, how about Ullswater? Or Crummock?'

'I'd like a sail,' Alan said, 'and you can't sail on Crummock. Ullswater, then, we'll drive to Pooley Bridge and catch the boat.'

'What about Dad?' she said.

'What about him?'

'If it's a Sunday, you know he has his dinner on a Sunday . . .'

'Well, for once he can't. Let Carole and Peter have him.'
'Carole and Peter are away.'
'Then let him stick, he's spoiled.'
'I wouldn't enjoy it. Can't we take him? He'd love it.'
'Well, I wouldn't. Take *him* . . .'

But they did. Alan was soft. She didn't have to blackmail him, didn't have to say she wouldn't go if Eric James couldn't come too. She just kept quiet, quieter than ever, and looked at Alan sorrowfully. She could have laughed . . . poor Alan. It was sad for him. He wanted to be just with her, that was what he had always wanted, even with Pat and certainly with Leo. The least selfish man in the world, quite unable to make sure he got what he wanted. So she invited Eric James and he infuriated her, typically.

'Ullswater?' he said, and, instead of showing the enthusiasm she'd been sure of, 'All right, if yer say so,' was the nearest to delight he could come. 'What time will us set off?'

She said she supposed about ten or eleven in the morning, to make a day of it. 'Why? Does it matter?'

'Course it matters, when us set off, course it does. Ten or eleven, eh? Which?'

'I don't know . . .'

'Well yer should. Ten *or* eleven?'

'Ten, then.'

'That's awkward.'

'Why?'

'I'll not be back until after ten. If I go. It'd mean not going.'

She was furious with him and said nothing. Very well, if ten was too early, if it conflicted with this urgent appointment he apparently had, then she wasn't going to change it. He could stay behind, stew in his own juice. Alan would be glad. But Alan spoiled his chance. Coming in at that moment, he hailed his father-in-law with, 'Looking forward to Sunday then? Has Sheila told you?'

'Ay. What time is us setting off?'

'Oh, about eleven, not before. That suit you?'

'Grand,' said Eric James, with indecent satisfaction, smirking, avoiding Sheila's eye. 'Give me time to git back from the cemetery. I'll be ready, niver fear.'

He could go to the cemetery any time, there was nothing sacred about going before ten on a Sunday. But he always went then, to pay his respects on the Lord's Day, as he put it, he who was the least religious of men. The only time he was ever in a church was for a wedding or a funeral. But once his wife died he became a cemetery visitor on a Sunday as though he were a God-fearing believer. Got dressed up in his best suit and trilby and shuffled off, even now, on the long walk to Jane's grave where he would remove his hat and cross himself. It was so silly. He used to take Leo and bewilder him. 'It's what you do on a Sunday at yer great-grandmother's grave,' was all Eric James would say when plagued with questions as to the meaning of this ritual. 'It's right and proper, just do as yer told,' was the only addition to this. Asked by Leo if he believed in God, then, Eric James said it was none of his business, but when Leo, at the age of twelve, just at the limit of revering his great-grandfather, said *he* certainly didn't, he was told to wash his mouth out and never say that again.

On the anniversary of her mother's death, Sheila always went with him to the grave. She ordered what was called a 'memorial posy', price £8.50, mixed flowers. Eric James loved her doing this, and putting a notice in the local paper: 'Jane Armstrong, died March 1, 1972, beloved wife of Eric James Armstrong and much-loved mother of Sheila and Carole. Sorely missed.' He kept the cutting. Every year he'd produce it and the whole thing would have to be gone through again. She made a day of it for him. They'd take the posy and walk up the centre path of the cemetery, always the same route. When he was young, Leo came too, allowed to carry the flowers, actually liking to carry them. Sheila hated it. All the way to her mother's grave she'd be thinking of Pat's, out there under the scorching sun, dusty and forgotten, the wooden cross perhaps disintegrated, eaten by ants, no stone angel to mark the spot, nobody putting flowers there, ever. She could hardly bear it. But her father thought her anguished face was due to grief for her mother and it pleased him. He'd even mutter, 'Now then,' and, 'Good lass,' on the way back, and he'd order Leo to keep quiet, his grandma was upset. Leo didn't need to be told. To him, eventually, she told the truth. After she had done so, he never went again.

They picked Eric James up at eleven. He was standing at the door, coat on, testing it was shut properly by pressing himself against it. He went in the front of the car, naturally, and she was in the back. Hardly was he in the car before he asked, 'What's us doing about dinner?'

'We're having it this evening, when we get back,' Sheila said, anticipating the horror he then expressed. 'And I've got a picnic for lunch.'

'Well, that's summat,' he said. 'What if it rains?'

'We'll eat it in the car.'

But it didn't rain. The sun shone brilliantly and the first glimpse of Ullswater dazzled. Eric James became quite perky and animated, asking her all the time if she remembered this day and that day, all the outings from her childhood. She always did. He'd brought them on the bus, a long journey, first to Penrith, then to Pooley Bridge. They were exhausted by the time they got there. The boat was the big treat, all the way to Glenridding and back. Leo had done it too, more comfortably, by car, only an hour or less to the landing stage. He'd loved it. Like Pat. She vividly remembered Pat, aged eight, her face upturned, smiling, excited, saying, 'I'm going to go on a big boat when I'm grown up, I'm going to sail the seven seas.' She'd laughed. It was from a story, of course. Pat didn't even know which were the seven seas. Leo was the same. He hadn't wanted to get off the boat. They'd had a terrible struggle the first time. He wanted to go to Africa on it.

The boat wasn't too crowded. They found seats easily, good ones, on the prow. Eric James sat as straight-backed as he could, staring around him, pointing out birds and other boats, in his element. 'Grand,' he said frequently, and, 'Champion.' Alan wandered off, to get a beer, she suspected. They were left happily feeling the sun and the breeze on their faces, Sheila's eyes closed. 'Makes yer think,' Eric James suddenly said. She said nothing. There was no need. He didn't want encouragement as others did, scorned the normal give-and-take of conversation. 'Aye, it makes yer think. First Pat, then him. And it only seems five minutes ago. Five minutes.' This was true Eric James enigmatic style. She knew nevertheless exactly what he was struggling to say. Let him struggle. 'You never know,' he went on, 'how anything will turn out. Who'd have thought it? Sitting here, holding my hand, nice as yer please. Makes yer wonder.' She had no patience with this, getting his drift, and opening her eyes turned round to look for Alan. Then he did surprise her. 'It was none of your doing, any road,' he said. 'Get that idea out of yer head, now then.'

'What idea?' She had to ask, unable to resist it.

'Never yer mind. That's all. Get it out of your head.'

'If I knew what it was, maybe I could.'

'*You* know.'

'You mean . . .'

'No need to spoil the day. I've said enough. Let it rest.'

She let it rest and it didn't spoil the day. It was a good day, all of it. As good as those others had been. They got off at Glenridding and found a place to have their picnic. Eric James walked well. Sometimes, if he wanted to be awkward, if he disapproved of where they wanted him to walk to, he'd claim he couldn't walk at all. But he was willing and able and sat on a boulder covered with Alan's jacket. Leo had loved picnics, just the eating in the open, and Eric James reminisced about all those he'd taken him on, sometimes just in the park with a packet of crisps, some chocolate biscuits and a can of coke, but a picnic all the same. Sheila suddenly realised, listening to him, that he spoke of Leo as though he were dead. Leo belonged, like Pat, to his memories, his happy memories, and that was all. She thought of where Leo was, what he was doing, while they sat here by the lake. Then she tried to think of Leo in the future. On a picnic. With them. All happy. A family. Leo maybe with wife, with children, Leo driving the car, his car, to Pooley Bridge. Leo in charge. Leo, having lived down the whole thing, with it all atoned for. But how could he atone for it? He hadn't shown any signs of wanting to, he'd expressed no regret or remorse. That was the worst of it. Nothing. Did he even know what he'd done to Joe Kennedy? Did he? Did anyone? He was intelligent, imaginative, he must. Maybe he would apologise, seek Joe out, as she had sought Harriet. Then everything would change, he would have a future.

He would drive to Pooley Bridge, with his wife, his children, with her. They would get the boat, have a picnic . . .

She couldn't see it. She just couldn't. Daren't.

★

The last school exam was on 23 June, Joe's seventeenth

194

birthday on the 25th. Harriet hardly dared mention the word 'celebration', and yet she so badly wanted to. Last year, Joe wouldn't even acknowledge it was his birthday. Birthdays were suddenly terrible. Forever after, his birthday would be smeared by the events just before it. And as for the exams, he didn't want to talk about them. They were not important, he said, though she knew they were, knew the predictions for his A Levels depended on them.

She never knew how he'd taken his GCSEs, which he'd been due to take that very June. Instead he took them when everyone did their retakes. All the rest of that agonising year, dragging himself to school, refusing any suggestion that he should defer them a whole year, and yet killing himself in the effort to concentrate. He'd lain on the floor sobbing over maths – he couldn't do it, he was just stupid, he was going to fail . . . She'd gone to the school, secretly, and they'd just stared at her, both teachers of maths, assured her Joe was so good he couldn't fail to get a 'B' grade at least. And he got an 'A', an 'A' in everything except Art; 'A' grades in eight subjects, 'B' in one. Oh, the euphoria she had felt! The triumph! All those 'A's *in the circumstances*. A triumph of mind over . . . she wasn't sure over what, but something tremendous. But there was no joy in Joe. None at all. It seemed to make things worse. 'What does it matter? he said, sadly. 'Doesn't mean a thing,' and she flashed back, 'When I said that, when you thought you were going to fail the lot, you said it did.' He'd been quiet. 'I just don't feel particularly glad,' he'd said. 'I don't feel anything.'

So no celebration. This year would be no different, except for the significance of driving. At seventeen he could get a provisional licence. They had it all ready for him, plus twelve lessons booked with an instructor. That was his present. She knew he would be pleased – to drive a car was one of the few remaining ambitions he would admit to having. It wasn't just the normal adolescent wish either. She knew why he wanted to drive so badly: to feel safe. If he had been driving that night, if he hadn't had to walk home alone from the cinema, if . . . it was foolish thinking, but not to him.

He'd taken to wearing boots, great big clumsy things. He wore them summer and winter alike, black lumps of lead at the end of his long, thin legs. He wouldn't be parted from them, abandoned his trainers and the moccasin-style shoes he'd once been so fond of. And he was quite open about the reason: in his boots, he felt more confident. He liked to hear himself walking, hear his feet echoing on the pavement. He said they helped him behave in a different way, a more powerful way. He said he felt he could kick in them. She'd had to turn away at that statement. So pathetic, pitiful. He would never kick. The boots were more likely to slow him down and be a handicap.

He wouldn't be able to wear those boots for driving, she was sure. They'd be awkward when he was learning, even if plenty of men wore them. She was hoping to persuade him back into trainers, a new pair, another present. It was to give her pleasure, not him, but what was wrong with that? New trainers, new socks, new Joe. New-looking Joe, anyway. She did so care about how he looked and knew it was wrong. She had her favourite shirts for him, favourite sweaters, as once she had had for Louis. After the attack, she'd kept the clothes he had been wearing. Detective Sergeant Graham had assumed she wouldn't want them. 'We'll have them burned when forensic are finished with them, don't you worry,' he'd said. They'd been in separate plastic bags, the garments. A blue short-sleeved button-down collared shirt, hopelessly ripped down the back and stained with blood; a pair of light blue jeans, intact but with darker, deeper patches of blood all down one leg; a black bomber jacket, canvas, unmarked; a pair of white Adidas trainers, untouched; a pair of white cotton socks, one perfect, one discoloured; and his underpants, blue, cotton . . . She'd fiercely demanded them all back, without telling Joe. She'd washed and repaired everything and hidden them. Furtively. In her wardrobe, on a shelf, at the back. Joe had naturally never asked about his clothes, only about his key and his bus pass.

Neither was returned. The bus pass didn't matter, it was soon out of date, and he had another, but the key bothered him. In the first weeks he asked about it all the time. Graham said it would be returned – the usual line, about forensic finishing with it – but it never came back and what would forensic do with a key, anyway? Joe was sure the police had lost it and worked himself into a rage over their carelessness. They had the lock changed, hoping this would calm Joe down but it didn't, he said they'd missed the point. Even a year later he was always muttering about the silly key. He'd tried to use it as a weapon. It had been in his pocket and his hand had gone to it when they jumped him and he'd attempted one desperate lunge with it, absolutely to no avail, only ridicule.

When he was small, they had always had parties for the boys, a joint one, since Louis' birthday was on 21 June. They celebrated the longest day or midsummer's day alternate years and the boys had six guests each. Sam organised the parties – cricket parties, crazy golf parties, canoeing parties, always some outdoor activity. Right up to Louis' sixteenth, and after that they'd stopped. Louis had his own parties and Joe didn't want one without him. But they'd still had celebrations, special meals, treats, his birthday had still been marked somehow. Until his sixteenth, just after. What a sickeningly sombre day that

197

had been . . . Happy Birthday, Joe . . . a farce. Detective Sergeant Graham had given him a present. A video game. None of them knew what it was like because Joe wouldn't even unwrap it. Even she had been moved to thank Detective Sergeant Graham for his kindness, and Sam had been fulsome. 'I'm too soft,' Graham had said, pleased, 'I can't resist spoiling the lad a bit after all he's been through.'

She had argued with Joe – 'It was kind of him, you can't deny that, Joe.' Joe had said he didn't want kindness, it made him feel sick. Most things, then, made him feel sick – kindness, compassion, tenderness, consideration and especially sympathy. The only people he really liked were those who were curt, uninterested, sharp and critical. Then he cried. He liked them, but they made him cry. The kind made him rage. To have a chance with Joe you needed to be a stranger who had come back to their little town after a prolonged absence, after everyone had forgotten the attack and didn't bother mentioning what had happened to young Joe Kennedy – then, Joe was prepared to give people a chance, then he might neither cry nor rage if asked about himself. He even enjoyed missing out this vital stage in his recent life. She'd heard him. She'd heard him say to a neighbour, newly back from Australia, when asked what he'd been doing with himself the last year, what had been happening. 'Oh nothing much, exams mostly, and working at the boat yard, boring really.' He'd smiled, been amused at the ease of the glossing over, and afterwards he had warned her not to dare enlighten these people.

It was why Sam was in a sense right and Joe needed to get away, to start a new life where no one knew anything about him. Staying here might give him security, among those who loved and protected him, but it was a false security and also a hollow one: he hadn't been protected.

Sam would've sent him off to Canada, to his brother in Toronto, that very first summer, as soon as he was physically recovered, but she'd said he wasn't up to it, he was too fragile altogether, he'd never cope with the journey and his cousins and having to pretend he was fine. Anyway, he hadn't wanted to go. 'How can I?' he'd asked, appalled, and that was that. He thought he carried a mark as visible as Cain's upon him.

She'd like him to invite a few friends for a meal, a barbecue if he wanted, though she hated barbecues, anything, so long as there was something. 'Which friends?' he'd asked. 'There's no one I like enough.' Timidly, she'd mentioned a few names, especially the names of two girls in his class who occasionally rang up. 'No,' he said, 'we're not really friends, it's all their idea, they just feel sorry for me. Anyway, Mum, nobody does anything on their seventeenth, none of the boys, it's only the girls.' So she tried for a family lunch, in the garden, maybe Ginny and his cousins . . . He groaned. Finally, they compromised: a Sunday lunch on his birthday but not *for* his birthday. And he wasn't going to stay in the whole afternoon, only for the meal itself, it was all he could stand.

Still, it pleased her, especially now, when things were difficult again.

★

When Sheila arrived on the next visit she was asked by the prison officer who checked her pass to go to the Deputy Governor's office. She felt only resignation. Leo might be refusing to see her now, not just Alan. Slowly, she followed the prison officer down the corridor, wondering what she should say. What were her rights? She didn't know. Even if she could insist on having Leo frog-marched into facing her, what would be the point, if he didn't want to see her? She felt tired, drained. All this worrying about him, for nothing. No real response.

The Deputy Governor was friendly. She had always liked him better than the policeman. He was older, less pompous, she felt easier with him. He asked her to sit down and offered her tea, which she took, apologising for the thick, white mug it was in. He had some papers spread out in front of him. They'd be about Leo.

'Now then, Mrs Armstrong,' he said, 'we've got a problem here with your lad.' She said nothing. What a waste to state the obvious. 'He's a good lad,' the man went on, 'no trouble, works hard, but he's taken a vow of silence somewhere along the road which makes things a bit tough, for himself too. He'll reply in monosyllables when he absolutely has to, but otherwise not a peep.' He waited, as though expecting her to say something, but she had no comment to make. 'You'll have heard about Gary Robinson being identified?' She nodded. 'Well, seems there may be a chance, a more than reasonable chance, that your lad wasn't more than a spectator.'

'Bad enough,' she said.

'Oh yes, bad enough, but not bad enough for the length of the sentence, that's the point. If Leo would tell us he was as intimidated as the victim . . .'

'He was drugged,' she said, 'he'd been taking LSD, he was out of his head.'

'I know that, but how did it happen? We don't know what he did and didn't do, so it was assumed he did the lot. Not fair, was it?'

'It was his own fault.'

'True, but it still doesn't make it fair.'

'Is that what you wanted to see me about, then?' She knew she sounded hard, truculent, but she was sick of this, she wanted to be done with it and either to be seeing Leo or on her way home. It was becoming too much, these ordeals. She couldn't stand another question.

'Partly. But there's another thing. Leo's soon to be released. I thought maybe I should remind you.'

'It isn't reminding,' Sheila flashed. 'I never knew. I wasn't given any release date. I've tried not to think about it.'

'He doesn't have to come to you, you know, there's . . .'

'Of course he does!' She felt her face redden. 'We're his family, he hasn't got any other.'

'It might be a bit much for you.'

'Yes, it will, but there's no use dodging that. It's always been a bit much but it's too late to think about that, he's my responsibility for a while yet.'

'He doesn't want to go home.'

She stared at him, at last surprised. He looked embarrassed, shuffled his papers around. She felt a combination of distress and anger rising within her and didn't know which was the stronger until she heard herself speak. 'Don't talk silly,' she almost shouted. 'Of course he wants to come home!'

'He's adamant he doesn't.'

'That's shame talking, that's all shame at last. He thinks he can't face us. He's nowhere else to go, nowhere, what would he do? He'd get into even worse habits, he'd have no stability, it would be the end of him . . .'

'Or the beginning. Maybe he knows best, eh?'

'He's only seventeen, he doesn't know best about anything, they never do at that age.'

'It isn't that young, seventeen,' the Deputy Governor said, thoughtfully, 'and he's mature for his years.'

'Not so mature he doesn't do daft things like take drugs.'

'Lots of adolescents experiment with drugs, Mrs Armstrong.'

'Yes, and look where it lands them.'

'My point is, he wasn't a drug addict. That was the trouble, his system couldn't take it, and he'd been drinking, and he didn't know that . . .'

'He knew he was taking a drug.'

She could see the man eyeing her warily. She knew he thought she was unforgiving, a cold woman full of self-righteous venom. He'd be thinking that if he was Leo he wouldn't want to go back to this grandmother either. He'd run a mile. It was her father coming out in her, Eric James arising unchecked. And he must be checked, this was no good. 'We can get over this,' she said, striving for a reasonable tone, though her voice shook. 'We can forget the drugs, everything. I didn't mean to sound as if I were holding it against him for ever. He's everything to me, Leo is. I'd love him to death whatever he did.' She swallowed hard. She hated talking like this, spilling out such intimate words to a stranger, hated mentioning love. 'He's just ashamed,' she repeated, 'and it's his way of showing it, not wanting to come home. We've never been able to talk about when he comes out, that's the trouble, never. It was too much, for both of us. I've never been alone with him since he was arrested, never. There's never been a chance.'

The Deputy Governor sighed. 'Well, I don't know,' he said. 'You've all my sympathy, Mrs Armstrong.'

'Can I see him?' she said.

'He doesn't want any visitors.'

'But I'm his mother – his grandmother.'

'We can't force him.'

The humiliation was utterly weakening. She didn't seem able to move or speak. She felt like a jelly, wobbling all over the place as she tried to stand. He came round his desk to help her. 'Have another cup of tea,' he urged, but she shook her head. Sooner she was home the better, if she wasn't going to see Leo. He asked if anyone was waiting for her and she lied and said yes, her husband, in the car. He took her to the door and would have come with her all the way out, but a prison officer came along, wanting his attention. She stood waiting for ages for the first bus. There was still half an hour to go. There was nowhere to sit. It was hot and the bus stop was full in the sun. She thought she ought to put the time in by walking around, but she hadn't the energy and her vision seemed blurred. It was such a relief to get on the empty bus the moment it arrived.

She didn't know what she was going to tell Alan. Or her father. The thought of Leo rejecting all of them, choosing to go his own way and never, ever come home . . . What was the matter with them that they had earned this? What had they done? What had *she* done, or not done? It hurt more than the discovery that Leo had taken part in all that violence, more than the pain of discovering he had had, must have had, some kind of secret life. She'd thought she'd known him through and through and she hadn't. The bond she'd thought so impossible to sever had broken at the first sign of strain. He was now strange to her – not a stranger, never that, but strange *to* her. And if he never came home he always would be. No answers, ever. No chance to understand. No opportunity to show her love and devotion could rise to the need, his need.

The anger had gone, anyway. She noticed that. Sitting on the second bus in particular, she noticed that. No anger. Distress had won hands down. And panic, she felt panic-stricken. The irony did not escape her – there she'd been, dreading him coming out, and all the time he'd no intention of coming to her. Now the dread was far greater and of a different kind. She might have dreaded the struggle to rehabilitate Leo once he was home, the struggle both to recover him, regain his trust, find the way back to him, and to help him face the future, but she was good at struggles, they brought out the best in her. Those sort of struggles, at least. But if he cut himself off, would not come home or speak to her, there would only be loss and bewilderment to cope with. She didn't think she could bear it.

Chapter Eleven

H ARRIET SAT IN THE waiting-room reflecting how little, as a family, they had had to do with doctors. Their notes must be wafer-thin. She saw people being handed such bulky packages by the receptionist before they went in to the doctor and marvelled at all the things that the size of these records would indicate had been wrong with them. Sam had been a few times with his back, strained playing tennis, Louis not at all, except for injections, given by the nurse; Joe only twice, once when he was four and broke his arm and, of course, after the attack, several times. Under duress, though, his dislike and suspicion of doctors almost matching his hatred of the police. Strange, really. When all the doctors had done was patch him up and heal him. This doctor, Dr Fenwick, had made a fatal mistake when he came to the house the day Joe was discharged from hospital. 'I think,' he had said, all jovial, 'your mother is in a worse state than you.'

Joe was contemptuous. 'How can he say that? How could you be in a worse state?' She'd agreed with him quickly. It was tactless of Dr Fenwick, though she understood very well why he'd said what he'd said. Any mention of him afterwards was always made by Joe with disdain – 'that stupid doctor'. Getting him to go to the surgery was a lengthy process, a huge fuss. It was lucky that the practice had a nurse whom Joe at least did not despise. Harriet preferred Jennifer herself. Jennifer did all the minor injuries, the taking out of stitches, the vaccinations and injections. She was gentle and cheerful and, however pressed, always seemed to have time. She was good with Joe, understood his embarrassment and, of course, knew all about what had happened. Harriet was glad not to have to see any of the doctors today, to have just Jennifer attending to her, Jennifer doing the routine but always unpleasant smear test and breast examination.

Jennifer was so clever at talking while she was putting on the thin rubber gloves and cutting open sterile packets, it all seemed so friendly and unthreatening, even the moment when she said to open your legs and spread your knees sideways, and her fingers were slow and careful as she slid the instrument in, whatever it was. She took the smear without giving the slightest pain. It wasn't even particularly uncomfortable. And then she made you feel you'd been so brave when no bravery had been called for. While she was popping the slide into a packet to send to the hospital lab, she asked about Joe. Harriet told her about the arrest of Gary Robinson and how difficult things were with another trial looming just as Joe had seemed to be coping better. 'When he gets off to college,' Jennifer said soothingly, 'that will help, I'm sure, with the trial over and the whole awful business . . .' She was stopped by the door of her little surgery crashing open and the receptionist rushing in holding a baby who seemed to be literally spouting blood, with blood arcing over the woman's shoulder, and behind, screaming, both hands held to her face, a young woman already herself covered in blood running in great dark crimson streaks down her pale blue dress. Harriet froze, shrank back into a corner as Jennifer took the baby and shouted out commands to the receptionist who ran from the room. Harriet couldn't see what was being done. She knew she should get out of the way, and began edging towards the door, still open. The mother of the baby was crouched near it, sobbing. She would have to pass her. Dr Fenwick rushed into the room, almost tripping over the mother and saying, 'Get her out of here, for God's sake, someone.'

Harriet put her arm round the young woman and murmured things in her ear, pointless things, untrue things, such as, 'Everything is going to be all right,' and, 'Don't worry,' and tried to lift her up. She was only a girl, slight, easy to manoeuvre. Her hands were still over the face from which the sobbing came, the awful tearing, hiccuping sobs. She let Harriet pull her upright and lead her away into the reception area where waiting patients sat transfixed. The receptionist who'd crashed into Jennifer's surgery was shouting down the telephone, her hand sticky with blood, the white receiver smeared with it. Harriet steered the girl in her arms towards the little cubby-hole where she knew the receptionist made tea and managed to lower her into the one chair and then to boil a kettle. She heard the siren of an ambulance. 'There,' she said, 'there's the ambulance arriving. I'm sure everything will be all right, try and drink this, just a sip, it will help . . .'

Afterwards, walking home, she couldn't believe she'd said any of this. So banal, so trite. She ought to have known better, she did know better, of course she did, she of all people. To tell that poor, hysterical young mother that everything would be all right! To tell her not to worry! To tell her she'd feel better if she had some tea! All things said to her, a year ago, said and found at worst so offensive she couldn't bear to hear them and at best so useless they might as well have been in a foreign language. She hadn't realised how shocking other people's intense distress can be. She didn't know this girl and yet she'd been so shaken by the drama, so horrified by the blood, so upset by the screaming . . . As others had been. Those, especially, who saw Joe first. Michael, she hadn't ever taken into consideration Michael's feelings, seeing his

nephew lying there, naked, bleeding, unconscious, filthy
. . . All she'd done was hate Michael for seeing him, and
the policemen who arrived on the scene with the
ambulance men. She remembered all of them, the young
policeman, the two ambulance crew, going to the trouble
of seeking her out in the hospital and expressing their
sympathy. She'd thanked them and cut them off.

She didn't know what was wrong with the baby. The
other receptionist had come in and taken the young
mother to the hospital. Everyone had been too distraught
and busy to offer explanations. Harriet thought how she'd
never realised that minor characters, people on the fringe
in these kinds of scenes, could experience such turmoil.
She felt sick and weak as she opened her front door and
was never so glad in her life to get into her kitchen and
fiddle about making coffee. She saw her hands were
shaking. She'd heard someone in the doctor's waiting-
room say, 'It was just a freak thing . . .' What was a freak
thing? What were they talking about? What had happened
to that baby to cause such blood? It was dreadful not to
know, she would have to ring the receptionist later,
tomorrow . . .

Joe came in, hanging about, watching her. She felt
irritated that he couldn't see her hands were shaking as she
measured the coffee. Why didn't he take charge? Why
didn't he put his arm round her and make her sit down and
ask her what had happened? If he hadn't noticed the state she
was in, she wasn't going to point it out, he ought to see.
She made the coffee without speaking. She ignored him,
took her coffee into the garden and sat on the bench beside
the south wall. She closed her eyes, tilting her face to the
sun, taking deliberately exaggerated breaths. She hoped to
hear Joe coming in search of her, but he didn't. She opened
her eyes and looked for him. He'd stayed in the house.
Well, perhaps she'd dissembled better than she suspected.

Perhaps she'd appeared perfectly normal, the shaking of her hands imperceptible. Perhaps.

Yet two hours later, when Sam came home, and they were all eating, Sam said, 'You're very pale, do you feel all right?'

Joe went on stuffing bread into his mouth and toying with the fish.

'No,' she said, watching Joe all the time, 'no, I don't feel all right. I feel terrible.' Not a flicker from Joe, instant concern from Sam. 'I had such a shock,' she said, and she described the incident at the doctor's surgery, finishing with, '. . . the poor mother was terrified, she was in a terrible state. I felt so sorry for her.'

She saw Joe smile, very slightly.

'Is that funny, Joe?' she asked, trying to keep her voice light.

'Course it isn't funny,' he said. 'I wasn't laughing.'

'You smirked,' she said.

He shrugged.

'Why?' she persisted.

'I don't know,' he said, 'that's if I did. I didn't know I did.'

She let it go, but when they were getting ready for bed she said to Sam, 'He *did* smirk, didn't he?'

'I don't know, I was watching you.'

'He did. Was I being pompous or something?'

'No, of course not.'

'I wonder why then. Maybe he thought I was glorying in it, enjoying the telling . . .'

Sam didn't reply. They both remembered too well the time Joe had heard his aunt, Ginny, describing what had happened to him. He'd caught her on the telephone relaying the horror of it with what he claimed was gusto. Nothing would convince him otherwise.

'Sometimes,' she said, 'I don't like Joe. It's horrible.'

'Sometimes I don't like him myself,' Sam said. 'He can be quite cruel.'

'It isn't that. It's feeling he doesn't care about anyone. Not any more. It's as if he thinks he's the only one who can ever suffer, or something. What's going to happen to him, if he's like that?'

'He'll change,' Sam said and, as ever, attempted a joke. 'The love of a good woman will change him, sooner or later.'

But Harriet took him seriously. 'But how could any woman love him when he's like this? When even I, his own mother, feel repelled?'

That night she didn't sleep at all. Babies, blood, Joe's smirk, all ran before her endlessly.

★

Sheila took her father's lunch round at twelve. He liked it at twelve-thirty precisely. He was standing scraping new potatoes at the sink.

'I'll do that,' she said, putting her bag down.

'Have to put m'time in somehow,' he said, without turning round. She thought there was something dejected in the set of his shoulders and paused before she said, 'Haven't you been out this morning, then?'

'No. Didn't feel like it. Got the meat?'

'Yes,' she said. Fillet steak, not that she told him what it was, just said it was a scrap of frying steak. She took the meat out of her bag and sliced it thinly and then went to the cupboard for the pan. He had to move to let her get into it. 'Oh,' she said, 'oh dear, what happened?'

His face, the whole left side, was black and blue. There were small cuts around his mouth and the lens of his spectacles, the left lens, was cracked. 'Fell over,' he mumbled. 'Damned silly.'

'When?'

'Yesterday. Getting m'pension. Just turned round outside the post office and I don't know what happened, flat on m'face, it felt like.'

'How did you get home?'

'Got m'self home, no bother. But I feel it now, that's the funny part.'

'Where, apart from your face?'

'Knees, elbows. The ribs, a bit. I'll manage.'

They ate in silence. He was eating well enough, anyway. Eight potatoes, the meat and half a cauliflower boiled to extinction, the way he liked it, plain and unadulterated by any muck such as cheese sauce. He wolfed it, in fact. Great greedy, messy mouthfuls. She'd always hated how he ate, without care, strings of fat hanging out of his mouth, gravy dribbling down his chin, taking slurps of tea all the time. His fourth fall, or was it his fifth, this year? He wasn't safe any more, but it was too sad to try to curtail his independence. Sad and impossible. Peter, Carole's husband, said he should be in a home. He was too much of a worry in his own house. She and Carole had turned on Peter. But of course he was right. One day soon he'd fall and break something, and then short of Carole or her moving in they'd have to find him a place. He knew all this. She could see he knew it. It was churning around in his head, depressing him.

They sat outside after their meal, on the stout garden seat they'd given him for his eightieth birthday. She'd made padded cushions for it. It was very comfortable. They sat and he pointed out the bees going in and out of a hole in the concrete path. She asked to see his knees and he pulled up his trouser legs and showed her. Both knees, the skin lard-white, were swollen and puffy but maybe that was his arthritis. The bruises on them were much worse than on his face, and she dreaded to think what they'd be like on his ribs. But he wouldn't undo his cardigan or unbutton his shirt to show her those. He insisted they were nothing. So she sat and watched the bees and wondered if his ribs might be cracked, whether she should risk his wrath and get the doctor to call. Not yet, give it a day or two. But the spectacles would have to be taken in and . . .

'How's the lad?' he asked. He never enquired after Leo, had said he never wanted to hear his name mentioned in his presence again. She didn't know what to say, didn't know how he'd react if she told the truth.

'He's fine,' she said.

'Doing his time well, is he?'

'Yes.'

'That's one thing, then. Not getting into more trouble, meking *your* life hell.'

'He hasn't made my life hell.'

'Yes, he has. Don't tell me that. I've got eyes. And it isn't as if you're his mother.'

'Dad, I don't want to hear . . .'

'There's a lot yer don't want to hear, that's your trouble, always has been.'

She was so annoyed she kept quiet and reminded herself that he wasn't well. She must humour him. If she didn't react he wouldn't get worked up, it was simple as that.

'I had an uncle,' he said, and stopped.

'You had seven uncles,' she said, relieved. 'Three on your father's side, now who were they, William, James and . . .'

'John. John. And four on my mam's, Matthew, Peter, Joseph and Luke. Luke was the bad 'un. Big fella, like a blacksmith he was. Won the wrestling at Grasmere twice. Killed a girl when he was young. They said it were an accident, he got off, scot-free, but nobody ever believed him, niver. Got another in the family way after that, wouldn't marry her. A bad 'un. Broke his mother's heart.

Used to annoy the others that much how she cared about that Luke. They were glad when he died.'

'How did he die?'

'Blood poisoning. Stuck a fork with manure on it into his foot. Thought nowt of it. Washed it, like, did all that, and thought nowt of it, but it went bad.'

'Septicaemia,' she said.

'Aye, that'll be it. A bad 'un.'

She refused to ask what all this was leading up to. Was he comparing Leo to his bad Great-uncle Luke? Was he wanting her to leave a pitchfork with manure on it lying around for Leo to step on? But still he hadn't finished, she could tell. The bees went in and out of the tiny hole and they both stared and went on sitting there.

'Yer sometimes get a bad apple,' he said. 'Nowt can be done about it. My mam wouldn't have it, though. Said he wasn't born bad, he wasn't brought up bad, she couldn't account for it except by blaming bad luck. Bad luck. My dad told her you mek yer own luck in this life, but she wouldn't agree. She were a religious woman, she wouldn't agree.'

'Neither do I,' Sheila said.

'Well, you should. Bad luck, that's all. Plenty of it. I've known plenty of it in my time and so have you. But you can't blame luck for everything, good or bad. Look at you, eh? After your Pat, how you got on with it. Didn't give in.'

She was lost. If he wasn't going to sort out this rambling of his for her, she couldn't do it herself.

'It's up to him,' he was saying. 'I've been turning it over and over and it's up to him. Not you. It isn't up to you. That's what yer've got to remember. He's old enough. You leave him to hisself, that's my advice. Meking yerself ill. Daft.'

When she left him, Sheila felt touched, not by his

213

'advice' but at his 'turning it over and over'. She could picture him, lying in that dreadful sagging bed he wouldn't part with – 'it'll see me out' – his bruises hurting him, thinking of her and going over and over the Leo problem. He'd have had a whisky to help him sleep and a hot-water bottle to soothe the pain in his ribs, even though it was a warm night. Then he'd lain there and thought about his Uncle Luke and decided Leo was a bad 'un too, a bad 'un who should be abandoned. If only he knew. She'd been tempted to tell him there and then that Leo was doing the abandoning, but she didn't have the energy to cope with his reaction. She couldn't quite imagine what that would be, but there would be rage of some sort and she couldn't face it, whoever it was directed against. It was odd, she thought, returning home, that Leo still never mentioned his great-grandfather. He was nearly ninety, after all. You'd have thought Leo could afford to ask how he was.

She hadn't told Alan yet about Leo refusing to come back to them, to his own home. What she couldn't bear was Alan's relief. It would be so obvious, it would hurt. She wanted him on her side, supporting her, and he wasn't going to be. Who would be?

*

Joe behaved better than she dared to hope, mainly because he was so thrilled with the driving lessons, all planned to start the next day. He smiled, really smiled, not one of those tight little half-smiles, but a big beam and a blush and a cry of, 'Oh, terrific, thanks!' His pleasure lasted all day, right through the family lunch party in the garden, right through his Uncle Michael saying how much better he looked, right through his cousin Natasha saying resentfully – she hadn't been given driving lessons a year ago when she was seventeen – 'Joe's always lucky.' He even put on a shirt, a proper shirt, and a pair of black cotton trousers she'd always liked him in. Harriet had to stop herself several times from saying to him, 'Look, how easy it is, being happy.' Once you started. Once you got your face used to it. Easy. Catching.

The difficult one was Laura, Ginny's younger girl. She was sullen, sitting there neither smiling nor speaking and refusing almost everything she was offered. Harriet felt the tension in Ginny, saw her sister endlessly biting her lip, screwing up her mouth in agitation. Laura was fifteen. She'd lost a lot of weight recently and for a diabetic it was dangerous. Ginny said she'd started being silly about the rigorous timetable of meals and snacks she was supposed to keep to, dangerously silly. She was no longer willing for her mother to monitor every little thing she ate and drank, she got irritable, said she didn't care. She was giving herself the daily insulin injections now and Ginny didn't trust her to remember. And she wasn't attractive any more. The Lycra shorts which clung to her pathetically thin legs were the very worst thing for her to wear. Incongruously, in view of these shorts and a shapeless black T-shirt, she had a pink satin ribbon in her hair, tied in a bow on top of her head. Perched above the scowling, unhappy face and black clothes it looked ridiculous; a piece of self-mockery, surely.

Natasha was the centre of attention, not Joe. Harriet realised what a coquette this niece had grown into. She flirted with her Uncle Sam and flirted with Joe. She pouted when told Louis had gone – 'Louis's gorgeous,' she said, 'it's not fair' – and they all laughed. She wasn't exactly pretty, Harriet thought, but had sex-appeal, undeniably. A way with her, as they said around here. She sat next to Joe, placed one beautifully manicured hand, nails varnished dark crimson, on his arm every time she wanted his attention, and she wanted it often. 'Will you drive me,

Joe, when you've passed your test? Will you run me to Manchester and back?' Joe looked embarrassed, squirmed, but still smiled and said he supposed so, if he was allowed the car. Sam said he wouldn't be having his car, no chance. 'Your mum will let you have hers, won't you, Harriet?' said Natasha. 'I know you will.' 'I might,' Harriet agreed, 'when I've seen how well he can drive, but I don't know about Manchester. Carlisle, maybe.' Natasha and Joe and even Laura all gave a cry of disgust – not Carlisle, what was the point of Carlisle, no clubs in Carlisle, no night life, nothing at all at night in Carlisle . . . who would want to go there for excitement?

There was a slight atmosphere then, but Joe rode the passing tension. He asked Natasha about Manchester, where she was going to university in the autumn. She said he should come and visit her, car or no car, she could put him up for the night and they could do the clubs. Joe, who had never been in a club in his life, nor ever, so far as Harriet knew, wanted to be, expressed interest. She was amazed to hear him say he wanted to get into Manchester University himself, it was going to be his first choice, then Liverpool, then Newcastle; he didn't want to go south, like Louis, he didn't fancy London . . . Sam exchanged looks with her, they both raised their eyebrows at each other. How encouraging, how reassuring to hear Joe make future plans. Good. They prayed for Natasha to continue the good work, and she did. She asked about the holidays. Joe said he was just going to work in the boat yard, he wasn't going anywhere, Mum and Dad were going to Edinburgh in August, though . . . Natasha said, 'Ooh, so you'll be on your own?' Joe said yes, till Louis was back. 'We could have a party here,' Natasha said, smiling dazzlingly at Harriet. 'Joe doesn't like parties,' Harriet said. Joe looked cross for the first time that day, and she added hastily, 'Not usually, anyway.' 'Ah,' said Natasha, looking at Joe through narrowed eyes, stroking his arm, 'it depends on the party, doesn't it, Joe?'

What had Sam said? The love of a good woman could change Joe. Natasha was not going to be a good woman. She was not going to be a bad one, but virtue was not something that shone out of her. Seduction did. And Joe was so vulnerable. Suppose some Natasha type fixed on him, now, when he was so fragile, and made him hers, and then chucked him . . . Harriet got up abruptly, shocked at herself, and went in to get more pudding. Ginny followed. The two sisters hung about the kitchen for a minute, getting ice-cream out of the freezer, washing a few spoons. There was loud laughter from outside. They smiled at each other, tentatively, a little nervously, each preoccupied with thoughts of the other's child, the other's problems. It was cool in the kitchen, a little dark after the brilliant light outside. 'She's sleeping with that Richards boy,' Ginny whispered, 'quite brazen about it. It's awful.' 'Why?' said Harriet. 'She's eighteen, it's normal. You sound like our mother did, back in the stone age . . . remember when . . .' 'No,' said Ginny, 'he's not the first, it's different, she's not in love with them or anything. Some only last three weeks. I can't stand it.' 'Oh, Ginny,' Harriet said, 'don't worry, she'll sort herself out, it's only a phase, she's clever and ambitious, she's in control, it's nothing.' Ginny groaned, then tried to laugh. 'Oh God,' she said, 'if it isn't Natasha and sex it's Laura trying to wreck herself. I can't *imagine* life without the worry.'

Life without the worry. Long after Ginny and her family had gone, Harriet found herself turning the phrase over. Ginny worried even more than she did. About so little. But was one daughter with an alleged voracious sexual appetite and another with mild (as yet) diabetes so little worry? She'd become arrogant, she could see. No one's troubles could be as big as hers. She remembered what she had started to say to Sheila Armstrong about choices. If she were given a choice, if someone had said, Choose: Joe can be attacked and injured (but not seriously) *or* he can have diabetes, which would she have chosen? Dear God, it was obscene, but she went on debating with herself. Diabetes, any other disease like that, was for life. So she'd choose the attack, of course. But the attack was for life too, its aftermath always there, its effect so deep-rooted, it amounted also to a disease . . . Why stop at diabetes, why not push it further – choose, choose . . . a deformity, Joe born with a deformity, or something horrific, spina bifida . . . choose, choose – oh, the attack, every time . . .

Joe would be so angry with her, playing these mind games, these *dirty* little games. It was a version of the glad game, she recognised it, that game played in the children's book she had loved. *Pollyanna*. Pollyanna, faced with some tragedy, small or large, was always playing the glad game, glad to find something to be glad about, whatever happened. It was sickening to Joe, that game. He was outraged at the idea of playing it, assured her that *never* did he think of himself as on a par with those to whom real disasters happened. Today, his birthday, watching him, it was as though he had convinced himself at last, that it was over, he had made the leap from the past, he was going to leave it behind.

But she wondered why she felt so uneasy.

*

Sheila knew she shouldn't go to the Kennedys' house. It was wrong. It was also difficult, nearly as difficult as visiting Leo, if not as far to travel. A train, two buses, the familiar story for anyone relying on public transport. She tried to think of it as just an outing for herself. Why shouldn't she go on an outing? There was no reason why not, absolutely no reason. Good gracious, for a woman who'd been alone to Africa it was nothing, nothing. It only took an hour and a half. She was lucky with the train, lucky with the buses, but maybe she wouldn't be on the way back. She had a cup of tea in a café when she got off the second bus and bought a street map at a newsagent's. She'd walk the rest of the way. It looked a pleasant walk, part of it with the lake in view.

I could commit a crime, she thought, and then laughed out loud at the absurdity of such a thought popping into her head. It was because she felt her very ordinariness so acutely, walking along in her nondescript clothes, an elderly woman, so harmless and respectable, so unnoticeable. I could have a gun in my bag instead of a purse and a comb and a map, and a handkerchief and my key. Nobody would guess, they'd never think of it. I could go up to someone and ask them the time and pull the gun out and shoot them. How extraordinary to be thinking along these lines on a summer afternoon in such a pleasant place. But then, she supposed her actual mission was ridiculous too. Completely. Aged nearly seventy, and going to hang about outside someone's house just to gawp. As if it made any difference what the Kennedys' house was like. She could almost guess what kind of house it would be and in what kind of street. Detached, probably, or at least appearing to be detached, the sort that you couldn't exactly see at first was halved. A garden all round, lawns, shrubs, that sort of thing. Maybe a double garage. An old, imposing house.

She was surprised to find it was a new house, and checked the address twice. And much more modest than she had envisaged. He, the father, was an architect, wasn't he? And weren't all architects well off? She'd just made the assumption, all the professional classes were well off. The garden must be at the back, there was only a strip of grass at the front. A neat house, blinds at the windows, she saw, not curtains. She wondered if it was a Scandinavian sort of house, maybe wooden floors inside, stark-looking, not the sort she'd ever fancied, except they must be easy to clean, no clutter. She didn't stop and look, she just walked quietly, fairly slowly, but not too obviously slowly, past it. Then at the end of the road, a very pleasant tree-lined road, she turned and walked back again, on the other side. She did this twice, and then sat on a bench beside a bus stop. She wasn't, of course, going to go and ring the bell. She'd never thought she would, not really. She wasn't bold enough, she didn't have an excuse. Harriet Kennedy's friendship was a delusion. She knew that, she wasn't silly, their second meeting had exposed that. A temporary thing, an acquaintance made under special circumstances.

When the car stopped she paid no attention to it. 'Mrs Armstrong? Sheila?' a voice said, and then she looked and saw Harriet leaning out of the car window. She was too old to blush, but she felt hot all over. She didn't get up, just smiled and nodded, as though she were perfectly used to sitting on this bench in this strange road. 'Are you waiting for the bus? Can I give you a lift?' Sheila shook her head. 'No, thank you, I'm fine.' She saw Harriet hesitate, and then give a little wave and drive on. She didn't turn to follow the car, just sat looking straight ahead and praying for the bus to come.

Harriet parked the car and sat there a minute. Obviously, Sheila had come here deliberately. Had she been to the house? Had she rung the bell? There was no other possible explanation for her sitting on that bench. So why hadn't she spoken, given a cry of recognition, been relieved to see her? Harriet had only noticed her because she looked so forlorn, in the middle of that uncomfortable bench with no back to it, a bench so hard, the wood splintered, that nobody ever did sit on it. She'd changed her mind, whatever she'd come for. Harriet went into the house and hesitated. She didn't want to embarrass Sheila. People should be allowed to change their minds, think better of their perhaps foolish impulses. She didn't want to ask Sheila into her home either. That was all done with, finished. She had absolutely no obligation to Sheila Armstrong. None. The reverse. But it was because of that, the sheer lack of any commitment, that she opened the door again and walked down her own road to the bench where Sheila still sat.

'Come and have a cup of tea,' she said, 'there won't be a bus for half an hour, honestly, the service is terrible.'

Sheila was clutching her bag as though it contained something precious. 'Really,' she said, 'it's very kind, but really no, thank you, no, I'd rather not.'

Harriet didn't know what to do. She couldn't force Sheila to come. 'Were you visiting someone?' she asked.

'No,' Sheila said, 'I was just on an outing. For pleasure.'

'Oh. On your own?'

'Yes.'

'Do you have outings often? How nice. My mother used to go off on her own sometimes, but I don't think she ever really felt comfortable, she always felt sort of conspicuous. Of course, she couldn't drive, driving makes it easier, going off on your own.'

Sheila said nothing.

'Please,' said Harriet, putting her hand out and touching Sheila's arm. '*Please* come and have a cup of tea.'

They sat at the back, on the terrace. 'Lovely garden,' Sheila said, 'lovely view.' She was over the awkwardness now, she was enjoying this.

'It was built for the view,' Harriet said, 'the house isn't much but the view makes up for it. It's hard to get everything right, isn't it? You have to settle for one or the other.' She remembered Sheila's drab terraced house, with no garden, no view. It suddenly struck her that it was silly to evade the issue with trite observations about houses. 'You seem different,' she ventured, then tailed off. Really, how *she'd* screamed at people who'd asked if she 'wanted to talk about it'.

Carefully, Sheila put her tea-cup down. Pretty cups, delicate, rose-buds on a white background, old-fashioned. 'It's Leo,' she said, 'he won't come home when they let him out. He doesn't want us. He wants to go to some hostel or something.' She picked her tea-cup up again and drank.

'How awful,' Harriet said, almost whispered, and then repeated 'awful' again. 'Maybe,' she went on after a long pause, 'maybe it's consideration for you, not wanting . . . you know . . . not wanting to put you through any more, feeling he should keep away . . .'

'Maybe. I expect so. Anyway, that's it. He doesn't want to come to us. We might never see him again.'

There was nothing Harriet could think of to say. Sheila's pain was so evident in her dejected expression, the tired face, the drooping shoulders. Other women, Harriet thought, might be relieved, they might have dreaded . . .

'Of course, it's a judgement,' Sheila was saying. 'I was dreading him coming home. I wanted him to, but I was dreading it. What I wanted was Leo as he used to be, when he was my boy. Not what he'd turned into. But I would never have closed the door to him, never. He surely knew that. My father would've done. He would now. He'll be pleased when I tell him.'

'You never found out, really, did you, what exactly . . .?'

'No, never. I thought it made no difference but maybe it did. He's not saying.' She sighed heavily. 'Here I am, troubling you again. It isn't right.'

'You're not troubling me. I brought you in, remember? I wanted you to come home with me.' Harriet paused. Whatever they said to each other always seemed full of pauses, so haltingly they spoke, long, long, consideration given to the shortest sentences. 'Things are better here,' she said, 'at last, they really do seem better.'

'Is it that other one, being caught?'

'No. No, I don't think so. That made it worse for a while. It isn't that, being over, and it isn't over yet, with the trial coming. Gary Robinson is twenty-two, he'll be named. It might be a Crown Court case. I don't know if Joe will have to go through it, but I expect so. No, it isn't over, it isn't that. It's more Joe looking to the future again. He hasn't, not for all this year. He didn't seem to believe in it, everything was the past. And for me too, I couldn't believe in any future for him, and . . .'

'I can't for Leo. That's it. He hasn't got a future, that I can see. He's finished, finished. You wouldn't believe what a good boy he was. But if I'd to start all over again I wouldn't know how to do any different, that's the point.'

I'm making noises, Harriet thought, clucking noises, I'm just making noises because there isn't anything to say. She shouldn't have allowed this to happen, it did her no good and it did Sheila no good. However hard they tried there was an immense gulf between them which was impossible to bridge. Nothing to do with one being the mother of the victim, one of the attacker; one elderly, one middle-aged; one poor, one prosperous. It was to do with suffering, the different nature of their respective suffering. This woman's was deepening, her own was lifting, and as it lifted she was already losing the language, distancing herself from such unhappiness, fearing to be dragged down once more. It was hopeless.

When Joe shouted, 'Hi! I'm home,' she was terrified.

Chapter Twelve

THERE WAS REALLY no need to have felt embarrassed, Harriet reflected. No need. Yet it was embarrassment which had threatened to overwhelm her and it was Sheila Armstrong who saw it, not Joe, and dealt with it, quickly, adroitly. 'I really must go,' she said, as soon as she heard Joe's voice, and then, when he could also clearly be heard running upstairs, shouting that he was getting his swimming things and going out again, she was out of the house in a flash, leaving Harriet scarlet-faced and dumb with shame. Because, of course, she wanted Sheila out of the house. She didn't want to have to explain to Joe who this strange woman was. She didn't want to persuade Sheila to stay.

She would be walking all that way to the bus station. There was no bus due, now she'd missed yet another. In this heat, in her rather heavy clothes. And she'd know, anyone would, that she'd guessed correctly, Harriet had wanted to get rid of her. What would have happened if she'd stayed, Harriet wondered. Another woman might have done so, out of curiosity, out of insensitivity. Another woman might have stayed and expected to be introduced, as a friend, if nothing else. Few teenage boys would enquire where their mother's friends came from. They weren't interested. She could just have said Sheila was collecting for the church bazaar, Joe would never have known, he wouldn't have cared. But she herself through her agitation would have given herself away. That was the only thing that would have alerted him, made him probe.

As it was, he did probe, just a little. She kept her face averted when he came into the kitchen before going off again, but she had to reply to his request as to what time supper would be. Even the simple, 'About half past seven, Dad's playing golf first, straight from work,' came out muffled, slightly indistinct in her anxiety to be natural. 'Got a cold?' he said. 'Mm, think so, starting one maybe,' she muttered gratefully, sniffing for authenticity. 'Don't give it to me,' he said, and was gone. What would he have said if she'd told the truth, told him who'd been having tea with her when he came in? It began to fascinate her. She had three fantasy conversations with him, trying out his reaction. In them, she said the same each time: 'Joe, the grandmother of one of the attackers, Leo Jackson's grandmother, has just been for tea, we've become sort of friends . . .' and he replied differently each time. In the first fantasy he was appalled, asked *who*, asked why the hell she wanted anything to do with that woman, slammed out in a rage; in the second he was contemptuous, sneered at her, asked if it made her feel virtuous, was she enjoying being so kind and good and understanding; and in the third he was simply indifferent, required neither explanation nor apology. Exhausting. It was just pointlessly exhausting. And she'd been so sure she'd grown out of it.

★

Sheila was late home, very late. She hadn't calculated on that hour with Harriet and she hadn't found her way back to the bus station with the same ease she'd found her way from it to the Kennedys' house. When she did get there, she'd missed one bus by two minutes and there was a long wait for the next one. The same pattern was repeated

225

when she changed buses and again at the railway station, always missing a connection by five minutes. She started to feel guilty as she waited for the train. She'd left no note, thinking she'd be home hours before Alan, who was down at the cricket ground helping the groundsman, an old mate of his, with heaven knows what. But he'd be back by now. It was long past his tea-time, and no sign of any tea. He'd be worried. He'd go round to Eric James and ask if he'd seen her, then they'd both be worried. For themselves, she thought grimly, their own welfare. At least it was summer, it wasn't dark. But she'd just decided that she ought to phone all the same when the train came and it was too late, and once she'd got off the train at the other end there was no point.

She anticipated Alan's face as she walked home. Contorted, it would be. She always kept her face as blank as possible, whatever her inner emotion, tutored in the school of Eric James, but Alan had no control over his, it was all over the place at the least thing, like a weather vane it was. He'd be standing at the door, literally standing there, peering out, as though waiting to pay the milkman. Ridiculous. Then, after relief – that exaggerated relief, brow unwrinkling, mouth opening – there would be the inquisition, the where, why, what for . . . And she'd be cool, as she always was in these situations, offhand. It was a sort of game. Leo played it too, though he was even better than she at it and she had never liked it when she was on the receiving end. No. It had cost her a lot to be the one asking where, why and what for. She hated lowering herself. She'd only done it when forced to, in the early hours of the morning, forced to it by Leo's alarmingly late return. Not often, though. He'd only come back so late twice. Alan had actually defended him. Only normal, Alan had said, only normal for a growing lad on a Saturday night. But she felt she had to know all the same,

226

know at least the where of it. She'd been reduced to asking him point-blank and he'd shrugged and said nowhere in particular. She'd echoed him – 'Nowhere in particular at one o'clock on a Sunday morning?' – but when he'd just nodded she'd let it go. She shouldn't have done. That was the start. She should have got it out of him, about Gary Robinson, or whatever was going on . . .

When she turned into her street she was quite surprised to find Alan was not in sight. Good. He would be sulking in the kitchen, pathetically trying to rustle up his own food. She'd told him often enough it wasn't on these days for a man to be so hopeless in the house, but he took no notice. The only time she'd ever been in hospital, for her hysterectomy, when they took those fibroids out, he'd gone to Carole's and to his sister Elsie's turn and turn-about, taking Leo with him. All that trouble just to avoid learning how to make a meal. But he was probably so hungry by now that he'd started scratching around in the bread-bin at least. It was sausage and egg tonight, but he wouldn't see the Cumberland sausage sitting in the fridge, or if he did he wouldn't know what to do with it. She'd take her time. She'd suggest it was too late and too hot after all for sausage. She'd say she wasn't hungry herself, though she hadn't eaten all day, and that she was only going to have a cup of tea and a cream cracker.

The house was empty. The key in the keyhole was enough to have brought Alan running, the merest scratch of a sound, but he didn't come, or shout. It was too early for him to have retaliated by going to bed, but she went upstairs to investigate, prepared to be furious if she found him there. No, no Alan. There was a pad near the telephone downstairs where they kept messages. There was nothing on the pad. Now *she* was going to have to ring her father, the last thing she wanted to do. It was half past nine. Three hours after Alan would normally be home, but then maybe he had been home and gone out again. Impatiently, she rang Eric James, who took ages answering and was bad-tempered, bellowing at her about the lateness of the hour and not even registering who it was for ages. She tried to be circumspect, asked only if Alan had dropped in at all.

'Alan? Alan? Why?' Eric James shouted. 'What would I want him for? Eh? It's Thursday.'

'I know it's Thursday, but I just wondered . . .'

'Why? Eh? What's up?'

'Nothing's up.'

'What yer ringing for then, disturbing me, on a Thursday, at this time? Eh?'

'I'm sorry I've disturbed you . . .'

'So yer should be.'

She wanted so badly to slam the receiver down that she had to physically restrain her right arm by holding it steady with her left. Disturbing him, from what? He'd have been snoozing in front of the telly, that was all. He could be such a pig, she didn't know why she bothered with him. And now he wouldn't let her go, he'd start getting suspicious . . .

'What's up?' he was saying again.

She wasn't going to tell him Alan wasn't there, or that she'd been out for the day. 'Nothing,' she said, 'just Alan said he'd pop in on you on his way to the cricket ground and I wondered if he'd remembered.'

'No, he didn't, and I don't want people spying on me.'

'He wasn't going to be spying . . .'

But at least they were off the topic of where Alan was, of why he wasn't at home. Eric James was in full flood now on the iniquities of those intent on spying on him just because he'd had a fall, and there was nothing wrong with him, he was champion again . . .

Sheila was glad when he hung up on her. The moment he did so, the telephone rang.

There wasn't much mail. Plenty of business stuff for Sam, even though the bulk of it went to his office, but few real letters. Picking up the scattered mail from the hall mat, Harriet saw the postcard from Louis and went into the kitchen, where Sam was still reading the paper over his toast and coffee, flourishing it happily. Louis was having a wonderful time, the work was tiring but easy, and the weather brilliant. On the side of the message he'd scribbled, 'Joe would love it, will put in a good word for him for next year perhaps.' They commented on this, extracted every ounce of pleasure from the puny card, and then she handed Sam the two buff envelopes. He handed one back, saying it was for her. One of those long official-looking, boring envelopes. She noticed, vaguely, that it had a Health Authority stamp on it beside the postage stamp.

When she'd opened it, opened out the one sheet it contained, she stared at it feeling puzzled. On the sheet was a list of printed alternatives: 'The sample was not sufficient to test adequately' was one, and, 'There is no cause for alarm but we advise a repeat smear in three months' was another. But beside these two was a dash. The tick was next to, 'We would like you to telephone your GP at your earliest convenience, though there is no cause for alarm'. She registered the tick not with disbelief but with a sense of irritation. Sam was still buried in his paper, though it was now five minutes past the normal time he left. She said nothing at all. If he doesn't ask what my letter was, what was in that dull envelope, then I am not telling him, she thought. A moment later his wristwatch had pinged the half-hour and he was on his feet, swearing, the paper flung on top of the things on the table. Carefully, as he rushed out, she lifted the paper up, wiped a smear of marmalade off it, and folded it neatly.

Then, as Sam's car started up in the distance, she cleared the table. She would go to her workshop as usual. Everything would be as usual. She would ring Dr Fenwick from there. With luck she'd be put on to Jennifer. She would ring from work, not from home, because Joe might hear. She didn't want him to. That was the only thing she was clear about: Joe must not be worried.

She didn't know, by the end of that morning, exactly how worried she was herself. Jennifer had been, as ever, reassuring. It was just that her smear test had revealed some change in the cells and a further investigation would be a good idea. It was better, Jennifer said in honeyed tones, that any doubts should be cleared up. Until she said 'doubts' Harriet hadn't had any, or hadn't admitted she had. That immediate feeling of bewilderment, yes, but 'doubts'? Jennifer said that if she came by the surgery on her way home she'd have a letter ready for her, a letter from Dr Fenwick to the hospital, and if she took the letter there and then they'd give her an appointment for a colposcopic examination. A colposcopy was just an instrument used to look at the cervix more closely and if necessary take a sample. It was painless, just a little uncomfortable. Harriet hung up, thinking what a lot of 'justs' Jennifer had used.

Joe need know none of this. Nor need Sam. She could cope on her own, she would prefer to do so. Some women milked situations like this. She'd seen them do it, build it up to a big drama, gain all the sympathy they could. It was a way of testing their own value and she had no need of it. She knew her value, especially to Joe. She knew how important it was that she was well and strong, able to withstand anything. He needed to feel she was his bulwark, that anything could crash against it and it – she – would not give way. Especially now, when the trial was coming up and his newly acquired contentment, all based on learning to drive, all based on such a flimsy development, would be tested. There was no room in Joe's life for her to be ill. She would not allow it, never.

She didn't tell Sam either. She almost did, but then she realised how he wouldn't care at all about Joe being shielded, he would say she was being ridiculous, he'd be exasperated with her, he'd give her away. An appointment was made for her that very day, so there were no more suspicious envelopes arriving, not that Sam had been suspicious, but he might have become so. Three days later, she went to the hospital, remembering of course all those times a year ago when she had gone in and out so frequently. She'd hardly noticed her surroundings, she'd gone from her car in one direction only, as though attached to Joe by an invisible thread, hardly aware of which corridors she went along, which corners she turned, which doors she entered. Everything had been a blur until she reached his bedside. But now she noticed everything, every face, every notice, every trolley wheeled past. It seemed a different hospital, less dramatic, the atmosphere quite lackadaisical instead of urgent, and the clinic where she eventually found herself positively soporific.

It was crowded with women. Before, when Joe was here, she had felt important, she was even treated as someone of fleeting importance. Now she saw at once that she was of little interest to anyone. She handed in her appointment letter and settled down to wait. She'd brought a book, a paperback, *Wild Swans*, a good, thick, absorbing book about life for women in China over this century, which she was half-way through, but she didn't read a word. She didn't even take it out of her bag. There was a pile of magazines on a central table and she took three of those. Flicking through magazines was more suited to this kind of waiting. She flicked, surprised that so few others did. Mostly, the women were just staring, sighing, looking at watches. Some had their eyes closed. Only one knitted, the focus of great attention. Harriet felt guilty when her name was called after only ten minutes. She passed a row of accusing stares and heard one woman go to the desk and complain, only to be told she was seeing another doctor and he just happened to be late.

She was shown into a cubicle like a horse led into a stall for a race, barely room to take her clothes off and put a gown on. Someone banged on the door at the other side, the door leading out of the stall, and shouted, 'Ready Mrs Kennedy?' and she went through it. There was a high bed there, a strip of thick white paper laid along the length of it. She clambered up obediently. The doctor came round the corner in a hurry, nodded, and stood reading some notes. He explained what would happen and got her propped up on the bed. She closed her eyes as the instrument slid into her vagina and at once began thinking about Joe. It wasn't logical. Joe hadn't had any instruments sliding into any part of him. It was to do with the humiliation of her position, the feeling of being helpless and trapped, at the mercy of others. It was true, there was no pain, only a smarting sensation, the merest scraping feeling, and there had been pain for Joe. There was no violence, but she thought of him, on that night, and knew she had at last come closer to something of what he had felt. She couldn't move, things were being done to her and she couldn't move and it felt degrading being so exposed. She understood why Joe had hated the kind, kind doctors who treated him. They were so distant, so aloof in their kindness. Joe had been an object, she was an object. How could it be otherwise? It was only her body. It wasn't her. The body was just flesh and blood and bone, a poor thing compared to the mind. She could rise above what was being done to her body, surely, literally rise above it, above this bed she lay on, and look down on the little scene and be detached. It wasn't his body he cared about, Joe had said. He did *then*, when it was happening, when it hurt and the pain screamed through him, but not now, not afterwards. It was his head, what remained in his memory, the fear. To know such fear, she thought. To be weakened by such fear. Her own fear, of cancer, was different. Lying there, being probed and prodded, she knew her fear was not yet realised. Joe's had been. He'd been gripped, held by it. It had overwhelmed him. Fear of death, then, fear that closed in on him and could not be conquered. He'd given in to it. It had swamped him, flooded into every fibre of his being, and that was what, even now, would not lift. He tried, she saw how he tried, but it was like trying to stem the tide. Again and again it came in, washing over the normal life he had reclaimed, and even though again and again it receded, it left its mark, and it left its threat of relentless return. She could never claim to know fear like that and it was a mistake to try.

'Well, Mrs Kennedy,' this doctor was saying, in his assumed jolly voice, 'that wasn't too bad, I hope?'

'No,' she said, clearing her throat. Of course it hadn't been. She blushed, but he couldn't know it was because of her shame at identifying with Joe's suffering when she had no right to, when any comparison was absurd, insulting.

'Good. Look, I think what we need to do here is have you in and do a cone biopsy. It's just not possible to be sure in your case. We could cauterise the area, but I think you'd need it done again soon and in view of the fact that you've a history, a family history, I think we should be sure, okay? We'll get it over with as soon as possible.'

A family history. She must have had to fill in a form some time, for Jennifer. For Dr Fenwick. Her mother had died of cancer of the cervix. That was the family history, that was what he meant. He'd already moved on, but a nurse was replacing the paper runner for the next patient. 'Do I have to be admitted?' she asked. 'Can't it be done in out–patients?'

The nurse shook her head. 'Two nights minimum,' she said.

Stunned, Harriet got dressed. How could she leave Joe for two nights without explaining? And Sam. She'd have to tell Sam. Without his help, she couldn't shelter Joe.

★

Alan had left a message, it was just that she hadn't seen it. He'd left it in a silly place and for a while that became the focus of her distress. It was all she said to him, over and over, why had he put a flimsy bit of paper like that on the table, didn't he realise the moment the door opened it would fly off? Why hadn't he propped it up against the flower vase, why hadn't he weighted it down, why hadn't he written it in huge capital letters on a large sheet of paper; why hadn't he used the pad beside the telephone? . . . And Alan, equally upset, had countered with similar accusations, why hadn't she said where she was going, why wasn't she back for his tea, why hadn't she telephoned and if she had he'd have been able to tell her and if she'd been at home, as she ought to have been, she'd have been the first to hear the news herself, and all this could have been avoided. She wasn't even thinking, he finished, of the double shock to himself, first the worrying about what had happened to her and then the phone call about Leo, it had all been too much.

It had. For both of them. Once home the next day, they both subsided into monosyllabic exchanges, barely able to communicate at all after the avalanche of mutual recrimination. Sheila was exhausted, drained. It was an appropriate description, she thought, to say to herself how drained she felt, as though someone had indeed opened her veins and let all the life-giving blood out, leaving her a sack of loose bones in a too-big skin. All she wanted to do was to lie down and sleep. She climbed the stairs slowly, each step made with aching legs, holding on to the banister and pulling as hard as she could. She wished she had her own room. She didn't want to share the double bed with Alan, she wanted to be on her own. There was no reason why she shouldn't, with two other bedrooms – one Leo's, one spare. Nobody ever slept in the spare, hadn't for years. They'd discussed Eric James having it, at times when he seemed to be growing more feeble, but they knew it would never do for him, not with those steep stairs and the tricky bend in them. If it came to having to have her father live with them they'd have to put him in the little living-room at the front. He'd have to use the outside lavatory if he couldn't manage those stairs. The spare room would stay spare, unless they took in lodgers, another often discussed and just as quickly dismissed notion. It had two beds in it, two single beds with only a few inches between. They hadn't decorated it for years and years. It was dingy, clean but dingy, and she hardly ever went in it except to take down and wash the curtains every spring.

Leo had Pat's old room. It had been natural putting him in there. Pat's room was different, quite different from the rest of the house, the only room, apart possibly from the kitchen, that indicated the twentieth century was well advanced. What a fuss when Pat took up the carpet and painted the floor boards *white* – white! Alan was angry, he said she'd no sense, the boards were now ruined. The wood was good strong deal and she'd ruined it, saturating it with white gloss paint. Why couldn't Pat just have varnished it? Varnished wood was very nice, he had no objection to that, and it was fashionable, wasn't it?

Varnished wood or whatever they called it, whatever they did to make floors look like that. But no, white gloss paint. And no curtains. That was what Sheila herself had objected to, the curtains and curtain rail taken down and a blind mentioned. She'd assumed it would be a Venetian blind, but what Pat had come home with one day was a flimsy straw thing. You could see through it, it kept out neither light nor prying eyes, she didn't see the point of it, personally. It didn't even go up and down properly. The strings operating it became quickly tangled and half the time it had to be rolled by hand.

Now, opening the door, she realised for the first time how little impression Leo had made on his mother's room. He'd been in it nearly thirteen years but so little had changed. Except there was a different blind, a proper one, dark blue. She could have put the curtain rail back and hung curtains again, but somehow she hadn't wanted to go against Pat's own wishes. A rug covered half the floor but it was still white and hell to clean. Otherwise, everything was more or less the same right down to the exotic bed cover Pat had brought home from that first trip to Africa, a gorgeous scarlet and black and white affair, impossible to wash and too precious to dry-clean. Twice a year she took it into the yard and shook it and put it on the line and let it air in the sun. That was all she could do, but she never even thought of getting rid of it, she liked it, it was beautiful. More than could be said of the black wooden carved heads on the walls. She hated those. She'd taken them down when Pat died, and stuck them in the cupboard, right at the back, and there they had stayed until Leo found them when he was about ten and insisted on putting them back on the walls.

Pat's maps were still there. One whole wall covered with a huge map of the world. It had flags stuck in places she'd been to, little pins with red flags on them. Another wall had detailed maps of Africa on it, she'd sent away to a shop in London for them. Sheila had always thought these four maps boring. They weren't colourful, like the map of the world. There didn't seem to be much on them, great acres of white space, others shaded beige or light brown. She went in and sat on the bed but she knew she couldn't stay there. It was too hurtful. Alan would be appalled, he would read into her desertion things she didn't want him to read, however true. It was silly, though, that they both still slept in their double bed. Why? Habit. Only habit. It wasn't comfortable any more. Their sleeping patterns had been different for years now. When Alan was asleep he snored, snored most violently, and kept her awake. And when he got up during the night he disturbed her as she did him when she, too, had to get up and pace about to try to settle the annoying tingling and cramps in her legs. They didn't cuddle any more, there was no point in being in a double bed for that. Sometimes, Alan's hand would seek hers and squeeze it, or his leg touch hers, that was all the contact they had had since Leo was arrested. But there was no connection really. She felt old, that was the truth. She was always reading articles in magazines about how sex could continue happily into people's eighties, but she found them ridiculous. She was only seventy, nearly seventy, but she had not felt amorous for a decade. Maybe there was something the matter with her, but she couldn't believe there was. It felt natural to her. She had had all that, it was over. Whether it was for Alan too she wasn't so sure. He knew and she knew that she had always been keener than he, something she had felt secretive about, something neither of them had openly admitted. And now she simply thought of sex as belonging to other people. In good time to Leo. Belonging to those who were young, their bodies unwithered, something she didn't begrudge at all. But it would be a relief to have her own bed, if only it would not cause such trouble to stay here in Leo's room, in Pat's room, when there was trouble enough. Anything for a quiet life. So she left the room and went to her own and lay down there instead, on top of the cover, the pink candlewick bedspread she had once thought cheerful and modern. It washed well, that was one thing. It went in the washing machine and came out every time good as new.

Downstairs she could hear Alan in the yard, watering the window-box. Then he'd trim it, take the dead heads off the geraniums, cut here, cut there with his little scissors. Once, it had been a pity Alan hadn't had a garden to play with, but now it was a good thing. He'd never have managed it. He wasn't like Eric James, he wasn't nearly as strong, and as he aged he seemed quite frail sometimes. A window-box, two window-boxes, back and front, and a hanging basket were enough. If the phone rang, Alan was nice and handy for answering it, but she hoped it wouldn't. She couldn't be bothered. They weren't going to find him today, it was very unlikely, and that was the only call she was interested in. It seemed absurd to her, perverse, that they seemed to think Leo would make for home at some time – why would he do that when he'd said he didn't want to come near it after he was released? If Leo rang, they were to keep him talking, and try to find out where he was. Again, they seemed to expect Leo to call. She didn't. He'd finished with them, she could sense that. This running away was all part of it, part of avoiding having to give explanations, having to satisfy her. If he succeeded, if he got away successfully, she thought it more likely that he would write some time, years ahead, when he was settled.

She might be dead by then, of course. His great-grandfather would certainly be, but maybe that would be no bad thing. Eric James would complicate any return of the prodigal son. But she and Alan might be dead too. She was seventy soon and her own mother had died at seventy, though she wasn't convinced this was relevant to any life expectancy of hers, because she was like her father, not her mother. Alan was seventy-one and both his parents were dead before that age so he might already be on borrowed time. They might both be dead when eventually Leo showed up, if he showed up. Or just Alan might be dead. She might be alive. Leo might come home and find her on her own. Then what would happen? With it all in the past, everything that had happened, would a reconciliation be possible? A real one? Involving at last being told exactly what had happened that terrible night?

Did mothers really die not knowing what had happened to their sons? Knowing they were out there in the world somewhere, but not knowing where or how they lived or with whom? The horror of it stole over her, her whole body grew cold, and then she was startled to feel the tears running down her face. She put her hand up and felt them and licked her fingers, disbelieving. To be crying, now . . .

★

Detective Sergeant Graham was furious. It wasn't his responsibility if Leo Jackson had absconded, it didn't reflect on him in any way whatsoever, how could it? But he was furious because if the boy were not found, then obviously he could not be produced in court when Gary Robinson came to trial. And Graham had been hoping great things from that confrontation, he was sure Leo would crack and very satisfactory that would be. He hated untidy cases and, though throughout his policing career he had learned that what he called untidiness and what others called loose ends were inevitable in the vast majority of instances, he nevertheless found them hard to accept. He couldn't be reconciled to never quite knowing that that was the case. It was what made him a good policeman, his determination to push and push for a complete story. Others usually wanted that final knowledge, because they worried that a wrong might have been done and they wanted to be sure it hadn't, but not he. It wasn't that he didn't care about justice, of course he did, but to worry about the absolute correctness of every sentence was the way to go mad. You caught the criminals, you presented all available evidence, and then it wasn't up to you, it was up to lawyers and magistrates and judges and juries. Leo Jackson had been convicted and sentenced without any shadow of doubt as to his complicity in the attack on Joe Kennedy.

Where the doubt came in was over how he came to be in Gary Robinson's company and over what precisely he had done. It niggled away in his head, this lack of knowledge, knowledge only Leo Jackson could supply. Even more maddening was the boy's attitude. It had remained consistent, very unusual with so young an offender, especially a first offender. The boy wasn't truculent, he wasn't aggressive, you couldn't even call him sullen. He was just silent and composed. He had appeared to have no interest in what happened to him. There hadn't been a single attempt at that well-worn plea of 'It wasn't my fault'. Yet maybe it wasn't. And now Leo Jackson had done a bunk. He'd informed the parents – the grandparents – himself as soon as he'd been told, even if it wasn't his job. Unfortunately, he'd got the father – the grandfather – unfortunately, because it was the mother – the grandmother – he would have preferred to catch. Catch was the word, he might have caught all kinds of hints, things he hadn't managed to pick up yet, indications of what really went on between that boy and his grandmother. But the grandfather was useless. He knew nothing, he was hopeless. There had been no point in catching him off guard. The fact that he didn't know where his wife was or when she would be back had been the only interesting thing he'd gleaned. It could even be said to be suspicious, a woman like Mrs Armstrong virtually disappearing for the day at the same time as her grandson doing a runner. Graham had a little chat with Mr Armstrong under cover of telling him about Leo. He heard all about how worried Mr Armstrong was about his wife who hadn't been right since her grandson was arrested. She couldn't accept it even when Leo confessed to it. And she was getting worse and worse, Mr Armstrong said.

Detective Sergeant Graham was most sympathetic.

★

Eric James was querulous, and when he asked for the hundredth time what in hell's name was *up*, Sheila simply wanted to silence him. 'Leo's escaped,' she said at last. 'He's run away from the prison place.'

Eric James considered this. His face was comical, poised midway between exaggerated astonishment and glee. Finally, he grunted a version of a laugh. 'Well, damn me,' he said, 'damn me. And he's got away, eh? Managed it?'

'So far.' She was depressed by his visible excitement. 'He hasn't any money, he's only got the prison overalls on. He can't get far.'

'Who says?'

'It's commonsense. He can't even buy himself a bit of bread, or a ticket to anywhere.'

'He can nick summat to eat, he can hitch a ride, course he's got a chance, clever lad like our Leo.'

She noted the 'our Leo' and put down the plate she was washing. He was whistling, shaking his head, enjoying this.

'Nothing clever about running away,' she said, sharply,

'or so you always told us, and him. "Stand your ground," you always said. "Never be a coward. Never run away from fights."'

He snorted, shuffled off to get the rest of his dishes on the table. 'Fights,' he said, chucking his knife and fork into the soapy water, which irritated her, 'fights are different. This isn't running away, any road, it's escaping, like in the war. Can't fight when yer in a camp, stands to reason. Escape's the only way. Over the wire and out.' He whistled again, reached for his tea-cup, but she was too quick for him and snatched it off the table herself. 'Don't glamorise it,' she said, 'he'll be in more trouble than ever.'

'If he's caught.'

'Of course he'll be caught, I've told you. Then he'll have to do longer. Where will that get him?'

'If he's caught,' Eric James repeated, looking superior.

Every day after that he rang her up, if she wasn't going to be seeing him, to enquire if there was 'any word'. She was so angry with him that she pretended she didn't know what about and made him ask her directly. When she told him, as she was obliged to, that no, there was no news of Leo being found, he would say 'Good lad' in tones of admiration – 'Good lad, giving them the slip, eh?' – and when she was in his company he took great pleasure in marvelling at how well Leo was doing. 'No money, eh?' he said. 'Not a penny on him and it's three days now, amazing. Wonder how he's managing it. Wonder if he's remembering what I taught him.'

'You *taught* him? And what might that be?'

'Oh, this and that, this and that, ways and means.'

'Don't talk daft.'

'Daft? Daft or not, he's doing grand.'

'You don't know that. You don't know he isn't lying in some ditch with a broken leg.' She made a great deal of noise with emptying the washing-up bowl to cover the shake in her voice. But he'd spotted it.

242

'He'll not be lying in any ditch, don't you worry, lass, they'd have found him if he were. Didn't yer say they'd search parties scouring the area for fifty miles, eh? And a farmer would see him. No, he isn't in any ditch. He's nice and cosy some place, biding his time, like his old grandad taught him.'

'I wish his old grandad had taught him to be good instead,' she muttered, 'then he wouldn't have got in this mess.'

A week after the escape and Eric James was jubilant. It annoyed Sheila intensely. She couldn't resist pointing out to her father what a hypocrite he was. 'I thought you wanted him locked up for ever? I thought you'd washed your hands of him?' she challenged him. 'Going on now as though he'd won a medal or something, as though you're proud of him. Changed *your* tune.'

Eric James was not a bit put out. 'He's done his time,' he said, complacently.

'No he has not, he hasn't done anything like his time, he's a coward now as well as everything else,' she flashed back. 'You should be even more ashamed of him.'

Her father just whistled and ignored her. All these months and months he'd disowned Leo and now, suddenly, irrationally, he seemed to be hailing him as a hero. It sickened her.

'Teks pluck,' he said, over and over, 'escaping teks pluck.'

'*What?*' she shouted. 'What? Pluck? What's that supposed to mean? Pluck to batter a poor boy half to death, eh?'

'Now then,' he cautioned her, 'now then! Nobody knows what went on. He wasn't letting on. Mebbe had his reasons.'

'*You* didn't want to know them at the time, I noticed. Very quick you were to cast him off.'

243

'I kept m'own counsel.'

'You did what? You did *not*, you never stopped cursing him . . .'

'I niver cursed him.'

'You did.'

'I did not.'

That was how their rows went, disintegrating into childish insults. It made her so angry but it left him unmoved. He simply didn't care what he had once said – it was forgotten, he was suddenly Leo's champion, endlessly speculating on where he would now be. He was convinced that Leo was aboard some ship, a stowaway, full of romantic notions Sheila found repugnant. But the police tended to agree that Leo had somehow found a safe place for the moment, even if it wasn't in a ship. They said he must have found a way to eat and get new clothes, or he'd have collapsed by now and been picked up. He was most likely, they thought, to have made his way to a big city, maybe Liverpool, maybe as far as London, and it would take time to spot him.

Life was supposed to be going on as normal again. Carole, calling to see her, said flatly that Leo running away could be a blessing in disguise. Sheila listened and enquired politely how that might be. Carole said it was a blessing because it let her, Sheila, 'off the hook for good'. She said that Leo had no more use for her, he wanted to be finished with her. To Carole this was apparently crystal-clear. Leo had cut loose and now she must face up to this and start a new life.

'What kind of life will that be, then?' Sheila asked.

Chapter Thirteen

'**D**ON'T BE SO STUPID,' Sam said, much more fiercely than he had intended. 'Harriet,' he began again, then stopped. They were walking. She'd told him as they walked rapidly along the lake path, meaning of course that he couldn't see her face properly, couldn't look her in the eye unless he leapt in front of her and stopped her. A typical Harriet ploy. Always, when there was anything important to tell him, she chose to do it when they were outside, on the move, never sitting quietly in the sitting-room, where surely the setting and atmosphere were more conducive to rational discussion. But Harriet didn't want that, there was nothing rational about her attitude and she didn't want any discussion. As ever, she had made her mind up, before telling him. To change her mind he would have to wage a sustained campaign and the thought exhausted him. She was so tiring like this. Her very strength tired him, however much he admired it, and he did.

He took a deep breath, slackened his pace and to his relief she slackened hers, showing at least a willingness to hear him, or maybe only recognising that she would have to. He decided to attack the logistics of her plan first even though that was to concede he acknowledged it, which he was reluctant to do. 'You cannot,' he said slowly, and then, correcting himself, '*we* cannot keep it a secret from Joe that you are in hospital. It isn't possible even if it was right, which it isn't.'

'We can,' she said calmly, showing she'd anticipated his response, 'we can just say I've gone to visit Aunt Mary. He'll be pleased. He's always complaining that I treat him like a baby.'

'And why would you suddenly go to visit an old lady you haven't visited for centuries? It wouldn't make sense to him, he'd be suspicious at once.'

'No, he wouldn't, and that's why he wouldn't, *because* I haven't visited her in ages, guilty conscience, that would make sense to him, he's always saying I'm so conscientious it bores him. He won't even ask where she lives, I bet you, he won't show the slightest interest.'

'So. You go to Aunt Mary's for two nights and then what happens if you have to stay in longer?'

'I won't. They said.'

'Things can go wrong . . .'

'Thanks very much, you're so cheerful.'

'You force me to all this. Suppose things go wrong and you have to stay in longer, what then?'

'Then I stay at Aunt Mary's longer.'

'I see. I just go on lying and lying, is that it?'

'If necessary.'

'And if I get found out?'

'You won't, you . . .'

'*If* I do – come on, consider it – *if* I do, which seems quite likely to me, when this is a small town . . .'

'No. I've thought of that. I'm going to have it done in Carlisle Infirmary. I asked the consultant, he works there too, it doesn't make any difference to him, he operates there twice a week. Nobody will know me there.'

'Oh God, Harriet.'

He felt so angry, so angry and bitter. She forged ahead, inventing these complicated scenarios when there was no need for them. Underneath the bravado, the control, he knew how distressed she was, but she wouldn't let him near it, he was kept away, his comfort rejected when he so badly wanted to offer it. If he touched her now, tried to embrace her, she would push him away, say that she couldn't bear his sympathy, that he mustn't offer it. The way he could help was by going along with what she wanted him to do – stay at home with Joe, tell silly stories about Aunt Mary, act normally. He wasn't even going to be allowed to visit her. She wanted him at home, with Joe, she didn't want to be visited. She would drive herself there and back, she would be perfectly sensible and wait until she felt fine and then drive herself back. But there he had put his foot down, he was adamant, he would drive her there and pick her up while Joe was at the boat yard. He made such a fuss that she gave in, but he knew that even that was a calculated concession. It didn't mean much to her, that bit, the going and coming, she could afford to be gracious.

All this talk about ways and means, all these plans to protect Joe, and meanwhile the real issue was neatly avoided. What in God's name was a cone biopsy? She'd shrugged off his questions – it was nothing, a very minor operation, very common. But they wouldn't do it for nothing, especially not today, with all the hospital cuts. They were doing it because they were suspicious. His heart almost stopped at the thought of those suspicions. Not Harriet, she was so healthy, it was impossible. She'd said the doctor had told her there was no cause for alarm. Right. He'd hold on to that, he was good at not crossing bridges till he came to them. But Harriet wasn't. She'd have crossed them several times already, seen the view on the other side. And now here she was, being brave and sensible, brave for Joe. It disturbed him, this misplaced selflessness. It wasn't good for Joe, he knew it wasn't. She wasn't giving him the chance to be brave himself. Worst of all, she wasn't giving him the chance to support *her*.

Had she thought of that? How Joe might welcome the opportunity to show his concern for *her*? Especially over something so harmless, something she swore was so minor. It wouldn't involve him in any sickening worry. He agreed that would indeed be bad for Joe, any prolonged anxiety, any real threat to his mother. But a small, routine op. was perfect, he could know about it and be helpful and it would all be over before he could panic.

They'd walked a long way by now, the lake left far behind. He allowed his dejection to show as they climbed the path through the wood. Hands in his pockets, he went on and up without looking back, in a way he would never once have done. It was how she wanted things more and more, to make her own way, go at her own pace, shut her real thoughts in her head. It wasn't that they no longer talked, of course they talked, talked far too much, but the talking complicated problems instead of simplifying them as it used to. He couldn't follow the strangely intricate patterns of her mind, he was always coming to dead ends while she twisted and turned into other routes. How this had happened he didn't know, but it was all to do with Joe, with what had happened to Joe. He found himself thinking of Detective Sergeant Graham and how the policeman had been surprised at the absence of any focused hate, of any straightforward desire for revenge, at the time of the attack. But he felt faint stirrings of hate now, not for what had been done to Joe, but for what it had done to him and Harriet through Joe. He didn't entertain any violent fantasies. He didn't imagine himself beating up Gary what's-his-name, or Leo Jackson. He couldn't even in his imagination force these brutes to see what they had done, because there wasn't anything to see. It was all invisible, invisible hurt, pain, damage . . .

On the top of the little knoll above the wood he stood and looked down at the lake, once more in view above the trees, a great, broad sheet of pewter-coloured water on this dull day. Harriet found all this beauty soothing, it made her feel better, but he found it too sad without knowing why. Sad, everything natural so beautiful, everything man-made ugly – something like that. Except immediately he contradicted himself. Everything man-made was not ugly. How could he, an architect, say such a thing, even to himself? He felt about buildings, some buildings, as Harriet did about lakes and hills. Venice. He'd like to go to Venice again. She was up beside him now, but he wasn't going to turn round. There was nothing more to be said. He would do as she wanted. Drive her to Carlisle. Stay with Joe. Talk about Aunt Mary. This would go on for ever, as far as he could see.

'What are you smiling at?' she said.

'Oh, nothing. I was just seeing Joe aged sixty being protected by you, even in your dotage.'

'And that's funny?'

'No,' he said, 'it isn't, not really.'

★

'Any news?' Eric James asked, as usual, and, as usual, she said there was none. 'Good,' he said, but before he could go into the patter he so loved, she cut in quickly, 'Do you want any shopping? I'm going up street, to the market.'

'Don't know what yer want to do that for, they've ruined it, damned shame, ruined the old market . . .'

'Dad, all I asked was do you want any shopping?'

'You can get me a pound of best back bacon. Nowt else. I'll get the rest meself, tomorrow.'

'But if I'm going you don't need to.'

'Have to put m'time in somehow.'

When their father's collapse wasn't so seriously imminent, they used to have bets, she and Carole. She said that Eric James would be digging in his blessed garden and he'd have a heart attack and that would be that, he'd be digging till the day he died, neighbours looking over their hedges at him and marvelling and setting him as an example for their own husbands. But Carole said that he'd be run over, probably by a bus. The way their father crossed roads had always been autocratic. He never waited for pedestrian crossing lights to change, hardly, in fact, used crossings at all, preferring to dash across the road when and where it suited him. Fine when he was strong and agile, but now he was neither, now he was stooped and slow and his sight not too good. But it made no difference, he still treated cars and buses as mere interruptions in his path, and Carole was right – one day soon he would be knocked down. Probably in the town, where the roads were wider and more congested. He'd stagger off the bus, then lurch from behind it into another and that would be that. Or he'd fall off one, fall off a bus. He could hardly negotiate the steps as it was. Sheila clearly remembered how, thirty years ago, he'd watched old people struggling to board buses and expressed the opinion that they shouldn't be allowed to use them, they were a danger to other folk. Quite.

It was odd that he wanted more bacon, surely there'd been plenty of bacon, she'd seen it in the fridge. But he was very fond of bacon, perhaps he was just eating twice as much, great fatty bacon breakfasts. He'd had them all his life, bacon and egg and fried bread, bread fried in the fat. Full of cholesterol, and look at him. Leo had loved breakfasts with Eric James, especially when she supposed she'd made them seem wicked, all that fat, the way she'd gone on about them, tried to make Leo a healthy eater. Her father had laughed at her, openly scorned newfangled ideas about diet. He'd been cross when, for a while, Leo had become a vegetarian, damned stupid in his opinion, an insult to his past working life as a butcher. He wasn't happy until he'd welcomed Leo back into the meat-eating fold, not very long ago either . . . But she couldn't bear to think about Leo and food, it was too worrying. Alan and Eric James both said how strong Leo was, how tough, how able to draw on his own strength for a long time, but she had visions of him starving, nightmares in which he was emaciated and begging for bread. She'd lost her own appetite as a result. Every bite she took she wanted to give to Leo, it was the only thing she had to offer him. Food. It had become their currency, those last couple of years. Making his favourite dishes, lavishing all her care on perfect apple-pies, perfect hot-pot, perfect soups and broths which he loved. And bread, she'd gone back to baking her own bread because Leo loved the smell of it when he came in from school, he'd pretend to swoon, when he came in and she was lifting a cob from the oven . . .

The shopping was soon done. She didn't know why she bothered going to the market, there was nothing better than she could get in the shops near her. It was habit. Her mother had always gone to the market, to the butter women for eggs, to a particular stall for home-grown tomatoes. The market had been all bustle then, but now her father was right, the soul as well as the trade had gone out of it. It was depressing going there even though the revamping had made the place so clean and the new building was very smart. She got his bacon and some tomatoes for herself and she went into the fish market and got some Solway shrimps for Alan's tea. He hadn't lost his appetite. Eating was the biggest pleasure in his life. If it wasn't she couldn't think what was. Watching cricket? Fishing? Not so much any more. Not drinking, Alan had never been a drinker. His tea was so important to him it annoyed her. Maybe she was jealous. There was nothing she enjoyed as much as Alan enjoyed his wretched tea.

Nothing. So what, missus, she asked herself, as she stood at the bus stop holding her shopping bag, what is your chief pleasure in life now you're in your seventieth year? Leo. It was simple. Leo, her only real pleasure, and he was gone for good. First Pat, then Leo. Farewell to pleasure . . .

She was frowning as she got on the bus, disapproving of her own mental meanderings. She didn't see her oldest friend, the one she'd known since school, Dora, Dora Sproat, as she now was. But Dora saw her and came to sit beside her, and Sheila, while smiling, cringed. All Dora would want to talk about was Leo. She'd ask questions, expect answers, and it was unbearable. She didn't even like Dora, only had to count her as a friend because of their long acquaintance. She was trapped in the window seat of this bus until it came to the stop for Eric James's house, and Dora had her at her mercy and knew it. 'Going to see your dad, Sheila?' she asked, and didn't wait for an answer. 'He's a marvel, I saw him the other day up street and I said to him, "Mr Armstrong, you are a marvel." How old is he now? Ninety?'

'Nearly,' muttered Sheila.

'Amazing, really it is, the way he gets about and that, fit as a fiddle, sharp as a needle . . .'

Sheila cleared her throat.

'And your Alan, Sheila, how is he? I haven't seen him in an age, is he well, eh?'

Sheila said he was indeed well. She asked after Dora's husband and her four children and her nine grandchildren, and hoped the encouragement to go round her large and nauseatingly affectionate close family would keep Dora going until it was time to part. But it didn't. Half-way through a recital of how her grandson had just had an accident on his motorbike due to the reckless driving of someone else, Dora slipped in the enquiry Sheila knew

252

she'd been waiting to make. 'And how,' she said, lowering her voice, a lowering Sheila particularly resented, 'how is *your* grandson?'

Walking up the path to Eric James's door, Sheila wondered why she was so spineless. Why was it so important not to let people like Dora Sproat, people she didn't care about at all, why was it so important not to tell them the truth? Why was the simple truth impossible to utter? Because it wasn't simple, that's why. The truth meant a lengthy speech and she wanted to be brief. So she'd said, 'Fine, fine.' Not, 'Mind your own business,' or, 'I can't talk about Leo,' or, 'Please don't ask me.' No, such evasions would only galvanise Dora into more questions. And if she'd said, 'He's run away from prison and nobody knows where he is,' that would have opened the floodgates of excited speculation. So 'Fine' was the only possible answer, but it had upset her to say that one word. It was like a denial, even a betrayal. Dora Sproat would find out in the end that Leo hadn't been fine, people like her always did, they always got to know and then they'd work backwards and pounce on the lie . . . '"Fine," she said to me, on the bus, I met her on the bus, and do you know he'd run away and half the police force in the county after him weeks before that, and yet she said he was fine. I mean, can you believe it?'

She shouted hello as she went in, but he wasn't there. She took the bacon out of her bag and left it on the table for him to see. Everything looked neat and tidy, she had to give him that. On closer inspection, of course, she knew she would discover it was all a surface impression. He cleaned the kitchen pretty well, army training he called it, but the bathroom wasn't quite as pristine and she could write her name in the dust on all the furniture in his living-room. Not that it mattered. The important thing was that he didn't become slummy, that he didn't start neglecting

253

himself or his house. She wondered if she ought to have a quick snoop in the other rooms, taking advantage of his absence, just to see everything was all right, nothing leaking anywhere which he hadn't noticed. But she couldn't be bothered.

He was turning the corner as she went down the street. Seeing him from that distance she felt suddenly alarmed – he was too old to be out on his own carrying that bag and needing to use his stick. And he was hurrying, it was ridiculous, actually trying to hurry, the stick going at a frightening rate, his walk erratic, the bag bumping away against his unsteady legs. She waited. He didn't look up until he was almost upon her and then he seemed to get a fright. He started and dropped his bag and then when she'd given it to him he covered up his surprise with bad temper. 'Made me drop m'bag,' he complained, 'standing there like that, what yer doing at my gate?'

'Brought your shopping, that's all.'

'At this time? Yer don't usually bring it at this time. What did yer do that for, eh, giving me a shock?'

'A shock? Seeing your own daughter an hour before you usually see her? Oh well, sorry I'm sure.'

'So yer should be,' he said.

She walked off without saying goodbye.

★

It was as easy as she had predicted. 'I'm going to visit Aunt Mary,' she told Joe. 'Remember Aunt Mary, your great-aunt actually? Lives in Newcastle?'

'Not really.'

'She's very ill, she lives on her own and I haven't been for ages, years, I feel so guilty.'

'You're always feeling guilty, it's stupid.'

There followed ten minutes of arguing about guilt, the kind of argument Joe loved and she found tedious. At the end of it he'd forgotten all about how it began.

'Anyway,' she said, 'I've decided to go and visit Aunt Mary, so I'll be away two nights.' He didn't say anything, didn't look the faintest bit interested. 'Dad will be here, I'll leave plenty of food . . .'

'For God's sake, Mum.'

'What?'

'What do you mean, you'll leave plenty of food, it's stupid, as if . . .' and he stopped.

'As if what?'

'Oh, nothing, nothing.'

He didn't ask to be reminded who exactly Aunt Mary was, or where she lived in Newcastle, or why she was going at this particular time, or what sort of illness she was suffering from. He didn't ask if she was going by train or driving. He asked nothing, and while she was grateful, glad not to have to extend the lies, it made her somehow depressed. She wanted him to care, to be concerned for Aunt Mary if not for her. Not this blankness, this self-obsession. His age, nothing more, she told herself. His age.

Sam drove her to Carlisle, as he had insisted he would. Quite unnecessarily. She hated leaving the house, pulling the front door behind her, suddenly thinking of hospitals and wards and how horrible the whole experience would be. Frightening, too, full of 'what if's. Sam was right, it could all so easily go wrong, her plans collapse, and he would be the one who had to deal with the result. She hadn't been fair to him, never gave his point of view any weight. Maybe she was protecting herself, not Joe, and doing him more damage in the process. She exaggerated everything, always had done, her imagination worked overtime and led her into supposing feelings in those she loved which they might never have had. And Sam had been odd ever since she'd told him about this business. Distant. It wasn't like him. He seemed newly secretive, contained, more like she knew herself to be.

They drove up the M6 in silence. The traffic was heavy, great lorries rumbling along on the inside lane. She tried to concentrate on the scenery, on the vistas of mountains to the left and the smooth humps of hills, much nearer, to the right. She wanted to tell Sam to stop, just stop anywhere, and let her off. She'd walk into the hills and keep walking and never go near the hospital. It was amazing how obedient people were, keeping their hospital appointments, facing it all, voluntarily entering these places, showing such trust. Happiness is coming out of a hospital, she thought. The day Joe came out she'd been so happy. He'd been so brave, so determined to get well quickly and put all that behind him. Her eyes filled with tears at the memory and she bit her lip furiously. Unfortunately Sam chose that moment to give her a quick glance. 'You're not crying?' he said, horrified. 'Of course I'm not,' she said, savagely, 'keep your eyes on the road.'

She made such a fuss he had to give in and leave her at the door of the hospital. She told him she'd ring him and tell him her ward, promised faithfully to do so. They kissed, an 'I'm–off–to–the–office' kiss. She didn't look back, trusted him to have gone to his car. There was a queue at the reception hatch. She joined it, shuffled slowly forward with the rest, inch by inch as each person was dealt with. The women dealing with the appointment cards were brisk. Not rude, just brisk. She was given her ward and stood studying the plan of the hospital, working out how to get there. Maybe she should have gone into their local hospital. This was so anonymous, but then it was anonymity she had craved. She followed the ground plan, walking along corridors and up stairs, scorning lifts, thinking this was the last exercise she would get for some time. She hated passing people in wheelchairs, people being wheeled on stretchers; it was too awful seeing how sick others could be. She thought of Ginny, backwards

256

and forwards to hospital clinics with Laura for so long. She'd been lucky. Only that once, for Joe.

The ward was bright, to her relief. Not one of those huge Florence Nightingale affairs. There were only six beds. All of them were empty, which confused her. Weren't hospitals bursting at the seams? Waiting lists miles long? 'Choose your bed,' a nurse said. It was like arriving at school, finding the dormitory, having first pick . . . She chose the bed furthest from the door, nearest to a window. She was told to take her clothes off, put them in a locker, and get into bed. Someone, it seemed, was meant to have come with her to remove her clothes, they weren't meant to stay in the locker. She felt reprimanded but for once didn't care, it was a small act of defiance. Once in bed, she got her book out, determined to become absorbed in it, but almost immediately someone came to take her temperature, and another her blood pressure, and a third to ask a long list of seemingly fatuous questions. One by one the beds filled up. Women started talking to each other. Incredible how quickly reasons for being there were freely given. All of them were gynaecological, a dreary list of scrapes and biopsies and hysterectomies. Someone asked her what she was in for and, though she replied politely, she lifted her book up as a shield. She didn't want to exchange medical histories. She didn't want to be chummy. She wanted to freeze, not to be there, until all this was over.

She rang Sam dutifully and was curt, though he was disposed to chat. It was too tantalising to think of home, she didn't want to. The night was long. First there was the evening to get through, bad enough with so many visitors crowding the place and her head aching with the hours of reading as well as the noise, and then the night began and she wished she'd taken the sleeping pill offered. She prayed she'd be first on the operating list. What did they do? Keep the little ops to the end, or get rid of them first? They kept her until the end. All morning she watched the other women being wheeled off, even the plainest made glamorous when clothed in a white gown and white cap, lying silently on a stretcher. It was unexpectedly moving watching these strangers being taken away, soft murmurs of 'Good luck' following them. And when they were returned the drama was intensified, the sight of the inert bodies being lifted touching, the sight of the occasional drip scaring. In spite of herself Harriet was swept up in it all, as anxious as the rest to know how each woman had fared.

She was exhausted by the time her turn came – it was bliss to be given the premedication injection. She closed her eyes and drifted off and was unaware of being taken to the theatre at all. When she woke, her throat was dry and there was a pad between her legs, but otherwise she felt she could not have had the operation at all. Cautiously, she reached for a glass of water and sipped it. She wanted to go to the lavatory. A nurse came past and she attracted her attention. The nurse seemed surprised she was awake. She helped her walk to the lavatory and stood outside the door. Back in bed, Harriet felt proud of herself – she was tough, she was up and about in record time, there had been very little blood on the pad and she was in no discomfort. The nurse told her there was an internal dressing still in place which would be removed later. Suddenly, she thought she would ring Sam.

The phone was brought to her on a trolley. She dialled, thinking how pleased Sam would be. He was out of the office. She left a message, very vague, said she would ring again. Then, not allowing herself time to think, time to change her mind, she rang home. It was four o'clock. Joe would be there by now. She just wanted to hear his voice. When he answered, she smiled. 'Hi,' she said, 'it's me, just

ringing to say everything's fine, I'll be home tomorrow.'
Joe grunted, half a snort of exasperation, she supposed,
and half a groan. She didn't know what else to say, so
badly wanted him to say something. 'How's Aunt Mary
then?' he finally asked. 'Fine,' she said, 'much better.' She
knew she mustn't ask how he was. How lucky he couldn't
see her, still in her white operation gown. The money was
running out. 'Okay then,' she said, 'I've got to go now.
Take care, see you tomorrow.'

Silly. A pointless phone call. Really silly to have
succumbed like that. Sam would be home soon. They'd
eat. Joe would do the cooking, more like assembling, with
everything left ready for him. She wondered how they
were together when she wasn't there. Did they miss her?
Were they aware that she wasn't there – heavily aware? Or
did it seem quite natural to be chaps together? Maybe she
overestimated her own importance. They wouldn't have
time to find out in two days, anyway, it would pass like a
flash for them, whereas for her each hour, except the hour
she was out of the ward, seemed endless. But it was over,
mission accomplished. They'd said she could go home
tomorrow. She was to ring Sam and tell him the time to
pick her up.

That night she slept very well, in spite of the moans
from the two hysterectomy patients.

★

She supposed she'd been expecting it, the phone call, the
message. Certainly, she acted as though she had. 'Thank
you,' she said calmly to the person who rang. 'I'll be there
right away, thank you for telling me.' She left a note for
Alan, a note very prominently, unmissably, displayed,
and then she set off for the Infirmary. She walked. It was
no good getting one bus and then another to the
Infirmary. Cutting through the back streets she could be

259

quicker than two buses. She walked briskly but without rushing. Rushing would only make her breathless and she'd arrive in a state which would do nobody any good. She should have phoned Carole before she left the house, but she thought she might as well see how Eric James was first of all.

By the time she reached the Infirmary, going up the slight hill to the front door, she was tired. It annoyed her. She'd always been such a walker, and now to be tired after a short walk, it was ridiculous. She gave her name in at the reception – so busy and offhand those women seemed – and was directed to where her father was. Directed, but she failed to follow the directions correctly and had to keep asking and was flustered by the time she found the right ward. She looked around for a nurse before she went in. Shrieks of laughter came from a room with 'Sister' on the door, but nobody answered her timid knock. She'd just have to find him herself. Not too difficult, for heaven's sake. The ward seemed dim in spite of the sun outside. The blinds were drawn and it was hard to make out the shapes in the beds. All old people, she could see that. Old people with their eyes closed, raised up on pillows. She was tip-toeing without realising it. When a voice said, 'Looking for someone?' she jumped.

Eric James was in a side ward, no wonder she hadn't found him. The nurse said he was not too bad, considering his advanced age. He was badly shocked and his left rib was cracked as well as his right wrist fractured, but he was coherent enough. Sheila advanced towards his bed dreading the sight of him, but he looked quite noble rather than pathetic. The sheets were drawn up to his chin and the whiteness of them and of the two pillows under his head emphasised his weather-beaten, ruddy look. One side of his face was cut, the same side as before, just little cuts all over, and he wasn't wearing his glasses.

'Took yer time,' he muttered as she sat down. She ignored that and gave him one of his own greetings, though she said the words gently. 'You've been in the wars.'

'Damned stupid pavement,' he said. 'Council wants prosecuting, wants suing ower them pavements.'

'Sue them, then.'

'Aye, I will an' all.'

'So, what happened?'

'I telt yer, didn't I? I tripped, ower that rotten pavement, a scandal them pavements.'

'Where?'

'Outside the paper shop, been paying m'papers, come out, bang, tripped, and now I'm in this place.'

'It's a good place.'

'My mother died in here, my father died in here, my wife died in here and now I'm in here.'

'Well, you're not dying, that's one thing. The nurse says you're doing champion. You'll be out in a week.'

'A week? Don't talk daft, I'm not stopping a week. I'll tell yer that. Shouldn't have brought me here in the first place, I telt them to tek me home, but bloody busybodies, phoning for an ambulance . . .'

'They did right, you've got a fractured wrist and a broken rib, you needed seeing to.'

'Well, I've been seen to and now I'm off home.'

'Dad, don't be daft, how'd you manage? Think on.'

'I'd manage. I've always managed. Get my clothes.'

'I don't know where they are.'

'Then look.'

To keep him quiet, she made a play of looking. His face was very red as he tried to shout at her to go and tell those nurses to bring his clothes. Sheila went, whispering to the first nurse she could find that her father wanted his clothes. The nurse went for the staff nurse, who accompanied Sheila back.

'Now, Mr Armstrong,' she said, pretending to be stern, 'I hear you don't like us, you want to go home, right?'

'Aye,' Eric James said, glaring, hating her.

'Come on then,' the staff nurse said, 'let's see you on your pins, up you get and I'll bring your clothes.'

Eric James tried. He tried so hard. Sheila could understand why the staff nurse had challenged him, but she couldn't bear to see him forced to admit his own weakness.

'Dad,' she said, stepping forward to push him back on his pillows. 'Dad, don't, just rest.'

He gave a groan and fell back.

'There you are, Mr Armstrong,' the staff nurse said, in the same tone, for which Sheila now hated her too, 'can't be done, can it? You just settle yourself and we'll see about going home later.' Then she left.

Sheila sat beside his bed, silent. One hand of his was hanging over the edge of the bed, dangling there, weightless. She wondered if she should take hold of it, squeeze it, that gnarled old hand at the end of the startlingly thin white arm. No. She couldn't. He'd think he really was dying. 'Just try and rest,' she whispered.

'How can I rest?' he moaned. 'I have to get home.'

'Your home's all right,' Sheila said. 'I'll go round myself, check everything's all right' That seemed to upset him even more, rather than relieve him. 'The gas, the electricity, the water, I'll check them all,' she said, 'and I'll lock up securely.' She wasn't quite sure what the word was that escaped him, but it sounded like 'food'. 'Food?' she queried. 'You don't need to worry about any food, I'll see nothing's wasted, what won't keep I'll take myself and use up, don't you worry.' He gave a big sigh.

'I don't know what's for the best,' he said.

'Your staying here and resting and getting better is for the best,' she said. 'That's for the best, so don't you worry.'

'I *am* worried.'

'No need, you've nothing to fret about.'

'I have.' Then he opened his eyes and looked straight at her. 'You're his mother, good as,' he said, 'yer wouldn't shop him?' It was a statement, made strongly, but she wondered if he was rambling.

'Leo?' she asked.

'Aye.'

'What about him?'

'Yer wouldn't shop him? You're his mother, good as, that comes first.'

It all came together. How slow she'd been. His delight, his glee. The bacon. Her stomach felt strange, queasy. She didn't need to ask him but she had to go through the motions to be sure. 'Dad,' she said, 'you mean you've been hiding Leo?'

He didn't speak. 'You're his mother, good as,' he repeated.

'He's in your house now?' she asked.

He nodded.

'Since when? All the time?'

He shook his head, wearily. 'Niver yer mind,' he said, 'niver yer mind when. The lad needs to lie up awhile, out of harm's way, that's all, then he'll be on his way soon enough. He didn't do nowt, any road, 'tweren't his fault, 'twas the other chap, all a mistake.' When she had been quiet for a long time, not moving a fraction, sitting rock-still, clutching her bag, he turned to look at her. 'You're his mother, good as . . .' he began again, and she cut him short.

'Stop saying that,' she hissed. 'Stop it! I'm his grandmother, it doesn't make any difference, anyway, I know what you mean. My God. Hiding him, so pleased with yourself, I might have known. What a mess, what a *mess*.'

'Promise,' Eric James said, and then, raising his voice, 'promise!'

'I'm not promising anything,' Sheila said, 'you've no right to be wanting promises. The idea!'

'If you turn that lad in,' her father said, 'I'll niver forgive yer, niver, mind. Niver. You're his mother, it'd be unnatural.'

'I don't know what I'm going to do,' Sheila said, almost sobbing. 'I just don't know.'

'You're going to remember you're his mam, good as.'

'I'll have to see him.'

'He doesn't want to see you. I said I'd keep my trap shut and I did, if it hadn't been for that bloody pavement . . . that's all that's got it out of me, not being able to get home and him there, wondering. I can't leave him there, wondering . . .'

'No,' she said, 'no, you can't.'

He was very agitated now, his head going from side to side, his hands gripping and ungripping the sheets, no longer smoothly under his chin, but rumpled, in a heap. She straightened them and gave him some water. He gripped her hand with his own good hand. 'Now promise,' he said.

She could break the grip easily, but she let it remain and looked at him steadily. 'For tonight,' she said, 'until I come tomorrow, until I've thought about it, I won't do anything until then. But I'll have to go and tell him where you are, won't I? I'll have to, you said yourself, he'll wonder otherwise, he might do something silly, he might just leave, go on the run again.'

'Aye,' her father murmured, 'he might that.'

She left the hospital in a dream.

Chapter Fourteen

'SHE'S AT YOUR AUNT MARY'S,' Joe said, 'you know, that old one in Newcastle.'

'Really?' Ginny was puzzled. 'She never told me. Why on earth has she gone to see her, for heaven's sake?'

'She's ill or something.'

'But, I mean, why does Harriet suddenly go and see her? It isn't her responsibility. Aunt Mary's in a Home, has been for years, and she doesn't recognise anyone.'

'Well, that's where she's gone. She's back tomorrow. Dad's picking her up from the station.'

'You mean she hasn't driven?'

'No.'

'Why ever not?'

'I don't know.'

'Aunt Mary's Home is miles from anywhere, she'd need her car. Why on earth has Harriet gone by train? I don't understand it.'

'You don't have to,' Joe said, quite rudely. 'Anyway, it's good. I'm getting lots of practice in on her car. Dad's taken me out every evening, doing reversing round corners and stuff.'

The excitement of driving was brilliant. He felt a rush of adrenalin every time he got into the driver's seat and all through the routine of adjusting the mirror, looking over his shoulder, making himself comfortable, he was longing for the moment he turned the ignition on and heard the engine. Sheer thrill, that was what it was, unbeatable. He loved changing gear, it was like a dance, the lovely way the stick slipped from first to second, the smooth rhythm of foot down on the clutch, the satisfaction of the car obeying him – he felt powerful, happy. It was the only place he was aware of being positively happy. His instructor said he was a natural, that he had good co-ordination and a feel for the engine. Sometimes he was too confident, he'd approach junctions and roundabouts too fast, forget to change down from fourth to second, but he always coped. Even the manoeuvres he enjoyed doing, those hill starts and parallel parkings others moaned about. The hour was never long enough, he hated it ending. His only reading now was the *Highway Code* and *Your Driving Test*, he carried them everywhere with him, memorising every single sign and symbol and instruction. He couldn't imagine how people could go through life as pedestrians.

His father shared none of his enthusiasm. 'A car is danger on wheels,' Sam said, pompously. 'Never forget it.' And, 'It doesn't matter how well you drive, other drivers will be fools, you have to expect disaster all the time.' What was he trying to do? Smash the one bit of confidence his son had managed to regain? Joe was annoyed but tried not to betray this – he needed Sam to take him out. They got on badly. Unlike his instructor, his father didn't think he was a natural, he didn't think there was any such thing. Sam sat beside him wincing every time Joe went over thirty miles an hour. Even in the large car park by the end of the lake Sam wasn't happy. The car park was empty, almost, by eight in the evening, and perfect for practising three-point turns between marked-out limits, but Sam said that he should be slower, more careful, when Joe knew he could do the whole thing with panache. 'I don't know what gets into you in a car,' Sam grumbled. 'I hope you're not going to turn into one of these speed merchants.'

He was waiting, ready to go out in his mother's car, when his father came home.

'Give me a break,' Sam complained. 'I want to get changed first. Has your mother rung?' Joe said she hadn't. 'Well, I'd rather wait until she has. She said about now. And I might have to go straight off to collect her.'

'Couldn't I come? It would be good practice for me, driving to Carlisle station.'

'Certainly not, you're not nearly ready for that, and anyway I'm going on the motorway. Learners can't drive on it. Are you sure she hasn't rung?'

'Sure. Only Ginny.'

'What did she want?'

'Mum.'

'Oh. What did you tell her?'

'What did I tell her?' Joe looked astonished. His father's face was all furrowed with sudden anxiety. 'I said she was at Aunt Mary's, of course, what else would I say?'

Sam nodded and went off to change. Joe sat, holding the car keys, on the chair in the hall, determined to be very obviously waiting. He could hear his father taking a shower. He began to think, as he had not done before, about his mother going off to this Aunt Mary person. He hadn't seen, until now, that it was odd. Ginny had. She'd thought it very odd. And his father had asked him what he'd told Ginny – peculiar thing to ask. When Sam came down, he said, 'Why don't you ring Mum at Aunt Mary's if you want to know what time to pick her up?'

'I can't. It's a Home.'

'So?'

'Well, they don't have personal phones, there's only the reception. They wouldn't know.'

Joe stared at him. His father had always been a rotten liar. Now he was in a hurry to cover up his lie by being keen to go out in the car. 'Come on,' he said, 'let's get cracking. I'm hungry, I want to get back as soon as possible.' But the telephone rang as they opened the front door. Joe saw his father run towards it and snatch it up and say, 'Harriet?' in a sort of panic-stricken voice. He seemed to listen a long time without saying anything himself. Then he looked worried. 'I see,' he finally said, and, 'Right, okay, but ring as soon as you know, promise?'

There wasn't quite the same pleasure in being in the car. His father was abstracted, hardly seemed to notice when he drove at fifty miles an hour in the built-up area, and when they got to the lake car park he said, 'Fine,' too quickly every time Joe turned the car between the stones they'd put out. Something was wrong. On the way back, Joe said, 'What did you mean, Mum had to ring you as soon as she knew? Soon as she knew what?'

'Oh, how Aunt Mary was going to be. She's very ill.'

'So Mum's staying another night?'

'Maybe. Mind this corner, it's up a hill, you can't see what's coming.'

'Where does she stay?'

'What?'

'Where does Mum sleep?'

Sam looked completely thrown. 'Oh, they have a spare room for visitors, I expect,' he said, hurriedly. 'Keep both hands on the wheel, you're far too flash.'

Joe waited until they were in the house and were sitting eating lasagne in front of the television. His dad wasn't taking anything in, he could tell. In one way, he didn't want to find out what was going on. He wanted to stay ignorant, it was safer, easier. He didn't want to know anything bad. He couldn't face it. It was worse than that – he actually couldn't be bothered to know, it was too much trouble. Especially if it was to do with his mother. Whatever it was, she wanted him to think she had gone to visit her Aunt Mary and his father had gone along with it and that was fine by him. If he pushed his father he'd probably get at the truth. Certainly he would, in the end. He could make a real nuisance of himself and his father wouldn't be able to stand it, he'd tell him, then make him promise not to reveal what he knew to his mother. It was tiring even thinking about it. Just when the driving was making him feel so happy. What he really wanted to do was pass his test, buy his own car, a cheap second-hand one, and roar off. Leave whatever was going on behind. Be by himself. With a car, in a car, he wouldn't mind being by himself. He'd never have to walk down a street on his own again.

It made him feel elated and yet miserable to think of it. He couldn't bear his home any more, this very house. Its familiarity, every corner of it, made him cry. It was a sad, sad place, full of his past self. He'd always loved it but now, ever since, ever *since*, he knew he couldn't bear to be in it. But he'd been afraid to leave it because there was nothing else. It upset him to be inside his home but, for such a long time, until now really, it upset him more to go out from it and feel lost and frightened. The sight of his mother made him cry too. Her face, so anxious, so concerned for him, so hurt, watching him all the time, alert to his every movement. He was cruel to her because it relieved the pain for him, it was like the exquisite agony of picking a sore. He longed for *her* to hit *him*, lash out at him, he wanted to see her expression change to one of loathing and contempt, though he knew if it did he would be devastated.

He didn't mind at all that she had gone away. It was a relief. He felt guilty thinking like that, but it was indeed a relief. So if she had gone for some other reason apart from visiting an aged aunt it didn't matter. His mind began to run over possible reasons why she might have gone and he stopped it, quickly. He didn't want to speculate. It was selfish, but he couldn't bear to be concerned about his mother. He had enough trouble thinking of himself, worrying about himself. He wanted to think about driving and cars and nothing else.

★

Sheila went straight to her father's house. She should have taken a taxi but there were none waiting outside the Infirmary and her impatience was greater than her exhaustion. But her legs felt distressingly weak and there was nowhere, along the way, to sit down. She should go to her own home and tell Alan and he would drive her over but she couldn't wait, she had to go and find Leo now. As she entered her father's street she realised she was afraid. Not nervous, afraid. Afraid of Leo, afraid of what might happen, how he might react, and most of all afraid of the decision she would have to make. Her father thought of it as so simple: of course she would keep quiet, help Leo to stay hidden, protect him. But it wasn't simple.

She had keys to both the front and back doors but she never used the front and neither did Eric James, except on state occasions. Often, he left the back door unlocked, which she and Carole were always pleading with him not to do, but he announced that it would be a foolish burglar who dared to try and burgle him and nothing would puncture his image of himself as frighteningly invincible. She tried the door cautiously. He had, after all, locked it. It was hard to open quietly – the lock was old and needed oiling, the key heavy, made of iron, a big old-fashioned thing. Once inside, she locked the door again and put the key in her pocket. Then she crept to the front door and turned the other key in that lock. Only then did she relax a little. She stood quite still, listening. Not a sound. If Leo was crouching, breathless, upstairs, what would he be listening for? The kettle. Eric James always put the kettle on when he came in. He didn't always go on to make tea, but out of habit, his dead wife's habit, he put the kettle on.

Sheila put the kettle on. When it had boiled she thought she might as well make some tea. It would steady her, though she was beginning to think nothing would. Her heart fluttered, rapid little beats, then missed a beat, her stomach churned and she couldn't stop licking her lips, round and round her tongue went trying to moisten them. She couldn't stand here for ever, it was ridiculous. She had things to do. Carole still hadn't been told about her father and neither had Alan. She went to the foot of the stairs and paused. Should she shout up? Force Leo to come down? Eric James would have shouted by now, Leo would be suspicious. Slowly, she walked up the stairs, her hand so sweaty it slid along the banister as though it was oiled. There were only two bedrooms, one of them divided by a thin plywood wall, put up to separate her and Carole. The door to this room was closed, the door to Eric James's own room open. Just in case, she looked in her father's room first. Nobody could possibly hide in it. A double bed, a dressing table, a chest of drawers, all crammed together. The only place was in the wardrobe. She opened it, silly though it was to suspect Leo might be there. She and Carole used to hide there when they were little, crouching among the shoes, their mother's dresses concealing their faces, but Leo was far too big, he'd never get into it even if he crouched. And he wasn't, which she had known he wouldn't be. Of course he wasn't. If he was anywhere he was in her old cubicle of a room.

Now that she knew that, she felt calmer, more ready for him. She mustn't sound timid. That would be fatal. Matter-of-fact, that's how she should sound. Give nothing away. She mustn't sound angry or hostile or give any indication of what she thought of him escaping and hiding there. She would find that easy because she didn't know herself. She went into Carole's old bedroom and towards the door into the one which had been hers. 'Leo,' she said, keeping any questioning note out of her voice. 'Leo, it's me. Your grandad has had a fall. He's in hospital. He had to let on you were here, he was worried what you'd think when he didn't come home.' She paused, quite pleased with how reasonable, how unexcitable she had sounded. She thought, but couldn't be sure, that she heard a faint sound from the other side of the door. She wasn't going to open it, she wanted him to do that. She sat down on the stool beside the window and looked out. Washing lines, there were a lot of washing lines. The woman next door, a newcomer, was taking her sheets in, such a nice sight, watching her unpeg them, tame their billowing life, fold them. Leo must be watching too, there was nothing else for him to do. He'd be used to keeping away from the window, though. Eric James would have impressed that upon him. Probably he went downstairs in the evening and watched television. No one would dare to call on Eric James unannounced and if they did it would be entirely in character for him to tell them to go away.

'Leo,' she said cheerfully, and hoped she sounded cheerful, 'come out of there, eh?'

★

The last thing Harriet wanted to do was fuss. She hated people who tried to throw their weight around, who tried to imply they were of some importance. She wasn't of any importance anyway, it would be hopeless. But they had said two nights – one before the operation and one after it – and she was ready to go. She'd been ready since nine in the morning, up and dressed and absolutely ready. She'd slept well, there was no bleeding, and the dressing had been removed. But they wouldn't let her go. The registrar, who'd done the cone biopsy, needed to see her, they said. She must wait for him and no, they didn't know when he would come. There were various emergencies today, she might have to stay another night. Harriet said she thought there were queues for beds, this was ridiculous when she was perfectly recovered. They ignored her.

As the day wore on, she began to suspect all kinds of things. Why did she have to be seen by the registrar? What was he going to do? What was he going to say? Had the biopsy shown cancer cells? Was that it? Would they know this, as soon as it was done? Why did they never tell you anything? Why was she being left in such ignorance? She tried to read but her mind wandered. She wanted to ring Sam but it was pointless when she had no news. It would only upset him unnecessarily. She knew she was being unfriendly, keeping herself apart from the other women. They would think her stuck up. She wondered why she'd been so biddable all her life – what was to stop her from simply announcing that she was going? Nothing. She could just go. They might not be pleased, but it would be up to them to contact her at home. So she rang Sam and told him that if the registrar hadn't come in another hour she would leave. She'd ring him again then and tell him, and if he still insisted he could come for her. She'd just sit and wait outside. It was a beautiful evening, it would be a pleasure to sit on a bench in the sun.

She packed her bag ostentatiously and put her book on top of it. It was half past six. She'd leave before they brought supper round, ring Sam from the reception area, that would be best, more tactful. She thought she'd check there were phones there, even though she was sure there must be. It would fill in a few minutes going to find out. She set off, pleased to find she felt perfectly steady, though she had been told the anaesthetic might take time to wear off completely. She walked down the stairs, to test her legs further. But she took a wrong turning, came not to the reception area but into another wing, an older part of the Infirmary. Here, the atmosphere was different. It seemed darker, it was darker, and dreary. She glimpsed old, very sick-looking people through the open doors. She was glad not to have old parents in need of her support. She couldn't bear the thought of having to visit and then look after one of those pathetic aged patients she could see lying there as though dead already. Whatever feeling she had had for her parents would never have survived the strain. Briefly, she thought of Sheila Armstrong and how she had spoken of her father, with pride and affection, she thought. All her own feelings like that were for her boys. She had never felt any strong emotion for her parents. Once she was an adult she had only wanted to be free of them. She would have been dutiful, if they had lived to be old and ill, but not truly loving. And she hadn't been devastated with grief when her parents had died. Sam, so fond of his own mother and father, even if his affection was hardly put to the test since they lived in Canada, had been rather shocked by her detachment. She couldn't explain it. She hurried on, trying to find her way out. She could ask a nurse, but she didn't want to, they were all so busy. She began to panic. She knew it was absurd but this part of the hospital scared her, she wanted to be back in that light, bright ward she'd been in such a hurry to leave.

By the time she found her way there, still not having reached the reception area but now no longer caring, she didn't feel so good. And the registrar was standing by her bed, frowning, looking at some notes.

'Here she is,' the staff nurse said. 'Mrs Kennedy, you shouldn't go off without telling us, doctor's been waiting.'

Harriet hated being in the wrong. She apologised, didn't even suggest she'd also been waiting, all day. She sat on her bed and the registrar looked at her quizzically. 'Had a walk?' he said.

'Yes.'

'Feeling okay?'

'Yes, thank you.'

'Good. So you're anxious to get home?'

'Of course.'

'Oh, I don't know,' he said, folding his arms, yawning, then excusing his yawns. 'We're quite popular with some people, you'd be surprised.'

She waited. She wasn't going to chat. If he had something to tell her she wished he would get it over with . . .

On her way out, relieved that she'd been told the biopsy had shown no cause for concern but that they'd like her to have smears every six months for the next three years, just to keep an eye on her, she couldn't keep the smile off her face. She'd done it, managed this little subterfuge so discreetly that Joe would never know a thing about it. He had been saved from even the smallest pang of anxiety, and that was how she wanted it. She swept out of the Infirmary and looked for a seat. Sam was on his way. She sat down, facing the late sun, and breathed deeply. Heaven to be out, to be free. A car stopped just in front of her. 'Wait, wait,' the driver was saying to the woman in the passenger seat, who was trying to get out before he'd stopped. She saw it was Sheila Armstrong.

★

He wasn't there. But he had been. There were tell-tale signs everywhere in the house. Toothpaste and toothbrush in the bathroom, when Eric James had had false teeth for thirty years; socks drying in the airing cupboard, socks of a size and type which made them definitely not her father's; screwed-up Mars Bar wrappers in the wastepaper-basket when chocolate of any kind was never brought into the house. He'd been there. His shape was still on the bed, still imprinted on the cotton cover, as clear

275

to see as though he'd been lying in sand. She could even smell him in the air, a mixture of that odd shampoo he used on his hair and something else, something indefinable. He'd been there and left in a hurry. There were crumbs on the bed cover and a plate on the floor. She ran a finger-tip round the plate. Toast. Toast and marmalade, her own home-made marmalade which she made every year and gave to her father, three jars to himself. A wet towel was thrown over the towel rail in the bathroom, thrown carelessly, as Eric James would never have thrown it. Soap suds were still warm in the bottom of the bath. He'd set off clean, then, clean and fed. That was something. What had he taken with him?

She didn't want to look. She wouldn't know how much Eric James had once more accumulated. It was a year since Carole had found and banked the last lot. Who could tell how many races he'd bet on since then, how many winners he'd had? He was incorrigible. Nearly ninety and still tottering down to put bets on, then denying he went near the betting shop. He always had denied it. 'Going to see a man about a dog,' he'd say, when they were young, and she'd always believed him, waited patiently to see this dog one day. It was harmless, kept him happy, gave him an interest. But it was dangerous keeping his winnings under the mattress. Carole had had a fit when she came to make his bed and found all the ten-pound notes. She'd had to confront him. He said it was his pension. Carole asked him what he'd been living on then, if that was his pension. Then there was the bedroom carpet. Carole had swept it – he didn't have a vacuum cleaner – and found the carpet all bumpy. She thought he was pressing something under it. More money, more bundles of tenners. They'd been amazed, how could he have so much money? He must have had winners at 100–1 several times over.

She didn't dare look. Even if there were nothing, it

wouldn't prove Leo had taken it. Only her father would know, and even he was unlikely to know how much. He hadn't the faintest idea how much he had tucked away, she was sure. She didn't know how she would feel if it turned out that Leo had taken money. Relieved? Glad to know he wasn't penniless? Or sorry he was now also a thief? Not that her father would see it as stealing, she was sure. Hesitantly, she went into his bedroom and lifted the counterpane, a faded blue affair which had 'seen better days' as Carole put it. It needed washing but Eric James couldn't bear a night without it for some unfathomable reason. She turned back the eiderdown and the flannelette sheets – he must be roasting with all this on his bed in summer – and slid her hand under the lumpy old mattress. Nothing. Bolder, she lifted the mattress right up and peered underneath it. There was one bundle of notes there, kept together with an elastic band. She withdrew it carefully, as though it were burning, and let the mattress flop back into place.

In the kitchen she sat down. She wasn't going to stay, so there was no point making more tea. There was a slip of paper tucked inside the elastic band on top of the money. It was a note from Leo. 'Dear Grandad,' it said, 'You said you wanted to give me all your money, so I hope it is all right to take some of it. I have taken £500 and left £200. I will repay all of it. I am sorry to go like this, but I can't stay for ever. Thank you for everything. I am sorry about everything. Give Mam my love and tell her one day I'll come back. Sorry.' There was a row of kisses. No signature. Five hundred pounds. Not a small sum, not an absolute fortune. He didn't have a passport, it wouldn't get him out of the country. It would get him to London, though, and keep him there for a while. Leo was clever, hard-working. With £500 he might have a chance. A chance to do what? She wished she knew.

She smiled slightly to herself. Leo had never known of his great-grandfather's loss of faith. He had probably imagined that Eric James stood by him whatever he had or hadn't done. They wouldn't have talked about that, of course. Leo would have been able to depend on that – no discussion. A few grunts and that would have been all. He hadn't had to fear cross-examination from Eric James, only from her. The minute he'd appeared at the door, the minute he'd whispered his name when his great-grandfather asked who was there, he'd have been impossible to resist. What kind of love was that, if it was love? Maybe the sort a mother should have and she'd been incapable of. Maybe it was mother love, uncritical, limitless . . .

Oh nonsense. She shook her head angrily and sighed. Well, that was that. Gone again. Eric James would be pleased he hadn't been caught, yet. She'd have to tell him about the money. That would please him too, it would make him feel useful. He'd boast about it within the family. Boast, too, that Leo had trusted him, not her. He'd known where to come, whom he could depend on. She washed the mug she'd used, checked the gas was off, looked around. Everything was so shabby. The cooker was fifty-odd years old, it was a museum-piece. Maybe while Eric James was in hospital Alan could decorate this kitchen. Her father would be furious but it would be worth it. A nice, cheerful yellow perhaps. And some new lino. This stuff was cracked and split to bits. All it did was harbour germs. Leo could have laid it for him, he could have done all kinds of things. She wondered how long he'd been here, she wondered if he had talked to his great-grandfather, did Eric James now know the whole story? Did he know Leo's plans, where he might go, what he might do? . . . Suddenly it seemed urgent to see her father again, get as much out of him as she could. Maybe she could make a bargain: *she* would promise not to go to the police, not to say a word, if *he* told her all he knew.

She locked the back door behind her and hurried home. She needed Alan. She couldn't dash on her own to the Infirmary again, he would have to drive her, then she'd send him to tell Carole in person, get him out of the way while she dealt with her father. She couldn't decide what she wanted to know most, the past or the future, what Leo could remember of that night, or what he was proposing to do. The past. It was true what was past was past, but if it was unknown it never seemed to be over. The future she could cope with. It would be a strain, but she could train herself. As they said, there was always hope where the future was concerned. She could hope Leo would make good and return. She could hope he would find a way, perhaps quite quickly, to get messages to her. Yes, she could cope with the future now, it didn't terrify her. This little note, it was a link. She'd keep it and get it out and read it when she was most down, she'd notice all over again that Leo had written 'Sorry' three times. It was all there, his remorse, his regret for what he had done to her. Others might not interpret his words to mean that, Alan certainly wouldn't, but she could and did. Better still if he'd left a note for her too, but she understood that that was asking too much at the moment, he couldn't trust himself, not yet.

She had Alan in the car in two minutes, bewildered and complaining, but in the car all the same. He tried to ask questions, but she had no patience with them, told him she'd explain later, told him just to drop her at the Infirmary. She didn't see Harriet Kennedy. As she got out of the car, Alan shouting at her to wait, she heard a woman's voice say her name, but she couldn't quite take in who it was, only vaguely acknowledged the greeting and rushed on, anxious to get to her father's bedside. She'd no time to be polite.

She had to wait for the lift, not trusting herself to climb the stairs in her present agitated state. She must calm down. People would look at her if her face went all red and sweaty. She felt it was already. This excitement, this terrible kind of excitement, that was all she could think of to call it, but the word wasn't quite accurate, this feeling made her ill. She liked life to be quiet, uneventful. She had never liked shocks, drama. And now everything seemed too dramatic, she shrank from this turn in her life. All drama. Pat would have relished it. She'd liked everything to be unpredictable, though she wouldn't of course have liked the drama to be because her son was in trouble. No, she wouldn't have liked that, no mother did. But Pat had had no time to know what it was like to be a mother, she hadn't even begun on motherhood. Mothering for the first three years was nothing, nothing . . .

The lift finally came. Sheila stepped in. It was full of doctors and nurses, there was hardly room for her. She felt apologetic. They were all talking but not about anything medical. Food, it seemed to be about food, who had last had any, who had had what and when. At least this time she knew where to go, that was some small comfort. But the door into Eric James's room was closed. She supposed it meant he was asleep, she'd be disturbing him, the staff nurse might be cross. She opened the door very, very quietly. The room was in darkness, semi-darkness, anyway. She could hear Eric James's heavy breathing. It was a shame to waken him, perhaps they'd drugged him and she wouldn't be able to. 'Dad,' she whispered, but there was no pause in the rhythm of his breathing. It would be cruel to shake him. She gave a little moan of exasperation, she'd have to wait until tomorrow, obviously. By then Carole would be here and it would be awkward trying to get time on her own. But it was pointless staying. She left the room and started guiltily as the staff nurse saw her. 'I just wanted to say goodnight,' she said, afraid she'd broken the rules. The staff nurse smiled, said her father had been given a sedative.

So she was out of the place in half an hour, not the hour she'd told Alan, who would be at Carole's house. She'd have to hang about, lucky it was fine. She looked for a seat. It was such a busy place this, cars forever drawing up, crowds forever coming in and out of the building. All action, all drama. She could never stand working in a hospital, it would be too much. Then she saw Harriet Kennedy smiling at her, waving.

'We seem doomed to meet on benches,' Harriet said. She looked radiant, pale but happy. Sheila knew how *she* must look. She sank down on the bench and couldn't prevent a great sigh. Really, everything was beyond her. She closed her eyes, tried to compose herself, heard Harriet ask, 'Have you been visiting?'

Sheila nodded, managed to say, 'My father, he fell.' She must be careful what she said. She mustn't even think about mentioning Leo, nothing whatsoever to do with Leo, especially not to Harriet. She'd just have to pretend the state she was in was due to worry over her father. Easy enough. Harriet was sympathetic, most concerned, but Sheila wished she would go away. She couldn't attempt a conversation, any conversation; she just sat there.

'Is your husband picking you up?' Harriet asked.

Sheila nodded.

'You're sure? Because if not we can drop you off, it would be no trouble. Sam will be here any minute.'

'No, thank you. Alan is coming. I don't mind waiting, it's warm enough, he'd wonder where I was . . .'

'Yes, it is warm. I've enjoyed waiting. It's lovely to get out of a hospital, isn't it? I hated being in there.'

Normally, Sheila would have asked how she did come to have been in there, but she was too tired to be curious.

Harriet was volunteering the information anyway. '. . . small op. . . .' Sheila caught, and tried to concentrate, '. . . but everything was fine, thank God. I don't think Joe could have stood anything being wrong with me. I didn't tell him. You'll think it silly, but I kept it a secret. He thinks I'm visiting an aunt. Awful, isn't it? I mean, my lying like this, keeping secrets from my own son.'

'I expect,' Sheila said, her voice a croak, 'he keeps some from you.' Why had she said that? She couldn't think.

'Perhaps,' Harriet said, 'but I doubt it. He's an open book to me. Sometimes I wish he wasn't. He needs to stand on his own feet, we're too close. He's seventeen, Louis was separate by then. I don't think Joe ever will be.'

'Oh, he will,' said Sheila, 'and then you'll wish he wasn't. It's worse, when they've been close.'

She wished Harriet would go. The arrival of her husband was a blessing. He drew up and sprang out of the car and kissed her. Very touching. Harriet blushed, said something to him before saying goodbye to Sheila. They looked so happy setting off together, a good-looking couple without a care in the world . . . Alan arrived soon after. He tooted the horn and she went and got into the car. 'Carole's all worked up,' were his first words. 'Says she should have been told earlier. And Peter says that's it, it'll have to be a home, he isn't safe any more.'

'Oh, be quiet,' she said.

'Eh?'

'Be quiet. My head aches, I'm worn out.'

'*You* are. I've done all the dashing about . . .'

'In a car. I've done it on my legs. Anyway, just be quiet, please.'

He was quiet. They drove home in silence. As soon as they got in – Alan threw the car keys angrily on the table and disappeared into the yard to begin watering his blessed geraniums – the telephone rang. It rang and rang and she took no notice. She had to have a cup of tea before she spoke to anyone.

'Are you going to answer that?' Alan shouted.

'No. Let them ring again.'

He came back in and said, 'With your dad in hospital? You're not answering, with your dad in hospital?' and he snatched up the receiver. 'It's Carole,' he said.

She'd known it would be. Alan was gesturing wildly. She turned away. He let the receiver dangle and went back into the yard. She could hear Carole's furious voice. 'Hello,' she said, 'what's all this shouting about? I've just got in and I'm worn out, you don't know the half of it.'

It took her five trying minutes to placate Carole, and then there was Peter to deal with, dutiful, only more concerned with plans for his father-in-law's release than his accident. She was tired of both of them. But she acknowledged to herself that she owed something to Alan. Over their tea, she told him about Leo and about the money. He was so stunned he didn't cross-examine her at all, just looked glazed, shook his head repeatedly. They ate, they drank their tea. Finally, he found his voice and said, 'It doesn't make sense, there's no sense in it.'

'There is,' she said, feeling kinder. 'There's a lot of sense. It does make sense. Where would you have gone, if you'd been Leo? Here? Of course not. Couldn't trust us. Couldn't trust me, could he?'

'No, no, it would be because he'd know the house was watched.'

'Don't be daft, they wouldn't watch a house, not just for a boy like Leo absconding. No, he knew not to come because I'd turn him in, I'd have told him to give himself up before I turned him in. I'd have said it was for his own good. He'd have thought of all that.'

'But you wouldn't have done, you wouldn't have turned him in, you know you wouldn't have.'

'Do I?'

'Of course you do. You'd have helped him, like you've always done, he knows you think the world of him.'

'Oh yes?'

'Well, you do, always have, apple of your eye, always, the best mother any boy could have, and he knew it.'

'Best isn't always best,' she said.

'What? Don't *you* talk daft.'

She thought of Harriet Kennedy being driven home by her handsome, caring husband, and Joe waiting for them, not knowing where his mother had been, and she so pleased with her duplicity. Little plots, little subterfuges. Nothing out in the open. Mothers sure their sons were open books, sons bored by the predictability of mothers. She knew why Leo couldn't trust her, why he hadn't even been able to explain to her what had got into him on that terrible night. Too close to hurt, that was the trouble. Whereas his great-grandfather was, by comparison, distant, beyond the pain he could cause her. He was afraid of her closeness to him, of those years and years of openly declared love, of her very devotion to him. She expected too much of him, thought of him as incapable of true deceit or cruelty, wasn't prepared to face the bad, the weak, in him. She'd made it unbearable for him to confide in her just by her very standards for him.

'I'm going up to bed,' she said, and when Alan looked aggrieved, and she knew was about to say it was only nine o'clock, still light, she added, 'I'm tired, done in, I can't think straight, and I'll have to be up at the Infirmary tomorrow, first thing, before Carole barges in, before she gets to Dad and wears him out. I want him on my own, get some matters straight before it's too late.'

Chapter Fifteen

IN MID-AUGUST, just before Harriet and Sam went to
Edinburgh, Joe passed his driving test, first time. He
came home, face flushed, trying to contain his euphoria,
and failing. Looking at him, seeing his excitement, his
sense of triumph, Harriet felt more shaken than happy. So
little, had it really taken so little? A driving test passed and
there was Joe, more himself than he had been for a whole
year. Or so it seemed. A transformation and yet it could
not be one, surely. Inside, he must still suffer, still be
scarred . . .

The agitation to have his own car began at once. He had
a few hundred pounds in National Savings Certificates,
left to him by his grandparents. He wanted to cash them,
buy a second-hand car. On and on the persuading went,
the pleading, the passionate advancing of his cause. All he
wanted in life was a car, a car he wouldn't be able to afford
to tax or license, or run. Sam told him straight that all six
hundred pounds would buy would be a load of trouble,
the kind of trouble which they would have to bail him out
of. And then Ginny played into his hands. She was buying
a new car, would get very little for her five-year-old Fiesta
and yet it was a good car, had never had anything wrong
with it. She would accept Joe's six hundred pounds.

So he got his car and there was nothing Harriet could do
about it. He said she spoiled everything with her anxious
expression. 'You don't want me to be happy,' he said, and
then, seeing her stricken face, 'Well, that's what it looks

like.' She tried hard to share his delight but could not suppress all the warnings of danger, the dangers of driving. 'It's not your driving I worry about,' she said (though this was not true), 'it's other people's.' He ignored her. Day after day he drove to the boat yard where he now had a full-time holiday job, loving his car, always impatient to get into it. Then he began talking of going on tour in it, just for the pleasure of driving. He wanted to drive round the whole of the British Isles on secondary roads, on his own, just him and his car. Luckily, lack of money stopped him. Everything he had had gone into purchasing the car, and all the boat yard pay gave him was petrol and pocket money for each week. It was a relief for Harriet to know he couldn't yet do what he wanted to do, couldn't cut loose and go off.

But it made going to Edinburgh harder, knowing Joe had a car and was never out of it. Suppose he had an accident while they were away? Harriet expected an accident daily. He was such an aggressive driver, he terrified her. She could hardly bear to watch him drive off, accelerating far too fast as he turned from the drive into the road. Sam said he was in fact a good driver, confident and in control, though he conceded that for someone inexperienced he had too much confidence. The trouble was, she could *see* him crashing. Quite clearly. She could see the front of the Fiesta smashed in and Joe's body slumped over the wheel and blood everywhere . . . It was hard to say nothing and sometimes a small protest escaped her. 'That van almost hit you this morning,' she would say. 'I saw it, I saw it coming round the corner and you hadn't seen it, had you? You must *always* watch out for that corner . . .'

'I do,' he said, annoyed.

'You swerved really wide,' she said, 'and if another car had been coming . . .'

'Well, it wasn't.'

'But *if*!'

'Oh God, Mum, I can't go on through life on "if"s. It didn't, no other car came along, and *if* it had I'd have coped.'

'That's what you think but . . .' Then she stopped.

'But what? You think I can't cope, don't you?'

'No, it's just that . . . oh, it's all so dangerous, things do happen . . .'

'And I'm not supposed to know that? You think *I* don't know that?'

'Of course you do . . .'

'Of course I bloody do, so shut up.'

He was so savage, so furious with her, and she saw he was right. Louis was thousands of miles away, driving in a strange continent, and yet she didn't daily agonise over him or fantasise about accidents. Joe was right, she had fallen into the habit of thinking of him as doomed, a person over whom disaster would always hang, an unlucky traveller in life. And it was so unfair, so silly. He was no more likely to have an accident than any other teenager who had just learned how to drive . . . but the moment she had reassured herself like this she couldn't help registering that it was little comfort because accidents were so high in this age bracket.

Then he met Claire. All because of the car, because of having a car. Claire, new friend of Natasha's, new to the area. He met her at Ginny's house and drove her home and after that he was with her all the time that he wasn't at the boat yard. He brought her home, full of himself, boastful because she was so pretty, such a catch (but a catch of his car, not of Joe, Harriet meanly thought). Claire couldn't have been more wrong for him. She was bold and brassy, Harriet decided . . . brassy, that old-fashioned term used about barmaids, and a barmaid was what Claire looked like. Blonde out-of-a-bottle, orangey blonde, dried-out-looking thick hair, lots of it. Large breasts barely contained in halter tops. Big, big smile showing irregular teeth. And very affectionate, touching Joe all the time, arm round his shoulders, arm linking his, hand ruffling his hair . . . He didn't push her off, not once. What were they doing in the car when he came in so late? 'What do you think?' said Sam, witheringly, and apparently unworried. 'He's seventeen,' Sam said to every objection Harriet raised. 'He's seventeen, Harriet.' He was indeed seventeen and she'd always longed for him to have a girlfriend, but not Claire, not someone like Claire who would ditch him when she had access to a better car. She began to issue more warnings, more muttered threats, or words that sounded like threats, because of how she spoke them. Joe ignored her. The more she went on about being careful, the more she suggested he should have other girlfriends apart from Claire, the more he blanked her. He, too, began to say, 'I am seventeen,' only he said it angrily.

To go away leaving Joe in an empty house with Claire around was folly. 'We can't go,' she said to Sam.

'Why the hell not?'

'Think,' she urged. '*Think*.'

'I am thinking. I'm thinking we haven't been away alone together for . . .'

'Oh I know that, it isn't what I meant, you know what I meant. Claire would just move in.'

'So?'

'*So*? Are you mad? They'd end up in bed together, God knows what would happen . . .'

'What usually happens in bed, I expect, though it hasn't happened so much in ours for the last year.'

'I'm going to ignore that.'

'Of course you are, you usually do, you ignore anything . . .'

'Don't be so smart, it's Joe I'm worried about.'

'So am I.'

'You wouldn't think it, to listen to you.'

'That's because you don't listen to yourself, because . . .'

'Oh be quiet.'

'. . . if you did you'd hear how stupid you sound, like a caricature, a caricature of, of . . .'

'Of what? Go on.'

'I can't think. You sound jealous, as though you can't stand the thought of Joe having fun . . .'

'Having fun? That's what it would be, is it? When this Claire dumps him? It would shatter him, he couldn't survive another blow, any more bad luck, he isn't ready for someone like Claire, it isn't *fun* he'd be having. She's having the fun . . .'

Sam was staring at her, pity in every line of his face.

'Don't look at me like that,' she shouted.

He shrugged, turned away. 'I'm going, anyway,' he said, 'to Edinburgh, I mean. I want to go. I need a break. Even if you stay, I'm going.'

'You can't do that.'

'Why?'

'Don't be ridiculous, think how it would look.'

'To whom? Joe?'

'Yes, Joe, everyone.'

'It would look how it is, that I'm fed up with your crazy ideas.'

'And what would that do to Joe, if he saw we'd quarrelled over him and you'd gone off . . .?'

'What would it do to Joe? Make him laugh, I should hope. You need to be laughed at, only I haven't the energy. Anyway, Joe wouldn't care if I went off without you. He'd probably be glad. You've made yourself into the indispensable one and me into nothing. I don't count.'

'Oh God, more self-pity, more whingeing, you're just so sorry for yourself these days, acting as though you've been somehow framed. It disgusts me.' She paused, but Sam said nothing, only smiled, and she picked up on his smile at once. 'There you are, you see, everything is a joke to you, everything has to be light-hearted, nothing is ever taken seriously. I haven't made you into anything, you've made yourself.'

'That doesn't make sense. What have I made myself into?'

'A coward, you're scared of Joe, you have been ever since he was attacked, you're scared of his distress and he knows it, he knows you can't bear it and he has to bear it, you just want to forget all the time – '

'Whereas you want to remember, and that's brave, is it? Revelling in the past is brave?'

'I don't revel.'

'You do.'

'In what exactly?'

'Suffering. You love it.'

'Are you mad?'

'No, you are, now you mention it, you're deranged half the time. You have no sense of proportion, you won't let life go on, every bloody thing is pulled back to the attack, as if – '

'As if? I warn you, Sam – '

'You warn me? I should have warned you long ago.'

'About what?'

'About how ridiculous you've become, how bitter, and about how much damage you're doing, and how I'm sick of this tragedy queen stuff. I'm sick of it and I couldn't care less whether you come with me to Edinburgh, I don't even know if I want you to come, you'd kill the weekend before it started. I'm going because I want to enjoy myself – yes, that filthy word, enjoy, have some pleasure again, and I'm not ashamed of wanting to do it. You can do what you like.'

And he left the house, banging the door, leaving Harriet with a frightening sick feeling in her stomach and the dreadful conviction, one she had never entertained before, that perhaps Sam's love for her was not as utterly solid and overwhelming as she had always believed.

★

In mid–August, Eric James died. Heart failure, nothing to do with his injuries, except in so far as the shock had weakened his strong, old heart. Only two days short of his ninetieth birthday. What a pity, Sheila found herself thinking, that he couldn't have hung on another forty-eight hours . . . it would so have pleased him to die, with such neatness, on the very day he was born. But he died on a hot, sunny day, two days before, two weeks after he'd come out of the Infirmary. It was the reminders which did for him, she was sure, coming home to the empty house where, for that short but thrilling time, he had sheltered Leo. He moped as soon as he came home, trudged round the small rooms, looking helpless, lost, picking things up and putting them down in a pointless way, and gathering up anything that Leo had used. Only he and Sheila, and of course Alan, knew why his own house suddenly seemed a mere empty shell for which he no longer had any affection. Carole, watching him, vowed he was ready to move into a Home. She said she was sure he'd realised he couldn't manage any more and he'd be happier surrounded by others. 'Rubbish,' Sheila said, and that was all.

She brought her father's dinner round every day and tried to talk to him about Leo. It took time, and a great deal of being glared at, to convince him that Leo had gone of his own volition and she had not betrayed him. 'He wasn't there, Dad,' she said again and again. 'Remember? I came straight to you in the Infirmary, only you were asleep, and then again the next day, and I told you he wasn't there. And I'd promised, hadn't I, to do nothing that night? I'd promised. And I didn't. He wasn't there, he'd gone already.' Over and over it they went and finally he'd believed her. But believing her hadn't helped much. He wondered aloud endlessly to her, when they were alone together, as to why Leo had gone at that particular time on that particular day. 'He said nowt,' Eric James protested, 'not a dicky bird, said nowt about moving on.'

'He wouldn't want you to know,' Sheila sighed. 'He'd know you'd be upset and it would make it harder for him to go and he had to go in the end.'

'He could've stopped a while longer.'

'How long had he been shut up here anyway?' Sheila probed. For some reason Eric James held on to this piece of trivial information as though it were precious, and it annoyed her. 'How long exactly?'

'Hard to say.'

'Hard to say? You mean you didn't notice? Don't be daft.'

'You watch your lip. Daft I'm not, else why'd he come to me, eh? Me, not you.'

He held that over her in a childish way all the time – me-not-you, me-not-you – until it sounded like bird song, that shrill, irritating cheep of an undistinguished sparrow.

'How did he look? How did he seem?' She was nevertheless obliged to ask, overcoming her resentment. And he liked her to ask that, it pleased him, gave him power.

'Champion,' he said. 'He looked champion, hadn't teken any harm in spite of wandering. Once he'd had a bath and got some clean clothes on he looked champion, even if there were no trousers to fit him, too short in the leg mine were, but we got ower that with . . .'

'Dad, I meant *in himself*, how did he seem, not how his clothes looked.'

'All right. Same as alus. Bit quiet but then he alus was.'

'And how had he managed, where'd he been, how did he get away?' The questions poured out of her, though she would rather not have given him the satisfaction of pleading with him like this.

'Niver said how he got away, wouldn't say, for fear . . .'

She didn't enquire for fear of what . . . it was an expression he often used when he wanted to indicate vagueness and usually it meant he didn't know something, but wanted to pretend he did. 'He got on a lorry, after he'd ran miles and miles. Turned his clothes inside out and put his shirt on the outside, and nobody said nowt.'

'Then what? When he got off the lorry?'

'Walked, all night.'

'What did he eat?'

'Took his bread with him, in his pockets, lived on that the first day, bread and water, army rations, I remember when we . . .'

'Dad, what then, after he'd finished the bread?'

'You'd best not know.'

'You mean he stole money, food.'

'I'm saying nowt.'

'So he's a thief now as well. Dear God, there's no end to it. It gets worse and worse, first violence then theft . . .'

'I niver said the lad were a thief.'

'How else could he have managed? It's obvious.'

'Ways and means, ways and means, things I taught him, army tricks . . .'

'Oh, *Dad*.'

It was silly for her to keep on about how had Leo got himself here when what was much more vital was to try to glean the smallest scrap of information as to what he had intended to do after he left his great-grandfather's house. But she soon found out that Eric James had no idea. Leo had never discussed plans. He'd come to rest and hide for a while and to collect money. Definitely to collect money, without which he had no chance of really getting away, money Eric James was only too glad to push on to him. 'I wish he'd teken the lot,' he told Sheila. 'What do I want with it? He should have teken the lot, it was all for him.'

'If it was, it wasn't fair,' Sheila couldn't resist saying.

'Eh?'

'You've other grandchildren, Carole's girls. It wasn't fair to give it all to Leo, to want to give it all.'

'What's fair got to do with it? You and your fair. Nowt's fair. Leo needed it, that's the point.'

'Needed it to go on doing wrong.'

'He's not doing wrong, niver did.'

'Did he say so?'

'Eh?'

'You know – did he say? Did he talk about it? Did he say what happened?'

'He took summat.'

'We know that.'

'Well, that was it, he took summat he shouldn't and that was that, out of his head.'

'But did he do it?'

'What?'

'You know – did he, did he – oh, I can't talk about it, those things, those awful things . . .'

'Mebbe he did.'

'Is that what *he* said? Mebbe he did?'

'Eh?'

She saw him look at her almost in amusement, shaking his head and half smiling. She couldn't stand it. If he hadn't been so frail and sad, she would have hit him.

'You mek it hard for yerself,' he said finally, 'alus have,

very hard. If the lad did what he did he's sorry. He can't undo it, none of us can. But yer won't let him, eh?'

'Let him what?'

'Let him be. What's done is done. You've only yerself to blame, lass. He'll not come near you like this, he knows what you think.'

'He does, does he?' Distress and anger made her voice shrill. 'He doesn't know anything, and neither do you. Neither of you, you don't know what I've gone through, what I still go through, and he just goes off.'

'No other way.'

'What do you mean, no other way? What do you *mean*?'

But he just shook his head and then coughed and the moment passed, as it did again and again. Every time, over those two weeks, they would get near what she strained to hope was some kind of enlightenment, something he could tell her about herself and Leo, and it would disappear. They would sink back into platitudes or sit silent for hours, both somehow mourning. The muddled implication was that he understood something she didn't and it enraged her. All that joined them was the loss of Leo, their love for him, and they never spoke of it openly, not even at the very end.

Sheila and Carole knew that the end was coming by the middle of the second week after he came home. They could see it. It was remarkable how visible his approaching death seemed. The flesh was suddenly stripped not just off his big frame – he'd been thin for a long time now – but from his face. It became first gaunt then took on a transparent look, the skin stretched so lightly over the bony nose, over the large cheekbones, that it looked as if it would split at any moment. And his pulse was weak. The doctor told them how slow and faint it was and then looked at them to see if they understood the significance of this. They did. They were ready, they had been ever since their father took to his bed, on the Wednesday, and wouldn't move. They took turns sitting beside him. He'd open his eyes and look at them, as though checking, and then close them again and keep them closed until an hour or so had passed and he felt the need to check again. By Friday he wasn't eating, not even soup. He took sips of water, that was all. Sheila thought how dignified he looked, how an expected death was dignified. She thought of the phrase used on the wireless when the King died – 'the King's life is drawing peacefully to a close'.

On what turned out to be the last day she'd gone in and out of his bedroom, and he appeared to be sleeping quite peacefully. There was no special atmosphere. At six, she came to tell him she was going home and Carole was taking over. He didn't reply, but then he hadn't spoken all day. The room was dim, but not dark, the curtains partly closed to keep out the sun. She sat beside the bed a moment. Any hour now and he might die, he would die. She wanted to be present but she had stayed last night, it was Carole's turn, and if they did not take turns they would fall asleep. She didn't know why she wanted to be with him when he died. It wasn't as though there would be any last words. The time for words had long since gone and anyway her father was not a man of words. Or a man to demonstrate feelings. That had always been the trouble. He distrusted words, distrusted touch, and that had left him only with actions. He believed he showed how he cared and what he thought by his actions. He took Leo in so it didn't matter what he had said. He stayed close to her, he had been there all through what had happened, so it didn't matter that he had never hugged or embraced or physically comforted her.

She must go. Alan would be waiting. She squeezed her father's hand but there was no response, his fingers did not

296

curl round hers. When Carole appeared in the doorway she got up. Carole raised her eyebrows but she shook her head and whispered, 'Sleeping.' She went home and made Alan his tea and then the phone rang, and yes her father had died. Well, that was that. She felt tired, listless. She hardly had the energy to go back round to her father's house but she couldn't leave Carole on her own. Alan drove her over but she wouldn't let him come in to pay his last respects, not yet, not before she'd paid her own. It bothered her, standing looking at the body with Carole, that she wasn't absolutely sure she had respected her father. Maybe. She'd respected his strength and loyalty and independence but not exactly him. It was hard to believe that great domineering force had gone for good. There would be nothing now to push against, to resist, but instead of this relieving her it depressed her.

Somewhere, out there, Leo didn't know. He couldn't possibly think his great-grandfather could live for ever, but he had last seen him astonishingly fit and well and couldn't be expected to realise how quickly he had failed. He might try to get in touch with Eric James, his chosen link with his family, with her. Without Eric James, there would be no means, except the most direct, for him to make contact, when and if he chose. Instead of this depressing her it somehow lifted her spirits. He could never cast her off for ever, of course he couldn't, and now he would be forced to realise this.

He couldn't hide behind his great-grandfather any more.

★

Harriet went to Edinburgh with Sam. She felt she had to. She knew he'd meant what he'd said, and without being able to admit there was some truth in his accusation, she knew she had to take heed and try. He was so happy when

297

she said she'd go with him. They stayed in Northumberland Street, in a bed–and–breakfast place. Sam had promised her the term was a misnomer, conjuring up visions of some cramped, cabbage–smelling abode and a landlady in curlers reeking of kippers, and it was. The house was Georgian, the rooms high–ceilinged and spacious, the landlady gracious. They had a room at the back, prettily furnished in chintzy materials and full of flowers, all exactly to Harriet's taste. She tried hard to feel happy but instead she felt adrift, completely adrift. All her thoughts were back at home, with Joe. She watched the clock all the time, working out what Joe would be doing. She wanted to telephone, just to say they had arrived safely, that was all, but Sam would not let her. His face went tense and angry when she lifted the receiver and so she put it back again.

At least they were busy, rushing around from show to show, all chosen by Sam. They ran from the Assembly Rooms to the Pleasance and collapsed panting just in time for the play and afterwards walked on to George Square and a late-night revue. There was no time to brood, but Harriet found it, little chinks of time during performances less than gripping, minutes sitting in the dark surrounded by the audience, when she flew back home and thought of Joe, coming in, in the dark, on his own – but no, with Claire . . . then her attention would be seized again and she'd be grateful, until the next lull, and then she'd see Joe driving, and she'd be off again, pulled back, pulled to where she should be, wanted to be, to where her real life was.

She didn't tell Sam. He was enjoying himself whole-heartedly, loving Edinburgh, loving his first visit to the Festival since he was a student. No pulling back for Sam. She wished, as ever, she had his capacity for pleasure, that she could relish it when offered as he did. She didn't ask him but she knew he wasn't thinking of Joe at all. As they walked back to Northumberland Street from high up beyond the Royal Mile, with the city brilliantly lit all around them and the streets full of happy crowds and lights winking on the sea over the roof-tops of the New Town, Sam was talking only of the next day, of what they would see, of the art exhibitions as well as the shows, and of where they would eat, how he had booked lunch at Pierre Victoire and dinner at The Witchery in the garden room . . . 'Lovely,' she kept murmuring, 'lovely, it will be lovely.'

He was so glad to be there, just with her, and his happiness showed so clearly. He looked handsome again, his strength and size not threatening any more but attractive. Beside him, walking back, she felt deceitful. She was pretending she was happy too. She smiled, she took care to respond to whatever he said, she never once mentioned Joe. And in a way it worked. Because her mouth was smiling it did have an effect on her spirits even though she knew the smile was a lie. She managed quite well to convince Sam that she, too, felt liberated from the strain of the last year, that it was a relief to be free of Joe. Sam wanted her to say it, she knew he did, wanted her to say something vague but significant, something coded such as, 'Isn't it wonderful to be here, *like this*?' But she couldn't quite go that far, not even to please Sam.

She wanted to please him, though. She was aware of that. He deserved her undivided attention. It was stupid to hold against him the fact that he had not been as wrecked by what had happened to Joe as she had been, and still was. A lesser man would have grown tired, perhaps even disgusted, with her obsessive grieving. Sam had been patient but his own breaking point had finally been reached. He was bewildered by the intensity of her suffering, but he had suffered too. Now was the time to show she understood, to show him she knew how fortunate she was that he had been able for the most part to stand her utter and absolute concentration on Joe. All Sam asked for was that she should shed her studied gloom and be light-hearted – nothing more, just light-hearted. Nothing needed to be said. No words were required. All she had to do was go with him, be once more really together with him without that black shadow of past tragedy between them.

When they drove home, the weekend over, Sam sang most of the way. He looked ten years younger. As for herself, she didn't know. Yes, she had had a good time too, but never without secret anxiety, never without, last thing before sleep, wandering down roads in search of Joe. Now, nearing home, she was rigid with apprehension, quite unable any longer to keep up holiday banter. Turning into their road her stomach churned and she had to take deep breaths to control her terror. The house, at least, still stood. No sign of life. She let Sam open the front door, not trusting her own shaking hand. All was still. The rooms were neat and tidy. There was a note on the kitchen table:

Welcome home, you ravers. Hope you had a good time. Gone with Claire to a party. Back very late – don't worry. Louis is back but has gone to Charlotte's. He's going to ring you after ten. Love, Joe xxx.

'We needn't have come back,' Sam said. She was still looking at the note. 'I said, we needn't have come back.'
'Yes, I heard.'
'What's the matter? Everything seems fine to me.'
'Mm.'
'You're not going to start again, are you?'

'Again?'

'Worrying. About Joe. He's at a party, he's having a good time, for *God's* sake.'

She walked upstairs without speaking to him. She didn't dare. Everything would be spoiled if she let him see it could never be over, not for her, she could never wholly suppress her terror in case anything else ever happened to hurt Joe. From the landing, she called down, sensing his despair, 'I'll just get changed. Why don't you open some wine and we'll have a late supper to celebrate everything being okay?'

That was the way to do it, if she could, from now on.

*

The Crown Court was different. It didn't look so different, since here, too, as in the Youth Court, everything seemed new and modern, but the atmosphere changed once the judge entered the court. No buzzer here, Sheila was pleased to note. Instead a woman in a black gown 'prayed' everyone to stand for the judge. It felt so much better, so much more proper. And the judge, in his purple, with his brilliant white cravat and his knobbly, grey little wig, impressed her, unlike the magistrates in the Youth Court. He was in control and the little knot on the floor of the court, of barristers and solicitors and clerks, knew it. They were wary, deferential, and Sheila approved. She had a sudden confidence in the law and wished Leo had appeared in this court.

Harriet, sitting behind her, was similarly approving, though busy reflecting that the arrangement of the courtroom left much to be desired. She felt as if she were sitting in a bus, a very small and cramped bus. There was no spectators' gallery, only four rows of three seats each, all close together near the entrance. If she had wanted she could have leaned forward and touched Claire, who sat in the very front, on the shoulder. The girl had been there when Harriet came in, hogging the limelight. That was how she thought of it – Claire was seeking to be prominent, more prominent than Joe's own mother. There was no question of going to sit beside her. Even if Claire had turned round and beckoned to her she would not have gone to sit with her, but the girl did not turn round, not once. She sat there in her white blouse – a great effort had been made to look appropriate, Harriet felt – and black skirt, staring straight ahead, her hair severely tied back with a large black clasp. Beside her, one seat between them, was Sheila Armstrong, wearing the same drab coat she had worn in the Youth Court.

Harriet sat at the back, next to two young girls, about Claire's age, she supposed. She wondered if they knew Claire or Joe, but neither of them spoke and she could pick up no clues. In the middle two rows there were four Chinese men and a woman, who seemed in charge of them. They must be a party, on some kind of tour of the city, perhaps. A court case in the morning, to see how British Justice worked, and a trip to the Roman Wall in the afternoon. That is how it would be, Harriet decided, Joe a mere entertainment for strangers. He was in a special room for witnesses. When she'd arrived and been unable to find him – he had been determined to come on his own, to drive himself and be by himself – she'd panicked. The reception area was like an airport transit lounge, full of people pacing about smoking, or sitting looking tense on the one row of seats, bolted to the ground, which ran down the centre. But one of the officials had guided her past the pay telephones and water fountain to the room where witnesses could wait. She saw Joe there, reading a newspaper, but she didn't go in. She turned and came back and went into Court 4, content to have seen him safely there.

She felt alone, isolated, and wished for a moment she had let Sam come. He had an important meeting, but he would have cancelled it with her encouragement. It was she who had insisted he should not, insisted there was no need for both of them to go. She noted Mr Armstrong was not there either and wondered if Sheila felt lonely too, sitting there by herself. It was silly that they were apart. If only Claire had not plonked herself there, if only there had been two spare seats next to Sheila, she would not have hesitated, she'd have gone and sat with her. It occurred to her that Gary Robinson could not have anyone present from his family, unless the two silent girls were related, which she somehow doubted. There was no mother of his here, that was for sure. No mother or father or grandparent to suffer. That was what made the atmosphere so different, Harriet decided, not the judge, not the regalia, it was the absence of the unbearable tension there had been in the Youth Court when everyone was so patently suffering, when all their nerve ends, hers and Sheila's, and even those of the two men had felt so exposed. Here, now, the suffering was dulled, it had been grown used to, it had settled down to a dull ache . . .

There was a long recital of times and dates which, to Sheila, seemed such a waste of time, though she conceded the need to be exact. The two barristers endlessly split hairs over tiny points and even the judge grew weary of their jousting and ordered one of them to sit down, announcing that he was sure all the salient facts had been most properly established. Then they brought Joe Kennedy in. Sheila saw his eyes go straight to the girl sitting one seat away from her and realised this was his girlfriend. Covertly, she examined her. A pretty, fresh-faced girl with lovely corn-coloured abundant hair, neatly tied back. She glowed with feeling for Joe, sitting up so straight, her expression so eager, positively vibrating with concern. And she saw Joe draw courage from her, saw him smile slightly in her direction – he was so near her, the witness box barely three feet away from the front row of the public seats. Facial signals were exchanged, eyebrows raised, little nods given. It was very sweet. What a changed boy Joe Kennedy looked. Not so much in appearance, though he had grown at least four inches since that first trial, as in demeanour. He didn't hang his head or hunch his shoulders and that awful strained look had gone. She remembered how he had looked before, standing between his parents, so pale and vulnerable. Now the girl had given him confidence, she could tell. She wondered what Harriet thought of her. Leo had never had a girlfriend, or if he had he'd never brought her home. Once or twice she'd timidly asked him about girls, did he have a girlfriend, and he'd said he wasn't interested and she'd been relieved. What if a girl of Leo's had been here now, with her? Worrying as she was worrying. It would have been company.

She tried to settle on the hard seat and wished she wasn't there, that she hadn't come. She need not have come, nobody had asked her to or required her presence. It was Leo they wanted, not her. At the back of her own mind was the absurd idea that Leo might turn up – ridiculous, she knew that. Wherever he was he would be a long way from the scene of his crime, if it had been his crime. That was why she was here, to try to find out how much of the crime against Joe had been Leo's and how much Gary Robinson's. Foolish, probably, to hope for enlightenment from that thug in front of them, but hope she still did.

Gary Robinson was horrible. They had tried to make him look as decent as possible and failed. The clean shirt only pointed up the ugliness of his scabby face, the open collar barely containing the thickness of the neck. No button would fasten over it. He slouched in the dock, leaning back against it and staring ahead, his eyes swivelling alarmingly. He had a big piece of elastoplast down the left-hand side of his chin and kept fingering it. There was the feeling that at any moment he might rip it off. Sheila kept expecting it. He was big but it was more bulk than height. He must weigh twice what Joe Kennedy weighed. Joe had no muscles. The sleeves of Gary Robinson's shirt were rolled back and the tattoos on his arms stood out. It was wrong, Sheila thought, to be so prejudiced by someone's appearance, but prejudice was what she felt.

It was obvious that this was what the court felt too, even though all the motions of a fair trial were gone through. It hadn't been like that when Leo stood there. People were not sure then. Leo had looked so impressive and of course his refusal to say a word had added mystery. There was no mystery about Gary Robinson. He looked what he was alleged to be, corrupt and evil. Sheila felt sorry for his defence counsel, who laid it on thick about his client's appalling background, but put no passion into his words – it was a familiar story of neglect, dreary, dismal, arousing no sympathy, although it should have done. When the facts of what Gary Robinson was alleged to have done were recited, all memory of extenuating circumstances disappeared. By the time Joe Kennedy was called there hardly seemed any point in making him give evidence, so strong did the case appear. Joe Kennedy identified Gary Robinson very firmly. Yes, this was the man he had picked out at the identity parade, yes it was the man who had attacked him. True, he had only seen him for a few seconds, but it had not been dark and he had seen him clearly. He had noticed the jagged scar, badly stitched, under the accused's left ear and had reported this in his statement to the police. This was confirmed.

Reddening only slightly, but his voice quite distinct, Joe

305

went through what had happened on the night of the assault. He had been coming home, alone, from the cinema. It was not quite ten o'clock in the evening. As he was walking up the hill towards his home he had seen Gary Robinson step out from an alley-way. He turned to go back the way he had come but the accused spun him round and held a knife to his throat. He was dragged into the alley, which was actually a narrow path between the backs of two rows of houses connecting the two main streets. The accused swore at him and asked for money. He gave him the few bits of change he had which seemed to make the accused angry. He was aware of the other assailant being told to blindfold him, which he did. Then he was kicked to the ground. The accused told him to strip. At first he refused. Then he felt a stabbing pain in his shoulder and realised the accused had used his knife. He took his jeans off and his jacket and shirt. He was kicked again and felt another pain in his stomach. The accused pulled his underpants off and stuffed them into his mouth. He felt himself choking. His hands were tied behind him and he was turned over on to his front. Two lots of feet seemed to be kicking him, but he could not be sure. He felt hot water on the back of his neck and then smelled the urine. He was turned back over and the gag removed from his mouth. The blindfold had slipped and he could see the black assailant, with a knife in his hand, standing motionless. The accused swore at the other assailant, who did not move. The accused then crouched down, with his trousers round his ankles, and defecated. He then picked up his own excrement and laughed and smeared it in his victim's hair. Then he pulled his trousers up and dropped the knife and told his accomplice to run.

Sheila had listened intently. Joe spoke quite slowly and was hardly interrupted at all either by the barristers or the judge. His voice shook only when he got to the bit about

306

the excrement. Sheila clutched her handbag tightly as she listened to that disgusting detail and looked at the floor, the very clean, polished wooden floor. Then Gary Robinson was called back and cross-examined. Sheila couldn't look at him at first. It was impossible after what had been said. He had a strangely light voice, almost high-pitched, not at all in keeping with his size. She heard him say, 'Wha'? Wha'?' over and over again, to everything – 'Wha'? Wha'?' The judge became impatient and it was explained that Gary Robinson had partially impaired hearing after a blow to the head when he was seven. Counsel for the Prosecution was ordered to speak up, which he did, and his loud tone contrasted with the soft, almost inaudible replies of the accused. He seemed to concur so readily with his guilt that Sheila realised some kind of agreement must have been reached before the trial: if Gary Robinson didn't waste the Court's time then this would be borne in mind when he was sentenced. Sheila could think of no other reason for Gary Robinson's compliance. He admitted the attack on Joe Kennedy and claimed to be under the influence of LSD. Questioned about his accomplice, he said he didn't know his name – he was just 'a black kid' he'd met that evening in a club and sold some stuff to. He'd made him come with him and join in the attack on Joe Kennedy. How had he made him? He couldn't remember. He couldn't remember anything in fact, and especially why he had carried out this attack at all. For money, he said at first, then for fun, he supposed. He was out of his head, he didn't know. He didn't even recognise the victim, it could have been anyone, and he couldn't remember anything about that night at all. He didn't know which club he'd met 'the black kid' in and was prepared to accept the evidence of those who had seem him (a doorman and a cloakroom attendant). He said he regretted the offence – in those words, 'I regret the offence,' spoken parrot-fashion, dully, without expression.

The judge, in a curt, snappy little speech, expressed his disgust for 'hoodlums' like Gary Robinson, disgrace to the country, etc., etc., and pointed out the suffering caused to the entirely blameless Joe Kennedy and his family. Nothing about Leo Jackson's family, Sheila noted. Gary Robinson had in effect exonerated his accomplice from the worst of the blame, but this wasn't mentioned, nor was it mentioned how Leo, at that other trial, had borne the brunt of it. Nothing about Leo at all, but then that was his own fault. He should have been there. He should have spoken up at the first trial. There were so many 'shoulds' and 'should haves'. Nothing was tidy. Even now, Sheila felt there were so many things that needed to be explained and nobody to explain them. That was life, totally unsatisfactory. The judge ended with a homily on the rise of random, mindless violence, violence not for gain or revenge, but 'fun'. It must, he said, be stopped. Gary Robinson got two sentences, one for drug-dealing, one for attacking Joe Kennedy, to run concurrently, bringing the total to four years.

The judge had looked steadily at Gary Robinson throughout his sentencing but his look was not returned and it appeared to have no effect. Harriet was glad not to have been naive enough to have imagined her son's attacker would break down and weep and beg his victim's pardon. She had expected nothing and got nothing. There was not a flicker of reaction from Gary Robinson. This lack of any response was somehow the most shocking thing of all.

The judge rose and left the courtroom. The moment he had gone through the door the atmosphere changed. The little cluster of lawyers and clerks in the middle of the room visibly relaxed and became animated. One barrister yawned and stretched, the other removed his wig, scratched, replaced it carelessly so that it did not sit quite straight. There was laughter. It angered Sheila. What was there to laugh about? It was only another day's work for them, she supposed. She wanted to leave but didn't know if she was allowed to before that cackling lot did. When the girl next to her got up, she followed. It was like shuffling out after a play and yet it hadn't been like a play at all because it wasn't over in the same way. It never would be. She had to accept that. She kept her head down, thinking about this, and not wanting to see Harriet Kennedy who she was sure must be close behind. She felt her sleeve being pulled and without turning round knew who it was.

'How are you?' Harriet said. They were caught in the middle of the Chinese party, as they came to the narrow door.

'Fine, thank you,' said Sheila, and tried to smile. She really didn't want to be obliged to chat, she wanted to be away as quickly as possible.

'I've got my car,' Harriet said. 'Let me take you home, *please*.' The 'please' was so forceful, yet so uncertain, that Sheila hadn't the energy to fight it. She allowed herself to be led to the car and managed only to say, 'What about your son?'

'He has his own car,' Harriet said, 'and his girlfriend.'

It was a short drive to Sheila's house. Neither woman spoke. Harriet was well aware that Sheila didn't want this lift and she didn't know why she had forced it upon her – it had just seemed imperative not to lose sight of her, not to leave her on her own. She knew there was no solidarity between them, that this awkward, uneasy, fitful alliance was not going to survive, but she was desperate to maintain it at least for today.

Outside Sheila's house Harriet stopped the car but

didn't turn the engine off. She knew Sheila didn't want to invite her inside and she wanted to make it easy for her.

'Thank you,' Sheila said, 'that was kind, I appreciated it. The buses aren't so frequent these days and my legs felt a bit shaky, I don't know why, I'm sure.'

'Well, it was an ordeal,' Harriet said. 'My legs are all right but my stomach isn't. I feel queasy, just the sight of that brute.'

'Would you like a cup of tea, to settle it?'

'No. No, thank you. I must get home. Maybe some other time. I'd like to stay in touch.'

Sheila got out of the car and hesitated. 'Are you sure? It wouldn't take a minute to boil a kettle.'

'I'm sure.'

'Goodbye then.'

'Goodbye.'

★

The house was very quiet. Harriet sat in her kitchen, motionless, doing nothing. Joe was still out with Claire, Sam not coming home until late. She had a premonition of disaster, but then such feelings were familiar. Heavy, tiring, claustrophobic feelings which sometimes did not lift for hours. Once, she had been sure Joe shared them, but now she was not so sure. If he did, he was hiding them well. All was action and excitement. 'He's normal, at last,' Sam had said. 'He's got over all that. I always knew he would.' She hadn't argued. Maybe Sam was right? She didn't believe he was, but it was possible. It was she who would never be over it. Never. The further Joe travelled away from her the greater the conviction that she would never readjust, even if he could. Always it was there and she could not seem to let it go. It was like a screen between them which blocked what had once been their effortless communication. She wanted so badly to rip away that screen but Joe did not. It was there, Gary Robinson had put it there, and there it stayed, everything changed in one night.

It was temporary, Joe's recovery, she knew it must be. He would crash again, he would be bound to need her again. The greater the apparent lift of his spirits, the greater the fall. It was a cheat, this 'happiness', the driving, the car, Claire. She was deeply suspicious of his buoyancy and he knew she was. He kept away from her because only she could detect how hard he was trying, how great was the effort to be what Sam called 'normal at last'. The hardest thing of all was to go along with it, *pretend* with him. But that was what he wanted, for her to pretend too, hard, and then he was free to escape the obligation she laid on him of always remembering. Claire had nothing to remember, she was a relief. And I, Harriet reminded herself, am a burden, my misery on his behalf is the greatest burden he still has to bear and I must lift it. But she didn't know how. She had tried, she had tried so hard, but the sadness still seeped through every pore, the bitterness, the resentment that her boy had suffered so. She still felt it was her fault. She always had done. What was the point of having children and loving them so much if you couldn't protect them? She had this curious, painful desire to be forgiven without being able to establish in whose gift forgiveness lay. Joe's? She shook off that thought, it was too alarming.

There was a meal to make, a simple matter. She attended to it. She must encourage Joe to invite Claire to meals, she must be friendly to the girl. She saw, quite clearly, a new phase of motherhood beginning. It made her nervous. She knew how to be the mother of a baby, a small child, even an adolescent, but of a grown-up? It was a mystery still. She carried so much baggage to her new posting and yet all her intimate knowledge, her great store

311

of memories, didn't qualify her. She had to learn, fast. Her status was not yet defined but whatever it turned out to be, it would be Joe who would do the defining, not she. And in a way that was a relief. She chopped and scraped and washed vegetables. She lit the oven, she set the table, and then she waited, patiently, humbly, for her boy to come home.

*

Sheila held the card in her hand. Post-marked London, WC1. Happy Birthday, it said. No signature but then none needed. Eric James would have been triumphant. Her own birthday was a month away. Maybe there would be a card for her too, but for the time being this was enough, all she could expect. A sign not just of life but of commitment. A sign that memories lingered. But what was lacking was the very thing denied to her, a chance for Leo to receive a sign from her. She had no way of telling him that she had stopped clinging on to ideals. Eric James had not clung. In the end, after his rage had subsided, he had accepted Leo as he was. She saw that she never had, never. She had struggled to make him, if not in her own image, then in the image of what she wanted him to be. There had been no place in this vision for any kind of transgression. She hadn't been able to be one of those mothers who could forgive anything. She hadn't been able to say it made no difference, what Leo had done, even if in doing it he hadn't known what he did. He was her boy and her boy wouldn't, couldn't, act so. And he'd known that, which was why she had lost him.

The trouble was that she still felt as if she herself had attacked Joe Kennedy. She had never been able to separate herself from what Leo had done. She felt dragged down, besmirched by his participation in such violence. It made perfect sense to her that parents were held responsible for their children's crimes because she felt exactly that, responsible. The hardest thing to do, even now, was tell herself that she had not been responsible, and yet even thinking that felt cowardly and she was no coward.

Alan would be back soon. He'd gone to remove the rose bushes from Eric James's garden. It was something Eric James had made him promise years ago – 'When I'm gone, tek them roses bushes, I don't want them left for somebody to neglect, tek them mind.' So Alan was taking them and planting them in Carole's garden. Then he'd be back and they were going for a drive out into the country. Alan wanted her to, and she'd agreed there was no point in moping at home. Now her father was dead and Leo gone they were free to do what they wanted, they had no ties.

She knew, of course, that ties were necessary to her. She'd always known, though, that Alan needing her was not the same as Leo needing her. Well, it would have to be faced. For the moment anyway Leo had shown he had no need of her. She longed to reclaim him, on whatever terms, but knew the terms would be his and he hadn't made them known yet. All she could do was prepare herself for them. It was important that Leo should not return to find he had broken her spirit. She must present a strong and resolute front, show she had borne the weight of the tragedy and not cracked under it. Then he'd be relieved, and even proud of her, and he might stay.

If he came back, if her boy ever came back and gave her another chance.